Step 1: Limbo

A GAMER'S GU1DE TO BEATING THE TUTORIAL

Step 1: Limbo

Palt

Podium

To Mamma and Pappa, who probably shouldn't read this book

Cover design by Leah Zink

ISBN: 978-1-0394-7288-4

Published in 2024 by Podium Publishing
www.podiumaudio.com

Podium

Step 1: Limbo

FLOOR 0

◆ Lo Fenrikk ◆

PROLOGUE

It Escapes, Irretrievable Time

By this point, it's really only a matter of days until I either starve to death or get killed in some desperate attempt to avoid the aforementioned. Personally, though, I'm leaning toward just starving to death. Worse ways to croak and all that.

More than that, I've got to admit that I'm kind of surprised that I lasted this long. Sure, I failed my homelessness-speedrun any%, but what can you do? Maybe I'll at least place somewhat high in the seventeen-year-old category, assuming such a thing exists. Then again, if you want to go even more in-depth, maybe there's even a category for *men*, and then the *lightweight* category.

Yes, all things considered, maybe I'll at least snag first place in the *loser-ex-pro-gamer-estranged-son-with-criminal-record* category. Then again, there probably aren't too many of those running around on these streets.

. . . Are there?

Ahh, who knows. I just feel cold. When did I last feel my toes? They don't wiggle anymore. If I tried to stand up, maybe they'd even snap off like icicles. There must be someone interested in watching that, right? A kid or two I could swindle some money off? Yeah. Somewhere, maybe. But as is, I can't even really think straight.

It's cold. Snowflakes have started settling on my ragged clothes. They're the ones I was arrested in, so they still have a little bit of his blood on them. Damned hack. I hope he got to the hospital too late for them to properly reconfigure his arm. If he's out of the game, that would mean I'm technically still the world champion.

. . . Assuming some other perky young colt hasn't popped up in these past six months to take back the title.

The thought makes the snow settling atop my body feel even heavier.

I can't feel my arms anymore but in some half-dying thirst for answers, I shuffle over a little and shove my bare hand in my pocket. I can't really feel anything in there, but I can hear a few coins clinking together. It's not much.

My stomach makes an all-too-familiar sound, but it's not like that's new. And in these times . . .

Even if I bought myself an entire cake with these coins, I still wouldn't live to see the next week. I'm pretty sure of that, at least. So, really, what's the point? I'm fine with dying. I've been dying for six months now. What does it matter if that darkness comes in a month or an hour? It still comes, like an undodgeable homing missile. Either way I'm screwed, so why not do something with it?

Actually standing up is a different matter. My knees make weird crunching noises, but they don't feel like anything. My hands are stiff and cold, like unwashed carrots. I bet they'd snap off just as easily, too. Standing up takes all the effort left in me, and it leaves me panting and heaving, choking out puffs of white smoke. Finally standing after so long, I can feel my legs tremble. My back is as hunched as ever. Right. So far, so good.

At my feet lies a backpack containing what few things I still have. A towel. A can opener. A few magnets. Stuff like that.

Looking at it, I feel a bit of disgust slither its way through me.

After staring at it for a full five seconds, I decide to leave it behind. I won't need it. On my way out of the snow-caked alleyway I pause at a drainage pipe and shove my hand into the mouth of it, pulling out a small bag of tiny cloudy but transparent crystals. I'm lucky I was smart enough to never start on this stuff, but it's still a good bribe for the people who weren't as clever. They never say no.

Limping my way out of the alley fully, I spy up and down the street. Lots of people walking by. Smiling. Chattering. Dressed nice and snug. Fashionably, not that I've ever been able to discern that sort of stuff. All I can see is that the fabric is good. For a minute or so, I scan the people walking by, ensuring that I don't recognize anyone. To stay on the safe side, I bundle my scarf closer to my face, covering most of it. The snow lining the creases doesn't melt when it meets my cheeks. The cold of the snow doesn't hurt anymore. Content with my preparations, I sneak out.

I know this city better than I ever did before all this. It's big, but it makes sense in its places. That's how I know where the nearest internet café is.

The sky is dark and starless, only lighted by the snow drifting down. It's the kind of night where all you want is to lie down and snuggle into your blanket and pass out of all of this without having to think too much about anything. But the world has never been that merciful.

Passing by the obnoxiously happy pedestrians, I make my way to the Point and Click, a café that may not have the cheapest rates but does have something much more valuable.

I stop just outside the front door, stiff hand hovering over the cold metal handle. My eyes glue themselves to a sign out front. To make up for my lack of glasses, I squint as best as I can to make out the words.

Closed for New Year's Eve—See you next year!

How cheeky. That's today? Makes sense, though I didn't think about it much. Nonetheless, the brothers who own the place both live in the apartment just above, so without much hesitation I press the doorbell by the side of the door, the sound of the chime echoing through the store and all the way up to the apartment above. Light flickers on in the apartment before traveling down into the café. I quickly take a step back, just in time to watch the door slide open. "Yes? How may I—" His eyes fall down on me and any curiosity and well-meaning dies out. "Oh, it's one of you. Listen, can't you read the sign? *Nu este deschis*—not open. How hard is that to understand? And P.S., no, I'm not giving you a free handout, so you might as well pick up your little poor-boy satchel and—"

I present the coins.

He gives an exaggerated sigh and rolls his eyes. "Buddy, we're closed. It's not that difficult of a concept to—"

I shuffle around in my inventory.

I present the little baggie of crystal meth.

His eyes shine up. "Well . . ." He licks his lips. "I can always make an exception for a friend, can't I?"

Proper item chosen. +5 intimacy gained with Co-Owner of Internet Café. Friendship with Co-Owner of Internet Café has increased from Mutual Resentment to Codependency Through Recreational Mineral-Collecting. +20 EXP. 3825 EXP needed until next level up. Access to Internet Café Point and Click gained.

After he's done his due by glancing around to check if anyone saw our successful interaction, he shows me his open palm and I deposit the little baggie in it. As soon as he has the item in hand, he shoves it into his pocket and opens the door fully. "Step right on in." Right as I'm about to do just that, he jams his foot in my way. "And, just so we're clear, you aren't here for a weeklong sleepover or a full-course New Year's Eve dinner. You play your games, I have my fun, and then you're *out*, get it? I really don't want to have you tracking dirt and lice and rat eggs and whatever it is your sort carries in here, you get me?"

A curt nod is all he needs, so that's all I give. The warmth inside the café hurts. It's stinging something awful and bringing a fair bit more attention to the fact that the insides of my ragged shoes and my ragged clothes and my ragged scarf aren't wet from molten snow alone. Every step hurts more than the last, but I didn't come here to live.

Once the co-owner takes his leave to go enjoy himself, I sit down by one of the many open computers. I log on. This is the one I always use, so it already has *Tendrils of Magic and Madness* downloaded.

Five years ago, it was the most popular MMORPG on the market. Every single lobby and every single server were always filled to the brim. Every item the game had to offer was on the market within only weeks of the game's launch. And still, it kept itself fresh. The in-game economy, miraculously, didn't collapse for several years, and even when it did, it did so gracefully enough that I could keep up even when most people couldn't.

But that was no surprise. I was, after all, *the* greatest TMM player in the world. Not just in the North Europe lobbies, not just on the Europe server, but in the *entire world*.

Entire groups of other players could face me, and I wouldn't even blink. It wasn't a matter of levels—that's not how TMM was designed. Skill was everything, and I had all of it. Secret Easter eggs, hidden bonus levels, ultra-rare items . . . I knew things the wiki hadn't even touched on yet.

I was, in every sense, unrivaled.

Whenever there was a tournament, I would join basically only as a spectator. The other players would all form parties and do combat in various ways, and then the final winner would face me. I didn't need to prove myself. Everyone already knew. That's how it was, and that's how it should have stayed.

If LetsFraternizeTogether had only known his place, it wouldn't have come to this. None of it would have happened. Really, it's all his fault for putting his nose where it didn't belong and getting so damn invested in a stupid video game.

But enough about him. Games like these cycle through WCs like toilet paper, so I'm sure he's been dethroned long since.

And now, the game has finally loaded. The music is the same as ever, but the game load screen is some sort of holiday variant I don't recognize. I don't like it. But it's whatever, you know? It's not important.

The game opens and I type in my username and password, *ThatGentleNight2*, make sure not to click *Save Password*, and press enter. Another loading screen.

<If you touch the tentacles of a Minos, you will take insanity damage until you recover with an incantation!>

Okay. Or you can use the exploit where you clip through the Minos until it goes into the floor and is never seen again, and the game forgets you're supposed to be taking insanity damage from it. Up to you.

The screen cycles a few times. Server: Europe. Lobby: North Europe 1. Enter.

It takes a while for the potato of a computer to render the lobby, something that took my old computer Zeus a mere millisecond. And there, standing in the middle of the screen, just as beautiful as the day I lost him, is my beautiful character. Massive black wings that could only be gained through the paid gacha during a Halloween event. Tentacle effects that shoot out every three seconds that I got for reaching the highest Job category of Old One Oracle. And then the Robes of Endless Fabric, Quasar Staff Manimous, Tendril Crown of Black Silver . . . Back in the day, just one of these items could bring about a huge bidding war within the entire Europe server. Obviously, though, what I'm wearing right now is only for show. I do have more powerful equipment, but it doesn't look as cool, so I only wear it for the *real* battles.

The last time that happened, though, was when—

When . . .

Well, it isn't important. What's important is that I missed this character. Long ebony black hair, icy blue eyes like limpid tears . . . the whole package. If I looked like this in real life, I wouldn't have any problems. The girls would be all over me, and the guys would all be jealous, and—

<FreshBiscuitsOhoy: lol what look at that guy>
<FreshBiscuitsOhoy: whats with the huge getup did u loose a bet>
<YoureMomFuqs33: is that the quazar staff? didnt that get outdated like five months ago with the new patch?>
<FreshBiscuitsOhoy: yeh thats the staff that got nerfed like a little *** lol>**

I stare at the screen. Nerfed?

<JonathanBanks[ADMIN]: It's not nice to make fun of returning players, FreshBiscuitsOhoy and YoureMomFuqs33. Welcome back, ThatGentle-Night2! We're always happy to have people pick the game back up ^^<3<3>

Blink, blink. I can feel my rotting teeth bite into my flaking lower lip. Slowly, I place my fingers on the keyboard.

<You: this is aktually the best gear in the game that i spent five hundred hours collecting and its super strong and probs way stronger than u guyses stuff>

I lean back in my seat. There. Roasted.

<FreshBiscuitsOhoy: oh ok ok so thats how you want to go geezer huh well ** you ok you ***** *** punk my gear is actually super strong and im in the top 100 players in europe i could whoop your *** anytime huh yeah exactly>**
<FreshBiscuitsOhoy has been issued a warning>
<JonathanBanks[ADMIN]: Easy on the language, FreshBiscuitsOhoy. This is a game for everyone. There is no need for harsh language.>

Okay. Alright. You know what? That's it. Six months ago, I would have let him go like a Cerberus ignoring the barking of a Chihuahua. But that's changed.

I've needed to cut loose a little. By now, my fingers have thawed, meaning that I am beyond ready.

<ThatGentleNight2 has challenged FreshBiscuitsOhoy to a duel!>

I lean back. If he was clever, he'd just surrender right now and avoid going gentle into that dark night . . .

<FreshBiscuitsOhoy has accepted ThatGentleNight2's challenge!>

But, obviously, you can't expect that sort of wisdom from some no-name standard-username peanut who can't even recognize the former ruler of this game. Everyone needs to learn a lesson sometimes. As they say, all kids need a good whooping to understand their place in the world.

I place my fingers against the keyboard and grab the mouse. The movements are coming to me easily now. This guy doesn't even have any flashy effects or mounts or wings. He's an obvious pushover, but still too stupid to do the simple courtesy of checking my level before accepting the challenge.

A grin rises to my lips for the first time in several months. It hurts. But it feels good.

A circle arena has formed around my avatar and FreshBiscuitsOhoy, separating us from the common rabble. A counter begins counting down from three and I ready myself. The second it hits that fateful zero, my brain shifts into gear completely and my character bursts to life with the press of only a few buttons, flinging himself across the screen and twisting and bringing down his gorgeous summoned black onyx sword on the opposing avatar, which is—

No longer there?

I blink at the screen. That's not right. Where in the world did he go? My brows furrow, which hurts but I don't have time to care as my character flings himself into another burst of movement, flying around the borders of the duel circle like a swallow, here and there. But he just isn't around anymore. Did he turn invisible? Can they do that now? What the hell is going on?!

My teeth grit themselves. What a coward. What a complete and utter coward.

I pause in my frantic running just enough to type in the chat,

<You: wher th ** ar u cowrd>**

And just as I click send, something smashes into the side of my character and hurls him across the map, where he crashes into the invisible barrier around the duel circle. I only just have time to gawk at how my health instantly slips down into the red before my fingers move on their own and narrowly toss my character out of the way of another horribly quick strike. It's so fast I can barely see it. Is that a hammer he's wielding? A *war hammer?!* This is a game about magic and sorcery! Why in the world would you even use a blunt weapon when you can just as easily summon weapons to—

He used a skill. I don't know which. It looked like his character tossed a small pig plushie at my character and somehow that was enough to stun me and then he caved my character's head in with his hammer and that was it.

The screen turns dark and monochrome and a single word overlays the whole screen, printed in horrible oversaturated red: **DEAD**.

<Duel is over—FreshBiscuitsOhoy is the winner!>

In my head, I can picture the screen on his end. A big green letterbox shouts **WIN!** and a spray of confetti erupts across the screen and all of the surrounding gawkers would use the Cheer and Jubilee emotes and spam the chat with astonishment and adoration and nobody could ever face you no matter how many they were because just one of you would always be enough to face them all, no matter what, no matter when.

But that's not what's on my screen. Just a big, red **DEAD**. That's all.

The chat is being spammed alright, but it's all just the same thing.

<FreshBiscuitsOhoy: gg ez>
<YoureMomFuqs33: lmaooo what a pushover>
<YoureMomFuqs33: GG ez for real lol>
<FreshBiscuitsOhoy: shoulda stayd offline>
<JonathanBanks[ADMIN]: Come on, have some sportsmanship. Good match, both of you! Very interesting techniques, ThatGentleNight2. If you grind a bit I'm sure you can have a great rematch! ^^>
<YoureMomFuqs33: yeah if he grinds a bit on MY NUTS LMAOOOO>
<YoureMomFuqs33 has been banned for foul language>
<FreshBiscuitsOhoy: admin vs user admin win gg ez>
<FreshBiscuitsOhoy has been temporarily muted>

I stare at the chat. After a few minutes it goes silent. Since FreshBiscuitsOhoy got muted I can't even challenge him to a rematch. If I look out the window, it's completely dark now. It feels almost like the world is holding its breath. The time is three minutes to midnight. What kind of loser would spend this time on New Year's Eve an online game, fighting randos?

I grind my molars.

Once I respawn, I quickly check the rankings. I must just have been unfortunate and run into some sort of underground legend, or some secret master. Maybe he was even an NPC hidden boss or something.

. . . No, that last one's a bit too unlikely.

But he could secretly be a super high-level player. I mean, how else would he just—just do *that* to *me*? I'm the number one player! If anyone's doing the curb stomping, it's *me*! That's how it works, and that's how it is, and—

And . . .

And he isn't even in the top hundred. Not for the world. Not for Europe. Not even for North Europe.

He isn't even in the top hundred for the *server*.

Neither am I. My ranking is very clear. It's right there, written in bold, purple text.

<Your Ranking: #12,494>

Twelve thousand four hundred ninety-fourth.

And what of my rival, nemesis, and enemy? Maybe I was a fool to have hope, to think he'd follow my footsteps and sink into the despair I feel, but . . .

He's number eighty-four. Internationally. It's not much. He used to be number one. But now he's eighty-fourth. At least, unlike a certain someone, he's actually on there.

<LetsFraternizeTogether's Ranking: #84 Worldwide, #20 Europe, #2 North Europe>

He's doing well.

I feel the buzz in my ears intensify, my vision blurring and blotting, my breathing becoming even more raspy, my joints aching and creaking, my flesh scraping together, and the fever more pronounced than ever. It hurts. Everything hurts. My face feels hot with everything that can make a face hot, but it won't seep out through tears. Had I always been this pathetic? Is this something new or was I always destined to be this sort of worthless, pathetic loser? My head is on fire. I want to die. Maybe I'm already dead. Maybe I died six months ago. Maybe this is hell. That'd be better. At least hell is perpetual. I'd rather be burnt than tormented like this.

Outside, far away, I can hear a thousand thousand people chant in unison.

Ten.

Nine.

Eight.

I wonder if my parents and sister are out there among them. Do they miss me? If it were me, I'd be happy I was gone.

Seven.

Six.

Five.

I mean, really. There's nothing to miss in the least. No skill, no trait, no dream of any value whatsoever. I wouldn't be surprised if they hate me.

Four.

Three.

Nothing to miss is almost an overstatement. What is there to miss in a void of a person like me? Certainly not my charming personality, or my looks, or my smarts, because God knows I do not have any of those. I am—by all means—nothing.

Two.

Nothing at all.

One.

And nothingness isn't something you miss.

Zero!

As the world outside the internet café windows lights up with cheers for a better year and fireworks and music, the inside of the café suddenly lights up as well. But not by any fireworks, no, rather, by a floating, shining text box straight out of a video game.

<You have been invited to join the tutorial.>

. . . What?

Oh, I see, so this is the light at the end of the tunnel you see when you die. Makes sense.

—No, hang on a sec, what the heck do you mean by *tutorial*?! Are you telling me my entire life was just the lobby period you spend before you even start the tutorial proper? Is this the menu screen?!

Okay, okay, let's just relax for a moment. This isn't real. Actually, it's not too bad. I'm dying, so I'm obviously hallucinating. Great, I really felt like dying right now. Wonderful. Glad someone up there's listening for once.

Which button do I press to die?

<Do you accept this invitation?>
<Yes/No>

. . . Well, if it means dying, then sure. Why the heck not. Take me there, ferryman.

A second passes.

. . . Oh, do I, uh, have to press it manually? Talk about outdated models for spiritual death, sheesh. Unbefitting of a dead man, I casually press the Yes button, and in that very second, a third screen pops up.

<**Please select desired difficulty.**>
<[**Easy**]>
<[**Normal**]>
<[**Hard**]>
<[**Hell**]>

Well, now you're just asking the obvious. Clearly, a pro gamer must prove himself even in the afterlife. What do you expect me to do if I choose Easy, go to hell, and LetsFraternizeTogether chose the Hell Difficulty and is doing much better than me? I'd try to off myself and go to whatever afterlife lies beyond the afterlife! Superhell would be my one and only fate. Can't have that, can I?

The answer is so simple I almost feel like chuckling. Instead, I just casually press the Hell button. Afterlife, here I—

FLOOR 1

A FOREST DARK

Screens and Buttons

Come?

Where—where am I . . . ?

Everything is so bright, and my head hur—

—No. No, it doesn't. My hand only barely has time to touch my temple before I realize that *my head doesn't hurt*. It's been months since my head has last felt this . . . *clear*. The eternal chill in my limbs is gone. The rattle in my lungs is silent. My knees don't feel crunchy. What in the world—

And then I realize that my eyes are also okay. My *eyes*. To reiterate, my vision has been piss-poor ever since I was six. I couldn't wear lenses because my glasses had to be so thick. And now you're telling me my vision is just . . . ? Listen, I can actually *see* the things around me with *near perfect* quality! And sure, it isn't much to look at, but there *are* things here!

I can see those white pillars in perfect clarity. The floor isn't blurry in the least. And, uh . . . No, wait, hang on, is that it? Is that seriously it? No, that can't be. There has to be something else around here apart from this infinite white void and the infinite white floor and the infinite white marble columns that seem to reach up thousands of feet into the distant, white sky.

If this is hell, then it sure doesn't look like it. I'd say it looks more like heaven, but this never-ending silence is kind of ruining the image. It feels eerie, somehow. Maybe it's limbo instead?

Rightfully confused and disoriented, I look around for a bit. My body truly is completely healed. My mind feels *clear*. Clearer than it has in ages; maybe forever. It's seriously tripping me out, but just as I'm about to accept that there's nothing more than these pillars, I can hear something like a door open behind me, and when I whirl around to face it, what I find is an open door and exactly no walls. It's just a door. It doesn't even lead anywhere. It's a door, and on the other side are six tables. But it's kind of like a gate without a fence because I can walk around it just fine.

And there we have them. Six tables. But it's not the tables I'm looking at. No, what's on the tables is *much* more interesting, and it makes me want to chuckle evilly.

Starter weapons.

An axe, a bow, a staff, a hammer, a spear, and a sword and shield.

Oh, it's beautiful.

I've changed my mind. Hell isn't so bad. This is starting to look like my life before this was the tutorial, and now I'm in the real game. Or something. Heh.

Okay, alright, let's wind down a little. This is probably the most important decision of my life, above choosing starter Pokémon and above choosing scholarships.

First up . . . I think I'll just discount the axe and hammer. I'm scrawny, okay? I'm short, and small, and that's just what I am, so there's no point trying to use a weapon I'm not suited for. Sure, once I get stronger, I'll be able to fling them around as I please and fulfill the small-character-with-big-weapon trope, but for now, I'll need to be able to actually kill things properly.

Regarding the rest . . . I'm not doing a spear. Sure, I read somewhere that spears are good for untrained combat, but I'm not going to be untrained forever, and besides, it's pretty inflexible in terms of range. I'm also eliminating the bow for that same reason. I'd obviously love to have some distance between myself and my possible enemies, but I need to also be able to fight at close range if the need arises.

That leaves me with the staff and the sword and shield.

I need to take a closer look at this. I creep up to the staff and put my head level to it.

<[A Termite-Eaten Staff]
Magic: 4
Probably more effective at bludgeoning people than magic.
Used item>

Alright. So, in other words, it's a magic staff. Despite what the description says, if I hit someone with a termite-eaten piece of wood, it's not going to bludgeon them, it's just going to burst into splinters and soft dust. Maybe if I'm lucky they'll get a splinter stuck in a weak spot and somehow die from it? Yeah, no.

How about the sword and shield, then? It's two weapons for the price of one, after all. Besides, that sword looks *really* cool!

<[An Ornamental Sword]
Attack: 4
A foolish knight brought the ceremonial sword to battle and died. It has a blunt edge.
Used item>

Oh, well, uh, that's—

<[A Termite-Eaten Shield]
Defense: 4
Makes for a good smokescreen. Beware the splinters!
Used item>

Are there termites in this entire starter weapon selection area?! Aren't we supposed to be in some sort of afterlife? Are you trying to tell me that ghost termites ate these weapons!?

But at least the sword, although blunt, doesn't seem to be on the edge of complete disintegration at any second, so I guess that's really my best choice. Unsure if it can be called anything close to *best*, but . . .

<Do you want to choose this starter weapon?>
<Yes/No>

I really don't have any choice, do I? Fine. Blunt sword and splinter-bomb it is. I press the Yes button.

And then the world below my feet disappears and I stumble and fall but someone catches me and for a second or so I just hang in their arms, staring down at the pristine white floor. "*Whoa there!*" that very someone says, just inches above my head. "*Was about to take quite the tumble there, weren't you?*"

English? With maybe a bit more force than intended, I push myself away from whoever caught me. He lets me go and even gives me a relaxed pat on the arm as he does.

And then we stand face to face. He doesn't look like a southerner. No, by all means, he looks completely normal. For a few uncomfortable seconds, we just stare at each other. "Why are you talking in English?" I ask in a low, almost growling voice.

He blinks at me. "You're Swedish too?" Oh, now he speaks the right language. Smiling, he scratches the back of his head. Meek. What a meek guy. That's the word. Much like almost every other non-teenager in the world, he's over a full head taller than me, and about as ordinary as you get. Average height, standard blond hair and blue eyes, wearing a pair of ordinary dress pants and a stained shirt. Going by the smell, it seems he's had a bit of a wild night before coming here. He's also wearing a New Year's Eve party hat hanging from his neck, so it's pretty clear where he came from. But it's not the hat I care about. Rather, it's his hair.

"Pffftt—!"

It's a crew cut. It's stupidly short, and it looks horrible on him. Everything else is so ordinary, except for that hairstyle. Did he lose a bet or something?

He furrows his brows at me. "Is something wrong?"

I boldly point at his head. "Your haircut looks stupid."

"My hair . . . ?" He gently touches his head, eyes widening as he does. But then he looks at me. "It would seem, in our appearing here, we both happened into the same predicament."

"Huh? What do you—" My heart stops. My hand flies up to touch my head. My hair isn't long anymore. Or greasy. Or knotted.

It's short, and washed, and would probably best be described as a *crew cut*.

Ah. Ahhh. I see. So, this is where the *hell* part comes in. Yes. I see. I see . . .

Gently, I lie down on the floor and bundle myself up in the so-called fetal position. My head feels breezy. So this is the thing that breaks me, then. After so many years of growing out the ultimate luscious hair . . . Gone. Taken from me at such a young age. This truly is hell. By the way, now that I'm lying directly on the floor, I can say that it isn't cold, nor is it warm. It's some atrocious, unfeelable middle ground. The whole place is exactly at room temperature, and not a degree above or below. It feels weird. I don't like it. The seemingly endless white is starting to hurt my eyes, too, but as soon as it begins to really sting it suddenly goes away. What.

A shadow falls on me and I glance up at my fellow sufferer. He gives me a meek expression. "Hey, man, just relax, alright? It's not the end of the world."

Oh, but it is. He's a fool not to think so.

"*If he wants to lie on the floor, let 'im!*" someone shouts in English from across the room. I raise my head just enough off the floor to see the face of this cruel man. He's as young as me, and by the looks of it, Finnish. Despite that, his English is really good, and the accent is hardly noticeable. His hair is dyed blond and cut in a crew cut, just as much a victim as me and this old guy. "*That makes two, and all that.*" Oh, and he's also holding a huge axe. Well, he's trying to, because for all his arrogance, the axe is still too heavy to properly lift. I smirk at him. His face twists in anger. "*What, you wanna go, punk? Huh!?*"

"*Hey, come on, relax a bit! He's just upset at . . . Well, whatever it is, it's his emotions, so be a bit nice, okay?*"

"Psh. Be nice. Yeah, sure." He spits on the floor. Then he lifts his axe and tries to wave it around. "I don't know if you can read, geezer, but unless we start practicing soon, we won't be ready for when the floor opens! Do I need to remind you that you can't even lift your pussy-ass spear properly?"

The average-age man above me frowns a bit.

Still, he's right. Lying here won't do me any good now, and what I really need right now is to prepare myself for the . . .

The floor opening?

I shoot up to my feet. And the second I do, another one of those screens pops up just before my eyes.

<Time Until Floor 1 Opening: 23:49:03>

A timer? It seems to be counting down . . .

So, if I get it right, in twenty-three hours and fifty minutes or so, the first floor will open.

. . . The first floor of *what*?

I guess it must be the tutorial, but it doesn't say anything else, either. How many floors are there? What happens after the tutorial? Does it even have an end? Where is this place? Why was I called here? And who are these other three people?

Three, because I only just now noticed someone on the floor. I think it's a girl, considering her slender frame, but her hair is cut so short it makes her look like a man. But she's wearing a pretty nice—if somewhat torn—dress, so I'm pretty sure she's a woman. I'm also pretty sure that she's sobbing because her exposed shoulders are trembling. On the other hand, I have no idea where she's from. She doesn't look like a southerner, or like she's from Norway or Denmark or even Germany.

The Finnish delinquent guy meets my eyes. "*On your feet now, eh? Guess you're at least a half man. How about you make yourself useful and show what kind of weapon you picked?*"

He's asking me to show my cards? Why? So that he can—

In only a few quick steps, he approaches me, now appearing close in front of me, axe raised, the edge of it pressing against my neck. "*If I wanted to kill you,*" he growls, "*I wouldn't be asking you to take out your weapon, now would I?*" I blink at him. Something cold slithers up through my veins and I begin nodding. "*Great, glad you understand basic logic. Besides . . .*" He shoves the axe closer to me, into my neck, drawing blood, making its cold blade enter my skin. A bit of blood trickles down my neck, but it heals within mere moments, leaving only a faint scar. I stare at him, wide-eyed. He draws back the axe, and the meager pain I felt dissipates. "*Even if I wanted to kill you, I can't. This place won't let you get hurt for real, much less actually die.*"

It takes a minute or so for my mouth to start working again. "*Wh—why?*"

"*Wuh—wuh—why?*" he asks right back, making a mocking face. "*Do I look like I've got a clue? I don't even know how I got here!*"

Now the only actual adult in the room butts in. "*As I've told you before,*" he says in that measured, even voice you only use with children, "*you got invited to the tutorial, you accepted, and you chose the Hell Difficulty.*" He sighs melodramatically. "*And then you chose the axe for some reason I can't comprehend.*"

"*I chose it because it looks awesome!*" the delinquent squeals as he hugs the massive axe closer to him. "*You—you never said why you chose that dopey spear, right? I bet it's 'cause you're a coward or something!*"

Spear this, spear that, I haven't seen any—

Suddenly there's a spear in the older guy's hand. Was . . . Was that always there?

"*The spear is the easiest weapon to use for a beginner. It's versatile, suitable for fighting wild beasts and humans alike, and—*"

"*Yeah, yeah, yeah. Shut up already, will you? You're a nerd, we get it.*" The delinquent turns to me. "*So? What weapon did you choose? Out with it already.*"

I have a feeling that if I were to talk now, I'd stammer, so I keep my mouth shut.

"*Just pull it out of your inventory, man.*" And the second he said *inventory*, a screen popped up in front of his eyes. "*Damn it, not again . . . Shouldn't this place be able to patch stuff like that? Such a bother.*" With a wave of the hand, the screen disappears again.

After a second or so, tentatively, I say, "Inventory." The window quickly appears, so since it works in both English and Swedish, that would mean anyone can use it, as long as they know it exists. Neat, I guess.

\<Community—Top—Status\>
\<Inventory\>

The screen shows a graph of small item icons, including a shield and a sword. They're shown as separate items, and apart from them, I also have five pieces of dried meat and five glass bottles of water. Wonderful. Just what I needed. I kind of forgot I was literally starving to death, but now that I see some food, I can feel my stomach's grumbling coming back in full force.

How do I get it out of there, though? The older guy didn't say anything to call out his spear, so do I just . . . imagine that—

A piece of dried meat wrapped in paper appears in my hand. I stare at it.

"*Pfff, that's your weapon, eh? Bet you'll kill loads of enemies with that!*" the delinquent says with a guffaw. But I don't really care. Without a moment's hesitation, I tear open the little paper package and rip out the meat from within before stuffing it into my face. It's bland and dry and tough, but it's food. I chew and

I chew and I suddenly realize that my teeth are no longer crooked and rotting, and it doesn't hurt to eat anymore. I almost want to cry, but I'm somehow able to keep it inside.

Once I've swallowed all of it, I take out a bottle of water and drink it all in one gulp. God, that was good.

But the window isn't closed yet, so I quickly pull out the sword and shield.

The delinquent stares at my weapons. "*So, another close-range dealer, huh . . .*" I tilt my head at him and frown. He rolls his eyes and jerks a thumb at the fetal-position girl. "*She also chose the sword and shield. That means we've got four guys who are all close-range damage dealers and nobody at a distance. If we face bird enemies or something, we're screwed.*"

My frown dips a bit farther down. What does it matter if we're all DPS? Whatever happens, I'm playing this solo. Who in their right mind would pollute the game of life by playing it co-op?

The delinquent huffs at me. "*What? You think this is some solo adventure?*" I shrug at him. Why wouldn't it be? "*Listen, if it was solo, we wouldn't all be in the same lobby, would we?*" I don't see how that's important. Even if you're in a lobby with a million people, you still don't have to play with all of them. "*Okay, listen,*" he says. "*Check the Community tab. Right at the top of the screen. Just press it.*"

I glance back at the window in front of me. No reason not to, I suppose.

‹Community—Top—Status›

I poke the Community tab.

‹Status—Community—Top›
‹Europe Server›
‹Easy Lobby: 130/130
Normal Lobby: 45/45
Hard Lobby: 11/11
Hell Lobby: 4/4›

There's seriously only the four of us? In the entire Europe server there's only *four* Hell challengers?!

Really now. Still, I guess this explains a bit of what's going on. From the looks of it, close to two hundred people have been called here, assuming the numbers indicate humans. It almost looks as though I should be able to press the lobbies to enter some sort of chat, but anytime I try I get blocked.

‹The Lobby Chatrooms and Server Boards will be unlocked once the First Floor of the tutorial is cleared.›

Right, okay. Gotcha. I guess that makes sense, but it's still kind of a bummer. Still, my point stands. There's no particular reason to form a party.

The only other Swede here sidles up beside me. "Press the Status tab."

His helpfulness is making me suspicious, but I can't really refuse him. Without much ado, I press the tab. And what appears is enough to freeze me in my tracks.

<Top—Status—Community>
<PrissyKittyPrincess
Human Level 0
Agility: 9
Strength: 4
Stamina: 9
Magic Power: 13>

In a different state of mind, I might have focused on the fact that my stats look kind of like hot garbage. Maybe I would've lamented over how I should have picked that termite-eaten staff instead. Or maybe I'd feel emasculated by the fact that my strength is pathetically low. Or maybe I'd wonder what it meant that I'm not even level 1.

But I don't. Because right now, all I can see is my username.

<PrissyKittyPrincess>

That—that can't be right. Shouldn't it be my name or something? Lo Fennrick? Or—or maybe just my former username? ThatGentleNight2? Maybe it could remove the 2 since there aren't too many with that username here, but . . .

I feel a tremble take hold of my body.

A hand falls on my shoulder. "Your magic power's good, but the rest is . . . You know, you can probably increase it once the tutorial starts, so I'm sure it'll be—"

And then he notices it. There was no way he couldn't notice it. It's blaring and bright and obvious and *right there*. Like a malignant tumor growing right on your face.

"Th—that's, um . . ." He gulps audibly. "You could have gotten a worse one, right?"

"What's yours?" my mouth says faster than my mind thinks it. "What username did you get?"

He freezes in place. A bead of sweat runs down his forehead. "It's randomly generated, so it's really not all that important to . . ." I stare him down. He buckles. His head falls to face the floor. "My username is SpearMaestro."

I feel a violent need to strangle him, but the last time I strangled someone I got arrested, so I resign myself to simply bringing forth the mental image of his face turning blue and then purple and then white. It's a good image.

"But, erm, uh . . . If you look at the bottom, you can see a clock for the—ah, the attempt."

I glare at him for a few more seconds just to watch him squirm before looking back at the screen. To be sure, right there at the bottom, there's a little clock calendar thing.

<Top—Status—Community>
<00:27:01 Day 1>
<The first attempt will begin in 23:32:59>
<Floor 1 will open in 23:32:59>

I watch the seconds ticking by for a few moments. I've got a lot of questions, but I have a feeling that the majority of them will be answered in twenty-three hours, thirty-two minutes, and . . . twenty seconds. Nineteen. Eighteen. You get the point.

For now, I should get ready for the first floor. I have no idea what it will contain, but if it's anything like the MMORPGs it's trying to emulate, then it'll probably have some goblins or wolves or rats or whatever that I'll need to kill. That's my best bet. I shouldn't discount the possibility that it's a gathering quest or something noncombative, but the chance that I'll be fighting something is too high to ignore. In other words, before I do anything else, I should spend these twenty-four hours training to use my starter weapon.

"If you want, I can just call you by your real name instead. Mine is Gustaf Larsen. And you are?"

"My name is—" But what if he saw the news of my assault? What if he knows what I did? What if he's related to LetsFraternizeTogether? What if he was his fan? What if . . . ? "—Lo. It's Lo. Just Lo."

"Lo, is it?" He smiles. "Well, alright, Lo."

Phew. Crisis averted. "That guy over there is Uu . . . Uu . . . something with Uu."

"*Hey, you talkin' about me, geezer?*" The delinquent snarks at us. "*The name's Uuno Klami! And before you ask, yeah, my parents are huge nerds. Don't even think of making a joke about it or I'll cave your skull in, you get me?*"

Right. Uuno, then.

I point a finger at the girl. "*And her?*"

He blinks at me before shrugging dismissively. "*Is it even important? She's not going to be any useful. If anything, she'll just be in our way.*" I'm not sure whether I agree or disagree with him. Even if I have no choice but to fight with these as my teammates, calling her useless is a bit . . . I mean, she'll be far from crucial, but if nothing else she can at least be a meat shield.

Ignoring his words, I disengage from the two and wander over to her. As I noticed earlier, she is indeed crying. Impressive stamina to be able to cry for almost half an hour. I squat down next to her.

"*Hey.*" No response. Hmm. "*Hey.*" Nope, not that either. When all else fails, use violence. I poke her in the side, making her jerk up. Yeah, that's a glare, alright. She's not saying anything though, so I poke her again.

"—*!*" That was apparently enough to get her to talk, because now she's proving her impromptu beatboxing skills by chattering at incredible speeds. No idea what she's saying, though. I feel like I might recognize a few words here and there, but it's going by too fast to make anything out at all. Either way she seems pretty threatening, so I quickly pull up my hands in a show of surrender. *Look, I'm not here to harm you, alright?* Right, exactly. Her words gradually slow down. Right, yeah.

She clearly doesn't speak English, so I just bring out my sword. She jerks back. Understandable reaction, I guess, so I just hold it out to her hilt first. She glances up at me. I nod. She touches the hilt. Then she takes it in her hand. The sword must be made of aluminum or something because it's pretty light, but it's still too much for her, and her arm soon starts trembling, so I take it back. Regardless, this proves that interlobby trading is both possible and simple.

Regardless, I think sticking a sword in her hand won't do her any good. Looking over my shoulder, I glance back at Uuno. "*Hey. How'd you make her show you her weapons?*"

"*Huh? Uh, I just made her repeat inventory and then*"—a screen pops up in front of his eyes and he waves it off with a huff—"*I guided her through the tabs. She's not stupid; she should know how to do it by now.*"

I nod at him and turn back to the girl. I point at myself. "Lo."

She furrows her prominent brows for a second before her face lights up in understanding and she points at herself. "Anna."

Okay. I point at her—"Anna"—and at myself—"Lo."

She follows suit, first pointing at me—"Lo"—and then herself—"Anna." And then she smiles. Almost unwillingly, I smile back at her.

It took a while of trying, but after a few minutes of back and forth, I was able to get her to open her inventory and bring out her sword and shield, which also brought forth her standing up. Safe to say, she was no longer crying. But just holding the sword in an upright position made her arms tremble, so I had to convince her through sheer gesturing that the sword just wasn't usable for her. She didn't like it, but she eventually accepted it.

Oh, and I also got a glimpse of her status. Agility: 12. Strength: 2. Stamina: 4. Magic Power: 21. I'm both envious and not. If she'd only picked the staff, then she could have made a great mage or healer or whatever it is that the staff makes you. As an aside, her username was TrepidationUnderCommitment. I only barely restrained the urge to whack her over the head with her own weapon.

But for now, I need to get her able to use the shield properly.

And to do this, we started sparring. She wasn't happy to do it, and I was initially worried the shield would explode into dust, but after a graze turned into a slice, we learned that damaged weapons would automatically regenerate inside the lobby. And while I trained Anna, Uuno and Gustaf sparred together as well. And after some time, we decided to switch partners. I guess I wasn't thinking too much about it all when it happened.

I suppose it was a good way to train without having to just blindly swing a sword up and down. But, honestly speaking, it was kind of nice.

Sometimes you read posts and things by ultra-macho blowhards talking about how the only way to get close to another man is to fight him physically. I always thought of those kinds of guys as chumps trying to disguise themselves as warriors, but I think I've changed my mind somewhat. You only learn so much by talking to someone. It's actions that count, and this is no different.

When the final hours until the opening of the first floor drew near, I felt closer to these three than I had with probably anyone in my life. Sure, your family is one thing, but friends . . . I don't think I've ever really had one of those, so I can't compare it.

It's not like I'd call these three randos something as absolute as friends, but . . . it's kind of close. Maybe.

<Top—Status—Community>
<23:48:20 Day 1>
<The first attempt will begin in 00:11:40>
<Floor 1 will open in 00:11:40>

"It's almost time, isn't it?" Uuno says for all of us.

I nod at him. "Yeah." The sword in my hand feels heavy despite being so much lighter than a real one. The shield, despite being eaten by termites, doesn't feel light in the least. It's like holding a small table. But right now, I think anything I'd hold would feel way heavier than it should. I look over our little band. "Is everyone ready?"

Gustaf smiles at me. The sleeves of his shirt are rolled up and the front of it is drenched with sweat. Even though we've been here for an entire day and night, none of us felt any real need to sleep. We took a break at the twelve-hour mark to eat some dried beef and drink, but after that we just went right back to it. Our bodies regenerated as we fought, and after a couple of hours all of us gained a relevant skill for the combat we were doing.

I got Basic Swordsmanship level 1 and Basic Shieldwork level 1, both of which then appeared in the Status tab. If I pressed them, I could see the details.

<[Basic Swordsmanship (Lv.1)]
Allows the user to use the sword in a rudimentary fashion.>
<[Basic Shieldwork (Lv.1)]
Allows the user to use the shield in a rudimentary fashion.>

Doesn't exactly paint it as an amazing skill, but just having it feels reassuring. There was a clear difference when I got them, and that could also be felt in the others. It wasn't anything groundbreaking, but they seemed to instantly gain a basic sense of how to use their weapons. None of us were able to reach level 2 in any of our skills, but we weren't disheartened.

We all feel ready.

<Top—Status—Community>
<23:59:03 Day 1>
<The first attempt will begin in 00:00:57>
<Floor 1 will open in 00:00:57>

I glance at Anna. She clutches her shield just a little closer to her, making sure to hold it so that it primarily defends her chest and abdomen. All the soft parts.

"Alright," I say. *"Let's go."*

I step in front of the three, them standing at my back, ready. The air around us buzzes with anticipation.

<Top—Status—Community>
<23:59:50 Day 1>
<The first attempt will begin in 00:00:10>
<Floor 1 will open in 00:00:10>

Ten,
Nine,
Eight,
Seven,
Six,
Five,
Four,
Three,
Two,
One.

<Top—Status—Community>
<00:00:00 Day 2>
<The first attempt will begin in 00:00:00>
<Floor 1 will open in 00:00:00>

I hold my breath.

<Floor 1 has opened. Do you want to enter?>
<Yes/No>

The same message appeared for us all. We all share a look, and grin.

<If no answer is chosen, [No] will be chosen for you and the floor may be accessed on the next attempt.>

"*Well, you read the message,*" I mumble. Turning back, I address the group as a whole. "*Let's all press it at once, on three, two, one—!*"

I poke the *Yes.*
And then the world shifts below my feet.

Pull and Push

Darkness. Howling winds. A strangle whistle reaches my ears, like a loosened arrow, and all of a sudden everything is very, very cold, like a late autumn evening. I stumble forward and find that the black ground beneath my feet is stiff with cold dirt and rocks. Goose bumps spread across my body in an instant. Roots like veins crawl across the ground.

Something feels wrong. Something feels very wrong. "*E—everyone, are you still—*"

Whirling around, I find that I am not alone. There stand my comrades, but they look different. I hear that whistle again. But it's so many. Splitting the horrible wind that threatens to topple me off my feet. Closer, closer, faster, faster. And then, they strike.

Arrows.

I don't know where they came from, I don't know who loosed them, but they strike like vipers.

Some pierce through Anna's soft back like a knife through tofu. Others thump thump thump into the shield in her hands, first getting stuck and then eventually breaking it fully, making it splinter and turn to dark dust. After that, there is nothing to save her anymore as the swarm of arrows pierces her lungs and deflates them before she can even attempt to scream.

And then she falls into my arms. She doesn't bleed as much as I thought people did. The holes are plugged by the arrows.

"Ahh . . ."

Gustaf sighs as he falls over, his back prickly like a porcupine. A spear apparently isn't too good at stopping arrows.

And neither is an axe. Uuno just falls.

Anna shudders and twitches in my arms. I can hear arrows whizzing past my head, but I'm not thinking about them. Thump, thump, thump. With every arrow that hits her body, her limbs twist and jerk. But she isn't saying anything. Her eyes are dull in the infinite darkness. I know she's dead. But she's still warm. I can't think. I wrap my arms around her and feel how the arrows stab into my arms and pin them to her dead, porcupine back.

And slowly, shuffling my feet against the ground, I drag her off to the side.

After only a few seconds my foot catches in the loop of one of the many roots snaking across the ground and I stumble into the shade of a dark, leafless tree, collapsing to the ground in such a way that I feel a few additional arrows stab into my legs. But once I'm in the shade, the arrows stop.

I breathe fast, just like my heartbeat. She's still in my arms. I can't let go of her anymore because the arrows bolted my arms to her back. I can't feel the pain. I can't feel anything but the warmth of her body slowly draining away.

I hold her tighter.

<You have learned: Piercing Tolerance Lv.1>

Alright. I see. So you get stronger . . . by getting hurt. I see . . .

Something rises to my cheeks. Something hot and choking and burning and it goes out of my eyes as cold streaks that run down my neck and into the mouth of my torn hoodie to make it soft and damp and warm.

If I look to the right, I can see glints from the arrowheads whizzing by, reflecting what I think might be a moon. But when I look up, what I see isn't a moon but rather an eclipse. A perpetual, unmoving eclipse of the sun. With the white-silver outline around that dark spot that is the moon, it almost looks like a massive eye, peeking down between the twisted branches of the leafless trees.

<Tutorial stage, Hell Difficulty First Floor: A Forest Dark>
<[Clear Condition] Reach the hill gazed upon by the black eye.>

Slowly, I let my head fall from that staring eclipse down to what lies below it. Just as the window said, it's a hilltop. It's tall and mainly composed of jagged, toothlike rocks. All I need to do is reach there.

I look back to my right. The wind whines and with it comes the whistle of endless arrows. By the tawny light of the eclipse, I can see the outlines of Uuno and Gustaf, both covered with so many arrows that they resemble urchins more than humans. The thought almost brings a chuckle to my lips.

Still holding her in my arms, I lean over to the left and release the contents of my bowels. An arrow whizzes mere millimeters past my head and by sheer instinct I jerk it back to the shade.

<You have learned: Field Instincts Lv.1>

My lungs hurt. After a full twenty-four hours in a place where I can't get properly hurt, this shuddering is nauseating. I don't even know how many arrows I've been hit by. How many arrows can you take before you die?

Leaning forward, I start counting. Five arrows in my arms. Two in my legs. One in my left shoulder. That isn't too bad. Anna took nineteen arrows, so unless I get hit eleven times more, I'll be fine. I should be fine . . .

<You have learned: Poison Tolerance Lv.1>

Aha . . . ahahaha . . . !

I see how it is—!

"Take me back!" I cry to the whistling winds. "Take me back to the lobby, please!" But the attempt only leaves my lungs feeling rattled. I feel like laughing but I can't muster the effort. Maybe I need to say the right word? "Return! Back to lobby! Leave floor! *End attempt!*"

Nothing. I'd say that silence meets me, but the arrows whizzing by all around me are way too loud.

There is no return. I'm stuck here until I clear the floor, or—more likely—die.

I hold her closer. There's no respawning. I can feel it. I can tell. She's just gone, and so are they.

<Status—Community—Top>
<Europe Server>
<Easy Lobby: 61/130
Normal Lobby: 5/45
Hard Lobby: 1/11
Hell Lobby: 0/1>

Yeah, I'm not surprised. It really is just me, then?

Everyone else is also doing their best. But I don't think any of them have died yet. And still, we . . . !

I shake my head. The movement makes Anna shuffle around atop me. I'm starting to lose any sense of touch in my hands and feet. I feel sick to my stomach for many reasons. And now that I think of it, my vision is sort of blurry, too. I can't tell if this is the poison or just the blood loss. So, in the end, this really is the way it happens.

I don't . . . I don't want to die. I thought I did, but . . .

I don't want to become stiff like she is.

<You have learned: Bleeding Tolerance Lv.1>
<You have learned: Unconsciousness Tolerance Lv.1>

For some reason, I feel neither more alert nor more *blood-full*. Just the opposite.

But I'm not dead yet. And really, what kind of loser dies on the first floor? Of the *tutorial*, no less? Not me. No, I can't be that person. I won't allow it. I need to live on. So I can stick it to LetsFraternizeTogether, and to Dad who didn't want to bail me out, and to everyone else who kept me down . . . !

I'll show them all the tenacity of a pro gamer—!

So let's just breathe in, and out. Let's relax. The poison spreads faster the faster my heart beats, and I bleed out quicker too. There's no time limit on this quest. It's just me, and that's it. I can take as much time as I need. I don't know if my wounds will automatically heal, but if there's a skill for that, then I'm sure I can learn it eventually. I just . . . need . . . to relax . . .

. . .

I let my eyes close.

Darkness surrounds me. Darker than the forest. In here, there is just me.

Me, and the pain. I can feel the arrows. The adrenaline fades bit by bit and the pain lurches onto me but I don't let myself get lost in the pain. There is pain, yes, but in the pain, I also feel warmth. My heart beats fast. But with every second that passes, it slows down, bit by bit. The sludge within my system that would bring total oblivion loses its tempo.

<You have learned: Poison Tolerance Lv.2>

Darkness. Darkness. Darkness.
But deep in the darkness . . .
Light.

<You have learned: Meditation Lv.1>
<You have learned: Lesser Auto-Regeneration Lv.1>

Internally, I smirk.

<A Canto appears to you.>

A what—

<[Nel mezzo del cammin di nostra vita mi ritrovai per una selva oscura ché la diritta via era smarrita.]>

. . . Okay?

When I open my eyes, the window is gone, but if I close them, it returns. I have no idea what that is or what it means. It's some sort of southern European language I think, maybe Latin? Spanish? Italian? Who knows. What I *do* know is that I have no idea what it's supposed to translate to. I mean, even if it is Latin or something, that doesn't help me. Hm. Now that I look at it, considering that *mezzo* is *middle* in Italian, I guess this must be that fateful language. And I only know that one because my parents had some unfortunate obsession with trying to turn me into a child musical prodigy. Shame on them that I got stiff fingers and suck at the piano, I guess.

But even if I knew every Italian music word, that still wouldn't help me here. It's Italian. It's a so-called canto. That means nothing.

Putting that aside, I got the healing skill, so now it's just a matter of time before I'm back on my feet and able to take arrows like they're spitballs!

. . .

. . .

. . . Or it might take a bit longer than that. Let's just take a quick look at the clock . . .

<Top—Status—Community>
<00:46:47 Day 2>
<The second attempt will begin in 29:23:13:13>

Forty-five minutes was all it took for all three to die, huh? That said, it seems the next attempt will begin in about a month. Whatever an attempt is . . .

I wave aside the window.

For now, let's just focus on not dying. Meditating seems to work, so I'll just keep doing that until I feel better. However long that'll take.

Slowly, over the course of several hours, I accrued both pain and tolerance skills and levels. After about two hours, I realized with a certain amount of unhappiness that there is no pain tolerance skill. And even the other tolerances, from piercing to bleeding to poison to unconsciousness, are very weak. I can hardly even notice the effect at all. But once poison tolerance reached level 4, it seemed to finally outweigh the poison enough to ward it off fully. But the arrows are still in my body, and it didn't take long for me to realize that even though auto-regeneration was at level 3, it couldn't heal away the arrows. There was only one way to remove them.

I'm not sure where I heard it, but the least damaging way to remove an arrow is to push it through completely, not to pull it out. This went pretty well for the ones in my arms and legs since they had already gone the whole way through, so pushing them the rest of the way didn't mean much. But the one in my left shoulder is different. It had only gone halfway in before getting stuck against my shoulder blade. I know this because if I move my left arm, I can both hear and feel the arrowhead scrape against the inside of my bones.

I can't just push it through willy-nilly Either I shift it enough to get it out below or above the shoulder blade, or I pull it out.

After gritting my teeth for a long time, I decide to simply pull it out. My vision is still dancing with white and black dots from the blood loss, but I still have to do it. My bleeding tolerance has reached level 5, but it will have to be enough.

Grabbing hold of the arrow's body, I prepare myself. Breathe in, breathe out. Just like when I meditate. One clean pull. That's all I need. One clean pull . . .

I tense my arms. Just one, clean, *pull!*

I pull with all of my strength and feel the arrow twist inside me and the last poison inside the arrowhead spread into my blood and my flesh gets carved as the arrow moves and my jaw snaps shut and I grit my teeth in pain but my fingers are trembling and slick with blood and the body of the arrow slips out of my grip and I almost fall forward, making her shift in my lap. "Argghhh . . . !" I unwillingly groan. God. Jesus. That was . . . not good.

<You have learned: Internal Damage Tolerance Lv.1>

Great. Wonderful. I bet that'll be extremely useful the next time I pull it out. Clean pull, my ass . . .

I grab hold of the arrow again. Touching it sends little electrical jolts of pain through my shoulder and chest, but it doesn't matter anymore. I clench my fist around the arrow. Two clean pulls. That isn't too much to ask for, is it? Of course not. But that's all I need, so here, we . . . go!

I don't even pull it a fourth of the way out before the arrowhead hooks onto what I think is my collarbone and in the absolute mind-blotting, toe-curling pain of this, the thin body of the arrow in my hand snaps in two. My breathing feels ragged. It didn't hit my lung but it's damn close. I . . . I really don't have any choice but to push it through, do I? Yeah. I don't.

The body of the arrow snapped off so close to my body that I can barely reach it anymore. But I need to push it the rest of the way in. Otherwise, I lose mobility in my entire left arm. I don't know if this stage has any monsters or enemies, but if it does, I'll need my shield arm. I grit my teeth again.

I just need to push it through. It'll have to go above the shoulder blade. That's the only way.

I clench my left fist and squeeze my eyes shut. And then, placing my right hand on the splintered end of the arrow, I push.

<You have learned: Internal Damage Tolerance Lv.2>

The arrow carves mercilessly through my flesh, severing tendons and gnashing through everything I have, scraping along my shoulder blade as it does, making the sound of metal against bone reverberate through my sore skull. Push, push, push. Once it finally no longer presses against my shoulder blade, the remaining half of the arrow has gone so far inside my shoulder that I have to stick my fingers deep inside my own shoulder to properly push it out, making blood squeeze out of the hole and run down my tattered clothes.

But after several minutes of this, I finally feel the arrowhead start to push against the hard and rubbery skin of my back. After a few unsuccessful attempts at pushing it through, I reach back with my left hand and hold down the skin while pushing with my right, which finally lets the arrow burst back out into the free air. I pull my right hand back out of my shoulder and pull the arrow the rest of the way with my left, tossing it aside once it's no longer stuck to me. The whole arrow is red, and so are both of my hands and almost half of my hoodie.

<You have learned: Internal Damage Tolerance Lv.3>
<You have learned: Bleeding Tolerance Lv.6>
<You have learned: Lesser Auto-Regeneration Lv.4>

I feel dizzy, but with this, I can finally rest a bit more properly. It might be optimistic thinking, but if this dark forest was filled with any beasts or monsters, they would have sniffed me out already. Unconsciously, I press her closer to me.

I close my eyes.

It wouldn't be right to say that I slept; I was in too much pain for that. If it was meditation, then it was an incredibly deep one.

<You have learned: Meditation Lv.2>
<You have learned: Hypnagogia Lv.1>

When I come to, my injuries are mostly healed. I still feel groggy, and my brain feels fuzzy and weird, but I'm not in any immediate pain. All of my resistances have leveled up pretty well, but I don't feel invincible in the least. One hit to the head and I'm dead.

How long has it even been since I entered this stage?

<Top—Status—Community>
<19:00:02 Day 2>
<The second attempt will begin in 29:04:59:58>

Nineteen hours. Nineteen hours just to recover from a few arrow wounds.

Then again, if this was the real world, I'd probably be dead. Dead and buried. I wonder how long it would have taken someone to find my corpse? If it was one of my coworkers, they'd probably loot me and leave me to the masses to find. Or something. I never did get too close to them.

But enough about that.

It doesn't seem like I'm going to be attacked by anything anytime soon, so if I wanted to, I could probably hang around here until that timer went down completely. The issue is that I don't know what happens when the second attempt rolls around. I was only able to survive like this because everyone was in the way of the arrows, so I was only hit in my arms and legs and stuff. If I had to redo this stage, I'd probably die instantly.

Now that I think about it . . . The arrows really do only come from one direction, don't they? Hm.

Let's see . . . If the hill is in the hypothetical north, then the arrows are coming from the hypothetical west. From what I can see, the arrows aren't being shot by anyone, but rather they're just guided by the wind. Since the wind is strong, it easily weaves between the trees, though a lot of arrows still hit the trees, getting stuck on their hypothetical west side.

If I get hit by these arrows head-on with no shield or shelter, I'm dead.

I hold her closer. Her shield had just burst. It made no difference in the least. From what I can see, the only things that can protect me are the trees, and . . .

I stare into her dead-empty eyes. Gulp.

But it's not as though I have any choice. If she were still alive, if she could still speak, then . . . Then, she would have told me to keep going. For their sakes. No matter the cost.

I glance to my right. Along a path weaving between the trees lie two urchin bodies and three gleaming weapons. A spear, an axe, and my sword. I'll need that sword. This floor is one thing, but if I don't have it for the next floor, I'll probably be dead. I really have no choice in all of this.

What's my best option for pulling my sword closer?

I turn my eyes to her. She could work, right? I mean, she's already riddled with arrows, so what's a few more?

Gulping, I straighten out where I sit. Lifting her up, I take a hold of her left foot and hold her chest up. She's pretty light. And with that as my tool, I toss her out toward the sword. Her body flops onto the ground in a weird, almost comedic position. About half a dozen arrows pierce her, three of them hitting her skull in such a way that it bursts open in a spray of goop. I pull her back in and throw her again. This time she gets a bit closer, but the gap is almost a full meter longer than she is. I pull her back in. Yeah, I'll need to go out there. I frown at her. *Sorry in advance.*

Propping her up in front of me like a shield, I stand up and inch out into the dastardly wind. Thump thump thump. A few arrows pierce all the way through her abdomen and graze mine, and a few hit my legs, but I can still keep on moving.

Once I reach my sword, I quickly grab it and will it into my inventory. But then I spy the spear and the axe.

It would be a waste to leave them to rot, right? Yeah.

Shuffling along, I take a few more steps, getting closer and closer, until I finally reach the two prime weapons. A single touch sends them into my inventory, and I feel a surge of victory and hope that's instantly dashed as an arrow flies by and completely severs my hamstring, sending me flying down to the ground with her on top of me. Pain spasms through me and I bite down on my lip so hard I taste blood.

Not good. Not good. Not good.

Damn it. I can't die here. Was it so bad to want a few more weapons?

Gritting my teeth, I try to drag myself across the ground but an arrow stabs into my hand, nailing it to the ground, and I give a hiss of pain. I can't let it stop me, though, so without any conscious input, I lift my hand high, pulling it off the arrow.

<You have learned: Bleeding Tolerance Lv. 7>

Great. Wonderful. Fantastic.

I'm leaving a snail trail of blood, but I don't have time to think about it. The tree is so close. I can almost taste it. Smell the bark. Touch it. My vision is darkening. But I need to stay awake. So I pull myself. Step by step. Inch by inch.

<You have learned: Unconsciousness Tolerance Lv.4>
<You have learned: Poison Tolerance Lv.5>

And then, finally, shade. My head enters the shade of the tree, and then my upper body, and then my abdomen, but I couldn't get my legs in before I felt my consciousness slip fully.

I'm still awake, but I feel asleep. I'm alive, but I feel dead.

<You have learned: Hypnagogia Lv.2>
<You have learned: Poison Tolerance Lv.6>

I don't know how many hours pass in this wakeful yet asleep state, but when I return from it, my vision is filled with status messages.

<You have learned: Piercing Tolerance Lv.7>
<You have learned: Poison Tolerance Lv.10>
<You have learned: Poison Resistance Lv.1>
<You have learned: Unconsciousness Tolerance Lv.7>
<You have learned: Bleeding Tolerance Lv. 10>
<You have learned: Bleeding Resistance Lv. 1>
<You have learned: Lesser Auto-Regeneration Lv.6>

I stare at them for a second. Then, once I've read them all, I pull myself fully into the shade of the tree. There I pull out the dozen or so arrows stuck in my legs. It's like pulling out splinters. I can't even feel it anymore. All I feel is the dull sensation of pressure and something giving way.

<You have learned: Cold Tolerance Lv.2>

When did I get that? Must've been the cold, I guess. God knows I could certainly do with some warmth . . .

On that note, it seems like my bleeding and poison tolerances both evolved into proper resistances, which is nice, I suppose.

<[Poison Resistance (Lv.1)] Evolved version of [Poison Tolerance]. Grants protection against poisons and venoms.>
<[Bleeding Resistance (Lv.1)] Evolved version of [Bleeding Tolerance]. Stifles bleeding and counteracts attacks that cause the [Bleeding] status effect.>

Right, that's about what I expected. Neither of them reached more than level 1, so it's fair to assume that it's harder to increase the level of a resistance skill than a mere tolerance skill.

With these two mildly competent-looking skills, I think I may actually have a chance of beating this floor. I have my weapons, I have her for protection . . . It's possible.

Looking off into the distance, I catch sight of the unmoving, unblinking eclipse and the hill just below it. By the looks of it, it'll take me several days to get there, and that's without accounting for the pain of dodging the streams of arrows.

At least, that would be true if I walked straight toward it. But I don't think that that's my most suitable strategy here. The arrows are coming from the hypothetical west, and the hill is in the hypothetical north. If I head straight for it, the arrows will hit me any time I'm not in the shade of a tree. Say what you will about her effectiveness as a shield, but I have a feeling that in a few days, she'll start to lose her arrow-riddled limbs one by one. Hopping from tree to tree without a shield would be suicide. However, if I had the arrows downwind or upwind—in other words, coming *from* the hill—then when I move toward the hill, I can line up the trees in such a way that the arrows won't hit me even as I jump from tree to tree. I won't need her protection anymore.

To do this, I'll need to walk in a roundabout manner. But it is doable.

<Top—Status—Community>
<03:21:20 Day 3>
<The second attempt will begin in 28:21:39:40>

Twenty-eight days. Yeah, I've got time.

I just need to get there.

And so, I set out to conquer the first floor.

Mentally, I made a map of the area. Trees all around, hill in the middle, and arrows from the hypothetical west. All I had to do was position the hill in such a way that it was in the hypothetical west so that the arrows were coming from the direction I was walking toward. That way, once I got close enough, it should also serve as shelter from the arrows. It was a simple enough plan, and for the first few days, it worked pretty well. I went from tree to tree, using her as a shield. After a day or two her limbs started falling off, but getting hit in an arm or a leg or a shoulder was no longer dangerous for me. As long as I kept my internal organs and head safe, I'd be alright.

<You have learned: Battle Focus Lv.1>
<You have learned: Enhanced Vision Lv.1>

At that point, I also learned a pair of immensely useful skills. Enhanced vision was passive, but once it hit level 3, I was able to actually see the path that the arrows would take before they hit. Battle focus was an active skill that drained my mental stamina to use, but with it, the world seemed to slow down. Together, they allowed me to dodge arrows. This was immensely useful once her head was shot clean off.

But after a few days, I found myself in a bit of a pickle.

The direction the arrows were coming from did not change. It was always from the hypothetical west, with the hill always in the hypothetical north. I had kind of hoped that I would eventually be able to use the eclipse as a guide since it *should* move as I do, but it doesn't. It hangs over the hill, no matter from which direction I look at it.

My strategy had been to walk toward the hypothetical east, which in my mind would have been the quickest to get me in the shadow of the hill, but after over a week of the hill not changing position and the arrows always coming from the hypothetical west, I realized my error.

The arrows aren't coming from the west, or the east, or even the north or south.

They're swirling around the hill in a giant storm. No matter what way I go, the arrows will always come from the left when looking at the hill, because they're moving counterclockwise around it.

By the time I realized this, I had already trekked for nine days and learned half a dozen new tolerance skills.

<You have learned: Starvation Tolerance Lv.1>
<You have learned: Dehydration Tolerance Lv.1>
<You have learned: Exhaustion Tolerance Lv.1>
<You have learned: Hypothermia Tolerance Lv.1>
<You have learned: Paralysis Tolerance Lv.1>
<You have learned: Wind Tolerance Lv.1>

Not to even mention the skills related to my stamina increasing, or anything like that. Even though it hardly felt as though they did anything in the moment, once they increased enough, it let me continue my trek of hell for days on end without stopping.

However, once I realized that my strategy was built on a faulty premise, there was only one thing I could do.

Sit down and redo my plan.

The Hill

And that's why I'm sitting here, in the shade of an especially large tree, using my meditation skill. Now that it's gotten pretty high, I can easily get into that place that took me hours before. The perfect darkness. It makes the pain feel more dull and brings me away from the horror and darkness outside.

<A Canto appears to you.>

The only trouble is every time I reach this state, this thing pops up. And, no, I checked, and it's still the same thing. Basically, it's useless. That aside . . .

I think I know what my best strategy is, now that I understand how this works.

Gently, I place a hand on her. I can't really remember her name anymore, and all I've got left is her upper torso. Her pelvis fell off a while back, but by holding her in my left hand and my sword in my right and keeping battle focus active, I can dodge, parry, and block arrows almost perfectly now. That's the only reason why I think my new strategy will work.

I will need to slowly walk in a gradually smaller spiral around the hill, several times over, until I finally get close enough to hopefully reach the eye of the storm.

To boot, I'll need to do this clockwise. The arrows move counterclockwise, but as I've discovered, it's a whole lot easier to block arrows if they're coming from the front. For the past few days, I've basically been walking backward. Sure, she's pretty battered by now, but I think she can last.

It's all just a matter of will.

<You have learned: Meditation Lv.10>
<You have learned: Recovery Meditation Lv.1>

Oho? The meditation skill can evolve? It doesn't sound too bad, either.

<[Recovery Meditation (Lv.1)]
Evolved version of [Meditation]. Recovery skills are enhanced as long as the
skill is active. Greater mental clarity is achieved.>

Is this what I think it is? The so-adored battle meditation that heals your wounds quicker? Well, well, well! Looks like I may actually have more than a noob's chance at surviving this!

And for once, the effects of the skill actually feel somewhat drastic, with the half a dozen or so holes in my abdomen and legs and arms quickly healing. Well, maybe not *quickly*, but I can feel that it will only take around half an hour as opposed to several hours. Is this how my legend as the unkillable player begins?

But maybe not under my current username.

If I die, do I get to choose a new username in the afterlife, or do I need to pay cash for a name change?

Hm. On that note, how's the community doing so far?

<Top—Status—Community>
<21:21:21 Day 12>
<The second attempt will begin in 19:02:38:39>

I've been in here for almost two weeks, huh. Somehow, it feels like it's been both more and less. Anyhow . . .

I poke the Community tab.

<Status—Community—Top>
<Europe Server>
<Easy Lobby: 61/127
Normal Lobby: 5/23
Hard Lobby: 0/6
Hell Lobby: 0/1>

A lot of people have started to die now, huh? Around five in the Hard, over twenty in the Normal, and a couple in the Easy. I guess the only way to know how this happened is when the lobbies open once I clear this stage. There's a fair chance that some of the others have already beaten this floor, but I don't know if the next floor opens instantly or only with the next attempt. I really don't know. Either way, dying isn't reserved for the Hell Difficulty alone.

Anyhow, my wounds feel pretty much healed, so it's about time I get moving. There are nineteen days until the next attempt, and I don't want to find out what happens if I haven't beaten this stage by then.

I get to my feet. Picking her up, I slide my hand into a hole I made around her spine to make for a sort of grip. She really does look like an urchin now. Better her than me.

And so I set out again.

I had only hypothesized it, but my theory was soon proven true. As I slowly, slowly, inch by inch made my way closer to the hill by circling around it, the winds did indeed get stronger. After some time, I was unable to physically move forward because of how strong the winds were. Only when my wind tolerance—a skill I had assumed useless—reached level 10 and evolved into wind resistance was I able to continue. Somehow, it made me more unshakable as I made my way forward. My stats were the same as when I began, but with the skills I had accrued, I was able to defend myself against the winds with some amount of skill. And it was going just fine, until one day, she poofed.

I don't know what did it or how or why, but exactly two weeks after she had died, her torso just up and poofed. I was so surprised by it that I got a couple of arrows in my abdomen, but by this point the arrows moved so fast that they just burst straight through me rather than getting stuck. In shock, I threw myself into the shade of a tree, deliriously staring at where she'd disappeared.

And there, like a mob in a game, lay a few item drops. Two pieces of dried meat and a glass bottle of water. I blinked at it, almost expecting it to disappear once I looked away.

I no longer had a shield.

But deep inside, a little question slyly chiseled its way into my brain.

Do I really need a shield?

After an hour of recovery meditation, the holes from the arrows were gone.

My skills were high enough to dodge and parry the arrows as needed. Did I really, actually, truly need a shield? And really . . . If the arrows hit the shield and not me, then I couldn't increase my tolerances from them.

A grin rose to my lips.

That's right. The more you get hurt, the stronger you become.

Boldly, like a lion facing an armed hunter, I went out into the fray.

Jumping, leaping, dodging, I held one sword in each hand, deftly parrying the arrows before they even got close to my supple flesh. Even after getting hit, I'm able to keep going thanks to my many skills. I think, by now, I'm mainly fueled by adrenaline and not much else. Any time I settle down without meditating, the pain seeps in and I have a strange, illogical need to get hurt again to get another fix, to keep the pain at bay. I have no idea how my brain is producing this much adrenaline, but I am certainly not complaining.

And so, slowly, I make my way closer to the hill, inch by inch, step by step.

I am now so close that the hill looms over me. But unlike my initial hypothesis so long ago, getting closer to the hill does not grant me any form of rest. The arrows now move so fast that even with all my skills, I can't see them. I just can't. The wind is also horrible and occasionally takes me off my feet despite my resistances.

I've been in almost the exact same spot for three days now. My only movement has been to jump out from behind the tree, get shot with arrows, and jump back in to pull them out one by one before meditating to heal again. In and out, in and out, in and out. My lesser auto-regeneration evolved into auto-regeneration, losing the *lesser* prefix. My regeneration meditation has reached level 5. By stabbing myself with an arrow and then comparing how fast the wound regenerates with or without the regeneration meditation, I can conclude that it currently grants a +50% healing rate, which is insane.

I can also use it in conjunction with hypnagogia to enter a half-waking, half-sleeping state where I can get some sort of rest without going to sleep fully.

The problem isn't this place. If I could, I would almost have liked to stay here for a few weeks until my battle focus and enhanced vision and the other skills were high enough to let me both see and dodge the arrows. At the moment, however, the problem isn't with ability and growth, so to speak, but rather with *time*.

\<Top—Status—Community\>
\<05:10:05 Day 27\>
\<The second attempt will begin in 3:18:49:55\>

In a little less than four days, the next attempt will begin. I need to beat this floor within that time.

I have no choice. I just don't have enough time left to try to get strong enough to beat this properly.

I need to brute-force this.

Looking to the sky, I can see how close the eclipse is, and the hill just below it. If I were to run straight at it, I could reach it within only a few hours, I think. The problem is that by the time I get there, I'll be as prickly as a porcupine.

But—but I can survive that, right? Sure, I mean, she didn't survive it, and neither did those two, but . . .

But I can. They didn't have any skills. They didn't even know what was happening. They didn't have time to know. *But I do.* I can. I can do it if I just push myself to the highest limits. Isn't that how your skills get better, anyway? I just need to go for it. Any damage I take can be healed easily. Piercing resistance level 2 is nothing to laugh at!

Yeah. Yeah. I can do it. I just need to set out.

Silently, drawing myself up, I get to my feet. I just need to run straight for it. No pauses, no healing unless I'm really about to die. I set my eyes on the hill.

My body tenses. A grin finds its way onto my lips.

And off . . . I . . . go!

My body flies out of the shade of the tree, both swords raised high, successfully parrying two arrows. Another arrow pierces straight through my arm but I can still swing it, so it doesn't matter. Battle focus is active, and my vision is good enough to notice a few of the arrows as the light of the eclipse glints off their heads. A leap, a twist, a buckle, and I'm in the shade of the next tree. Without pausing at all, I jump toward the next, catching an arrow to the knee but still continuing. This isn't enough to stop me. I won't let it be.

From tree to tree like a shadow just as ghostly as the leafless trees themselves, accruing more and more arrows as I go, like medals pinned to my limbs, I keep going. The intoxicating adrenaline dulls the pain and I'm able to focus only on dodging and parrying. When an arrow shoots at my head and I can't parry it, I sacrifice my limbs. They'll heal, but my brain sure won't.

After half an hour, my razor-sharp focus begins to wane. I've lost a lot of blood, but that'll regenerate in time.

The arrows are moving so fast now. I can't see them, much less parry. So, after a moment of silent thought, I put the swords back in my inventory and pull out the axe. It's ridiculously broad, so it actually works as a shield, large enough to hide both my head and upper chest. My lower abdomen isn't quite so lucky.

It doesn't feel like I've got a head anymore. My body feels bereft of blood. I think most of it got stuck to my clothes. I want to take them off but they're the only defense I've got left.

I have no choice but to go on.

\<Top—Status—Community\>
\<02:00:10 Day 28\>
\<The second attempt will begin in 2:21:59:50\>

And then, after lord knows how many hours or days or years, the arrows let up. No more arrows hit my body. I haven't seen where I've been going ever since I started using the axe as a shield.

Numb from head to toe, I fall flat on my face, my skull meeting rock and mud because I'm a fool to expect a pillow. For the past few hours, I haven't been looking at the status messages I've been getting because, frankly speaking, they distract me. Looking at them in the middle of a battle is a death sentence.

In a little less than three days, the attempt ends.

Slowly, groggily, I open my eyes and look up. Before me looms that hill overlooked by the black eye. I'm here. I cleared the floor. I think.

I stare up at the hill.

<Tutorial stage, Hell Difficulty First Floor: Boss Stage.>
<[Clear Condition] Reach the top of the hill and greet him.>

B—boss stage? Hey, the floor description didn't say anything about some boss stage; this is horsecrap! Have you even seen the top of that hill!?

I mean, seriously, aren't boss stages only supposed to appear after, like, ten floors or something? And then a midboss at the halfway point? This is ridiculous!

But, then again, if all I have to do is get to the top of the hill, then it could be worse, right? Get to the top of the hill. Compared to dodging and/or getting hit by a gazillion arrows, it's basically a piece of cake. Even though it's steep enough to be called a cliff or a small mountain rather than a hill, I bet I could get up there with several days to spare until the next attempt.

And then I'll greet him and be done with this whole floor.

Whoever *he* is.

Looking down, I scan my current injuries. I've taken too many arrows to my legs and arms to count, but my abdomen and head are mostly clear. Nothing to my lungs either, so I should be alright.

<You have learned: Bleeding Resistance Lv.3>

Great, very useful. Snark aside, once a tolerance evolves into a resistance, it actually becomes really useful. Who woulda guessed?

Back to reality, I've got less than three days left until the next attempt, so I should have enough time to heal up before I start. I want to get to it straightaway and get back to the lobby to get back to my full health, but that will have to wait.

So, even though it pains me, I take a seat and begin meditating. After an hour or so, I've healed enough holes and scrapes to be able to start pulling out the arrows. First my legs, one leg at a time, and then my arms. Once these have healed fully, which takes about two hours, I can pull out the half a dozen stuck in my abdomen. Pulling them out reminds me of the fact that I haven't eaten in almost a month.

<You have learned: Starvation Tolerance Lv.10>
<You have learned: Starvation Resistance Lv.1>

It's a funny thing, no matter how high a resistance gets, the actual pain from it doesn't go away. My body feels less weak, and I can move better with the resistances, but the arrows and the poison and the starvation and the dehydration still make me lethargic with the pain. It's still better than dying, though, so whatever. I start pushing out the arrows stuck deep in my bowels.

\<You have learned: Internal Damage Resistance Lv.2\>

Fun.

After digging around a fair bit and feeling the squishiness of my organs and pushing out the final few arrows, including one arrowhead that got snapped off, I pull my arm back out. If you're running around a lot, then if you get an arrow stuck in a certain part, the head may often stay stuck inside while the body itself snaps off, which is a huge bother. Normally speaking you shouldn't even run with just a single arrow in your body, but I don't exactly have a choice here.

With all the arrows dislodged, I spend a few more hours fully healing the rest of the damage. Once my fingers feel alright again and my body is no longer anemic to the point of half death, I know it's time.

\<Top—Status—Community\>
\<05:01:10 Day 29\>
\<The second attempt will begin in 1:18:58:50\>

Alright. Two days. I can do this.

I heave myself onto my feet and survey the hill. Since I've circled around it a dozen times now, I know very well that all sides are equally jagged and horrible. Might as well just head for it, you know?

As for preparations . . .

I check my inventory.

\<Top—Status—Community\>
\<Inventory\>

Yeah, all I have is what she dropped, alongside a spear and a shield and sword. Two bits of dried meat and a glass bottle of water. I've eaten all of the rest and drunk all of the water. Going without food for a few weeks is alright, but you can really feel the loss of water. I'm lucky my dehydration tolerance evolved after only a week or so or I might really have died.

I think it would be best to prepare myself for the worst, so I pull out my wooden shield and put the axe back in my inventory. Although I've been carrying it and swinging my sword around so much, none of my base stats have increased, not even my stamina, despite getting exhaustion resistance. It seems that I really can only get stronger by increasing my level, which I assume comes from beating monsters. Assuming there are any monsters in this God-abandoned hell of a tutorial.

First stage my ass.

Closing the window, I clutch the shield in my left hand and my sword in my right.

It's time.

Looking up toward the eclipse, I boldly make my entrance.

The hill is angled in such a way that it has a slow slope that eventually ends in a sharp, rocky ascent, so for now, I'm just stepping forward, keeping my eyes and ears at the ready. Battle focused out of my mind and all that.

And for almost an hour, it goes fine. And then, the boss monster appears.

<Leopard (Lv.8) [BOSS]>

"Ha . . . hahahah . . ." It's literally just a leopard. Big and spotted and with legs as long as spears. That last part was an exaggeration, but this is absolutely a leopard. Long, thick tail. Almost round ears. It's not exactly as big as I imagined, but it is absolutely larger than me. Not in terms of pure height or anything, but it is clearly in a completely different weight class. Now that I think of it, it might have longer legs than I do . . . B—but that means nothing!

It's just a leopard. Sure, it's fast, but I'm not planning on running. Its speed does not grant it immense agility. If I just keep calm, I can handle it.

"GRAUUUURRR"

<Lion (Lv.7) [BOSS]>

Leaping five feet into the air, I simultaneously whirl around just in time to see the massive maw of the maned lion that suddenly appeared close behind me. We—well, hello there, um, king of the jungle . . . What are you doing on this horrible hill?

It moves closer to me, bold as can be. Gulp.

I take a step back, but my mind reacts for me, and I quickly angle my body to the side and leap back, allowing me to turn my front toward both of the large cats. Slowly, I creep back, pulling my sword and shield closer to me. D—don't come any closer. I am trained in the art of jiujitsu! I can toss you both clear off this hill without the slightest sweat! J—just you believe it!

"Grrrrr . . ."

I freeze in my step. Silently, I give a prayer to any god that will listen before glancing over my shoulder.

Yup. That's a wolf.

\<Wolf (Lv.7) [BOSS]\>

My internal mental processes speed up into a blur.

According to the clear conditions, I don't have to defeat these creatures. I just need to get to the top of the hill. If I run with all my might and get to the jagged rocks, they will no longer be able to pursue me. It wouldn't be any trouble. None at all.

But what if the next floor has a massive load of enemies? What if all of the enemies are level 20 while I'm still level 0? I need to survive, but if it just means dying a bit later, then there's no point.

I need to beat them. I need to kill them with my own two hands.

But who says I need to do it in a fair fight?

\<The God of Cowardice sees you.\>

The world briefly pauses and holds its breath. The three boss monsters don't move. I can't hear the weeping of the wind and the whistling of its arrow brethren.

. . . Huh?

And then the world starts moving again and my feet whirl beneath me faster than I can think, throwing me down the side of the hill. With this acting as a starting shot, the three beasts throw themselves at me, barking and growling and roaring, but since we're all running downhill they can't properly run, demonstrated as the wolf briefly tries to speed up to catch me and ends up falling ass over teakettle and tumbling down the side of the hill. Taking that opportunity, I slash my sword at it, forgetting that it's literally blunt. Instead of doing any damage whatsoever to the exposed abdomen of what I now see is a she-wolf, it simply bounces off, less than ineffective.

Damn it!

My failed attempt unfortunately stalled me for just a second, an opening that the leopard happily takes advantage of by leaping at me and catching hold of my exposed left arm. I don't have time to try to counteract, so all I can do is stab my sword into its mouth, chipping off one of its front fangs and making it mewl in pain, the surprise of the attack making it lose its grip on me. By this point the she-wolf has gotten back to its feet, but I'm already gone, back to running like high hell. My breath is starting to grate in my throat, but I can't stop.

Just a bit farther down, I can see the whistling woods grow nearer and nearer and some form of hope latches onto me just as I hear a loud growl.

Purely by instinct, I throw myself into a roll to the right, just in time to watch the lion fly by, paws and claws raised and ready but missing me by only a hair. My breath hitches as I tumble to the ground, rolling once and then twice before somehow leaping back to my feet.

The forest is close now and the sound of the whistling arrows that I had almost forgotten once again assault my ears. Fleeting hope comes to my chest and like a dehydrated desert-walker spotting an oasis, I bound for the trees, leaping with near desperation into the way of the storm of arrows, my shield raised to cover my head and chest and my sword in the same position.

About a dozen arrows stab into me as I fly across a clear spot before rolling into the shade of a tree, my arms and legs and abdomen and chest all pierced with innumerable arrows, and just as I force myself into a stop, I'm given the satisfying visage of the pursuing beasts, just a hair behind, also leaping into the fray of arrows. Watching their bodies get pierced by dozens if not hundreds of arrows before falling over reminds me of *them*, but seeing the horrible beasts die is too delicious to avert my eyes.

<Wolf (Lv.7) [BOSS] Defeated.>
<Lion (Lv.7) [BOSS] Defeated.>
<[Level Up]>
<You have reached Level 4.>
<Agility has increased by 11.
Strength has increased by 9.
Stamina has increased by 12.
Magic Power has increased by 4.
Hypnagogia has increased by 1.
Enhanced Vision has increased by 2.
Battle Focus has increased by 1.
Field Focus has increased by 2.
Regeneration Meditation has increased by 1.
Bleeding Resistance has increased by 2.
Poison Resistance has increased by 1.>

Oh good lord in heaven. It's . . . it's beautiful . . . !

I feel like crying. It's so not cool to cry, but it really does make me feel like crying. A bunch of hard-to-raise skills just suddenly got a huge boost. And my normal stats have also gone way up. It really is like a light from heaven.

<Top—Status—Community>
<PrissyKittyPrincess
Human Level 4
Agility: 20
Strength: 16
Stamina: 26
Magic Power: 19>

I don't like looking at my status because it reminds me of what username I have, but for once, I'm glad to see it.

My only problem is that, well . . .

Why did I only get messages for the she-wolf and the lion?

Looking toward the hill, the answer to that is obvious. There, on the other side of the hail of arrows, stands the leopard. It's got an arrow stuck in its paw, but that's it. I guess it was a little bit cleverer than its two coworkers.

No matter. I've only got a dozen or so arrows stuck in me, so I'm basically fit as a fiddle. Yup, I could absolutely do a tap-dancing routine right now.

<Top—Status—Community>
<20:32:11 Day 29>
<The second attempt will begin in 1:03:27:49>

Alright. How do I solve this?

Since I can starve for an unknown number of months, my best bet would be to make this into a battle of attrition. If I just stay here, the leopard should eventually starve or get thirsty to the point where it will have no choice but to brave the arrows in order to get to me and my supple flesh. For once, I wish the poison in the arrows were stronger, because as is, the leopard won't die just from that single arrow alone.

And since there's only a little more than one day left until the next attempt, I need to settle this now.

Looking at the leopard, I can tell that it's too intelligent to be goaded into attacking. If I'm going to do this, I'll have to be the one to take the leap. But if I do it as is, I'll be too battered by the arrows to put up a proper fight.

I need to heal up first.

I hate this strategy, but there's no other choice.

Since I'm at a lack for time, I choose to just bite the bullet and pull out all the arrows at once. My stamina and bleeding resistance should be high enough to cover it properly.

As I pull them one by one, I dampen the pain by just counting them as I go. In the end, I pulled a total of seventeen arrows out of my limbs, abdomen, and chest. It hurts like hell, and I think one of my lungs may have collapsed, but the other works just fine so I should be okay. I'm two arrows short of death, so I should be okay.

Even though I can hear the hissing breaths of the leopard, I let my eyes close and slip into meditation.

With the clock in front of me, I count every second and every minute and every hour. I can't spend more than nine hours at this or my schedule will suffer. I can't let that happen.

Deep in the darkness of my mind, I focus on that and nothing else.

<You have learned: Oxygen Deficiency Tolerance Lv.1>
<You have learned: Auto-Regeneration Lv.2>

Most of the damage heals standardly and is well and good after only around three hours, but the lung is different. Being so complex, it takes much longer, and despite getting a tolerance skill for it, the oxygen deficiency still gets to me in the end, and after only a few hours, I enter hypnagogia.

And by the time I awaken . . .

<Top—Status—Community>
<14:50:50 Day 30>
<The second attempt will begin in 0:09:09:10>

I have only around nine hours left? That's . . .

I feel sweat bead on my back, turning the dried blood on my clothes watery once more.

I don't have any more time. I need to act, and fast. On the other side of the arrows, I can see the leopard still there, pacing to and fro. After I take the leap, I'll need to get straight into combat. There will be no other choice.

I . . . I can do it. I've gotten this far, right? Just a little bit more. That's all.

Silently, I put my sword back into my inventory and bring out the axe. It will protect me.

I stand up. The leopard meets my gaze, and for one long second, there is perfect understanding between us. I know what it's thinking, and it knows what I'm thinking.

There's no need for words.

"*Graaarrgghhhh!*" Roaring, I leap into the fray of arrows, holding up the axe so that it protects my head and chest, ignoring the adrenaline-dulled pain of a dozen arrows piercing my arms and legs, and the second I reach the arrowless eye of the storm that surrounds the hill, I throw the axe forward onto the leopard in an attempt to distract it.

But it's far too quick-witted, and it easily dodges the axe with a small side step, quickly throwing itself toward me in the opening I created. But in the small moment of the leopard dodging before leaping, I've already pulled two arrows from my legs and armed myself with them, and when the leopard leaps at me, jaws wide and claws on display, I waste no time stabbing the arrows toward its exposed face, one in its open maw, the other in its eye.

Despite the obvious pain, the leopard snakes its claws around me, hooking them into my flesh as its jaw first clamps down on the arrow and then into my shoulder. With this as a start, the leopard clings to me with the rest of its body, its claws stabbing deep into my bowels, but I can't afford to think about it. Pulling more arrows from my legs, I stab them into the supple skin of the leopard's underside. One, two, three, four arrows and counting. I don't need them to go far in, I just need them to poison the leopard enough to make it unable to continue for much longer.

More and more arrows, but its jaws are powerful and their harsh clamp is enough to render my bones to dust, crunching them loudly as it chews and tries to reach my larger arteries.

But I'm not just letting this happen apathetically.

Once I stab a second arrow into its other eye, blinding it fully, the leopard finally shrieks and leaps back, disoriented and pained. But I won't let it get away. Throwing myself at it, I grab two arrows from its bosom and stab it into its neck, and in some pure, feral need for vengeance, I begin to bite down into its neck, searching for veins, for blood, for anything that will let me kill it. Once the skin bursts and the blood flows into my mouth and tongue, the month-long dehydration comes back in full force and I lap at the warm liquid with sheer desperation.

\<You have learned: Bite Lv.1\>

The leopard mewls and swats at my face with its massive paws, gouging deep gashes across my face and neck. Blood is rushing to my head and making me feel drowsy, but it doesn't matter. All that matters is killing this beast.

When I no longer have any arrows in my body to stab it with, I start using the arrows in its own body to gouge deeper and deeper, and once I've got a hole big enough, I shove my own hand in there and start digging around, eventually hooking my hand around what I think is an intestine that I then pull out.

\<You have learned: Rip Lv.1\>
\<You have learned: Tear Lv.1\>

And after a long and desperate fight, I finally feel the heavy breaths of the leopard die down.

\<Leopard (Lv.8) [BOSS] Defeated.\>
\<[Level Up]\>
\<You have reached Level 6.\>
\<Agility has increased by 7.
Strength has increased by 4.
Stamina has increased by 5.
Magic Power has increased by 2.

Bite has increased by 3.
Dehydration Resistance has increased by 1.
Starvation Resistance has increased by 2.
Bleeding Resistance has increased by 1.
Basic Swordsmanship has increased by 1.>

That's . . . That's good . . . Yeah . . . I'm strong now . . . Way stronger than a leopard . . . Eat my ass, feline miscreant . . .

\<Top—Status—Community>
\<PrissyKittyPrincess
Human Level 6
Agility: 27
Strength: 20
Stamina: 31
Magic Power: 21>

. . . No level clear message, huh . . . Guess I really do have to climb up to the top of the hill . . .

Tiredly, I push the leopard's body off me. By this point, I think my entire outfit is brownish red. The blood I beat out of LetsFraternizeTogether isn't visible anymore.

. . . What's the time?

\<Top—Status—Community>
\<15:11:00 Day 30>
\<The second attempt will begin in 0:08:49:00>

Eight hours. Eight hours is a lot of time. Sure, it took me a couple of hours just to get to where the beasts attacked me, but this time I'll do it much faster. Super-fast. Faster than anyone's ever seen anyone do it before. I just . . . need to . . . take a small rest.

Gently, I curl up in a ball.

\<THE GOD OF COWARDICE BEAMS WITH PRIDE.>

That thing again. Listen, I don't know what or who you are, but I'm not buying. God this, god that, I don't see you up on a cloud. This must be like with the cantos—in other words, complete horseshit.

\<THE GOD OF COWARDICE LOOKS AROUND FOR A STICK.>

He's doing what—

<THE GOD OF COWARDICE POKES YOU WITH A STICK.>

—Yowch!

That—that hurt, you bastard! What the heck was that for?!

<THE GOD OF COWARDICE SNICKERS AND GRABS A BAG OF POPCORN BEFORE RETURNING TO SILENTLY WATCHING.>

Y—you . . . !

Well, fine! Guess dying's off the table, boys. The poke was enough to get me to my feet, so I guess I've got no other choice. Grumbling, I stagger up toward the hilltop, but only after I pocket my axe again. But before I leave, I squint at the leopard. Its body is still there. I don't have the time to wait around forever, but I have a feeling that it should at least drop *something*.

Summoning the spear, I poke the leopard's chest. It spasms a little.

In sheer curiosity, I stab the leopard's corpse around five dozen times, at which point the heavily mutilated corpse suddenly disappears, leaving a chunk of meat and a neatly folded leopard hide behind.

<You have learned: Basic Spear Arts Lv.1>

Well, well, well. What do we have here?

Pocketing the items, I start heading up the mountain, staggering with each step and basically using the spear as a crutch. If I get attacked by another beast, I'm probably dead.

After a few hours of walking, I reach the part of the hill where it becomes basically nothing but sharp, jagged, toothlike rocks that go in a completely vertical incline. I really do have no choice but to climb. Unwillingly, I stash the spear. At the same time, I also give the inventory a quick once-over to ensure that there really isn't anything useful in there.

But that would've been too kind, so there's obviously nothing. I turn back to the rocks and frown.

To be completely clear, before this, I couldn't even do one pull-up, which explains why my strength was at a mere 4. But now it's at 20, which would suggest I'm more than twice as strong. The thing is . . . I don't feel strong in the least. Maybe the stats aren't linear? But, then again, it's not like I have a choice, right?

Steeling myself, I place both hands on the rocks and begin my steep climb.

It didn't take long for the exposed skin on my fingers and palms to get rubbed off, and once they started bleeding like a stuck pig, the rocks got so slippery I fell several times, bashing my head on the rocks far below.

<You have learned: Blunt Tolerance Lv.1>
<You have learned: Falling Tolerance Lv.1>

And still, I continued. Rock by rock, I climbed. The flesh on my fingers was ground down to the point where I could feel my bones scrape against the rocks, but I had no choice but to continue. If my fingers wouldn't work, then my teeth would have to do. And if I had no teeth left, then I still had my gums.

Foot by foot. Every time I fell, I got up again, because I had no other choice.

And every time I looked up, the black eye of the solar eclipse was just a little closer.

<Top—Status—Community>
<23:10:00 Day 30>
<The second attempt will begin in 0:00:50:00>

But in the end, I got to the top. I had gotten so close so many times, and whenever I got close enough to see the light at the top, I would grin and my grip would loosen and I would fall far enough to kill any normal human being, but I would just get a new form of horrible tolerance.

<You have learned: Organ Rupture Tolerance Lv.4>
<You have learned: Fracture Tolerance Lv.3>
<You have learned: Concussion Tolerance Lv.1>
<You have learned: Hemorrhage Tolerance Lv.1>

But now, finally, I'm at the top.

And I can see him.

A shadow. A shadow with eyes that see me.

His hand is stretched out. Ready to be grasped.

My feet click and clack as I walk, my exposed heels making quite interesting sounds against the rocks below. It's so bright up here. There's light. A few patches of the ground are covered with grass, and flowers, and plants. But I'm staggering blindly, my own hand, now lacking fingers, grasping toward his.

He's tall. Standing in front of him, I feel small.

Greet him.
Greet him.

GREET HIM.

I know what I must do.

My bloodied and mangled palm grazes against his open hand, and he closes it around mine. I look him in the eye, shake his hand, and say, as toothless as any toddler, "Hewwo."

<**You have cleared the first floor.**>
<**You have received 1,000 points for clearing the floor.**
You have received an additional 1,000 points for being the first to clear the floor.>

<**For clearing the stage completely, you will receive an additional reward.**>

<**There is a God that sees you. You have received 500 points.**>
<**A God has shown a positive response to you. You have obtained 1,000 points.**>

<**A CHANGE HAS BEEN MADE.**>
<**THE GOD OF COWARDICE WISHES TO GRANT SOME OF HIS POWERS INSTEAD OF THE NORMAL STAGE REWARD.**>
<**WILL YOU ACCEPT?**>
<**YES/NO**>

The world has stopped around me. All that there is and all there has ever been is the window, and my shallow breathing.

"Yesh," I mumble. Using the stumps of my fingers, I press *Yes*.

<**You have obtained:**>
<**[Fetal Position Blowover(Lv.MAX)]**
The God of Cowardice, who watches over those who exhibit caution above logic, has granted some of His powers to His potential apostle.>

I see. Okay. That makes . . . sense . . .

As the world turns dark, I feel myself stumble forward, into the arms of the eyed shadow, and everything goes black, and then I face-plant on the eternally white floor of the lobby and pass out cold.

FLOOR 2

THE RUGGED PASS

Making Good Financial Decisions

I awaken with a startle.

Wh—where am I? Did I win? Did I kill the leopard? Did I greet him!?

Haah, haah, haah, haah . . .

This is . . . This is the lobby, right? Yeah, with that eternal whiteness and the pillars and the . . .

—My body. My body feels fine. It—it even feels good! I'm okay! My teeth are back, and all of my fingers are here, and my *tongue*, oh, I never thought I'd miss my *tongue*, and my palms, and my feet, oh, this is . . . !

<Time Until Floor 2 Opening: 18:01:09>

Th—that's . . . ?

. . . No. No way. I am *not* throwing myself back into that craziness. I—I almost *died*! I could have died five hundred times over for how many arrows I took! No. Absolutely no way.

Eighteen hours . . . is not enough. No, not in the least.

But—but maybe I'll change my mind in eighteen hours? Eh, probably not. But it's possible, and, well, this *is* a room that heals everything. Eighteen hours is a long time in that sense, I guess.

Growwwwwwwwl.

My stomach growls.

I guess, for now, I should try to eat something. I doubt everyone else is just perpetually starving, so there really ought to be some sort of shop window.

<Top—Status—Community>
<05:59:30 Day 31>

<The third attempt will begin in 29:18:00:30>
<Floor 2 will open in 18:00:30>

We really are on the second attempt now, huh . . . Whatever that means.

By searching around a bit, I'm able to find a shop window, where I also find out I currently have 3,500 points. Nice. Now, what to buy . . .

I look down at what I'm wearing. Yeah, no, my first order of business is to buy some proper armor. Let's see, light leather armor would be best for my play sty—

<Leather Armor Set (Light)>
<A full-body set of light armor that protects the user from harm while still keeping them agile.
Defense: 15>
<Price: 8,500 points>

E—eight thousand—!?

Eh, uh, well, um, maybe that's just an especially high-quality piece of equipment, right? If I check the *used* section, I'm bound to find some goodies!

<"Leather" "Shirt">
<A thin piece of what might have once come from an animal fashioned into something that may in some circles be called a "shirt."
Defense: 2
USED ITEM>
<Price: 2,250 points>
<Prop Knife>
<An aluminum knife used for playing pranks.
The blade retracts.
USED ITEM>
<Price: 1,000 points>
<Leather Foot Bindings>
<The skin of a drake's scalp, tanned and refitted into a form able to be bound around feet.
Slippery when wet.
Defense: 1
Agility: –2
USED ITEM>
<Price: 1,200 points>

. . . Right. So, uh, yeah, I think I'll skip that, okay? Okay.

After much deliberation, I decided to invest in a knife for 1,500 points. Say what you will, but as is, my sword is blunt and I'm almost completely unable to use the spear and axe. I need some way of defending myself, right? Right.

And then I also bought a simple tracksuit for 1,650 points because I can't run around in stiff, bloody hobo clothes all my life. The tracksuit even came with proper shoes, though I can tell that even a single slice will have them imploding on themselves.

But—good news—my items and equipment regenerate in the lobby, so I should be fine as long as I have the scraps left of them.

That leaves me with a full 350 points left to splurge on whatever I want!

For many long minutes, I simply stare at the food section.

Food is good. Humans need food to live. But I technically don't. I can make it just fine without it. I don't need it. I'm basically superhuman. No food and no water for thirty days does not make me a hungry boy. Absolutely not. I. Am. *Fine.*

I gaze into the screen.

The screen gazes back at me.

My hand hovers over the dried meat.

I don't need it.

I don't need it.

I don't need it.

. . .

At the very last second, my hand swerves to the side and accidentally presses the Princess Cake button, and then it slips again and enters *1* as the amount for purchase, and then tries a few discount codes before accepting fact and pressing *Summon Directly.*

Oh, no! Oh whoops, there go my 350 remaining points! What a bummer. What a shame. No dried meat for me, I guess!

I stare at the cake in my hands and drool. It's perfect. It's absolutely amazing. A simple smell of almonds, an easy waft of scrumptious vanilla sneakily hiding just below the marzipan surface . . . Oh, it's enough to make any man a true believer.

I summon my newly purchased knife. It's smaller than I thought.

Oh, well.

Tossing it away, I instead use only my hands and fingers to attack the princess cake with ravenous, bestial desire, tearing into it like a man gone wild, going so far as to eat the marzipan rose and leaves right at the beginning, barely even chewing it before I gulp it down like a fish swallowing water and then going back to it, ripping out layers of cream and vanilla custard, thrusting handfuls of fluffy sponge cake directly down into my guts, eating, swallowing, almost choking it all down, my hand acting like a plunger to press it all into my gluttonous stomach.

\<You have learned:
Choking Tolerance Lv.1\>
\<You have learned:
Rip Lv.2\>
\<You have learned:
Tear Lv.2\>

And by the end of it, I'm left lying straight on my back, staring up at the endless white. My eyes flutter closed, and without a care in the world, I fall asleep. And not half-asleep or half-awake, or even some sort of deep meditation. I just sleep, and that's it. Not because I need to heal, not because I need my body to recover—simply for the sake of sleeping because, for once, *I can*.

And I guess it's the magic of the lobby, because when I wake up, I feel so inhumanly refreshed I might as well receive a status message reading:

\<You awaken feeling refreshed.\>

But I don't because that ability would be too powerful. At least there's no such skill as *sleep*, that'd be one step too far. On the topic of skills, I quickly bring up my status and read through them, checking what they're for and all.

The skills section of the Status tab is separated into active and passive, of which I have seven and forty-two, respectively. Most of the passive skills I have are tolerances or resistances, which is kind of insane. But right now, I'm much more interested in the active skills. To be specific, a certain MAX-level skill I just happened to receive from some guy up above . . .

\<You have obtained:\>
\<[Fetal Position Blowover(Lv.MAX)]
The God of Cowardice, who watches over those who exhibit caution above
logic, has granted some of His powers to His potential apostle.\>

And there it is. Frank question: what in the world is this?
Oh, there's more of a description down here! Let's see . . .

\<Should the user go into the fetal position, they will become invisible to all
enemies and otherwise unsmellable, unhearable, and untastable.\>
\<[SOVEREIGN SKILL]\>

It—it makes me *what*?
Isn't that, uh, really overpowered? Like, that's the kind of skill that'd get nerfed in the next patch because of all the complaints. Fetal position blowover . . .
Um . . . Do I really have to go into the fetal position to use it? I mean, might just be me, but that feels a bit, I don't know . . . pathetic?

<THE GOD OF COWARDICE SNICKERS.>

Y—you're still here?! I thought you'd stay on the first floor or something! Well, then again, I'm not sure what he is at all, so . . . Yeah. God of cowardice.

God of cowardice . . .

Hang on. If the god of cowardice has taken to watching me, even calling me a potential *apostle*, then that would mean . . .

Are you trying to make fun of me?!

<THE GOD OF COWARDICE BREAKS INTO LAUGHTER.>
<THE GOD OF COWARDICE GESTURES FOR SOMEONE ELSE TO COME LOOK.>
<THE GODDESS OF IGNORANCE AVERTS HER EYES.>
<THE GOD OF COWARDICE SULKS.>

. . . What the hell kind of sitcom is this?

Okay, to be frank, I never had an issue with streamers trying to stream me and showing everyone their pathetic attempts at beating me. Being watched is fine. It's nothing new and all that, but this? This is worse. I don't like this. I feel like I'm on the set of a sitcom and I'm the only one who can't hear the canned laughter. I want to die.

Hmm . . . I wonder if the fetal position blowover skill works on *everyone*?

Smirking, I lie down and hug my knees to my chest.

<THE GOD OF COWARDICE LOOKS AROUND FRANTICALLY.>
<THE GODDESS OF IGNORANCE RECOMMENDS HIM TO LOOK UNDER THE COUCH.>
<THE GOD OF COWARDICE GRUMBLES AND ASSERTS THAT YOUTHS OUGHT TO SHOW RESPECT FOR THEIR ELDERS.>

Mwahahahaha, my plan is working perfectly . . . !

. . .

On the other hand, lying down on the floor like this isn't especially fun. After a few minutes of messing with what I have been told is a literal god, I eventually give in to his demands and undo the skill. Hm. Now that I think about it, that damn god might just be playing along for the sake of it, like a parent pretending not to notice their giggling child hiding behind the curtains in a game of hide and seek.

<THE GOD OF COWARDICE WHISTLES AND LOOKS THE OTHER WAY.>

That damn coward geezer . . . !

Then again, I suppose, with a name like that, there's not much you can do. Hm. All this talking has sort of reminded me that I've unlocked a new feature of the menus.

Leaning my back against one of the endless white pillars, I bring the window back up again.

<Top—Status—Community>
<19:05:03 Day 31>
<The third attempt will begin in 29:04:54:57>
<Floor 2 will open in 4:54:57>

Five hours, huh? Anyway, with a quick poke, I make my way to the Community tab. The chats should be open now, which means I can—

<Status—Community—Top>
<Europe Server>
<Easy Lobby: 211/237
Normal Lobby: 76/87
Hard Lobby: 18/21
Hell Lobby: 7/7>

Th—there's more people?

My eyes fly up from the screen to look around the lobby.

But there's no one here! It's just me, so why . . . ?

Maybe they're farther away? Maybe I can walk there? Maybe . . . ?

"*Hey!*" I shout into the endless white. "*Anyone there? Hello!*" But there's no response. Gritting my teeth, I pull myself to my feet and start moving. First, I'm just walking, shouting "*Hey!*" over and over again, but then I start running, and shouting, and screaming as loud as I can, hoping for someone—*anyone*—to hear me. But there's no one.

And in the end, when I've gone as far as my feet can take me, I find myself back at the slippery, cake-soaked part of the floor where I ate that delicious princess cake.

Defeated, I drop back down to the floor with a thump.

Silently, I press the Hell Lobby button. And now, unlike before, it actually takes me somewhere.

<Status—Community—Top>
<Hell Lobby: 7/7 First Floor Lobby: 6/6
Second Floor Lobby: 1/1>

We have different lobbies? I—I guess that makes sense, sort of—somewhat. I mean, really, in the other difficulties, they'd have to get really crowded. The Easy Difficulty is way over two hundred people now. No way they'd have enough space in a single lobby.

But we can't even meet? I can't even tell them what awaits them and how to deal with it? There—there has to be a way to send them a message, right?

In desperate denial, I press the Hell Lobby button.

<Status—Community—Top>
<Hell Lobby: 1/7 Active>

And then just a huge, blank screen.

Silently, without so much as breathing, I type in a message.

<PrissyKittyPrincess: hey>

And then I wait. One minute. Two minutes.

But I know they can't respond. They can't even see my message. Until they beat that circle of hell, they won't even know I exist.

But, then again, it *is* six people this time, right? Six whole people. That's, uhh, a third more than we were? Is that how math works? Something like that.

No, wait, 50% more. Yeah. I think.

Either way, they're more. They might even get an archer! Imagine how useful an archer would be in a stage that's nothing *but* arrows! Hm. Now that I think about it, maybe I should have picked up a few of those? It might have let me use them as, you know, actual weapons. Like how I beat the leopard.

Not that it matters anymore. There doesn't seem to be any way to descend the floors at will, which is just as good for me. I don't think I could redo the first floor even if I tried.

But enough about those heavy thoughts! Let's check the other chats to see if there's any information to be shared.

<Status—Community—Top>
<Europe Server>
<Easy Lobby: 211/237
Normal Lobby: 76/87
Hard Lobby: 18/21
Hell Lobby: 7/7>

Let's try the Hard Lobby first. Good gamers think alike, as they say.

<You do not have access to this Lobby.>

Right. Okay. That, um, makes sense, maybe? Okay then, let's try the Normal Lobby.

\<You do not have access to this Lobby.\>

No? Not so? Then, the Easy—

\<You do not have access to this Lobby.\>

Okay, fine, I get it. I *should* be able to access the Europe server as a whole though, right?

\<Status—Community—Top\>
\<Chatrooms\>
\<Discussion Boards\>

Another choice, huh? Well, into the discussion boards I go!

\<Status—Community—Top\>
\<Discussion Boards\>
\<Love4Life[F3]: Best strategies on beating Floor 3 without killing all the goblings?[2]\>
\<SuperMoleman[F11]: Moleman's guide to the shop feature [DO's/ DON'T's][19]\>
\<UrchinLurchin[F2] What is this place am I in hell what[0]\>
\<FranticSwordSlapper[F2]: What happens if You die? Is there respawn or do You meet Shiva[121]\>
\<MilkInACupboard[F2]: How To Make The Magic Happen????[1]\>

That's . . . a lot, and it's not even the entire first page. There are literally dozens of pages. The first thing I can make out is that the F1 and F2 is not talking about formulas, but rather the floor you're on. I'm guessing mine would say either two or one. The other thing is that the number at the end seems to be the number of responses. To check, I test by clicking the post about magic.

\<MilkInACupboard[F2]: How To Make The Magic Happen????\>
\<FriendlyFanatic[F2]: You Don't Lmaooooo.\>

Theory: proven.
Hypothesis of inherent human evil: likewise.

Checking a few of the other threads yields the same results. A lot of questions, very few concrete answers. How many floors are there? "Eat a boot." Which starter weapon is the best? "Whichever your mom prefers." How do I effectively get stronger? "Go die." In other words, it's a very standard forum. More importantly, though, all of it is in Swedish. It reads like it was written by a native, but I doubt that this accurately reflects the actual state of things. Even in the Hell Lobby, only half of us were Swedish. Assuming half of these are also Swedish, it still makes no sense that all of them are fluent, and to this degree as well.

No, a much more likely answer is simply that everyone sees everything in their own native language. Regardless, this doesn't mean that there is no divide.

\<LionMawMadness[F5]: everyone who is North European answer to this message and I will invite you to North European chat>
\<MirthOfTheEarth[F2]: hi>
\<AvantAnGarde[F3]: Yo Dude //AAG>
\<ShootsOwnShadow[F3]: are Danish also invited?>
\<LionMawMadness[F5]: no>

How civilized. Nevertheless . . .

\<PrissyKittyPrincess[F2]: add me plz>

And now, we wait.

In the meantime, I check a few of the other boards and find out some data.

According to SuperMoleman, the tutorial has a hundred floors and after that you get to go home. The way he found this out was that every ten floors, you get to meet with the administrator of your difficulty and have a wish granted. He asked for a bit of information, and now he's kindly sharing it with the rest of us out of the sheer goodness of his heart. How sweet, kind, and not at all suspicious.

Luckily, he was actually able to get quite a lot of information through this. For one, every thirty days, a new attempt will occur, which will cause those currently on floors to be sent back to the lobby for twenty-four hours, at which point they have to redo the floor. In other words, I dodged a bullet by around thirty minutes. Scary. The actual use of the attempt itself wasn't explained, but when the attempt begins, a new batch of challengers will be invited to the tower.

According to SuperMoleman's calculations, last time, one hundred and ninety challengers were summoned, and this time, about a hundred and ninety-five new challengers have been summoned, which sounds like a lot, but considering that only one hundred and fifty-seven remain from the first attempt, calculated by SuperMoleman, he doubts that the lobbies will get flooded anytime soon. After that he went on to write a massive statistical analysis of what's happened so far by calculating the death rate for each difficulty and comparing them and all that sort of stuff, so I just got bored and zoned out. But he needs to hear my appreciation, so before I left his post, I decided to show my gratitude.

<SuperMoleman[F11]: Moleman's Tutorial
Statistical analysis of casualties and Q&A (. . .)>
<MilkInACupboard[F2]: Wow!>
<LanternInTheDark[F4]: Very detailed, thank you so much for this. It's a shame we've lost so many, but getting numbers soothes the ache.>
<InItToWinIt[F2]: ^^^the guy above me is a *****>

< . . . >

<SnakesOnAPlane[F9]: Mr Moleman how did you beat floor 10 my party keeps getting stuck plz help we keep having to go back to the lobby>
<SuperMoleman[F11]: "Git gud," haha, no, just kidding.
I would suggest you check out my Moleman's Guide to clearing the 10th Floor. It seems suitable.>
<SnakesOnAPlane[F9]: thx>

My fingers hover above the keyboard. Hang on a sec. What do you mean, *go back to the lobby*?

Mind bustling, I'm still somehow able to push through and write my reply.

<SnakesOnAPlane[F9]: thx>
<PrissyKittyPrincess[F2]: nerd>

Unable to savor the moment, I quickly press SuperMoleman's profile, which brings me to a list of what posts he's written. Somehow, in only a month, he's gotten to floor eleven. From what I can see, considering that he's written an extensive guide on how to use magic properly, he must be a mage of some sort. But I don't care about that. What I care about is his collab post written together with two other challengers from the two other difficulties. As might be obvious, considering how fast he's able to climb these levels, SuperMoleman is on the Easy Difficulty, which means that his field of analysis is compromised. Being a nerd, he will clearly want a complete range.

That's what he does in this post.

<SuperMoleman[F11]: Moleman's Collaborative Guide to Difficulty Differences.
Hello all and welcome back to my guide! Today I've been helped by OrthodoxPox[F3] of the Normal Difficulty and JonesMcScones[F2] of the Hard Difficulty.
They agreed to assist me on account of how I only know the Easy Difficulty,

and they hope that their guidance may live on through here. On to the differences . . .>

The guide then goes on to explain first—for those who didn't know about it in the audience—that those who die in the tutorial have their messages and posts deleted. Probably to make space or something, who knows.

They mention a lot of unnecessary differences, and also how there's little data about the Hard Difficulty because almost everyone who challenged it died. I scrolled past everything pretty fast, but I'm pretty sure he lamented at some point that they couldn't get any contact with the Hell Difficulty challengers, so considering how tough Hard is, they might as well give up on them.

Well, ex*cuuuuse* me, princess.

And for about fifteen pages, Moleman went on and on about minute differences and similarities and this and that and completely unnecessary details that nobody on Earth could possibly care about. But, thankfully, at the very end, he mentioned the lobbies and how returning to them worked.

In Hard, there's a portal that leads to the lobby from where the challengers spawned in. The portal remains open for twenty-four hours.

In Normal, the portal remains open for the duration of the floor attempt.

In Easy, if you just shout "Return to Lobby!" you'll return.

I don't even know how to react. These people are literally getting a free heal-up, whenever they want, for nothing! And then they can just return to the floor again without having to redo anything! This is beyond bullshit; this is the whole damn animal and all four stomachs included!

Blind with rage, I take to the comments.

<PrissyKittyPrincess[F2]: ok this is dumb and ur dumb and ur a nerd hack and im bonking ur mom>

There. Take *that*, you inglorious troll-nose! Bet he's quaking in his boots right about now, heh.

Content with my sloughing, I exit the post. But just as I do, my eye spies a little post.

<SuperMoleman[F11]: Moleman's guide to the 2nd Floor>

Although I feel suspicious of the nerd, I give the post a quick read-through just for the sake of it.

<SuperMoleman[F11]: Moleman's guide to the 2nd Floor. Welcome back, friends! This floor is pretty simple and as long as you have a good ranged

**fighter in your party it should be an easy fight. The only enemies that
appear are Lv.1 or Lv.2 vultures, but they'll only attack if the heat and
trekking weaken you too much. As long as you bring water, food, and cold
potions you should do fine. The boss is also simple.>**

Right. Not as detailed as I would have expected.

But you know what I've noticed? This total nerd hasn't made any guide for
the first floor! What a dumbo. Absolute idiot. I'm going to show him so hard . . .

Grinning, I enter the main community boards. But just as I do . . .

<Floor 2 has opened. Do you want to enter?>
<Yes/No>

Huh? It's that time already?

Well, my body feels alright, but . . . Listen, in Moleman's difficulty differences guide thing, he said you could still enter the stage even if you answer no.
And, I mean, honestly, even if I can't, who cares? I'll just wait until the next
attempt, no biggie! Easy peasy.

**<If no answer is chosen, [No] will be chosen for you and the floor may be
accessed on the next attempt.>**

Yeah, yeah, I get it, who cares.

Dismissively, I poke the No button.

<Floor 2 has been closed.>

[WHITE] and [RED]

<Time Until Floor 2 Opening: 28:23:59:59>

So, it really did circle all the way back to a month, huh? Well, it's not like I can die in the lobby, so who cares. With a wave of my hand, the window disappears. I look back at the normal window.

<Top—Status—Community>
<00:00:01 Day 32>
<The third attempt will begin in 28:23:59:59>
<Floor 2 will open in 28:23:59:59>

With a few scrolls and pokes, I'm back to the boards. Cracking my knuckles, I begin writing.

<PrissyKittyPrincess[F2]: MY guide 2 floor 1 (4 pro gamers ONLY) ok so step 1 is u got to hide behind the trees n when the arrow come from the left u jump out n just like hit them away so pick shield or u die and also when u fight the boss monsters make them die by arrows 2 ok also when u climb the hill if ur hands not work then use ure mouth>

Perfect. Moleman, go die in a ditch. Or something.

<You have gotten a response.>

Oh, already? Why, I wonder who that might be!

<LionMawMadness[F5]: everyone who is North European answer to this
message and I will invite you to North European chat>
<MirthOfTheEarth[F2]: hi>
<AvantAnGarde[F3]: Yo Dude //AAG>
<ShootsOwnShadow[F3]: are Danish also invited?>
<LionMawMadness[F5]: no>
<PrissyKittyPrincess[F2]: add me plz>
<LionMawMadness[F5]: ok but only if you explain your username>

I stare at the window. It doesn't move. The lobby suddenly feels very empty
and stale.

<PrissyKittyPrincess[F2]: add me plz>
<LionMawMadness[F5]: ok but only if you explain your username>
<PrissyKittyPrincess[F2]: go die>

And just as fast as I opened the window, I close it once more.
Slowly, I cross my arms. Mm-hm. Yup.
Yeah . . .

<You have received a message.>

I press the response faster than humanly possible and only realize once it
opens that it isn't for my post.

<Status—Community—Top>
<Personal Messages>
<[NEW]OrthodoxPox[F3]: Invitation to The Delegate Commission.>

The heck is this?
Out of sheer confusion more than anything else, I poke the message.

<OrthodoxPox[F3]: Invitation to The Delegate Commission.
Hello PrissyKittyPrincess. I am Pox, Delegate of the Normal Difficulty 3rd
floor. I found you by collaborating with my fellow Delegates to compare
the members of each individual Difficulty Lobby against the full list of
members found on the Europe server. I know that you have beaten the
first floor of Hell Difficulty. I know that you are the only one to survive.
I am cordially inviting you on behalf of HuppiGupp[F10], the Delegate
of the Easy Difficulty, JustAPrankBro[F5] of the Normal Difficulty, and

TalonsOfRage[F4] of the Hard Difficulty to join our ranks as the Delegate of the Hell Difficulty.>

What? What even is this? Delegates . . . ? It's not especially strange that they were able to find me, but to invite me to do something like this is a bit, well, strange. They aren't wrong. I *am* an ex–pro gamer after all, so if they have me among their ranks they'll be sure to boost their power significantly. There isn't any question along the lines of *Why me?* either because, so far, I'm the only one to survive this difficulty.

So far.

Huh. Since the first floor opened, does that mean . . . ?

<Status—Community—Top>
<Europe Server>
<Easy Lobby: 168/235
Normal Lobby: 22/80
Hard Lobby: 9/16
Hell Lobby: 2/2>

Yeah, as expected, they're all—

Hang on a moment.

Two?!

Th—there's still another person in the Hell Lobby alive? Did they already beat the level?!

Like an absolute maniac, I swivel my head from side to side, checking the lobby. Nobody there.

Well, yeah, now that I think about it, that would be way too fast, right? It's only been like a few hours at most. No, the much more likely answer would be that they for some reason decided to stay behind in the lobby. Pretty clever one, I'd say. And, as expected, all the others died. Five people was not enough. Will there ever be enough?

Something hollow hums inside my chest.

But one of them survived. I don't know how, but they did. And if I could just contact them, then . . . Then, they could survive. I think. They just need to do almost exactly what I did and then they should be okay.

Assuming they don't try to beat the first floor before then. Sure, they might have a small chance, but I honestly only survived the first floor because they took the first arrows. If it hadn't been for that, I'd be just as dead as them.

Anyhow, let's get back to that Delegate Commission thing.

I'm not sure what to do. I mean, it doesn't sound too bad, but there has to be some sort of trade here, right? I give them something, they give me something. Just having a title, as dope as it sounds, isn't quite enough.

Frowning, I enter my PMs and type up a response.

<PrissyKittyPrincess[2]: ok. what do i get tho>

And a few minutes later, a response dings in.

<OrthodoxPox[F3]: I'm so glad you asked, PrissyKittyPrincess. You may not be aware of it, being alone in your lobby, but there are quite a few people in ours. Order is needed with so many people. Rules, laws, punishment, and reward. All of that is necessary to make the Tutorial a better place for all of us. This includes you.
At the moment, few of the responsibilities and obligations of a Delegate will fall on you. Rather, you will hold the title as a formality until you are needed either by us or by other Hell Difficulty challengers.
Suffice it to say, once you are needed, you will likewise be rewarded. And if you want to renounce your position, we'll simply hold on to it until you want to give it another shot.
Should you accept, you will also be invited to the exclusive Delegate Commission chatroom alongside the even more exclusive Executive Delegates chatroom.
And, if you must know, the title of Delegate is quite the boast in and of itself.>

In my head, a picture is forming. A picture of me, writing up a post. Someone calls me a dork. I contact my fellow Delegates and have him shot and executed. All is good. There are no more wars. The world is at peace.

A trail of drool goes down the side of my chin and I quickly wipe it off.

<PrissyKittyPrincess[F2]: im in.>
<OrthodoxPox[F3]: Always happy to hear it, PrissyKittyPrincess. I will invite you in just a moment, and I hope to see you in the chatrooms soon. Thank you for the audience, Hell Delegate. By the way, do you have a name or title you would rather be referred to by?>

I almost want to shed a tear.

<PrissyKittyPrincess[F2]: call me . . . Hell Delegate Gentle Night . . .>

As I lean back, a relaxed, joyous grin easily finds itself my lips. The world is good. I had forgotten that this was a good world. Yes, it is good indeed . . .

<OrthodoxPox[F3]: Okay. See you soon, Hell Delegate Gentle Night.>

Oh, I'm practically giddy with excitement.

Like a child stumbling down the stairs on Christmas morning, I poke my way back to the Community tab, poking the chatrooms button as fast as my fingers allow.

<Status—Community—Top>
<Chatrooms>

There's nothing there. The heck kind of joke is this? Shouldn't I at least be in—

<Status—Community—Top>
<Chatrooms>
<NORTH Europe chat>

Whoa, that took me by surprise! It just popped right out of nowhere! But it isn't the Delegate Commission chat. Instead, it's that European chat I was sure I'd bummed out my chances of getting into. Huh. Well, since I've got some time to kill before the Delegate Commission puts me in their chats, I may as well give it a look.

<Status—Community—Top>
<NORTH Europe chat>
<SuperMoleman[F11]: I still think we should allow Danish to join the chat. As far as I can see, they haven't tried to make a chat yet, so there's no reason to refuse them.
<LionMawMadness[F5]: they are literally satanists.>
<SuperMoleman[F11]: Just because they live in a satanist society doesn't make them all satanists. Are you a Christian for living in Sweden?>
<LionMawMadness[F5]: I am tho.>
<PrissyKittyPrincess[F2] has joined the chat>
<SuperMoleman[F11]: Welcome, Kitty! Always a delight to get new people to join. Where are you from? I'm from Skåne, Sweden!>

This guy again? Why is he everywhere I go? Next thing I know he'll be a Delegate, too. But in that case, since I'm an Executive, I'll have power over him, so maybe that would be for the best? Anyway . . .

<PrissyKittyPrincess[F2]: im not doxxing myself u slag>

If he finds out we're from the same damn place then I'm hanging myself.

<SuperMoleman[F11]: There's really no need to be rude about it. Kitty . . .
is Kitty okay? Would you rather be called something else?
<PrissyKittyPrincess[F2]: call me Gentle Night or i will send a pipe bomb
to ur family>
<SuperMoleman[F11]: Gentle it is :). Did you join the tutorial recently?>
<PrissyKittyPrincess[F2]: no ive been here for like a month now
****head>

I can't believe a real-life game of life and death would censor cursing. Literally 1984.

<SuperMoleman[F11]: I hope you won't take offense to the question, but
what difficulty are you attempting?>
<PrissyKittyPrincess[F2]: hell>
<HookedOnBach[F3]: Yeah we're all in Hell but what difficulty are you
doing. :)>
<PrissyKittyPrincess[F2]: hell>
<LionMawMadness[F5]: Oh hey Bach back from the second floor already?>
<HookedOnBach[F3]: Yeah it was no biggie. Vultures didn't even take one
hit from my bow haha. :)>
<SuperMoleman[F11]: I'm so happy my guide helped you! Congrats!>
<HookedOnBach[F3]: Yeah it didn't but thx anyways Mole. :)>

Silently fuming, I exit the chat.

They just ignored me. Completely! It's like I turned into some sort of ghost and just went completely invisible. I'm not even in the fetal position! God, I hate people. The second they no longer like the bone I'm presenting them, they jump for the next one like hyperactive puppies. The very moment I get dethroned, they're all over the new guy and nobody cares anymore about the former WC because he's less than a prince now. Barely even a shadow.

Grinding my molars, I return to the Community tab.

<Status—Community—Top>
<Chatrooms>
<DC Executives Council>
<Delegate Commission Chat>
<NORTH Europe chat>

Well, well, well. What have we here? Hmm, which to enter first . . . Eeny, meeny, miny, moe!

<Status—Community—Top>
<Chatrooms>
<Delegate Commission Chat>
<RedHanded[F7]: Report: Minor Squabble on NL7. Both offending parties were punished in accordance to Article 2. RedHanded[F7] acted as Judge and punisher.
<HerringFerry[F3] Report: Second Degree Homicide on HF3. Victim: StarFriend[F3]. Perpetrator: HospitalityOnParade[F3]. In accordance with Article 3, HospitalityOnParade[F3] was Executed by being sent to Floor 3 alone. He is now presumed dead. HerringFerry[F3] acted as Judge and punisher.
<ParliamentWho[F8] Report: Attempt at High Treason on EL8. Five challengers attempted to overthrow the DC's rule. All offending parties were punished in accordance with Article 1 and have since been executed.
<PrissyKittyPrincess[F2] has joined the chat.>

Huh. That's, um, a lot of very serious stuff. Isn't execution, like, a medieval punishment . . . ?

Then again, it might just be that today is a very busy day for criming. Who knows?

<PrissyKittyPrincess[F2] has been removed from the chat.>

H—hey! Why did the window just close all of a sudden? What'd I do?

This is bullshit, I didn't do anything at all! Why, I oughta . . . !

Fuming, I smash my way into the Executives chat. There I'll be sure to find someone who'll reverse this. I'm an Executive, damn it!

<Status—Community—Top>
<Chatrooms>
<DC Executives Council>
<TalonsOfRage[F4]: We're getting close. I can feel it.>
<HuppiGupp[F10]: I don't get it tho, why is it mainly norwegans doing it like thats weird right im not the only one who thinks thats weird right?>
<TalonsOfRage[F4]: It doesn't matter. What matters is that soon, there won't be a single player in this entire tutorial who can question our authority.>
<JustAPrankBro[F5]: OK. ^w^>

\<JustAPrankBro[F5]: When were done lets eat cake together UwU>
\<PrissyKittyPrincess[F2] has joined the chat>

I take a deep breath.

\<PrissyKittyPrincess[F2]: **** **** mother****** banned me ****** *****
let me back in or ill **** ur ******* daughters and *** in their ******* like
the ****** they are>
PrissyKittyPrincess[F2]: ******* **** ******* **** ***** *** mother******
eat **** and die ******* ***** ***** *** ****** ****** ******* **** **** ***
****>

There's a long pause in the chat as they obviously deliberate my very serious injustice, and another minute or so passes as most likely as one of them hurries to fix this most grave of offenses, possibly by executing the offending parties.

Another minute goes by.

\<JustAPrankBro[F5]: OxO>
\<HuppiGupp[F10]: thats . . . uhh . . . wow>
\<TalonsOfRage[F4] . . .>

Hm? That's a pretty weird respo—

\<PrissyKittyPrincess[F2] has been removed from the chat.>

They—they—they . . . !?
This is just . . . !
I can't believe they would remove *their own Executive* from the group chat! Who does that? What kind of stupendous stupidity-wielders would go and REMOVE THEIR OWN COMRADE!? This is insane!

If I knew this was the kind of group the Delegate Commission was, I never would've joined!

I wonder if I'm still technically an executive? Hm. Well, I need to message Pox about this great injustice anyway, so I might as well ask him about it.

Quickly swiping over to the personal messages, I type up a letter for him.

\<PrissyKittyPrincess[F2]: ok i joined u cuz it sounded fun but like u and
ur group are total jack***** and a bunch of ***** so like i didnt do no thing
bad an they just banned me 4 NO REASON!!!! im like literally ur executive
and like ruler so ummmmm y dont u treat me like it literally sooooo dumb
u guyz are all dumb delegate commission more like delegate commPISSion

haha get it cuz ur full of **** isnt that just so funny its cuz its TRUE ok but srs can u put me back in da chats ill be good from now on thx>

Aaaaaaand send. Perfect. Now I'm sure he'll understand my perspective and stand on my side even when the rest of the commission attempt to unfairly renounce me. He's had my side since the beginning, so there's no reason for him to turn me down now.

And after only a few minutes of suspense, a little answer drops in.

<OrthodoxPox[F3]: I have reviewed your case and decided not to revoke the removals conducted by RedHanded[F7] and TalonsOfRage[F4]. This is on account of the fact that you were in clear violation of the Rules on both occasions. I have discussed the matter personally with the executives, and we have decided not to remove you from your post at this time. However, you are on thin ice. It is safe to assume that, should another challenger of the Hell Difficulty reach the second floor, they will be presented with the position as executive. If you in this position should choose to do away with them, then this will be considered foul play and you will be fully removed from your position. Furthermore, should you ever meet with any Delegate, they will do their best to punish you for your heinous crime. Thank you for understanding.>

I stare at the message. Then I read it again, just to make sure my eyes are working.

Well, there's only really one thing I can respond to that one, right?

<PrissyKittyPrincess[F2]: **** u>

Silently, I close down the window. The endless white stretches in front of me. I can feel my right eyelid twitch. I wonder what time it is. It can't have been more than a few hours, but I don't bother to check or anything, so who really knows?

<Top—Status—Community>
<01:10:23 Day 32>
<The third attempt will begin in 28:22:49:37>
<Floor 2 will open in 28:22:49:37>

It's only been an hour? Wait, seriously? But I've been writing and chatting and messaging like crazy! That should have been *at least* a full day or something. This makes no sense. There must be something afoot here. That's the only explanation.

But, well, uh, since I've got almost a full month to train until the next floor, I'd better get to it. I'm lucky you can still gain skill experience in the lobby without the added threat of dying. To boot, you also have the thing that all wounds get healed in a flash, so there isn't much pain.

And so begins my training. I'm still annoyed that my only available sword is too blunt to use for anything other than parrying, but it's good enough. Swoosh, swish, up and down, jumping around as I do. Bonking the pillars does nothing and just makes my sword bounce off. I wish I had a training dummy, but I spent all my points on a cake.

After a while I switch to a knife.

<You have learned: Basic Knife Arts Lv.1>

And so I train with that.

Running to and fro, up and down. I can't tell how long I've been doing this. The battle and field focus skills make everything slow down and I can't tell how long a second is supposed to be. I couldn't tell sunset from sunrise on the first floor because it was always dark, but it's worse here. I can't even try to use hypnagogia because it's so bright I can't see.

You know when you were a kid, and your mom told you not to look at the sun, but you did, and then wherever you looked, there would be a big white blot? I think I've developed that, but, like, for my entire field of vision. Closing my eyes doesn't help. Winding the clothes I bought around my face doesn't help.

It's all just WHITE.

<Top—Status—Community>
<01:15:11 Day 32>
<The third attempt will begin in 28:22:44:49>
<Floor 2 will open in 28:22:44:49>

It's only been five minutes? No that can't . . . that can't be right.

I must be hallucinating, or something like that.

Five minutes . . . It must be because of the battle focus, and the field focus. In here, I regenerate, and my brain does too, so it must be that they just . . . don't stop. At—at least, that's what I think may be happening. Maybe. I don't know. I can't think clearly.

I keep training. If I train, I don't have to think. Isn't that neat?

<You have learned: Exhaustion Resistance Lv.3>
<You have learned: Basic Knife Arts Lv.7>

Funny, I can't remember that one hitting level 2, or level 3, or level 4, or level 5, or level 6.

But I guess I'll just keep going.

<You have learned: Intermediate Spear Arts Lv.2>

There's a spear in my hand. I don't remember summoning it.

"Inventory," a voice says, but it's not me, but there's no one around either. It's just WHITE. But even though someone said *Inventory*, no such window will pop up. All I see is a blot of WHITE, like when you've stared into the sun for too long. There's no inventory.

<You have learned: Starvation Resistance Lv.6>

My stomach hurts. I don't know why. I ate a cake only earlier today. Just a few minutes ago. It kept me nice and fed. Why do I feel hungry now? That's so weird.

"Community."

Nothing pops up. It's WHITE.

"Status."

Nothing pops up. It's WHITE.

"Clock."

Nothing pops up. It's WHITE.

When I look at my hand, all I see is a blot of WHITE, like when you've stared into the sun for too long.

I think I'm moving, but I'm not sure anymore. I'm not sure if there's something in my hand or not. Everything around me is WHITE. I can't see the pillars anymore. The pillars used to have shadows, weird shadows, like they were badly rendered, and the sun was shining down from straight above, but they had shadows. I remember it. They had shadows, but I'm not sure I can remember what those shadows look like anymore.

Experimentally, after what could be a few minutes or a few hours or a few days or a few months or a few years or a few millennia, I try bringing my hand to my face and taking a big, yummy bite. Warm and wet stuff goes into my mouth and like a baby cow tasting its mother's udders for the first time and I drink my fill of my milky WHITE blood and it is so sweet and delicious like the first milk from a cow and it makes me want to cry but even when my world turns blurry it's still WHITE and WHITE like when you've been staring into the sun for too long.

Yummy. Yummy.

Yummy. Yummy.

I try getting more of the milk out of my veins. I'm not sure if there's anything in my hands or if I even have hands anymore so I start scratching at where I think my wrists are and scratch and scratch and scratch and scratch and after only a few years the milk comes out again and I drink, starved, even though my skin and my flesh and my blood and my bones is all WHITE like when you've been staring into the sun for too long.

WHITE.

WHITE.

WHITE.

WHITE.

I have decided that the fault must lie in my eyes. My eyes are wrong. They are bad. The WHITEs of my eyes are bad. They are bad and they are wrong and I must do something about that, so I put what I think is my fingers into what I think is my eyes and the WHITE turns RED and then the RED turns black and I cry tears of joy because the WHITE is gone and the WHITE is gone and the WHITE is gone and the WHITE is gone and the WHITE is gone

But

Then the WHITE returns, but I can see the pillars, and I can see the messages before me, but I don't look at them, I look at the WHITE floor, and the WHITE pillars, and I see that the floor beneath my feet is not WHITE, not anymore. It's gone all RED, from the milk in my veins.

And it's still there. It isn't gone. Much like the cake I ate, the milk from my veins is not removed. Never removed. Always there.

I decide, now, that the WHITE must be gone. Gone. Removed.

My wounds heal fast but not as fast as I can tear them open with my own fingers. It heals slashes and nice gushers faster than when I rip the arteries out and point their pulsating openings at the ground, because the lobby gets confused, and doesn't know how best to heal me. And once the RED milk in my veins is on the floor instead, I get down on my knees and hands and spread it out more, farther, everywhere the eye can see, across the floor as far as the floor reaches, and up the pillows as far as my little feet can carry me, and if I stab the spear and the axe into my feet and use them as stilts I can put the RED even higher up, and I do, because the more of the WHITE that isn't WHITE, the better.

And in the end the lobby isn't WHITE anymore.

And I smile, and sigh, and lie down.

\<You have learned: Bleeding Resistance Lv.10\>
\<You have learned: Bleeding Protection Lv.1\>

I see. I see . . .

\<Floor 2 has opened. Do you want to enter?\>
\<Yes/No\>

"Yes."

I press the Yes button.

VI

Yummy

When I appear once more, the world is in color. Beautiful, nuanced, exotic, intricate, wonderful, Faustian color.

I am in a large pass, right in the bowels of a tall ravine, taller than the hill, too tall and too steep to climb. High above, the blue, blue, blue, blue sky smiles down at me. I can't see any sun but it isn't important. It's blue. I love blue. Blue is my favorite color. I've always loved blue. It's so melodic, and harmonic, and symphonic. Just a beautiful color right down to the composition.

Behind me, the ravine closes. In front of me, it stretches on for what seems to be miles upon miles upon miles upon miles, to no end but a shadowy, unseen destination. And along the way, growing in luscious bundles along the side of the simple road, there are hundreds and thousands and millions and billions of wonderful, beautiful, colorful *flowers*. Like little dancing ladies, or little dancing ladies, or little dancing ladies, with their skirts all flowing in the wind. Oh, how I love them.

Bending down, I pluck a yellow flower by the stalk, bringing it to my nose and giving it a nice whiff. Mellow, yet sweet, like honey, or honey. No—actually—it reminds me way more of honey. Yes, rich, sweet, golden honey. That's what it is. Yellow. That's my favorite color. I love yellow. Like the sun on a warm day, or a warm day where the sun shines bright, or a day that is both warm and sunny. How I adore that color.

And here, see, another flower, of gentle countenance, bowing so sweetly in the wind, that upon seeing it, I gently bow in turn, before plucking it from its place and bringing it into my fold. The pink leaves of this bloom, speckled by black, almost shimmer in the light of the blue sky above. Pink—now *there's* a color for the ages. I love it. It's really my favorite color. Like a gentle, loving version of RED. So sweet. A maiden's kiss it brings me, and to it, I bring a gentleman's *nomch*.

Yummy. Yummy. Yummy. Yummy. Yummy. Yummy.

My tongue feels dull. Experimentally, I eat the yellow one, too. And then I try to eat the sky, but the sky is very unwilling, and refuses to go into my mouth. Naughty! I shall give it a stern talking-to once I've helped the rest of these lovely maidens into my inside mansion, where tea and cookies and tea is awaiting them.

I go down on all fours and start chomping down flowers. The maidens dance into me.

Yummy. Yu

<You have learned: Poison Resistance Lv.4>

Oh, haha, they are making a party within my bowels! What a rumbustious bunch. Haha. Ha! Hahaha. Oh, God.

<You have learned: Poison Resistance Lv.5>
<You have learned: Paralysis Tolerance Lv.9>
<You have learned: Organ Failure Tolerance Lv.1>

Party animals! They are animals! Yes, I must speak to them in their language! "Woof, woof! Hiss! Meow! Moo! Blub blub! Pikachu! Hiss! Meow!" But being so bestial, they do not respond to my courteous attempts.

Ah, but the world is looking so pretty now, with all the colors and the fireworks and the colors and the colors and the colors and the colors and the colors.

<You have learned: Hallucination Tolerance Lv.1>
<You have learned: Hallucination Tolerance Lv.2>
<You have learned: Hallucination Tolerance Lv.3>
<You have learned: Hallucination Tolerance Lv.4>

Haha, what is this, what, am I, uh, haha, inside, um, like, a video game? Isn't that just so funny, haha, it's like, video game screens! Wowww, I love video games, ever since I was a kid, but Dad didn't want me to be a pro gamer, but, uhh, I sure, haha, showed him, right? Got 'im! Haha!

I wonder how he's doing. He should be okay, right? I think so. I love him. He doesn't know it, he probably doesn't think so at all, but I do. And deep inside, I think he loves me, too. If he didn't love me, he wouldn't care.

Not that there's much to care for anymore, haha! Look at me! Oh, these beautiful colors . . .

<You have learned: Organ Failure Tolerance Lv.2>
<You have learned: Poison Resistance Lv.6>

I miss Dad. I miss Mom. I miss Sis.

"They don't miss you."

The darkness at the edge of my vision speaks.

Oh, begone, foul apparition, I need not your pity nor your honesty! Begone, specter! Or . . . something!

"You're going to die."

Well, yeah, obviously. But at least I beat the first floor, so now it's okay if I die. You get me?

"No."

Sour toad. I bet you're like, uh, a hallucination, or, um, something. Whatever.

"I am what you want me to be."

And right now, I want you to be gone. There. Leave me to my ladies, O specter. They are making a hell of my insides, but at least they're having a party, so I'm down. Like, physically, I'm lying down, and there's all these ladies around me, and I think I'd do best to eat, like, all of them. I mean, don't they look yummy? So colorful . . . except that WHITE one. It looks something foul, and it reeks, and nobody likes it, and everyone wishes it would just stop coming to the party and bringing down the mood.

A dark hand reaches across my vision, pointing, guiding, putting a single night-black finger against the petals of the ugly little WHITE flower.

"Eat it, and you will live."

. . . No. Look, all of these flowers are yummy but that one. No way. I can already tell it tastes like the inside of a washing machine, or a toilet bowl, or even the inside of a washing machine. No way in hell.

"It is your only way."

And you know what I don't get? You. I told you I don't want to see you, and yet here you are, goading me on to eat the one lady here I would rather grind to a fine paste beneath my Gucci soles. Is this just to taunt me, O specter? You spooky dork?

"Eat it."

No.

"Eat it."

Nuh-uh.

"Eat it."

Nuh. *Uh.*

The specter quiets for a second. After a moment, it steps to the side, making the darkness in my vision shift, revealing a flowery lady just out of sight, in a rainbow gown with streaks of all the colors of a prism in her hair, with the most radiant smile you'd ever see. The specter plucks her from her place and holds her in its black hand.

"If you eat the WHITE flower, I will give you this."

. . .

. . .

—You got yourself a deal, partner!

In one smooth movement, I bring my wrist to my face, gnaw into the veins, and once the blood flows like wine in a frat party, I hold it over the WHITE lady, turning her RED.

And then I face-slam her with my mouth open.

. . . Yummy. I suppose.

<WHITE Death consumed. Prepare yourself.>

Huh. Hm. That's, uhhh . . .

<You have learned: Poison Resistance Lv.7>
<You have learned: Poison Resistance Lv.8>
<You have learned: Poison Resistance Lv.9>
<You have learned: Poison Resistance Lv.10>
<You have learned: Poison Protection Lv.1>
<You have learned: Organ Failure Tolerance Lv.3>
< . . . >
<You have learned: Organ Failure Tolerance Lv.10>
<You have learned: Organ Failure Resistance Lv.1>
<You have learned: Organ Failure Resistance Lv.2>
<You have learned: Necrosis Tolerance Lv.1>
<You have learned: Necrosis Tolerance Lv.2>
<You have learned: Necrosis Tolerance Lv.3>
< . . . >
<You have learned: Necrosis Tolerance Lv.10>
<You have learned: Necrosis Resistance Lv.1>
<You have learned: Coma Tolerance Lv.1>
<You have learned: Coma Tolerance Lv.2>
<You have learned: Coma Tolerance Lv.3>
< . . . >
<You have learned: Coma Tolerance Lv.10>
<You have learned: Coma Resistance Lv.1>

\<You have learned: Oxygen Deficiency Resistance Lv.1\>
\<You have learned: Oxygen Deficiency Resistance Lv.2\>

I . . .
Don't . . .
Feel . . .
So . . .
Good . . .

The Specter Embraces Me And Brings Me Into Its Loving Arms

VII

Courting the Ladies

My sister stands in front of me. She's crying. I say something. She cries harder. Mom comes in and hugs her. She doesn't hug me. It makes me say something else. Mom makes a conflicted face. I don't say anything after that. My sister says something. I didn't like it. I raise my hand to her. But mom is in the way. My dad comes in. He screams. At me. At my sister. At mom. I feel horrible. It makes me want to make them feel horrible, too. So I say more things. Even though I didn't want to. I say the things. None of them like hearing it. I don't either. But I say it. Because if I don't say it. Then the silence will be there. And the silence hurts more. The silence is WHITE. But the words are RED. And something is always better than nothing. Even if that something is **hate**.

\<You have learned: Death Tolerance\>

I awaken. I'm standing.

There's a flower clutched in my hand, as colorful as a rainbow. I stare at it as though it's about to grow a head and arms and face and whatever else humans have.

Hum. I have a feeling that something very strange just happened.

\<THE GODDESS OF WANT SEES YOU.\>

A message floats in front of my eyes. It feels like it's always been there, at the same time as how it may have popped up just now. It could have been there for hours or even days and I just . . . I wouldn't know. It feels nonlinear in time.

But it is there, and I can sense that the time around it simply does not move too much.

It's there. It was always there.

. . . The goddess of want, is it?

I'm not *that* greedy, am I?

Silently, I glance down at the flower.

Before I can have another breakdown—the nth this day-week-month-year—I quickly pocket the little flower and send it into my inventory, where it gets labeled as *Mysterious Rainbow Flower*. How useful, guys.

I don't know how or why, but I think my brain feels clearer now. A bit. A little.

Did I die? *Again?*

I don't know. I don't want to think about it. But I have a feeling that I'll know it once I actually read the floor description. Which was suspiciously hidden behind a message from a certain goddess of *you're greedy*. You know, big shocker, but I'm starting to get really irked by these supposed divine beings. Can't I get noticed by a nice god? Like the God of War, or the God of Tenacity, or the God of Adventure, or something like that? No? Just the mean gods? Got it.

<Tutorial stage, Hell Difficulty Second Floor: The Rugged Pass> <[Clear Condition] Reach the door.>

Another *reach this place* quest, huh. Well, assuming that it doesn't want me to literally climb the sides of this cliff, I don't think I'll have too much difficulty with all of this. When do I get the *kill X amount of goblins* quest? Right now, I really, really, really, really want to do some of that sort of stuff. You know.

But *nooooo*, I have to reach a *door*. Yeah, because obviously there's going to be a door down in this ravine. Just stuck to the side of it. Or something.

. . . I don't feel good.

I'm trying to remember what Moleman's guide said about this stage. Something about vultures? Something about heat? I don't know. It isn't especially warm here, and the sky is blue, so I don't get what the issue here is supposed to be. Or, well, I do, but Moleman—being the dumbo he is—didn't touch on it.

Namely, these pretty ladies. Uh, flowers. I mean, flowers.

The entire path, all the way down the rugged pass, is covered with them. And they're all extremely colorful, alongside just plain pretty. But that's not really the issue. There aren't just hundreds of thousands of these flowers. They make up a veritable bush, covering the entire bottom of the ravine, and the variety that they show is to the point where it's hard to spot two of the same flower. Going by the experience I had just now, I have good reason to believe that a large percentage of these flowers are poisonous to the point where eating them would probably kill me. Not to mention just grazing by them.

Normally, just touching a poisonous plant doesn't necessarily kill you, but this must be dawn or something, because these ladies are covered with a fine layer of dew. For some reason, I don't think this will go away anytime soon.

Climbing up the side of the ravine is out of the question; despite my resistances, a fall from that height would still kill me.

Trying to use the cliff to avoid the flowers would also not be possible, as the side isn't actually entirely perpendicular, but at a slight outward angle. I'd fall. Simple as that.

My only option in this scenario is to push my way through.

At least, that is if I want to clear this place as fast as possible. But, you know—I don't know if you've noticed—but I'm not exactly an ordinary gamer. For now, resistances and tolerances are all that I have. Well, that, and two *protections*. Whatever those are.

<[Poison Protection (Lv.1)]
Evolved version of [Poison Resistance]. Grants powerful protection against poisons and venoms.>
<[Bleeding Protection (Lv.1)]
Evolved version of [Bleeding Resistance]. Grants powerful protection against bleeding out, increases speed at which bleeding is stifled, and more blood can be bled before negative effects are incurred.>

Right. With this . . . I mean, "powerful protection against poisons"? It's basically a shield against dying by poison! Considering what it took to get it, I probably won't be leveling it up anytime soon, and the same remains true for bleeding protection. But that doesn't mean I can't make use of them anyway, right? Exactly. I mean, the flower that got me to that point was that—that—rude little lady called WHITE Death, so I doubt any other flower will get me to that point.

This floor is a veritable all-you-can-eat buffet of status effect resistances!

Oh, assuming the flower doesn't override my tawny tolerances and kill me on the spot. Of course.

Since my memory is kind of shit, I suppose I'd do best to keep a log of the ladies just to ensure that I don't accidentally eat the same deadly flower twice.

Pulling up the Community tab, I get to writing. But just as I check my posts in order to write, I notice something new.

<PrissyKittyPrincess[F2]: MY guide 2 floor 1 (4 pro gamers ONLY)>
<CatBatBarrage[F2]: my dude what are you on>
<ArrowToTheKnee[F6]: Haha, look guys, new LOLCOW dropped.
Hahaha.>

<RadicalMedical[F5]: I'm actually a former pro gamer and this is not for me.>
<YourRockSucks[F2]: so this guy basically waited for the eclipse to complete and then pretended that the floor was super hard huh>
<BlueEyesWHITEArcher[F6]: You can at least try to be original in your delusions. Even the Hard Difficulty only has a Leopard as boss monster. Did you you forget to take your meds, schkitzo?>
<YourRockSucks[F2]: btw nice username *** lol>

I can feel a tremble take hold of my body.
Fire and brimstone seeps into my skull and my fingers flash to the keyboard.

<PrissyKittyPrincess[F2]: **** u **** u **** u
u all r ***** nd im bonking ur moms **** u **** u **** u
eat my ****>

Silently, like a commander killing the final enemy on the battlefield—the only other survivor other than himself, I close the post. Then I open another one. My memory of the pretty ladies is fuzzy, but I can remember them well enough to write down a guide for them.

<PrissyKittyPrincess[F2]: guide to ALL DA LADIES by a PRO-GAMER (ONLY 4 REAL GAMERS!!!!!) fuk U h8trzzz
spotty black shimmery pinklady: she makes u c stuff das not ther. mayb a little posion fluffy yellowlady: strong poison prob kill u. a little paralyse but mayb only in brain
WHITE death: dontt eat this 1 u die
rainbowlady: i dunno wat this 1 does but a goddess gave it 2 me>

After a few more minutes of writing down the ladies I can remember, I put down the Community tab. My best bet is to just not think about all of the haters. They don't get me, and they never will, and that's just how it is.

<Top—Status—Community>
<00:37:37 Day 61>
<The fourth attempt will begin in 29:23:22:23>

I raise my eyes from the clock. In front of me, a near-endless path overgrown with flowers of all sizes and colors stretches out. I'd better get to it, then.
Maybe I should call myself lucky that I was in such a state upon arriving here, because instead of already standing in a huge patch of ladies, there's a small bald

spot where I've already eaten everything. Hm. I wonder if it's physically possible for me to eat every single lady here?

<THE GOD OF COWARDICE WORRIES THAT HE MAY LOSE A PROMISING FUTURE APOSTLE.>

Shut it! You are not part of this, so you better go away!

I'll probably get negative effects just from touching these, so I might as well go ahead and munch down. But since none of them show their effects or names in the form of boxes or windows, I'll just have to do it myself. One lady at a time, all the while writing down the effects as I go.

Taking a long, measured breath, I sit down, crossing my legs as I do. Let's get started.

Lady number 1: a light blue skirt with large, lacy plumes, her crown held by a body of silver. Taste: mellow, with hints of metal and copper. I then realized that this was because her coarse body tore up the inside of my mouth and left me bleeding. When swallowed, she did the same to my throat, so I have reason to believe her entire form was covered in small, imperceptible barbs. Status condition: [Bleeding]

Lady number 2: periwinkle buds crowded around a blank center of gold. Taste yummy. It left me hallucinating for several minutes on end wherein I saw God and He laughed at me. In anger, I ate Him too. Status condition: [Hallucination]

Lady number 3: God. Shadowy form, salty taste. Made me puke. Ew. Status condition: [Nausea]

. . .

Lady number 662: Yummy!

Lady number 663: Yummy!

Lady number 664: Yummy!

Lady number 665: Yummy!

Lady number 666: Yum—

"Caw!"

Hang the on the on, Mr. long-neck duck, I am countrying a *woman* here.

"Caw, caw!"

Go away rendezvous point, I told you that I am in no mood to dillydally, my readers are depending on me for this lifesaving information!

<PrissyKittyPrincess[F2]: eq011

11n1n 101000 dnenenen jjdjfjf

Wnnnnnnnnnnnnnnnnnnnnnnnnnnnnnnnnnnnnnnnnnnnnnnnnnnnnnnnnnnnnnn

Mmrmmmrmm

yeyye 29292 188 1881 88
Ladyladyladylady
Efnnnn errre rr erroroo oon. nenn. euff>
<AdvanceDestroy[F3]: fellas, I think she's lost it.
<CottonEyedJeff[F4]: RIP>
<FrondBeyond[F3]: she made a good effort. RIP>
<HowWhatWhy[F6]: rip>

They need me, my good fellow!

"Caw."

And like the melodramatic vulture-man he is, he extends his beak across the table far more than is normally acceptable, and takes a peck at my face, removing my eye. How rude! As I've told you many times, Sir Archebeak the Third, there is really no need for such vulgarity. We have plenty of appetizers—Lady 77 and Lady 320 are especially plentiful this season. Here, won't you try Lady 43?

Grabbing hold of his slender, lady-killing neck, I shove Lady 43 down his throat.

"C—cawwhhwkk, cawwhhkkhhh . . . !"

Oh, and now you're rejecting her advances. How cruel a bird you are, Master Wingley. You are hurting her feelings!

<Vulture (Lv.3) Defeated.>

But much like the rest of his kind, he just starts foaming and flapping his wings like a lunatic, before dropping dead on the spot. How boorish. I should never have agreed to dine with these gents. Nevertheless. Would you like more tea, Mistress Lovethorn? Milk from my own veins, steeped in Lady 200. It's quite marvelous!

She, much like her brusque brothers, attempts to refuse the tea, but I will not have any more of this circus act within my tea party, so I force the yummy tea down her throat.

"Cwaaaaahhkkkk—!"

<Vulture (Lv.2) Defeated.>

The rest of my guests look a bit restless but nonetherest I must restore their restpite in this restpectable restaurant. Restolutely.

"C—caw . . ."

Oh, don't you sass me, woman!

It would seem to me that the lot of you all have yet to respect me and my attempt to please the lot of you! It is very upsetting, and I have no choice but to bar you from this gathering. I hope that none of you will take this personally, as it is far from my intention. But I hope that, until next time, you will reflect upon your actions, well and truly.

I greet them with the butter knife.

<Vulture (Lv.5) Defeated.>
<Vulture (Lv.3) Defeated.>
<Vulture (Lv.4) Defeated.>
<Vulture (Lv.2) Defeated.>
<Vulture (Lv.2) Defeated.>
<Vulture (Lv.5) Defeated.>
<[Level Up]>
<You have reached Level 8.>
<Agility has increased by 3.
Strength has increased by 2.
Stamina has increased by 4.
Magic Power has increased by 1.
Coma Resistance has increased by 1.
Internal Damage Resistance has increased by 1.
Intermediate Knife Arts has increased by 2.
Hallucination Resistance has increased by 3.>

I hope to see you all next—

<You have learned: Hallucination Protection Lv.1>

. . . Huh.

Huh?

Huh . . .

This is . . . weirdly enough not the weirdest position I've woken up to. I'm surrounded by dead half-eaten vultures and not much else. In front of me, a few meters away, the flowers and the ravine continue. Behind me is a long stretch of bare ground. Not even a single leaf remains.

So, in conclusion, I've been eating a lot, but I don't feel bloated. What a neat feature. Are ladies nutritious? I don't know.

Hum.

What was I doing again? Oh, yeah. Eating flowers. Better get back to it, I guess.

I stretch my hand toward a flower but stall inches before its petals.

No, if I touch this lady's stem it'll hurt. I need to eat the flower first, then wait a few minutes to grab the stem.

. . . How do I know that? Where is this . . . ?

It's Lady 93. It's only common sense. Right, right, just standard common sense . . . of course. Quietly, a little speechless, I chomp down on the flower. And there, next to it, is Lady 6. She's very spicy, and will kill your organs one by one, starting with your spleen, so your best bet is to just remove your spleen before it spreads any further.

. . . It doesn't feel like this knowledge belongs to me. I can barely even recall gaining it. And yet . . .

<Top—Status—Community>
<13:50:50 Day 68>
<The fourth attempt will begin in 22:10:09:10>

It's been a full week. I can't remember much from it aside from the start; however, I can tell that I've been using this time in some mode or manner. I'm not sure how, but it wouldn't be exactly fair to say that it was a waste. I can remember eating. That's about it.

If I look in the Skills tab, I've gained a lot of new tolerances and even a fair number of resistances, though I only have three protections so far. Personally, I think that this is for the best. Mainly, though, I feel a bit winded. When I look at the flowers ahead of me, I can kind of tell just what each of them will do to me if I eat it. There are a few unknowns left in my vision, though.

I wonder for how long this ravine stretches on? It's supposed to end eventually, right?

Besides . . . I'm starting to feel a bit hot. I'm not sure when, but the temperature down here has risen sharply, and now it feels downright humid. Furthermore, now that I'm actually looking at it, it seems I've gained a heat tolerance skill, though it isn't doing much.

Well, enough about that. There's still plenty of ladies left to court, so I'd better get to it.

Wearily, I return to eating flowers. I can deal with the poisonous and hallucinogenic ones relatively well, but some cause *really* exotic symptoms that my resistances basically have to work together to counterattack. Lady number 667 has a nerve toxin that makes you unable to feel your tongue, and since it doesn't exactly work as a normal poison, it doesn't trigger my poison protection but rather my paralysis tolerance. If it hadn't evolved into paralysis resistance just in time, I might have choked to death on my own tongue.

Lady number 9 makes me feel horribly, horribly hungry, like I've got a black hole in my stomach. All I can really do to counteract it is to try to only eat the flowers that I can already handle well enough, though this is often far from enough.

Lady number 690 made my stomach uncontrollably itchy, and I thought that only the skin would be affected by the itchiness, but then it was still itchy even after I'd scratched off my skin, so I just kind of kept scratching even after it went through my thin fat layer and a bit of the muscle. I almost opened up my own bowels, but then I got so desperate I purposefully ate Lady number 444, which makes me manic, but that didn't really help because it just made me eat more flowers and dance around naked.

Once I got to Lady 1,000, I decided to take a breather.

I tore off my clothes. I don't know where I put them. I think I might have eaten them because I suddenly gained an indigestion tolerance. I didn't mention it before, but my body no longer makes any waste. A lot of the ladies make me puke uncontrollably, but none give me anything from the other end because for some reason my body doesn't do that anymore since I entered the tutorial. I'm scared. What happened to my clothes? Can they still come out or am I screwed?

Since I can't afford to buy new clothes, I pulled out my leopard hide and now that's what I'm wearing. I put its head on my shoulders and tied its arms around my neck, but then I had to somehow cover my groin, which I did by tying its legs around there, and now I just feel bad for it because it looks like I'm wearing a big diaper. I don't know what to do with the tail so it's just hanging behind me but I keep stepping on it and stumbling. I just feel bad.

<THE GODDESS OF WANT APPROVES OF YOUR SENSE OF FASHION.>

What is there to approve? I'm wearing this poor thing's skin as my only clothes! Ah, if I could only wear my normal clothes . . . A hoodie. A pair of jogging pants. A nice pair of briefs. That's all I'm asking for. Why did I have to eat my underpants, too? Why can't my brain survive this sort of stuff?

Oh, Lady number 877 with the effects of inducing coma, take the pain away!

But, of course, since I have coma resistance level 2, all it does is make me feel drowsy and numb. And, you know, I've been thinking, but . . . there really is a tolerance for everything. I mean, just the other hour I ate Lady number 769 and got hormonal imbalance tolerance level 1.

But the fact that there are so many different tolerances is not a good thing. I mean, sure, I've got super strong poison resistance, but the second something attacks in a slightly different manner, I'm gone.

Silently thoughtful, I chomp into Lady number 1,247. Hmm. An aftertaste of hazelnut, with more mellow notes of ginger and burnt tires. As for the effect . . . Yes, I'm starting to go blind. Interesting.

<You have learned: Blindness Tolerance Lv.9>
<You have learned: Blindness Resistance Lv.1>

Phew, nice to have that one in the bag. Shame my vision is still being filled with nothingness. Seems Lady number 1,247 has a stronger effect than Lady number 67, so there's only really one way to deal with this.

Putting down the flower I was about to eat next, I quickly shove my fingers into my eyeballs and pull them out. Since it's a waste to just throw them away, I put them into my inventory to use as vulture bait once I get thirsty. And after a few minutes of meditation . . .

\<You have learned: Auto-Regeneration Lv.4\>

I can sense that I got a level up, but I can't see it. It seems that whatever the lady did, it targeted not my eyeballs themselves but rather my neural centrals for vision. My eyeballs have regenerated, but I'm still blind. Hopefully this won't last too long. It's kind of silly, but before all this, I assumed being blind was like having your eyes closed, like everything is black, but that isn't it at all. You just can't see at all.

\<You have learned: Bacteria Tolerance Lv.1\>

Oh, that's going to be a bother.

Well, it's not like I can tell the ladies apart by touch alone, so . . . I mean, I probably could, but then what's the fun?

. . . Okay, fine, I'll keep going. But I'll only do the ladies I've already had a taste of!

Now, let's see here . . . Ruffled skirt . . . Soft, delicate leaves . . . Slightly curved stem . . . That's got to be Lady number 690. Let's have a taste to check. Mm. Just as flavorful as usual, and within only half a minute, I can already feel my abdomen start to itch.

\<You have learned: Irritation Tolerance Lv.7\>

Though, thanks to my tolerance, it only sort of makes me want to disembowel myself. By groping around for a while, I'm able to find Lady number 881, whose acidic slime is enough to corrode my hand down to its bones and leave it unable to regenerate for several hours, and with no hesitation, I press her to my stomach.

\<You have learned: Acid Tolerance Lv.10\>
\<You have learned: Acid Resistance Lv.1\>
\<You have learned: Corrosion Tolerance Lv.5\>

Ahhh, that's *much* better.

. . . Hm? Is that a flap of wings I hear? I guess the smell of my stomach melting was enough to rouse their attention. This might be a problem. I'm not sure what sort of impression I've given you, but I'm no [insert famous martial artist here]. Flap flap flap, and now I can't hear the flapping, so I think they've landed. Hm. Choice one: try to feed them ladies. Choice two—

Oh, something just went into my soft stomach. Yup, that's a beak. My skin got kind of goopy thanks to the acid, so they don't really need to make much of an effort to slurp it up. The problem is . . .

<Vulture (Lv.3) Defeated.>

Yeah. Acid, dude. You ever heard of it? It's not very edible.

But the other vultures don't really care, so they just kind of bustle around me. I can hear their feathers rusting together. Their beaks poke into me, one by one, pecking and slurping and poking and grabbing. First my stringy muscles, and then my organs. Well, mainly my bowels and stomach. But see, you know, I haven't exactly been eating a nutritious diet as of lately. My body has neutralized most of it to the point where I can handle it well, but these vultures don't really have those sorts of resistances. So, once they get to my stomach . . .

"C—caw!"

"Crawwaaahkk . . . !"

"C—caw . . ."

<Vulture (Lv.2) Defeated.>
<Vulture (Lv.3) Defeated.>
<Vulture (Lv.5) Defeated.>
<Vulture (Lv.2) Defeated.>
<Vulture (Lv.4) Defeated.>
<[Level Up]>
<You have reached Level 9.>
<Agility has increased by 2.
Strength has increased by 3.
Stamina has increased by 4.
Magic Power has increased by 1.
Coma Resistance has increased by 1.
Blindness Resistance has increased by 1.
Organ Failure Resistance has increased by 1.
Bacteria Tolerance has increased by 3.
Internal Damage Resistance has increased by 1.>

Yeah, take that, you bird-brained beak-for-brains! Take . . . that . . .
Falling flat on my back, I feel my consciousness fade.

. . .

Ugh . . . Man, what a hangover . . . Where is—?
Oh, my vision is back! Great stuff, that's—
Is that a door?

VIII

Fire

No, it isn't *just* a door, it's . . . It's *my* door.

But we moved out of that house when I was like nine, why would . . . ?

<You have learned: Heat Tolerance Lv.10>
<You have learned: Heat Resistance Lv.1>

Yeah, that's . . . man, it is *hot*. It feels like my skin is on fire, and still I've got heat resistance. No pun intended, but it really does feel like I'm standing in front of the door to hell. Except that it's my door. The door to my childhood bedroom. I want to ask why it's here, but this is some weird tutorial watched by weird gods, so what's even the point?

More importantly, there are no more flowers. I must have eaten them all while I was asleep or something.

<You have learned: Hypnagogia Lv.7>

Yeah, I get it, but it still feels anticlimactic.

There is seriously just a door right there. Stuck in the rocky wall of the far-thermost edge of the rugged pass like a badly placed prop. It looks completely out of place, and it's even worse because of the—you know. It's *my door*. It's even got the little poker-face sticker my sister put on there just before we moved.

<Tutorial stage,
Hell Difficulty Second Floor:
Boss Stage>
<[Clear Condition] Open the door and enter within.>

I just need to open it? Is that seriously it? Considering that Moleman made literally no mention of the boss, I guess that really is the whole deal. Open a door. Is it even locked? Is there something in it? Will it explode in my face? What is the purpose of living? All very good questions. But, before that, I want to check two things.

\<Top—Status—Community\>
\<10:00:05 Day 70\>
\<The fourth attempt will begin in 20:13:59:55\>

It's only been like ten days since I came here, but since there is physically nothing more for me to do since all the flowers are eaten and all that, I guess I should just get to it. But first, I want to meditate a little. I've been kind of out of it this entire floor, so I haven't really looked for it, but . . . Yeah.

Sitting down on the ground, I close my eyes and meditate.

After only a minute or so . . .

\<A Canto appears to you.\>

Alright, let's see if it's any different this time around.

\<[O muse, o alto ingegno, or m'aiutate;
o mente che scrivesti ciò ch'io vidi,
qui si parrà la tua nobilitate!]\>

Uh-huh. Uh-huh. Um . . . It's different? But it's still Italian. The only real difference here, though, is that it almost says *miau* on the first line. You know, like a cat? Miau? No? Okay.

Sighing, I break the meditation and stand up. The door is right in front of me. An almost burning heat is emanating from it. I step toward it, holding out my hand to the brass doorknob, letting my palm hover over it. I haven't touched it yet, but the warmth coming from it feels like holding your hand over a flaming fire pit. It's not going to kill me, right? It's just a door. There's no need to be afraid. Just open the door.

Simple.

I grab the door handle.

\<The Goddess of Want is disappointed.\>

Fire.

Burning. My hand erupts into flames and my skin melts off and my flesh melts off and my bones start to crack from the heat but I can't let go and within mere seconds the fire eats more and more and more and more of me, snaking up my arm, leaving my skeleton black and cracked, up to my shoulders, through my entire rib cage, making my chest empty, down my pelvis and legs, making all of me black, and then up through my neck and spine, turning it black like the keys of a piano, and then the fire reaches my skull and I explode into black dust.

"If you don't want the salmon, I can heat up some of yesterday's chicken for you, son. You don't need to eat it if you don't want to."

No, I need to eat it, Mom. It's good for me, and you spent all evening making it. Wouldn't it be mean of me not to eat the fruits of your hard labor of love?

"You're so mature for your age."

Thanks, Dad. I wouldn't be who I am without you. I love you, Dad, Mom.

"When did you turn so sappy, brother?"

I don't know, sister. I suppose I've learned to appreciate life. I mean, it's so feeble, you know? One day it's here, and the next, it's all gone.

"Like your pro gaming career?"

My sister snickers.

It might sound weird, but . . . I don't think I miss it. Being a pro gamer wasn't good for me. It made me mean, and vindictive, and when it all came tumbling down, I really did become the worst version of myself. But now, I'm better. Working down at the store with you, Dad, makes me feel like a valuable member of society. Like I'm actually useful.

My dad smiles.

"You've always been useful, son. I'm sorry if my words ever made you think the opposite. I was just worried about you, because I care. Not because I don't want you to be happy, but because I didn't believe that your happiness lay in gaming."

And you were right, Dad. It didn't. I just thought it did, because it made me feel blindly superior to those who were playing the game because they liked it. In hindsight, I don't think I ever actually enjoyed a moment playing it. I was constantly searching for the next piece of strong gear not because I enjoyed playing the game, but rather to beat down those who did. All and all, the entire obsession just boiled down to an inferiority complex taking the form of undue hatred. It was wrong of me to take it out on you, Dad. And you too, Mom. And Sis.

My mother giggles.

"Now you're talking gamer lingo again, son. Can't you leave the work talk for after dinner?"

Oh, come on, Mom. I'm not technically a pro gamer anymore, so it's hobby talk rather than work talk, wouldn't you say?

We all share a laugh.

I thank God in my heart that instead of foolishly lashing out, I instead shook his hand, and gave him my title with grace. It was the best decision of my life.

Mom, Dad, Sis . . . I love you all. Thank you for being in my life.
"I love you too, son."
"I'm sorry that I haven't said it enough, but I love you too, son."
"Ew, stop being so sickly sweet! Though, in the end . . . I guess I love you too, bro."
Mom smiles.
Dad smiles.
Sis smiles.
I smile.
A screen appears before my eyes.

<[DO YOU WANT TO DIE?]>

What?

I'm not at home anymore. Mom isn't here.
Dad isn't here.
Sis isn't here.
They don't care about this.
They never cared, because they don't love me, and they never have.
They hate me and I hate them.

"And the new World Champion of Tendrils of Magic and Madness is . . .
LetsFraternizeTogether!"

Cheering.
Horrible, grating, loud, addictive cheering.
But not for me.
It was never for me.
On the other side of the room,
I can see him.
He's grinning from ear to ear.
But there's a purity to it.
He's not grinning because he loves the taste of my misery,
or because he wants the world to see how great he is,
but rather for the simple reason that he is happy.
He won.
I lost.
The world shifts off balance.
Everything turns on its head.
Mice chase cats,
cats chase dogs.

"Good fight, thank you for the exciting match!"

He's in front of me now,
flanked by his slightly older brother.
He isn't older than me.
He isn't younger than me.
We're the same age.
But, somehow, he looks more energetic.
Bright-eyed, optimistic, and
happy just to be here.
I feel my hands ball into fists.
If he had lost, he would still be smiling,
just because he found the challenge exciting.
He would still thank me, he would still shake my hand,
and I would still feel like the pit of my stomach was filled with black sludge.
I can't stand his type.
I can't stand them.
I won't shake his hand.
To restrain myself, I simply cross my arms.

"Good work today. I hope I'll see you next championship so we can have a proper rematch!"

And he slaps my shoulder.
And for some reason,
For some inexplicable reason,
that's what does it.

My world turns RED and I fly at him, grabbing his arm and twisting it around, and even though my arms are normally so weak, now they are strong, much stronger than his even though he looks so much healthier, and I grin at the way his arm crunches and twists, and I want to hear that sound even more, so I keep pulling it and snapping it every which way I can think of, and the bone is much more brittle than I had thought, and we fall to the floor, me on top of him, and him struggling, desperately, but still not making a sound, his eyes wide and beady like a bug caught in a trap, not really capable of understanding what's happening, but now I'm on top of him and his right arm is all bent and sharp shards of WHITE are sticking out of his skin but I'm not happy with that so I begin pummeling his face, winding like a mechanical figure, beating and beating and beating and beating, until his nose crunches under my bruised knuckles, a trail of RED going down his lip and splattering onto my hoodie, and it's only been a few seconds so now people try to respond, but I'm stuck to him, and even though my fingers hurt and my hands hurt and my knuckles hurt, I clutch a hold of his neck, pulling my grip tighter, tighter, tighter, tighter, watching as his face turns RED and then blue and then . . .

<[Do you want to die?]>

I tumble.
Down, down, down.

The world is dark.

It burns. Mommy, it burns.
I don't want to, anymore.

I miss my family.

Why did I say that? Why did I do that?

Help

Help

Help
I
Want

To

Die

"Your father doesn't know I'm here."
. . . Mom?
"And he can't ever know. Son . . . If you go home, he will kill you."
He didn't even come to the trial.
"You can't go home. But I can't let you stay here. I . . . I took out a loan.
In the family's name. It's not good. I put down the store as collateral.
If your father finds out . . . No, when he does, you have to be as far away as possible.
I'll take the hit. He won't understand a mother's love, but he won't be able to kill
me. Not while Astrid still lives at home.
And after she's moved out . . . I won't care anymore. But you can't be home when
that happens."
What do you expect me to do?
Go homeless?
"We all have to make sacrifices, Lo. The only reason I was able to bail you out
was because I happen to know a few people down at the courthouse. You can't be
ungrateful."
I hate you.
I'm going to starve in the streets and you don't care.
"I care, and I love you.
But sometimes, you're a very hard boy to love."

<[Do you want to die?]>

Fire.

Burning.

Searing, blistering pain.

There is no recourse from it.

Sometimes, when I go to sleep, I dream about it. It feels good to choke him. To see his grin falter and his eyes bug out. It's a nice dream. And when I'm dreaming about it, I never remember the consequences. What happened afterward. Because it didn't matter in the moment. All that mattered was to put the light out of his eyes. To make him remember who the true winner here was. But then I always get pulled out of the dream, and back into the real world. And the real world is dull. It always is, and it always has been. I hate the real world. I hate it so much.

I wish the real world didn't exist.

<[Do you want to die?]>

I don't.

I don't *want* to die. It's just that, for some reason, I always find myself in situations where dying seems like the simplest solution. But even then, it's not like I just lie down and die. What kind of gamer would just give up once the level gets difficult? When the boss changes to a different form, or heals itself, that's when the real battle starts. No true pro gamer would simply give up. They keep going, because the pain of losing, over and over and over and over again, can never compare to the joy of winning just once. Even if everything else goes wrong, even when you're surrounded by nothing but enemies, there's still a way to win, and once you do, the rewards you reap will be all the sweeter. The higher the difficulty, the better the loot.

I don't want to die.

If I die, I lose.

<The God of Cowardice repeats Himself.>
<[Do you want to die?]>

No. I don't.

My skeleton hand clenches around the doorknob. Slowly, it turns in my hand, and as I creak the door open, a wave of soul-rending fire rushes out, basking my charred, coal-like body in the fiery blazes of hell. But even though it hurts, even though it makes my brain boil and bubble and burn, I still press onward, pushing against the door with my shoulder, forcing it open with all the power that the remains of my body possesses. Inside, I can see the darkness within poking out, staring into me with eyes of black fire. And still, I don't flinch.

I push onward. The door opens, inch by inch, and once it is open fully, once the very pits of hell show themselves to me, in their full, fiery glory—

I step inside.

The fire takes me and I join with it.

<You have cleared the second floor.>
<You have received 1,000 points for clearing the floor.
You have received an additional 1,000 points for being the first to clear the floor.>
<There is a God that sees you.
You have received 500 points.>
<A God has shown a positive response to you.
You have obtained 1,000 points.>
<A God has shown a negative response to you.
1,000 points have been deducted.>

<A CHANGE HAS BEEN MADE.>
<THE GODDESS OF WANT WISHES TO GRANT SOME OF HER POWERS INSTEAD OF
THE NORMAL STAGE REWARD.>
<WILL YOU ACCEPT?>
<YES/NO>

The last time I accepted a god's offer I got a useless, embarrassing skill that did me no good, and according to the posts on the community boards you can usually get a pretty good piece of equipment for clearing a stage, which I desperately need because I think I ate all my clothes. But on the other hand . . .

How bad could it be?

"Yes."

I press the Yes button.

<You have obtained:>
<[Great Values Sniffer(Lv.MAX)]
The Goddess of Want, who watches over those who exhibit desire for what they should not possess, has granted some of Her powers to Her potential apostle.>

Okay.

Whatever charcoal remains of my skeleton turns to dust and I disappear into the hellish winds around me. And only as my dead dust drifts skyward, do I realize . . .

I didn't get the reward for completely clearing the stage.

Shoot—

FLOOR 3

THE ACHING CITY

The Haters and Disbelievers

The very second that I reappear in the lobby, I fly to my feet.

My eye twitches.

WHITE. There is WHITE all around me. WHITE pillars, WHITE floor, WHITE sky . . .

It makes my stomach flip. But, thankfully, now, I know just how to deal with it.

I'm so happy bleeding protection doesn't stop me from bleeding, or I wouldn't be able to make the lobby livable. I don't think I could stay in here for a whole twenty-four hours if it wasn't RED.

Since I've already done it once, painting the whole place RED doesn't take as much time as it did last time, and once I'm done, I can do nothing but wipe the sweat off my forehead and gloat at the sight. Now, as for the next floor . . .

<Time Until Floor 3 Opening: 23:11:32>

Looks good. And how's the time as a whole?

<Top—Status—Community>
<10:49:30 Day 70>
<The fourth attempt will begin in 20:13:10:30>
<Floor 3 will open in 23:11:32>

Hm, so if I compare this to that, the whole . . . *door thing* only took three seconds? That whole thing was just . . . three seconds?

I—I'm just . . . Not going to think about it. It isn't important, what happened and all. It isn't. What's important is that I cleared the floor, and that dumb goddess of want gave me a skill, and . . .

—And I failed to fully clear the floor! How? Why?! I even tried to use my eyeballs as bait and no more vultures would come even if I exposed my bowels! So how did I not fully clear the level? I even ate all the flowers! Each and every single lady without a single exception! So how did I *not* 100% clear the floor?! This is an outrage, and I demand a refund!

Fuming, I stomp my feet on the floor, but apparently the paint hasn't fully dried yet, because I soon slip and fall, exposing the WHITE. Sh—shoot, heck, that's not . . . Bad. Bad. Not good. With increasing desperation, I slit both my wrists and spread the paint as far as I can, covering up the mistake. Bad. The bad is gone.

It's gone now . . .

S—so, uh, I think, my best bet right now would probably be to check out that nifty new skill I got, huh? Right? Yeah.

<[Great Values Sniffer(Lv.MAX)]
The Goddess of Want, who watches over those who exhibit desire for what they should not possess, has granted some of Her powers to Her potential apostle.>
<Using their nose as guide, the user can smell what they want and thus drive them in the direction of their desires. The more they want it, the stronger the smell.>
<[SOVEREIGN SKILL]>

So, it's, like . . . Either this is my most useful skill yet, or it's completely worthless. It depends on how I use it.

Well, I might as well give it a try, I suppose.

. . . Uh, do I just . . . smell? Do I need to turn it on somehow? It weirdly doesn't feel like an active skill, so maybe I just . . .

Sniff. Sniff sniff.

Sni—ff.

Okay. One major problem: right now, all I can smell is blood. Like, that's literally all I can smell. Well, there *is* also this gentle flowery smell, but that's probably just because I've eaten so many flowers that the smell is basically stuck in my system forever now.

Or, well, I mean, then again, it *is* sort of coming from my inventory. I don't know how or why I can tell that, but that's just what it feels like. There's a flowery smell coming from it, is all I'm saying.

That's suspicious. I don't like it.

But it's not like opening my inventory could hurt any, so . . .

"Inventory."

My inventory pops up. We've got the usual stuff. Two swords, a shield, a spear, and axe, a rainbow-colored flower, two pieces of dried meat, a bottle of water . . .

Hang on. Flower?

My mind flashes back to a certain suspicious shadow. Don't tell me . . . ?

I remove the flower from my inventory.

She's pretty. Her petals are long and shimmer in the light, almost pearlescent. It isn't so much multicolored as it seems to shimmer and shine in the light, as though it were made of crystals. I wonder what kind of horrible status effect it could inflict on me. Organ failure? Uncontrollable bleeding from every orifice? Necrosis? There's only one way to find out!

With reckless abandon, I pop Lady number 1,777 into my mouth. Silky texture. A slight hint of vanilla, with a touch of stained glass. Crisp stem, soft but fluffy petals, with a gently chewy inner core that tastes sweet of residual nectar, like honey, only so much sweeter. And once the lady is chewed to absolute homogeneity, I swallow.

<CRYSTAL LILY CONSUMED.
ALL WOUNDS WILL BE HEALED.
THROUGH THE BLESSING OF THE GODDESS OF WANT, YOU HAVE RECEIVED:>
<[TOUCH OF REVERSED TOLERANCE (LV.1)]
ANY [TOLERANCE] SKILL CAN BE USED IN THE REVERSE TO CAUSE THE EFFECT THAT
IT PROTECTS FROM, TO THE STRENGTH OF THE SKILL. THE TOLERANCE LEVEL THAT
MAY BE REVERSED DEPENDS ON THE SKILL LEVEL. THE TOUCH MAY ONLY BE USED
ONCE PER TOLERANCE LEVEL.
CURRENT POWER: LEVEL 1.>

It does what now—

**<<<<<<<FFFF4or clearing the the [STAGE.002] completely, you will
receive an additional reward.002>**

That, uh, doesn't look very . . .

**<You have [OUT OF MY GRACIOUS GENEROSITY] received [Clawed Panther
Hide]>**

For some reason, I feel nauseous. But, uh, listen, Mrs. Want, if my guess is right, even though I am of course *very* grateful for this, uh, *gift*, what I don't exactly get is . . . Why? Specifically, if you're going to all this trouble to—and don't take offense to this—*twist the tutorial to make me clear a stage while I'm in a lobby*, why in the world would you then give me a *panther hide* of all things? I mean, don't get me wrong, I love panthers as much as anybody, but why not some item that's, you know . . . useful? Like, for example, a *sword*. I'd love a sword. Right now, I only have dull, ornamental swords. They're barely even sharp at the tip, so why, for all that is good in the world, would you give me *this* of all things?

And when I already have a leopard hide, too?

<THE GOD OF COWARDICE PEEKS OUT FROM BEHIND A COUCH.>
<THE GOD OF COWARDICE GIVES A THUMBS-UP IN SUPPORT.>

I wasn't talking to you! I'm talking to—

Actually, shelve that thought; I can tell she's already gone. Darn it.

Ignoring the whole ordeal with the hide, let's check out that skill, shall we?

I feel pumped already. I mean, it's a real skill! Not just martial arts or battle focus or another damn tolerance skill, this one *actually does something*! Isn't that wonderful!?

I think I should check a certain forum.

<Status—Community—Top>
<Discussion Boards>
<SuperMoleman[F13]: Moleman's Guide to The 13th Floor[18]>
<OrthodoxPox[F3]: Information From
The Delegate Commission.[198]>
<UnderSunder[F8]: why are we here[1]>
<ThroughTheLookingGlass[F9]: Seeking Allies to beat floor 10 Easy Diff
(mage wanted)[0]>
<SharkAttack[F4]: I've heard rumors that floors can B completely cleard.
How??[7]>

Same old, same old.

Moleman . . . !

He and his lies must be quelled! Now that I've beaten the second floor, I will waste no time to disprove his falsities and explain how best to defeat this floor.

Like a wrathful god, I get to typing.

<PrissyKittyPrincess[F3]: a REAL guide 2 floor 2 (BY A REAL GAYMER
NO H8ERS ALLOWD)>
welcome back frends JUS KIDDING welcom back H8TRZ
ok now that all da H8ATRS r gone hers da guide
2 totally clear da stage u need 2 eat all da ladies an kill all da birls 2 kill
all da birds u need bait and ur eyeballs or othr flesh will work gud so just
use dat

an then when u get to da door u just say "no i dont wanna die"
an u win bt make sure u eat ALL DA LADIES or u dont get da comeplete
clear reward which u want even tho it may jus b a ****** pelt or whatevs>

And then, we just post it. Now that SharkAttack guy can even learn how to completely clear the stage, so, you know, there's that. Easy stuff. I really don't see how anyone could be having trouble with this.

That said—

\<You have gotten a response.\>

Oh! I forgot I was keeping a list of all the ladies. Seems someone else may have found use for it after all.

<PrissyKittyPrincess[F3]:
Lady 1669 vomit
Lady 1770 vomit
Lady 1771 vomit
Lady 1772 vomit
Lady 1773 vomit
Lady 1774 vomit
Lady 1775 vomit
Lady 1776 vomit>
<TrackRecord[F6]: RIP miss Kitty>
<JustifiableDefeat[F2] RIP>
<ProtectAndDestroy[F4]: kitty dont have nine lives irl so RIP i guess>
<LearnFromIt[F3]: okay listen . . . This is going to sound super strange but
stick with me.
I'm on Hard and I just beat floor 2 thanks to this guide.
I'm serious. I checked the boards and on Easy
There aren't any flowers (referred to by miss Kitty as "ladies")
But on Hard there are tons of flowers and a lot of them are poisonous.
Some have antidotes and heal you but a lot cause severe hallucinations and
Vomiting and stuff. My buddy [Removed From Tutorial]
Ate a "Lady Number 43" and dropped dead. The effects were exactly
As miss Kitty described them. Also I don't think Miss Kitty is dead because
now her floor updated to F3. She beat the second floor.>
<TrackRecord[F6]: lol no ******* way>
<HowWhatWhy[F7]: yo no wayyyy>
<TrackRecord[F6]: omg lol look she just posted a bat**** guide to the
second floor lmao whattttt>

Well, well, well. They've been chatting up quite a storm here, huh? As they say, while the cat's gone, the rats dance on the table.

But right as I start to write, another few responses tick in.

> <TrackRecord[F6]: omg lol she just posted a bat**** guide to the second floor lmao whatttt>
> <LongBottomJohn[F13]: Lol just read it . . . She's totally crazy . . . >
> <FragmentsOfHope[F9]: Her guide to the first floor is also insane. Why would you even make a guide to floor one. Who is even going to read it.>
> <TrackRecord[F6]: either she's literally schizophrenia or she's faking it for the attention>
> <HowWhatWhy[F7]: i think she just looney>

They're all coming in so fast I barely have time to type. But after gritting my teeth for long enough, I'm finally able to get a word in.

> <TrackRecord[F6]: let's face it tho no one can survive hell i mean look at the state of the lobby>
> <LearnFromIt[F3]: it's possible. Two people
> Have survived it so far.>
> <TrackRecord[F6]: ok but if they survived it then why haven't we heard from them huh this would be huge i mean even Hard is like next to impossible unless you're a literal soldier>
> <PrissyKittyPrincess[F3]: if he 8 a bunch of Lady 2 an then moved lotz he woulda survivd>
> <TrackRecord[F6]: yo kitty . . . . . . not cool>
> <LearnFromIt[F3]: miss Kitty that is
> Honestly very insensitive. Please don't
> Say such things.>

I—I was just trying to be helpful! Geez, talk about being touchy.

> <PrissyKittyPrincess[F3]: tbh im jus sayin it like it is i dont c da prob>
> TrackRecord[F6]: you literally told a guy his friend died cuz he didn't follow your unreadable guide to "da ladies">
> <LearnFromIt[F3]: listen it's okay I was just surprised. I'm still grateful for the guide, since it let
> The rest of us survive. We were even able to
> Compare the flowers in the guide to those
> On the floor to learn which were healing or antidotes, Since they weren't in the guide. That wouldn't have been

Possible without miss Kitty's guide.>
<PrissyKittyPrincess[F3]: o so u guyz get free heal n antidotes dat is so
dumb how u gonna raise ur tolerance an resistance if u jus get healed bet u
eet food n drink watur 2 dumb***>

There. Owned. Now he won't be able to—

<RedHanded[F7]: Hello, I am Delegate of Normal Floor 7. The DC was
alerted regarding possibly offensive language usage and were asked to step
in.
PrissyKittyPrincess[F3], what Difficulty do you herald from? If no answer
is given your position will be determined forcefully.>
<LearnFromIt[F3]: ok who alerted the dc? We can settle with without that
sort of stuff.>
<RedHanded[F7]: LearnFromIt[F3], for questioning the motives of the
DC, I have contacted HerringFerry[F3], Delegate of the Hard Difficulty
Third Floor. He should speak with you shortly. Pray that he will be merciful in his judgment.>
<LearnFromIt[F3]: oh come on,
There's no need for that s>

Okay, this is *really* getting out of hand. Did that guy just get, like, executed? . . .

<TrackRecord[F6]: RIP LearnFromIt[F3]>
<RedHanded[F7]: Are you suggesting that the DC is unjust in its governing
to the point where we would unfairly execute a challenger?>
<TrackRecord[F6]: no sir>
<RedHanded[F7]: Would you like to convince your Delegate of your good
intentions?>

Okay, that's a bit too far.

<PrissyKittyPrincess[F3]: hey cmon man cut it out he didn do nothun
wrong b chill>
<RedHanded[F7]: Don't think you can weasel your way out of
your due punishment simply for being out of our long reach,
PrissyKittyPrincess[F3]. Once the Server Symposium arrives, you too will
receive your due punishment.>
<PrissyKittyPrincess[F3]: nuh-uh>

The server what now? What am I even being threatened with here?

Doesn't matter. He doesn't know anything, and I know everything. I hold all the cards, mwahahaha!

<RedHanded[F7]: We will be swift in our judgment. You will not be able to run. You will not be able to hide. If only for making light of this great organization, you will be made an example of. There is no question of that. Only pray that your end will come quick.>
<PrissyKittyPrincess[F3]: nuh-uh no way ur dumb an i dnt hide from dumb ppl>

I can feel the pure seething hatred emanating from his end, but at the same time, I feel uneasy. For some reason, he seemed assured in being able to get me.

What if he can? What if he does?

Dying in player-vs-player mode is slightly less embarrassing than dying to mobs or the terrain, but it's still easily worse than not dying at all.

Server Symposium . . . If he's so certain about it, then there has to be some information on it, right? Right.

By searching around on the community boards, I'm quickly able to find the following post. I don't know how trustworthy it is considering that it was uploaded by those guys, but, you know. Still.

<OrthodoxPox[F3]: Information From The Delegate Commission.
It has recently come to our attention that some doubt the justification of our presence. This is a ridiculous notion based not in fact, but rather on some superstitious idea that everyone here has the same abilities and resources in clearing the tutorial, has access to the same information, and is able to procure what they need in order to do the above. This is wrong.
The Delegate Commission has only been here for as long as you have, but our goal is as simple as any. We simply want peace and security within the lobbies and community boards. To do this, rules must be decided upon, followed, and enforced. That is simply how society works.
If we have no rules, and if we have no punishments for breaking them, then this society we call the Tutorial will fracture and die. In order for this all to work, for all of us, we must follow the same rules. Delegates, Executives, and all the rest of you alike.
In order to do this, the Delegates who remain in the lobbies must also be able to eat and drink. You, as challengers, will easily be able to gain enough points to feed both yourself and others. This is not a matter of us "taking" your precious resources, but rather that you pay us for our labor as Delegates and Executives.

Furthermore, we are also collecting gear and points to be invested in stand-out challengers who need the resources to climb higher. The allegations that many of these stand-out challengers happen to be part of the DC or affiliated with us is strictly untrue. Furthermore, suggesting that constitutes treason and your Delegate may judge it as such.>

Then the post continued on for waaaay longer about how this was for the best and we all follow the same rules, yadda yadda yadda. It was all a very weird way of saying "follow our rules or else," but if I'm getting this right . . .

These guys are taking food and water from the challengers? And also gear? I mean, sure, it's for the good cause of clearing the tutorial, but do you really need to steal from unwilling challengers to do it? I have a choice in this matter because they can't physically force me to join, but these other guys . . . I don't know. It feels icky. Frankly, if these stand-out challengers can't clear the tutorial with their own merit alone, I don't think they deserve the sponsorship.

But, that all aside, what really interests me is what was written at the bottom.

<. . . There have been rumors circulating regarding a so-called Server Symposium. Many of these rumors are unabashedly false, while others are close to the truth. In order to uncover what this is about, Normal Challenger PetrifiedEggs[F11] used his exclusive, one-off Wish to ask for information regarding this event, after which he graciously gave it to us so that we may spread it further.
The Server Symposium will be held on the last day before the fourth attempt. It will include all challengers from all difficulties on all floors, including the first. We will all meet. The purpose of this meeting is unknown, but it will last a total of 24 hours, during which time we may speak to each other and mingle properly. This will be an important moment, and the DC will for this special occasion demand that, on the Server Symposium, a ceremony will be held to swear in a special surprise guest as our formal ruler and leader. He will lead us from now on, in sickness and in health, through every floor and every lobby, until we can all beat it, together.
This will be a special occasion and marked as a future holiday.
Attendance is mandatory.
Thank you for your attention.>

Okay. That's . . . a lot.

But I get the gist. We're all gonna meet, and while they do, they're also gonna publicly execute me because I called REDHanded a dumb and a dumb. Makes sense.

Frankly speaking, I kind of hate it. Don't get me wrong, the whole being-executed thing also upsets me, but . . . mandatory attendance? Just to come watch these grease-tongued sacks of corporate manure swear in our new almighty leader?

I hate mods. I bet their first order of business will be to put a complete ban on free speech. Oh, alongside executing me.

But aside from that, this is kind of worth the excitement, if only for one specific reason.

That person in the Hell floor 1 lobby that stayed behind. Assuming he's still alive, that is.

<Status—Community—Top>
<Europe Server>
<Easy Lobby: 78/199
Normal Lobby: 19/66
Hard Lobby: 7/13
Hell Lobby: 2/2>

Yeah, he's still alive. Great.

In that case, we have a chance for the Hell Difficulty to not become a veritable bloodbath. This is the kind of game where information is key. Sure, even if I'd known exactly everything there was to know about the first stage, I would still have had a hell to endure. But if I'd known to use an axe to shield my head and chest from the start, and to try to increase my resistances as much as possible, and to make sure to move clockwise around the hill, then maybe it wouldn't have taken an entire month, and maybe I would have come out of it with something better in hand than fetal position blowover.

<THE GOD OF COWARDICE HUFFS AT THE NERVE OF YOUTHS NOWADAYS.>

Yeah, yeah, I get it, so shut up already.

If I can make sure that people in the first-floor lobby can receive this information, then they may have a chance of surviving this place.

Unfortunately, I can't really do that if I'm dead and executed. As it is, frankly, I just don't have enough information to make sure that this doesn't happen. It's a weird thing to say, but I have no idea how weak or strong I am compared to the other people in the tutorial. In the time it took me to get to floor two, they were already doing floor ten and beyond. They could be like human-shaped bearsharks at this point for all I know. As unhappy I am to say it, what I need right now is information.

And, unfortunately, I know just who to talk to. But I certainly won't like it.

<HookedOnBach[F5]: Yeah but it's still your wish. You should be upset. :(>
<SuperMoleman[F21] It's okay, really. If it helps them share the information with more people then it's all for the better. My post wasn't getting much traction anyways.>
<LionMawMadness[F8]: Dude mole you should totally take a breather you've been doing nothing but challenging floors for like the past half a month>
<SuperMoleman[F21]: I'm fine. The DC lost us at floor 18 but I have a feeling that they won't stop there. We need to keep moving. It's that simple.>

I crack my knuckles. Time to intervene.

<PrissyKittyPrincess[F3]: hey moleNERD gimme info im gona b exercise>
<SuperMoleman[F21]: Nice to see you again Night, congrats on beating the second floor! What can I help you with?>
<LionMawMadness[F8]: Moleman PLEASe let me ban this guy he's obviously just a troll>
<HookedOnBach[F5]: Yeah you know Mole for once I have to agree. This guy is kind of mean. :(>
<PrissyKittyPrincess[F3]: mole i need u 2 tell me hw strong u r>

Simple question. Anyone can answer that, assuming they aren't being unnecessarily mean like these two dumbos are. What'd I ever do to them?

<HookedOnBach[F5]: Mole don't. Don't answer that one. :/>
<LionMawMadness[F8]: Ok lol tbh if this guy wants to try and take on Mole at the symposium then sure like why not I really wanna see him get his *** beat>
<HerringFerry[F3]: hey guys whatd I miss?>
<LionMawMadness[F8]: Lmao Ferry this guy's at floor 2 and he wants to try and take on Moleman>
<HerringFerry[F3]: haha yeah thats pretty funny i wanna watch.>

I am writing a list. I am checking it twice. On the Server Symposium, I will complete my hit list. Whether they like it or not.

<SuperMoleman[F21]: It's alright, everyone. I'm sure he has a good reason. Having a goal in this tutorial aside from clearing it is far from a bad thing.>

<SuperMoleman[F21]: That said, I am currently Level 42. My stats are well-balanced, with an obvious focus in Magic Power.>

Level 42 . . . that's, um . . . That's kind of high, isn't it? . . .

<PrissyKittyPrincess[F3]: ur lyin>
<LionMawMadness[F8]: Hahaha and now he's backing out, classic troll coward move>
<PrissyKittyPrincess[F3]: i m NUT a cowurd SGHUT UP>
<HerringFerry[F3]: ooohh tr oll is mad lol.>
<PrissyKittyPrincess[F3]: NUT A TROLL FUKKKK UUUUUUUUUU>
<LionMawMadness[F8]: I've changed my mind this guy can stay he's great lmaooo>
<HookedOnBach[F5]: I just checked Miss Kitty's post history and um guys we need to stop misgendering her. Sorry about assuming you were a man Miss Kitty. :)>
<PrissyKittyPrincess[F3]: M NUT WMN>
<HerringFerry[F3]: shes speaking in code now.>
<LionMawMadness[F8]: Let me decipre. "I am a big stinky woman who loooves to eat flowers and hallucinate all day and im gonna fight mole to the death" lolol>

I can feel my vision begin to tremble.
Oh. Oh. Yeah. Oh. I *need* to kill these people.
They must die by my hand.
But I can't kill them as I am. I'm too weak. Only level 9 won't hurt them. I'll need to level up as much as I can on this floor. That's my only choice. I'll level up to the point where I could wipe the floor with a winged *T. rex* and then some more. Moleman is level forty-two? Hah, I'll be level forty-THREE! He won't stand a single chance against my superior and incredible skill.
I will defeat him. No, even more than that; I will *destroy* him.

<PrissyKittyPrincess[F3]: jus u wait moleman. jus u wait.>
<LionMawMadness[F8]: We're really quaking in our boots now, soooo scared>
<SuperMoleman[F21]: See you at the symposium, Night! If you really want it, I wouldn't mind a duel. I'll see you soon!>

Damn that Moleman. Why's he always got to be so cheery all the time? That aside, now I know the range I'm aiming for.

It's high, but if I hurry like heck, I might be able to beat floors three and four before the symposium. I mean, how hard can it be? I've done a little speedrunning before. Mostly Tamagotchi Death any% but, you know. Potato potato.

Let's see, what's the time . . .

<Top—Status—Community>
<9:49:30 Day 70>
<The fourth attempt will begin in 20:14:10:30>
<Floor 3 will open in 11:32>

Perfect timing. Almost so perfect it scares me . . .
I guess I'll just meditate a little until the pop-up arrives.
And within only a little more than ten minutes . . .

<Top—Status—Community>
<10:01:02 Day 70>
<The fourth attempt will begin in 20:13:59:58>
<Floor 3 has opened. Do you want to enter?>
<Yes/No>

Without so much as a hint of hesitation, I press the Yes button, and the lobby disappears.

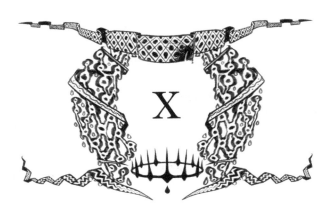

Kill X Goblings

I feel it before I smell it. Soft grass beneath my bloody, bare feet.

I smell it before I taste it. A waft of pollen in the air, fresh flowers, earth.

I taste it before I hear it. The slightest hint of fresh fruit, touching my tongue before fluttering away.

I hear it before I see it. Birdsong, wind rustling the treetops, off in the distance, hooting, and the sound of children laughing.

And now my eyes open.

It's a forest. A luscious, green, fresh, earthy, massive, bright forest. It's more green than I may have ever seen in my life. Maybe on a field trip, or a family trip, or some other sort of trip, I might have seen something similar. But even that wouldn't have been enough green. It might be because I haven't seen proper green in so long, but it's making my eyes water a little. Or it's how bright the sun is. Or some other negligible reason.

I wipe at my eyes, quickly glancing from side to side to make sure nobody can see the pathetic display. Thankfully, I seem to be alone. Good. Sniffle.

And just as my body calms down a little, a message pops up in front of me.

<Tutorial stage, Hell Difficulty Third Floor: The Aching City>
<[Clear Condition] Escape the forest.>

There it is. The forest in question is obviously this one, but it can't be as simple as just darting out of it at full speed, right? If I want to completely clear the stage, I'll probably need to defeat all enemies, as usual.

In a forest, I assume the enemies in question would be the wildlife that exists there. Hm. Do bugs count? I mean, maybe if it's a spider, but . . . On that note, do the trees also count as enemies, since they're technically blocking my way to the exit—wherever that is? I'm starting to feel very confused by the whole situation. Still, considering that this tutorial place was clearly designed by *someone*, it makes sense that the rules might change a bit between the stages. I suppose.

But, first up, there's something I really need to take a look at.

Because I can still hear it.

Children's laughter. Sticks hitting sticks. Talking. Squeals of joy. It's not that far away, either.

Without really thinking, I move toward the sounds.

I love the feeling of grass beneath my feet. I'm leaving a little trail of dried blood, but that's okay. Should I take off the leopard skin? I don't want to scare them. The rustling of the trees and the soft winds are so nice. It feels like summer. Warm. Not cold, not hot, just pleasantly warm. Not so warm my leopard skin feels too hot, no, it's *just right*.

As I draw nearer, I start to think. It's always interested me a little, but all children sound the same. No matter the language they're speaking in, they all have the same accent. It's weird. You can always tell when the voice actor is a real child and when it's a woman pretending to be one. Maybe that's just one of the many wonders of the human ear, but that's how it is. You can just tell.

And that's why it's such a surprise when I finally reach them, and I step out from within a brushage, that what I'm met with isn't children at all.

<Gobling (Lv.1)>
<Gobling (Lv.1)>
<Gobling (Lv.2)>
<Gobling (Lv.1)>
<Gobling (Lv.1)>
<Goblin (Lv.10)>
<Gobling (Lv.1)>
<Gobling (Lv.1)>

There's about seven of them. They're small, and green, and all dressed in the kind of clothes you'd see on peasants in the Middle Ages. Brown and beige wool, little wooden shoes, stuff like that. And now they've noticed me.

A lot of them are carrying sticks. Not clubs—just normal sticks.

One of them is bigger than the rest, though still hardly bigger than a regular child, which may or may not be unlike common goblin archetypes. He has a bald head as one would expect, but he also has a fluffy, dark green mane around his neck and upper back. At the moment, he's currently on all fours on the ground, pretending to be a horse with two of the smaller goblins riding on top of him.

I have no idea what to say or do. I mean, it's goblins. Standard enemy, relatively standard appearance, and I'm ready for a fight. My body is basically itching to fight. I want to. I really want to. I've got a lot of pent-up energy from those damn bullies in the chatroom. And that one big goblin has a pretty high level—even higher than mine—so he'll be great for leveling up, but . . .

They aren't attacking.

Maybe it's some old instinct in me, some pacifistic need for peace, but I don't want to attack first. Until now, I haven't had to attack first. The vultures descended anytime, the ladies were basically courting me first, and the three beasts . . . Is that the test for this level? To be able to take the initiative?

That might be it. It might also be a test of your will. I don't know if you've noticed, but these little creatures happen to look a whole lot like human children. Just that they're green. And bald. And with huge pointy ears. It's almost funny, because I'm next to naked, and they're dressed like typical civilians.

I shake my head. I need to get it together! They're *goblins*! I bet they stole those clothes from *real* human children. Yeah, that's it. Goblins are . . . they're scavengers, and bandits, and looters, and all those kinds of things. Like 99.9 percent of early-game quests are always *kill X goblins*, or *clear out the goblin lair*, or stuff like that. This is no different. I just need to . . .

One of the smaller goblins is approaching me. For some reason, I can't move. I think I'm sweating.

It's so small.

"Kier tu un'lau?"

My hand moves so fast I don't even have time to think, and it strikes plainly across the little goblin's head, making it fly to the side. I look down at my hand. It's trembling. Slowly, I clench it into a fist.

<You have learned: Hit Lv.1>

"*Lifrit!*" the large goblin cries as he flies at me, the two goblins on his back tumbling off. He's pulled a sword out of a hilt on his belt and somewhere deep in my brain I feel calm now, because I'm being attacked, which means there's nothing wrong with what I'm about to do. I summon my little knife. But apparently, I don't move exactly fast enough, because his sword slashes across my vision before I even have time to notice how close he'd gotten.

<You have learned: Slashing Tolerance Lv.1>

A new tolerance! Nice.

He seems to think the fight is already over because his body is visibly relaxing, but I'm way quicker than that, so I stab at his maned neck, already grinning in satisfaction.

But then the world shifts on itself and I fall backward, flat on my back, and he stabs the tip of his sword toward me like King Arthur sticking the sword back in the stone, and I'm so stunned by the fact that a mere goblin feinted me and kicked my legs out from under me that I do nothing as his sword stabs itself deep into my bowels.

<You have learned: Slashing Tolerance Lv.2>

Shoot. Okay. That's not good. I feel light-headed. That's not good.

The goblin suddenly turns away from me, over to the left, where that little goblin is still lying. It's pulled itself together into a tiny ball. I didn't get any message about defeating it so it must still be alive. "Lifrit, kier tu un'lau?" the large goblin asks as he kneels down and takes the little thing into his arms. New piece of information: goblins bruise purple. Interesting.

But he's made a critical mistake. Namely, thinking I'd die just from getting a sword to the bowels. Well, I guess most people would die, but I'm a super-special gamer, so I'm fine. For now, at least. Ah, the world looks spotty. That's a pretty cool effect . . .

Argh, got to stay awake! Okay, okay, yeah, I've been in worse situations, I can manage. I think he only stabbed through my intestines, and there's nothing in them anyway, so it's fine. I've been stabbed before, and there's a very simple way to undo it. You just pull out the stabby object.

Slowly, with trembling arms, I reach for the grip of the sword. But my arms are too short. Damn it, I guess this is why my parents never let me pick up the trombone. But if I can't reach, then I just need to bring myself high enough to do so.

It hurts, it makes my entire body give little electric spasms, but I'm rising up. You know when you were in elementary school and you were still agile enough to crab walk on all fours? Yeah, it's like that, but I'm just trying to stand up. I'm actually able to almost completely stand up until my wound gets stuck on the hilt of the sword. But now I can reach it, so with maybe some amount of undue confidence, I start pulling at it.

Pull pull pull.

. . . It's not coming out of the ground. How deep did he push this thing in?! This guy really *is* some sort of reverse King Arthur! Damn it, I guess I'll just have to try to wiggle myself off the hilt. This is going to hurt.

Stretching my own wound as far as it can go, I even use the blade itself to widen the wound, making it just big enough to put in one of the crossguards, and then I just need to do a little more, and . . .

"Gur fra hik . . . ?"

I look up. The big goblin is looking at me. Our eyes meet.

Oh, uh, um, I was just, ah . . .

He takes a step toward me and with agility I didn't know I had I pull out the final bit of the sword, leaping through the air and forming myself into a ball as I do, hitting the ground in the perfect fetal position.

And from a worm's perspective, I have an interesting view of how the big goblin starts looking around, startled, without even the slightest indication that he might know where I am. For some reason, I had hoped I'd never need to use this ability. But here I am, and being in the fetal position just feels right. I'm hugging my legs to my chest, putting pressure on my wound, stifling the bleeding just a little. I can't really meditate here, but . . .

Uh-oh. A small goblin is walking toward me.

B—but, I mean, logically speaking, it can't smell, hear, see, or taste me, so I should be fine. Yup. Totally fine. The fact that it's walking toward me is just a coincidence. In fact, I can clearly see that its eyes are focused on something completely different. It might just be me, but it feels a little like the small goblins don't understand the situation too much. The big one has pulled his Excalibur from the ground and is currently in a battle-ready position, looking around like he might be attacked at any moment, and the small goblins are sort of just . . . being. Except for this one that's walking toward me. Getting closer. And closer. And . . .

—And it just stumbled over me!

"Ah!" it cries as it stumbles and falls.

Damn it! Invisible or not, I guess I'm still tangible. Flying to my feet, the FPB is undone, and the cry of the little goblin alerted the big one, so now I'm in a bit of a pickle.

I glance back at the goblin that stumbled on me. Or am I? . . .

The big goblin charges at me, sword raised high, but not even he could see this one coming, because I deftly leap back, grab hold of the little goblin, and hold it up toward him. As expected, his sword stops midswing, just a few inches above the small goblin's bald head. Haha, gotcha! Can't attack me now, can you?

"H–hoeksak . . . !" Oohh, now it's growling at me, how sca-ry. What are you going to do next, try to bite me or something? But, no, he quickly turns his head and meets the gazes of all the small goblins. "Trie, friie! Friie, par und!" And as if on cue, after a single moment of glancing at each other, all the small goblins start running away into the woods. Are—are they running to get reinforcements? Hey, not fair! I'm outmanned eight to one and you're still not happy? Cruel beasts!

However, as long as I have this little goblin, he can't attack me. Hehe.

<The God of Combat is appalled.>

Huh? Who the heck asked y—

A tiny foot smashes into my family jewels and I instantly buckle over. You . . . little . . . Flea . . . !

The little goblin that was previously in my arms runs away.

Attacking a man while he's distracted, huh? . . . H—how cowardly . . . !

"*Haaah!*" the big goblin shouts as he raises his sword once more, the blade falling right toward my neck. But if I'm already on the ground . . .

I pull my legs into my arms and his sword suddenly loses direction completely. Because of the momentum, it still slashes into my left arm anyway, slicing right through the skin and flesh and making a huge gash before getting stopped by my bones.

<You have learned: Slashing Tolerance Lv.3>
<You have learned: Slashing Tolerance Lv.4>

D—damn it—!

Leaping back to my feet, his sword slips out of me. Shoot. Shoot. Shoot. I need to kill him fast, before those small goblins can call over five hundred more of their green kind. In pure combat, he's my obvious superior. For one, he has a real sword. But I think there's one thing I have that he doesn't. Namely, an inventory. How can I tell? Let's just say that if he had an inventory, he wouldn't need a hilt.

That's the only way I can defeat him. Through *sheer surprise*.

I grin and ready my hands. The moment he attacks, I'll begin my fight back.

But he isn't attacking, and neither am I. We're both as tense as drawn bows, but neither of us will fire our arrows. Carefully, we begin to rotate, around and around, looking for weaknesses in each other's defenses. Unfortunately, he has one huge advantage. All he's trying to do is buy time, while I'm desperate to kill him. The longer he waits to attack, the more he wins. Damn it.

As much as it hurts, I need to be the one to attack first. But I know exactly how to do it, and exactly what to try.

At a random instance, guided less by an actual opening in his defenses and more by simply making up my mind, I leap at him. As expected, his sword quickly stabs into my abdomen, in through my soft belly and out through my back, skewering me on it. But I can survive that, and he knows it. He's trying to pull his sword back out for another attack, but it isn't hard for me to force it farther in, threading my entire body on it like a piece of shish kebab, and once I get him within reach, I put one hand on his face and the other on his shoulder.

<[Touch of Reversed Slashing Tolerance (Lv.1)]>
<[Touch of Reversed Piercing Tolerance (Lv.1)]>
<[Touch of Reversed Heat Tolerance (Lv.1)]>

<[Touch of Reversed Dehydration Tolerance (Lv.1)]>
<[Touch of Reversed Falling Tolerance (Lv.1)]>

The hand that touched his clothed shoulder didn't do anything, but for every finger that touched his face, I could apply one touch of reverse tolerance. I grin.

He stares at me. He looks mostly confused.

Uh. Huh. Um.

He blinks at me.

Okay, so, it seems to me, that TRT might not be especially stro—

With a mighty push, he throws me clear off his sword, in the process also slashing open my entire side. Ow. Ouch. Ow-ow-ow. Okay. That's . . . Not good. Shoot. Heck.

A bit of my intestines is spilling out. Not good. I'm on the ground again. Also not good. I don't want to die like this. Not against some damn goblin. Shoot. This is really bad. It hurts. Mommy, it hurts. I don't want to be here anymore.

"Friie mit tu, grathtet hoeksak."

Oh, come on, don't speak like you're the hero here; what'd I ever do to you? Nothing! That's exactly what. Nothing at all!

Growling, I reach for his ankle. It's exposed. My fingers can touch him. If five tolerances weren't enough, then . . . How many will do the job? . . .

<[Touch of Reversed Organ Rupture Tolerance (Lv.1)]>
<[Touch of Reversed Coma Tolerance (Lv.1)]>
<[Touch of Reversed Hypothermia Tolerance (Lv.1)]>
<[Touch of Reversed Poison Tolerance (Lv.1)]>
<[Touch of Reversed Choking Tolerance (Lv.1)]>

He stumbles.

"Hef . . . ?!"

Yeah . . . take . . . that . . . !

I grab his other ankle with my other hand.

<[Touch of Reversed Fracture Tolerance (Lv.1)]>
<[Touch of Reversed Necrosis Tolerance (Lv.1)]>
<[Touch of Reversed Hallucination Tolerance (Lv.1)]>
<[Touch of Reversed Blindness Tolerance (Lv.1)]>
<[Touch of Reversed Nausea Tolerance (Lv.1)]>

He stumbles again, falling backward, grunting as he does, before finally dropping to the ground, his body twitching a little. "Hef ut myr—?" He's mumbling something. I don't care. The TRTs can't kill him, but I don't need them to kill him.

I crawl on top of him and put my hands right below his chin, just above where the mane starts. And then, gleefully, I *squeeze*. None of his bones are fractured, he isn't blind, not one part of his body is experiencing necrosis, he isn't puking, and he isn't seeing anything that isn't there. But I can tell that he feels something is wrong within him. And that's all I need. He's stronger than me by far, but this isn't my first time choking.

<You have learned: Choke Lv.1>

Die. Die. Die. Die. Die.
You took everything from me.
Die. Die. Die. Die
Because of you, I have nothing.
Die. Die. Die.
My home, my family, my title.
Die. Die.
Everything.
Die.
His eyes turn dim.

<You have learned: Choke Lv.2>
<Goblin (Lv.10) Defeated.>

No level up, huh? Guess not. Shame.

Normally, when you kill something in a game, it drops what it owns. However, the leopard only dropped a hide and a tiny bit of meat. In other words, to get everything out of this goblin, I can't just hope it drops everything of worth. I'll have to do the looting myself. Now, how about I get right to it?

Let's see here . . . A set of clothes that are too big, a small pouch of colorful rocks that seem to be painted, a letter written in a language I can't read, a crudely carved wooden animal, a small ring, and other worthless trinkets. I grab it all and put it in my inventory. Hm, now that I think about it, in games, goblin ears and fingers and noses and eyes can sometimes be sold, or used for alchemy and similar. I don't know if that's the case here, but it's a waste not to grab what I can, right?

I remove my knife from my inventory and grab what I can.

<You have learned: Butcher Lv.1>
<You have learned: Butcher Lv.2>
<You have learned: Butcher Lv.3>

Two goblin ears, ten goblin fingers, one goblin nose, two goblin eyes, thirty-two goblin teeth, one goblin tongue, ten goblin toes, twenty goblin nails, two goblin lungs, one goblin heart, two goblin kidneys, one goblin spleen, one goblin pancreas, one goblin brain, one goblin skull, one goblin stomach, one goblin appendix, one hundred thirty-eight goblin bones, one goblin liver, about thirty kilos of goblin meat, one goblin hide, and one goblin tumor I found in its neck. Into my inventory it goes! See, if I'd just poked it until it poofed, it would probably only have left like a goblin hide and a piece or two of goblin meat, which would have been a huge waste.

. . . Oh, I forgot completely about the small goblins! Well, it didn't take too long to completely loot the goblin, so they can't have gotten too far. Hopefully.

Standing up, I take a deep breath through my nose.

I was sort of worried that the enchanting smell of the forest would get in the way, but nope, I can smell them just fine. Going by the intensity of the smell, I can even tell sort of where they went. Most went toward the hypothetical east, but a few lost their way. They smell more when together. The scent is a lot like this one sweet I used to eat as a kid that was discontinued before I could fully appreciate it. It's making me drool pretty badly. I wonder what goblin meat tastes like? Sure, I'm trying to level up my starvation resistance so it can reach the protection level, but there has to be some sort of exception, right? Right. Perfect.

Smiling, I set out.

Obviously, my first objective is to get to the biggest group that are moving with the most confidence toward the hypothetical east. I don't know how fast they are going, but considering that the smell of them is getting stronger, I'm just a bit faster. Good.

<You have learned: Sprint Lv.1>
<You have learned: Sprint Lv.2>

Sprint is technically an active skill that uses up your stamina like a fat kid at an all-you-can-eat buffet, but since I have exhaustion resistance, I can keep running anyway. It makes for a surprisingly good sort of synergy, as while I'm sprinting, my resistance is increasing, too.

<You have learned: Exhaustion Resistance Lv.4>
<You have learned: Sprint Lv.3>
<You have learned: Sprint Lv.4>
<You have learned: Exhaustion Resistance Lv.5>

Nice. Nice. Nice. Nice. Veeery good.

Ah, the smell is becoming overwhelming. They're so close. I can practically taste them. If this were a cartoon, this is the point where I'd lift from the ground and start to float toward them. Ahh, I'm so excited. I'm so excited.

<THE GOD OF HUNTING SHAKES HIS HEAD.>

Are you envious? Is that it?

Ahh, it smells so good.

It's so close. I can tell.

Right in there, just inside a little hut made of sticks. I see what they did. They took sticks, and they leaned them against the tree and then wound them with ropes. But the sticks are too heavy for the small goblins to carry, and way too high up, and I don't think they could make such ornate knots. They must have gotten help from bigger goblins. Interesting.

But there's only one entrance to it. Isn't that just silly?

Smiling, I pop inside the small wooden hut.

It's dark in here, but I can see them with perfect clarity. There are four of them. Huddled together. At seeing me, one of them jumps in front of the others, stick raised.

<Gobling (Lv.2)>

Oh no, a level 2! Whatever will I do?

I pull out the sword I stole from the bigger goblin and stab the smaller one through the chest.

<Gobling (Lv.2) Defeated.>

<THE GOD OF COMBAT IS ENRAGED.>
<THE GODDESS OF INNOCENCE LOOKS AWAY.>
<THE GOD OF ADVENTURE WINCES.>

Who the heck are all of these? A bunch of weird—

One of the goblins notices my distraction and runs for the exit.

Ah, nope, not letting you do that!

I slash at its bald head but the sword kind of bounces off, gouging a huge flap of flesh out of her skull without actually piercing through the skull itself. Man, I'm bad with this thing. Not that I'm good with the spear, either. Or the axe. Or the dagger. Or my own two hands. Maybe I'm just not suited for combat at all? It wouldn't be too strange—I *am* a modern human being, after all. I'd like to take my time defeating them, but now the little goblin at my feet has started rolling around and emitting the most ungodly wail, so I don't really have a choice other than to put this animal out of its misery. I step on its neck.

<You have learned: Choke Lv.3>

Hm. I think there might be a more humane way to do this.

With a twist of the heel, I instantly break its neck, quickly and painlessly. See? Easy.

<Gobling (Lv.1) Defeated.>

<THE GOD OF HUNTING COVERS THE EYES OF SOMEONE.>
<THE GODDESS OF CHILDREN IS BLINDED.>

This time, I consciously keep myself from looking at whatever these weird gods and goddesses are trying to do. Instead, I look at the two remaining goblins. It's hard to believe someone would call these things children. Sure, they're small and kind of pathetic looking, but they're obviously monsters. Enemies. I mean, I get experience from defeating them, right? Isn't that proof enough? You don't get experience from defeating non-enemies.

Since these gods are so adamant about all of this, I decide to put down the two last goblins in a more . . . humane way. I discover here and now that my hands are just the right size to perfectly slip around their necks, to the point where I can hold them both at once with no problem. And although I'm far from strong, I can actually lift both of them at once! Man, this feels so cool. Should I do a Three Stooges bit and bonk their heads together? Hahaha, that'd be hilarious! But if I do that, it won't be humane, and the gods might get upset again. Psh. I thought divine beings weren't supposed to care about *mere mortals*? Well, whatever.

I clench my hands as hard as I can, but it's not quite hard enough to instantly break their necks. But almost. I can feel their spines creak a little in my grip as they struggle and flail wildly. Just . . . a . . . little . . . more . . . !

<You have learned: Choke Lv.4>
<You have learned: Clutch Lv.1>

Kra—ack!

And just like that, both of them go limp. One of them is kicking a little, but after a few seconds, it stops.

<Gobling (Lv.1) Defeated.>
<Gobling (Lv.1) Defeated.>

—And no reprimanding words from any of the gods and goddesses! Humane killing: successful.

<THE GOD OF CRUELTY IS AMUSED.>

Oh, come on!

<THE GOD OF CRUELTY SEES YOU.>

Hey, quit that! I didn't do anything wrong! All I did was defeat a few bipedal animals in a super-humane way! If this were the meat industry, I'd be able to slap on a *Cruelty-Free* label no problem!

This is ridiculous. Every time I do something right, these guys go and spin it in the exact opposite way.

<THE GODDESS OF WANT PRAISES YOU.>

I want to be happy, but for some reason, I don't want to thank *her*, specifically. This feels kind of like getting a pat on the back from a bear.

<THE GOD OF COWARDICE TRIES TO MUSTER A COMPLIMENT FOR YOU BUT FAILS.>

Gee, thanks, Coward. That means a lot. You too.

These gods really are an eyesore. I wonder if there's some way I can find the settings to turn off all divine pop-ups? That would be swell.

Anyway, before I do anything else, I quickly poke my head out of the little hut and take a great big sniff. The other three have gathered, but they aren't heading anywhere from what I can tell, so I have time to look at these four first.

I pull out my knife but change my mind.

There's a skill for everything. Maybe there's a skill that lets you grow claws or something? That'd be sweet. My nails are kind of long as is, so I might as well give it a try, right? Right.

I get to it.

XI

Devil's Experiment

<You have learned: Butcher Lv.4>

My first attempt is, uh, not quite a success. But halfway through the skinning-part, after I'd grown desperate enough to use my teeth, I got this skill, so, uh, semi-success, I guess?

<You have learned: Fang Lv.1>

And then, almost exactly when I finished up the first one, I finally got it.

<You have learned: Claw Lv.1>

It isn't much, but it's enough.

Butchering the four tiny bodies with only my bare hands took way longer than when I had the knife, but for some reason, I have a feeling that it wouldn't be good to rely on items too much.

And by the end of the final one . . .

<You have learned: Butcher Lv.5>
<You have learned: Claw Lv.6>
<You have learned: Fang Lv.4>

Good stuff!

With this many goblin hides, I could probably make myself a pair of trousers or something. Unfortunately, I am not gifted in the art of sewing. What's that? I could learn to sew very quickly within this tutorial where effort is rewarded with skills? No way, I didn't have any idea! Anyway, I throw all the organs and meat and hides and child-sized clothes into my inventory and get going.

. . . Whoa.

The sky . . . it's turning orange-red! The sun is going *down*!

Th—the passage of time! It's happening! I can't believe this, I'm just, oh my God, the sun, it's, and the sky is so colorful and *pretty*, and, oh, my word, it's . . . Damn it, I'm crying again. Glad there aren't any goblins around to notice. Sniffle.

Let's see, what time does this put us at . . .

<Top—Status—Community>
<18:45:01 Day 70>
<The fourth attempt will begin in 20:05:14:59>

It looks about right. I wonder if the time shown on the floor was altered to match the time that I dropped in, or if it would have been dark had I appeared later, or if the fact that the times match is just a coincidence. Guess I'll learn that if I get to a similar stage in the future, but it doesn't feel like a coincidence.

Either way, I should try to catch the goblins before nighttime or things might get complicated.

Sprint, activa—

The second I activate sprint, my right leg snaps in two and I fall to the ground.

<You have learned: Fracture Tolerance Lv.8>

Okay, that's not good. Ow. Not good.

Hm.

Crawling back inside the hut, I start meditating.

Okay, so, maybe, just maybe . . . constantly using sprint doesn't just affect my stamina-slash-exhaustion, but also my legs. Like, physically.

But doesn't that still mean that it's a great moment to train, or something? Sure, breaking my own legs puts me out of commission for a little while, but it's a great way to get higher levels in fracture tolerance, and maybe even to reach fracture resistance! Great, glad we've got that deci—

<A Canto appears to you.>

Oh, whoopie, this again. Sure, show me what the deal is this time.

<[Lasciate ogne speranza, voi ch'intrate'!]>

Okay. Wonderful. Anyway.

After maybe half an hour or so, my leg finally heals fully, alongside the sword wounds I still had left.

<You have learned: Auto-Regeneration Lv.5>

Nice, good to have.

Well, off I go to catch a few goblins!

Stepping out of the hut, I activate sprint again, and the second I take off, I feel a few of my toes break.

<You have learned: Fracture Tolerance Lv.9>

I keep running. As my sprint skill increases, the damage it does to my body increases as well.

<You have learned: Sprint Lv.5>
<You have learned: Exhaustion Resistance Lv.6>
<You have learned: Starvation Resistance Lv.7>
<You have learned: Sprint Lv.6>
<You have learned: Fracture Tolerance Lv.10>
<You have learned: Fracture Resistance Lv.1>

My body is physically becoming so weak that enough energy is being siphoned from my muscles to increase other resistances as well. I never considered it before, but should I take up jogging?

And right as I have that horrifying thought, my brain suddenly goes completely black and I fall over, my last conscious thought being the echoing sound my skull made hitting the ground.

. . .

. . . I'm awake! I'm awake.

Okay, reminder to self, maybe jogging for too long might not be for the best. But now that I'm awake, I can tell that a few other resistances increased too, so, you know . . . Hooray?

<You have learned: Coma Resistance Lv.4>
<You have learned: Unconsciousness Tolerance Lv.8>
<You have learned: Unconsciousness Tolerance Lv.9>
<You have learned: Unconsciousness Tolerance Lv.10>
<You have learned: Unconsciousness Resistance Lv.1>

<You have learned: Blindness Resistance Lv.3>
<You have learned: Hypnagogia Lv.8>

Lots of fun stuff.

Anyhow, it seems like my feet have healed. However, more worryingly, it is completely dark. Bummer. And I don't mean that it's, like, kind of dark, or that it's hard to see, or something weak like that. No, it is literally pitch black. But, somehow, I can still see. And I'm not entirely sure how. Well, I can guess, but does being resistant to blindness really let you see better in the dark? It's weird.

Hopefully, the remaining goblins weren't able to escape during the time I spent unconscious/in a minor coma.

Sniff sniff sniff.

. . . Smoke?

I can still smell the goblins, but I can also smell smoke. That's . . . odd.

I can't see anything down on the ground, so after a few seconds of deliberation, I hook my sharp fingernails into a nearby tree trunk and begin climbing.

<You have learned: Climb Lv.1>
<You have learned: Claw Lv.7>

Up, up, up, up I go until I can peek my head out above the treetops.

. . . Whoa. Normally, I'd probably feel obliged to mention the fact that there are a number of what I think are moons in the sky, but they are easily overshadowed by the sheer number of stars up there. It looks, to me, like wherever this fantasy planet is supposed to be, it is currently in a galaxy crashing together with another one. I don't know how else to describe it. The darkness below the treetops was misleading because this is beyond bright. I don't think I've ever seen this many stars before, which isn't strange when you live in a place like Malmö, but seriously. This is more than should be possible.

Awestruck, staring at the stars, I completely forget about the fact that I could smell smoke. Hm. Smoke. Stars are fire, but where's the smoke? Isn't that weird? Don't you say no smoke without fire? How strange.

. . . Oh, yeah, smoke!

Smoke, smoke, smoke . . . Ah, there! A pace or so away, right next to a shiny, moonstruck lake, I can see a plume of smoke, slowly rising into the sky. And if I take a deeper whiff, I can tell that all three of my targets are right there. How convenient!

Hmm . . . It's not like I'll lose track of them if I go down on the forest floor, but with the stars this pretty, wouldn't it be a waste? Might as well train my new climb skill while I'm up here.

Happy with my decision, I begin leaping from treetop to treetop, heading toward the smoke with excitement.

<You have learned: Climb Lv.2>
<You have learned: Climb Lv.3>

And within only a few minutes, I get there. But I don't attack straightaway. No, before I even get close, I have an idea. A very clever, very useful idea that makes use of something I had assumed to be useless.

Silently, I stick my leopard-hide back into my inventory, and before anyone can see me in my true form, I summon the Clawed Panther Hide. As expected, it's black. In other words, unlike my naturally ashen skin color or the leopard's bright yellow one, this one is camouflaged for the night environment. See, I want to try something. As quietly as possible, I put on the hide, doing my best to cover up as much of my pale skin as I can. Funnily enough, the hind and front paws both have weirdly large claws, way more than a normal big cat should. After staring at it for only a few moments, I realize the facts of the matter.

The claws are weapons. The front paws are made in such a way that they can be worn as gloves. For some reason, I both adore and hate it. Sure, I've become a clawed stalker of the night, but at what cost?

Grumbling, I use the paws as gloves.

Making sure not to make a single sound, I creep nearer, slowly moving from tree to tree. And, as hoped . . .

<You have learned: Stalk Lv.1>
<You have learned: Stealth Lv.1>

Awesomesauce. If my theory is correct, as long as they don't notice me, I can rack up the skills as much as I please, hehehe.

Huh? What need do I have for a stealth skill if I have fetal position blowover? Can you even hear yourself? *Obviously*, almost *because* of the FPB skill, I need this sort of stuff. These mobs clearly can't tell the difference, but at the symposium—once I'm in PvP—I can't let them understand that I have FPB, or what it does. If they understand that I can go invisible by going into the fetal position, they will have a much easier time countering against it. I need them to think that my stealth skills are just really high overall, and not that I have a single broken skill. Easy as that.

And that's why I need these goblins not to notice me even though I can see them perfectly.

They've set up a little campfire by the side of the lake and are currently grilling a small fish over it. How quaint! I'm sitting up in a nearby tree, consciously not in the fetal position, watching them. That's all. It's a pretty nice scene, you know. Just us four chums, all watching the fire crackle and pop.

"Kier Rufe un'lau?" one of the little goblins asks, sitting on a big, smooth rock. The others don't respond. It pulls its feet to its chest. Now that I look closer, it's got a dark bruise on the left side of its face. I wonder where it got that from? "Ish kier fra'u . . ."

One of the other little goblins puts its hand on the goblin's shoulder. Uh-huh. Right.

And then none of them talk again.

<You have learned: Stealth Lv.3>
<You have learned: Stalk Lv.4>

I'm learning skills effectively, but . . . God, I am *so* bored. Beyond bored. I can't even use any skill to increase my focus because I've always got battle focus and field focus active, so it changes nothing. The goblins aren't even doing anything of interest. Every couple of minutes one of them will say some weird line in a weird language with a childish accent and then the two others don't respond. It's damn awkward, that's what it is.

. . . Okay, yeah, I can't stand this anymore. This has to end.

I tense my body.

One of the three goblins quickly turns to my direction, but it's too late.

Leaping through the air, I grab two of the goblins by the throat. The last one, the bruised one, doesn't move. I kind of expected it to start running, but it doesn't. It's just staring at me, and now I'm staring at it, because I can't find anything else to do.

"H—hoeksak . . . !" it says. Okay. I still don't know what that means. You're aware of that, right?

Oh, shoot, the goblins in my hands have started struggling again. Should I just kill them?

Actually, no, I have a better idea. I pull my hands slightly tighter, though not enough to activate Clutch.

<You have learned: Choke Lv.5>

It takes almost half a minute, but the two of them eventually stop struggling. And for that entire duration, the little one in front of me didn't move an inch. It just sat on its rock, obediently staring at me. I hold the two tiny necks for a few more seconds before releasing them, making their unconscious bodies thump to the shore lifelessly.

I approach the final one and squat down in front of it, so that we're at the same eye level. I stare at it. It stares at me.

Oh, I only now noticed it's trembling. Does trembling count as moving? It does, right? At least, that's what I—

Ew, gross, it just pissed itself! Man, that's disgusting! The heck did it do that for?!

Grabbing it by its smooth, bald head, I lift it off the rock before bashing its head back onto it, once, twice, thrice, too many times, until the skull cracks open and spills pink brainy goo everywhere. Damn. That was disgusting. Are all goblins incontinent or something? Is that a physical trait of goblins? I should make notes.

Normally, I'd want to loot it right away, but I mean . . . seriously? No way. That's gross. I guess I can't win every time. I don't even want to touch its soiled clothes. Ew.

Back to the two goblins I've captured. They're still blacked out, and they will hopefully remain that way for at least a couple of minutes. I don't know how long this sort of stuff takes, but a few minutes is all I need. Well, that and a rope.

Rope . . . Sure, I could buy a rope in the shop, but I'm kind of saving up to buy some real clothes. Also, I don't think I can access the shop while I'm on a floor. There has to be a better option, right? I check my inventory.

Let's see here, goblin eyes, goblin tongue, goblin bones, goblin hide, sword, goblin spleen, dried meat, goblin ears, goblin meat, goblin intestine (small), goblin intestine (large), goblin fingers, goblin toes, goblin—

Hey, wait a minute. Goblin intestine? Well, well, well!

Unlike what you'd think, intestine is surprisingly strong and rubbery, so it will work perfectly! Great, I'm so glad everything worked out. Pulling out two lengths of goblin intestine (small), I tie the two goblins to a tree each, using one intestine for each. Perfect. My only hope is that they won't try to gnaw through the intestine, which is possible, but I mean . . . So far, they don't seem like the kind of creatures to do that. Then again, what I'm about to do might awaken some sort of deep bestial instinct within them, but if that happens, I'll just kill them, so it's fine.

While I wait for them to wake up, I pull out a piece of goblin meat from my inventory. Sniff sniff sniff. It's like my nose is seeing double. I can smell the meat as both meaty bloody juicy yummy meat and also as that old nostalgic sweet. It's very weird. I'm not sure if the smell will transfer into taste, but anyway.

I move toward the still-crackling fire, but then I stop.

Cooked meat is safe to eat. It doesn't have any living parasites or bacteria in it. In other words, it doesn't give any tolerances. Damn it. Then again, I did always like my meat rare, so it shouldn't be too bad. I think . . .

Hunching down beside the fire, I begin chewing into the meat. Yummy. Yummy. Yummy. Yummy. Not bad. It doesn't taste sweet, but smell and taste are really interconnected, so it still has a semisweet taste. Not overpowering. Yummy. Yummy. Yummy. Ah. I guess I didn't realize how hungry I was. This is *really* hitting the spot. Yummy.

"I—Ifrit!"

Someone shouts but I don't really hear it because, man, this meat is *really* yummy. I'm not sure what I expected out of raw meat, but this is way beyond it.

<You have learned: Bacteria Tolerance Lv.5>
<You have learned: Parasite Tolerance Lv.3>

Here it comes. I can already tell that I'm going to have a heck of a stomachache in a few hours, but it's fine. This meat is worth it.

<You have learned: Ulcer Tolerance Lv.1>
<You have learned: Nausea Tolerance Lv.8>
<You have learned: Indigestion Tolerance Lv.6>

The only bummer is that, like all good things, it eventually comes to an end. Man. Keeping in the tears takes everything I have. Can't let the goblins catch me on the weak side. Mournfully, I lick my fingers. Then, I finally turn to my two live ones. One of them is silently weeping, and the other is staring unblinkingly at the third one that pissed itself. It's almost a little funny, I mean, they're just mob enemies. Is this another test of one's resolve? If that's the case, then it's really not needed.

Standing up from my hunched position, I walk over to them. Let's see here, which should be which, hmmm . . . Eeny, meeny, miny . . . moe!

My finger falls on the one on the right. It's staring at me, unflinching. Is that determination I see? Not that it really matters. Once I'm close enough to touch it, I put my finger to its forehead and carve *TRT 2* into its flesh. It's trembling, but it refuses to make a sound, which is nice for me because so far these things have only made annoying sounds. I turn back to the first one and quickly carve *TRT 1* into its forehead. Perfect! Now I can keep track of which is which. I don't have Touch of Reverse Tolerance level 2 yet though, so I'll have to start with number one.

I step closer to it. It flinches with every move I make, like a glitching NPC. I put my hand to its face and slowly drum each of my fingers onto it, one at a turn.

<[Touch of Reversed Bacteria Tolerance (Lv.1)]>
<[Touch of Reversed Virus Tolerance (Lv.1)]>

\<[Touch of Reversed Ulcer Tolerance (Lv.1)]\>
\<[Touch of Reversed Indigestion Tolerance (Lv.1)]\>
\<[Touch of Reversed Parasite Tolerance (Lv.1)]\>

Still no level-up, huh? I really hope I don't have to use every single tolerance skill I have to make this work. It'd be even worse if it turned out that I only got experience for it if I killed an enemy while it was under the effects of the skill. That'd be a real bother.

Normally, I would hate to use anything that's one-use in vain outside of dire combat, but this is an exception. It's one-use, but if I use it enough, it should hypothetically level up and let me use it more times. I think. If that isn't the case and I'm doing all of this for nothing, then there's nothing I can say but *shoot.*

Anyhow, back to guinea pig one!

I put my hand back to his face.

. . . Hm? No effect? But I'm sure that I have tolerances left . . .

. . . Don't tell me—?

I put my other hand to his face.

\<[Touch of Reversed Fever Tolerance (Lv.1)]\>
\<[Touch of Reversed Internal Damage Tolerance (Lv.1)]\>
\<[Touch of Reversed Unconsciousness Tolerance (Lv.1)]\>
\<You have learned: Touch of Reversed Tolerance Lv.2\>

Nice, finally! I was starting to run out of tolerances there . . .

Now, let's quickly check on the guinea pig's state. It's mostly just confused, but that can probably be explained more by the fact that I'm tapping my fingers against its face for no real reason. In synopsis, for TRT1, you'll need to use at least like fifteen or twenty times to cause any sort of actual damage. All and all, for now, this is less of an actual skill and more of a distraction. But that's only the case with TRT1. What I want to know is how much stronger TRT2 is. Probably not much, but it should be enough, right?

I think I can remember what tolerances I used on guinea pig one, so if I just replicate it on guinea pig two, I'll be able to compare the effects. Hm, I kind of wish I could measure somehow what the exact differences are, but I don't have that kind of equipme—

. . . Oh my God. Am I becoming a nerd!?

Moleman, you insidious bastard . . . ! I'll have my vengeance, you subterranean mammal!

If I were one step worse off, I might try to win by outnerding him, but I don't think I'm that far gone yet. I think . . .

Shrugging, I put my fingers to guinea pig two's face and start tapping. Apparently, I need to use one finger at a time, from one hand at a time, in a certain order. Thumb, index, middle, ring, little, and then the next hand, in the same order. That's a pain. Hopefully, within time, it'll become sort of like an automatic reflex, and I won't have to think about it too much. But, for now, I need to keep it in my head, very much consciously.

<[Touch of Reversed Bacteria Tolerance (Lv.2)]>
<[Touch of Reversed Virus Tolerance (Lv.2)]>
<[Touch of Reversed Ulcer Tolerance (Lv.2) is currently unusable.]>
<[Touch of Reversed Indigestion Tolerance (Lv.2)]>
<[Touch of Reversed Parasite Tolerance (Lv.2)]>

Huh? What's that? What do you mean it's—

Oh, I haven't gotten ulcer tolerance up to level two. Bummer. Eating meat seemed to do the trick, though, so I quickly summon a piece of goblin meat and eat about half of it.

<You have learned: Ulcer Tolerance Lv.2>
<You have learned: Parasite Tolerance Lv.4>
<You have learned: Indigestion Tolerance Lv.7>

There we go!

<[Touch of Reversed Ulcer Tolerance (Lv.2)]>
<[Touch of Reversed Fever Tolerance (Lv.2)]>
<[Touch of Reversed Internal Damage Tolerance (Lv.2)]>
<[Touch of Reversed Unconsciousness Tolerance (Lv.2)]>

With this, my experiment is concluded. Good work, guinea pigs, your reward is to be put out of your misery!

Before they really have time to do much of anything, I crush both of their necks.

<Gobling (Lv.1) Defeated.>
<Gobling (Lv.1) Defeated.>
<[Level Up]>
<You have reached Level 10.>
<Agility has increased by 2.
Strength has increased by 3.
Stamina has increased by 3.

Magic Power has increased by 1.
Enhanced Hearing has increased by 1.
Battle Focus has increased by 1.
Field Focus has increased by 1.
Claw has increased by 1.
Fang has increased by 1.
Sprint has increased by 1.>

Level up; nice! That just proves they're enemies, right? I mean, I leveled up from them, so there's no other way to look at it.

And, again, just to prove how virtuous I am in my acting, not a single high-and-mighty god or goddess comments on it. Is there anything that I can do wrong anymore? Probably not. Anyway, let's start looting these—

Hang on a sec. I can hear something.

<You have learned: Enhanced Hearing Lv.3>

Yeah, I am absolutely hearing voices. From this far away, it almost sounds a bit like humans, but I can tell that it's goblins by the weird language. Don't tell me that one of the goblins somehow escaped? No way. I am absolutely certain that I killed all of them. Maybe this is a scripted event that happens no matter what? Yeah, that's possible. I still don't really like it, though.

I glance at the bodies of the two guinea pigs. I really want to loot them, but I don't think I have time.

Smoke reaches my nose and I glance back at the still-burning fire. Whether they're looking for me or the smaller goblins is unimportant, because whichever it is, they'll be heading toward this trail of smoke. It's too late to douse it. Shoot. I don't think I'm screwed quite yet, but unless I handle this with some amount of grace, there won't be anything left for me to do. First things first, am I able to bring the two, erm, *untainted* bodies with me?

I try to put them in my inventory. Nothing happens. Alright, that's a bust, then. I can't really tell how close the goblins are to getting here, so I don't think I should make any risky gambles like trying to take just their heads.

On the other hand, those heads are looking mighty ingredient-full . . .

Okay, fine, but let's be quick about it. Since I need to be fast, I'll have to save my bare hands for later. Summoning my knife, I get to it. Saw saw saw saw saw saw saw.

I think I might be getting really bad, because the exposed flesh on display here is making my mouth water. Am I bad enough to eat an entire head raw? Well, that's . . . It all depends on what head, you know? There are people out there who eat pig head. It's not *that* weird. Personally speaking, I probably wouldn't eat a human head, but this is . . . this is different, right? Yeah. Right.

I stick it in my inventory.

Above the treetops, I can hear shouts, closer now. I can't tell how close, but close enough to make something deep within me say, *Maybe it's time to go now.* But, on the other hand, there's still a whole head left here! Sitting right there, perfectly usable. Am I just supposed to leave it behind?

No. A true completionist strives for 100% and nothing less. Every chest and every cupboard must be looted. Otherwise, you might miss an important item or clue. Nodding to myself, I put the knife to the goblin's pallid throat and start sawing again. Saw saw saw saw saw saw saw saw saw.

The voices are getting closer.

Saw saw saw saw saw.

I can hear what they're shouting now, as loud as they possibly can.

"Ifrit!"

"Rufe!"

"Joru!"

"Ki'ur!"

"Valer!"

"Sui!"

"Arfis!"

"Bunthe!"

I think, if I'm not being delusional, that it might be names. Maybe. Anyway . . .

Saw saw saw saw saw saw saw saw saw saw saw saw saw saw saw . . . *Pop!*

There we go; perfect! Now, time to dip before someone—

"Joru?"

Ah. Oops.

Scooby-Doo Shenanigans

<Goblin (Lv.7)>

There's a goblin standing right there, by the entrance to the woods. He's holding a torch and nothing else, and I'm pretty sure it's a guy because of the mane and the build. To preface, I didn't exactly have time to put the goblin's head into my inventory before this guy popped up, so I'm still holding it in both hands like a football.

Uhhh . . . It's not what it looks like—?

The head disappears from my hands and into my inventory.

The goblin stumbles back a step. "A . . . *AAAAAAAHHHHHHHH—!!*"

Hey, hey, hey, no need to scream like a damn raid siren! What's that for?!

Moving like greased lightning, I fly up to him, shoving the butt of my knife into his maned throat.

"Gck—?!"

Grabbing him by the neck with both hands, I jump onto the side of a nearby tree and use my teeth-climb no jutsu to make my way up. The whole thing probably took less than ten seconds.

<You have learned: Fang Lv.6>

And once I'm up, I quickly sink my sharp teeth into his neck. Yummy warm blood flows into my mouth as he begins to kick. I consider using touch of reverse tolerance on him, but I don't think it's needed. Once my teeth have made a big

enough hole in his neck, I use my claws to rip up his airways and whatever arteries can be found in there. Badda-bing badda-boom, goblin no more.

<Goblin (Lv.7) Defeated.>

My position has already been more than given away, so without even trying
to loot the body, I drop it down to the ground again.

Hm. I'm not sure what to do. I don't know how many goblins there are, but
I'll need to defeat them all to completely clear the level. At the moment, I can't be
sure of anything. If I hide, they'll probably go away eventually, but I don't think
I'll get another opportunity to defeat them.

However, if all of them are at level 7 or so, I won't be able to take them all
on. Not at once, at least. I'll need to make them spread out and pick them off,
one by one. The issue is that I'm not omnipotent. How will I know where all of
them are at all time—

Sniff sniff.

Sni—ff.

Yeah. I can smell them.

Let's see . . . Sniff sniff sniff . . .

Twenty, no . . . Twenty-seven? Yeah, twenty-seven goblins. They don't smell
very sweet, but they smell like goblin meat. And I like goblin meat. Since there's
so many of them it's harder to tell where any one individual is, but I'm lucky,
because they seem to have split up into five smaller groups. Always the first mistake. And, in many cases, much like this one, the last.

The closest group is heading here at a relatively fast pace, probably in response
to the scream. Two of the other groups are also heading this way. Speedwise, it
would be fastest to take out the groups closest to me, but that gives the groups
farther away more time to run. If I shoot for those farther away, it will also con-
fuse the ones closer to me, so that's the best choice.

Let's see, the group farthest away . . . Sniff sniff . . . Seems like they're at that
wooden hut I defeated those four goblins at earlier. In that case, I know the way.

Confident in my own abilities, I set out, leaping from tree to tree like some
unholy cross between a cheetah and a chipmunk. Jump jump jump jump.

<You have learned: Claw Lv.9>
<You have learned: Climb Lv.4>

And within only a few minutes, I arrive.

<Goblin (Lv.6)>
<Goblin (Lv.9)>

<Goblin (Lv.5)>
<Goblin (Lv.12)>
<Goblin (Lv.6)>
<Goblin (Lv.7)>

And there they are. There are six of them, and all of them are big. This would suggest that the small goblins are spawnlings or whatever, while these big ones are the normal ones. That would also explain the name difference now that I think about it. In the end though, a small goblin is just a yet-to-be big goblin.

Four of them have kind of low levels, but two of them are almost as high as my own or higher. The most important thing for me is to remove their advantage in numbers, so my number one objective is to kill the weaker ones. I need to hunt them like a stalking lioness, except that I'm a guy. The moment one of the weaker ones leaves the pack, I strike.

<You have learned: Stealth Lv.4>
<You have learned: Stalk Lv.5>

Silently, I creep closer to the level five. I think it's a woman. The lack of head hair makes the otherwise feminine clothing look out of place. Somehow, she also looks a fair bit younger than the others, and shorter, too. If I compare their height to my own, the men seem to be about slightly taller on average than the women, though both are still only about as tall as older children. Not counting one guy, who's almost as tall as a tween. At least, that's what I think. Somehow, it feels thrilling to for once in my life be the tallest in the room. Forest. Whatever.

It makes me wanna squish 'em.

Oh, chance!

The level five just stepped behind the hut to check it out, and in swoops the great I, grabbing her by the throat and dragging her up into a nearby tree. And then . . . Chomp.

<You have learned: Bite Lv.5>

Our eyes meet. She seems more confused than afraid. She doesn't even have time to struggle before her eyes go dim.

<Goblin (Lv.5) Defeated.>

Still keeping my attention on the goblins down below, I climb higher into the tree and hang her body way up where it can't be seen. In games and movies, goblins are shown to be nocturnal, or at least have night vision, but these are using torches and lanterns to move about. Maybe they stole so much from humans that they developed hubris and now use human technology even for things that don't need it? Not sure.

Anyway, after a minute or so, the other people in the group notice that she's gone and start shouting a new word. I think it might be her name, but since she's a goblin, it might just be a title, or what she works with. Unsure. Whatever the situation is, the fact that they're looking for someone new means that they are now even more divided than before. From what I could see, the level twelve was the one that coordinated this split. But since the number left is odd, one goblin had to be left on its own. And like the good leader he apparently is, the level twelve decided that he should go on his lonesome. How inspiring.

I leave him to himself and go after the group with the level six and the level seven.

As I have come to learn, a good sneak attack is worth more than any ally. Dropping down from above and biting and tearing up the level six's throat quicker than she can even try to scream is so effective it's almost scary. In seven seconds flat, she's dead.

<You have learned: Fang Lv.7>
<You have learned: Bite Lv.6>
<Goblin (Lv.6) Defeated.>

And the one goblin left is so startled by my appearance that he doesn't even have time to react before I descend upon him like a fury of the night, clawing and ripping and tearing. Maybe it's weird to say, but ripping things to shreds is oddly stress-relieving. All I need to do is imagine that this guy is LionMawMadness or some other bully and my hands just move on their own to tear open his chest and crack his ribs in two and tear out his organs. Very relaxing.

<You have learned: Rip Lv.10>
<You have learned: Tear Lv.10>
<The skills [Rip (Lv.10)] and [Tear (Lv.10)] have combined into the skill [Eviscerate (Lv.1)]>
<Goblin (Lv.7) Defeated.>

That's a new screen. Eviscerate, is it? Hm. I like it! I'll make sure to try it out the next chance I get. Since the other two small groups aren't nearby, I don't bother trying to hide the two bodies; rather, I head straight for the next one.

<Goblin (Lv.6)>
<Goblin (Lv.9)>

A level six and a level nine. Nine is only two above seven. It should be fine, I think.

Once I have the upper ground, I leap for the level six, crashing down on top of her.

[Eviscerate].

Ohh, that's effective! My hands are going through the goblin's guts like a hot knife through butter. Honestly, the feeling is almost mesmerizing. Squishsquishsquishsquishsquishsquish . . .

<Goblin (Lv.6) Defeated.>

Mmm. Gloopy—

A hot piece of fire is shoved into my face, but mostly into my eye. Ouch! What was that for? Rolling back, I grip at the wound. I can hear my flesh sizzling.

<You have learned:
Burn Tolerance Lv.1>

I think I might have gotten shards of coal stuck in my eye. Not cool, level nine. Not. Cool.

"F—friie, hoeksak!" the goblin stammers, waving the torch from side to side. Shouldn't he have a real weapon or something? All he seems to have is that torch. Not even a knife or something. In that case, there's no real need for me to feel any real danger from him.

I rush him. In desperation, he waves the torch more, jabbing it at me to try to cause me to feel some sort of fear, but I don't really care that much, so once I'm in range, I grab the torch by biting into it of my free will. My teeth crack like popcorn and my tongue sizzles as my saliva instantly evaporates, but I'm too focused on jabbing my fingers into his throat to really care. The way I act apparently startles him so much that he doesn't even try to fight it as I check if the eviscerate skill can be used on a neck. It can!

<You have learned: Burn Tolerance Lv.2>
<You have learned: Burn Tolerance Lv.3>
<You have learned: Eviscerate Lv.2>
<Goblin (Lv.9) Defeated.>

Hm. Unlike that first big goblin, these ones aren't exactly fighters. I wonder what that's all about. Eh, it doesn't matter too much. All it does is make my quest easier, so I have no complaints.

I head for the final member of this group.

<Goblin (Lv.12)>

I don't like this guy. I don't know how or why, but unlike all the other goblins, he's somewhat close to my own height. To make things worse, whereas I'm slim and sticklike, this guy has a robust, steady figure. Worse yet, he's carrying a sword with him. I wonder what poor human warrior he looted it from.

But right as I start to consider when the best time to strike might be, he suddenly moves out into a brightly lit meadow. Carefully, he puts the torch into the soft ground, jimmying it down far enough in the dirt to ensure it doesn't topple over. Then he straightens back out, and like a man going to war, he unsheathes his sword. He turns to me and beckons toward himself. Inviting me.

He shouldn't be able to see me. I am very well-camouflaged, so there's no way for him to—well, there is, but I don't want to think I might have gotten outwitted by some stupid goblin of all things.

However, that doesn't change the fact that he has sighted me, and instead of trying to draw me into an ambush or whatever, he's inviting me to a duel.

. . . Suspicious. He must have laid a trap here somewhere. If I were to just walk into this obvious trap, I'd never be able to live down the embarrassment. No, there's a better way to handle this.

After I don't emerge for several minutes, he takes a slightly more relaxed pose. He knows I'll have to get him sometime. He's in no hurry. He'll still be here when I return.

Hmm. We're kind of close to where I defeated that level 5, and I still have some goblin rope, so . . . yeah. It's possible.

After a few minutes of preparation and painstakingly dragging a body through the treetops, I return to the glade. Yup, he's still there. Waiting patiently. But not for much longer.

A few meters into the forest, fully visible from his meadow, I drop her down. The goblin-gut noose around her neck tightens and her descent stops just a few inches about the forest floor. In the light of the stars, it would be obvious that she was no more, but in this dark forest? Not quite so much.

Looking back to the meadow, I have a perfect line of sight to how the level twelve's eyes widen, and all pretense of calm evaporates. "P—Patrieff!" he exclaims as he dutifully leaves the protecting light of the meadow and enters the dark, dark forest. He doesn't even reach her body before he realizes the jig is up, and yet, maybe guided by some desperate, feeble mob hope, he continues all the way until she's in his arms. The time is right.

I let go of the goblin-gut rope, making her body slump into his stiff arms, and at that exact same time, I drop down, right atop his head and shoulders, my fingers clawing at his throat.

But as shocking as my scheme was, it wasn't quite enough, and after less than a second of my attack, he shrugs me off, leaving me to clatter down to the ground. However, he made a fatal mistake. Right now, we're in my territory. The darkness is mine. Here, his sword will hurt him more than it will hurt me.

My surprise attack was able to inflict a few deeper wounds to his face and neck, but it isn't enough. Without a single second of hesitation, he throws himself toward me, sword raised. I had hoped he would drop it to catch her, but as demonstrated you can hold both a sword and a maiden, I guess.

Crouching down, I dart for his legs. His sword easily lodges itself into my lower back, but that's okay. Leaping up from below him, I aim for his bowels but change target at the final second to attack his neck and face instead, but he foresaw my feint and has already raised both arms in protection. But it's not like his arms don't contain any arteries, so I just go for them instead, scratching up both of his wrists to leave him bleeding like a geyser. And still, he didn't make a single sound of pain. It's almost a little anticlimactic. At least the question of *What do I need to do to make him scream?* elicited a bit more passion in me as I quickly leapt back to avoid a swipe of his feet.

Taking a step back, he prepares to attack me again, but I'm just a step faster, though since I don't aim directly for him, he can't counter with anything more damaging than a look of pure confusion.

I pull the level five's body off the ground and lift her up in front of me. I briefly catch a glimpse of his eyes widening before I rush at him with her in front of me. Man, this is kind of nostalgic.

And just before I reach him, I plunge my clawed hands into her soft dead back and burst through like a chestburster, right into his horrified, pale green face. He didn't even try to defend himself against her, and I, covered in her cold intestines, have no trouble clinging onto his upper body, eviscerating his neck and chest and face and bowels just like I did with her.

<You have learned: Eviscerate Lv.3>

Once I'm done, since I was only able to pop halfway through her bowels, I have to step out of the rest, kind of like taking off a frilly skirt. N—not that I would know what that's like!

<Goblin (Lv.12) Defeated.>
<[Level Up]>

<You have reached Level 11.>
<Agility has increased by 3.
Strength has increased by 2.
Stamina has increased by 2.
Magic Power has increased by 1.
Enhanced Vision has increased by 1.
Eviscerate has increased by 1.
Stealth has increased by 1.
Claw has increased by 1.
Fang has increased by 1. >

Oooh, nice! Now that I think about it, I haven't checked my stats in a while . . .

<Top—Status—Community>
<PrissyKittyPrincess
Human Level 11
Agility: 40
Strength: 30
Stamina: 46
Magic Power: 26>

There it is. Not too shabby, if I have to say so myself. I still hate my username, but I think I'm starting to get used to it. If I just delude myself into thinking everything's okay, then there are no worries! Hakuna Matata and all that. I mean, isn't there a saying about how, uhhh, there's no use worrying about what you can't change, and if you *can* change it, then there's also no use in worrying about it? Yeah. I'm pretty sure that's a thing somewhere in the world.

No worries allowed!

Hmm.

I look down at the level twelve's body. He really is almost my size. I have an idea, but it's . . . I mean, can I? Sure, I can, but it's a bit . . . Then again, they are just enemy mobs . . . Yeah. That's right. Goblin hide is just like cheetah hide or panther hide, so there's no reason not to wear it in a bit of a, you know, *creative* manner.

Squatting down, I give the body a long, hard look. I sharpen my focus into a razor's edge. Goblin body skinning speedrun any% begins . . . now!

<You have learned: Butcher Lv.6>
<You have learned: Claw Lv.10>
<You have learned: Sharp Claw Lv.1>
<You have learned: Butcher Lv.7>

Aaaaaaand . . . *time*!

\<Top—Status—Community\>
\<03:30:30 Day 71\>
\<The fourth attempt will begin in 19:20:29:30\>

Fourteen minutes and twenty-two seconds, a new world record! The first and only world champion of goblin skinning has been crowned: Lo Fennrick!

Hehehehehehehehehehehehehehehehhehe.

Basking in my invisible glory, I overlook my work. Yup, it's good. Somehow, I got good at this way quicker than you should be able to. And with nothing but my fingers, too? I am absolutely *dominating* the no-tool category. That said, now that I have a full and complete goblin hide, I can move onto phase two: skinwalker strategy.

I remove my panther hide and put it back into my inventory. Then, in the same way you'd put on a onesie pajama, I thread the goblin hide over my nude body. Man, I should really invest in a pair of boxers. Anyway, using a few goblin teeth, I'm able to secure the hide in such a way that from a distance, I might, at least for a moment, be confused for a real goblin. On closer inspection any such thoughts would vanish, though. I mean, fact number one: this skin is way too big for my slim body while still being too short, so it's totally sagging in some places and stretches thin in others, not to mention that the face is doing some weird kind of stiff thing where it just doesn't move at all. But, as I said, from a distance? Goblin time.

And once I'm up close, this will spook their socks off so bad they won't even be able to think a moment about fighting back as I eviscerate them. This is such a wonderful plan! Why didn't I think of this earlier?

Alright. My body and mind are ready.

Sniff sniff sniff. Yup, everyone is still here.

Time to pull some Scooby-Doo shenanigans!

And pull some Scooby-Doo shenanigans I do. Except in this situation, unlike the beloved monsters of the mystery dog franchise, I just literally kill all the goblins I come across. As I quickly found out, it isn't that hard to make a group split up. I only really need to take out one member for the dynamic to completely collapse on itself, and then I pick them off one by one. I have to say, waving to a goblin only for it to stupidly stumble right over to you and then scream as it notices that you aren't actually a goblin has to be one of the funniest things I've ever seen. Shouting *"Boo!"* just makes them completely lose it every time. This is the most fun that I've had all tutorial, which isn't really an achievement. Not much competition.

I'm not counting my time with Lady 444, for the record.

And just like that, I picked them off one by one. By the time the sun rose, I had completely cleared out the goblin invasion of the forest. Great success!

<[Level Up]>
<You have reached Level 12.>
<Agility has increased by 2.
Strength has increased by 2.
Stamina has increased by 3.
Magic Power has increased by 1.
Butcher has increased by 1.
Enhanced Vision has increased by 1.
Eviscerate has increased by 1.
Stealth has increased by 2.
Stalk has increased by 2.>
<You have learned: Disguise Lv.1>

Love hearing it. Ahhh, I love the smell of goblin epidermis in the morning . . .

That said, this skin is starting to get stuffy, so I'm going to take it off now. It was fun while it lasted, but running around in it for all the obligatory Scooby-Doo chases did a number on it, so it's gotten torn in a bunch of places. Shame. Still, throwing it away feels like a bit much, so I'll just put it back in my inventory.

Ah, leopard skin, my old flame . . . I can't resist you any longer.

It seems the goblin-related events have kind of calmed down now, so I think I'm going to do the only sensible thing possible and hunt every animal in the forest to extinction.

<THE GOD OF HUNTING FROWNS AT YOUR DISREGARD FOR THE ART OF HUNTING.>

You know, mister sourpuss, I'm only using the word *hunt* because it fits the whole track-and-kill operation I've got going on here. In reality, this is more of an extinction type of thing. Really, if I had the choice, I would have loved to set fire to the entire forest to make sure it was totally cleared. Sadly, I don't think I'd survive that sort of situation, so I won't. So, no; I am not committing myself to the art of hunting—I am simply hunting.

<THE GODDESS OF FORESTS FROWNS AT YOUR DISREGARD FOR THE GRANDEUR OF NATURE.>

You too, huh? How many of your sort can we get in here? On a different note, how many of you are currently watching me doing this?

Really, if you hate me so much, mister god of shoots-thing-with-bow, why are you still here? Shouldn't you have left the moment you saw me doing things that your itty-bitty teeny-tiny coping ability couldn't take?

Oh, and now I get the radio silence again, of course. Always with these things . . . They want to tell you that you're doing it wrong, but the second you bite back, they run behind the couch with their tails tucked between their legs.

<THE GOD OF COWARDICE PEEKS OUT FROM BEHIND A COUCH.>

. . .

. . .

. . . Not you. I suppose.

<THE GOD OF COWARDICE SIGHS IN RELIEF.>

Yeah, yeah, I get it, so scram already! Man, I really can't handle these beings.

If I'm lucky, there might be a system in place to keep them from interacting with me too much. Should one of these glorified deities decide to zap my behind to the nearest moon—unless the tutorial itself protects me—I don't think I have much of a chance at surviving. Then again, there *was* that time when the Coward poked me, and Want *did* stretch the system just to sugar-mommy me, so . . .

Yeah. Okay, I think, right now, my best bet is to just not think about it. From what I've seen, there's a god for pretty much everything, so no matter what I do, I'll always displease at least one. If they could just kill people they disliked willy-nilly, there'd be a lot more divine casualties by now. Assuming that said casualties didn't get erased from reality or something, of course.

Damn it, I wish I had answers. But I don't think there's anyone I can ask. I mean, if Moleman knew about this stuff, he would already have posted a stupidly detailed guide about *How to get noticed by the Gods.*

Euck.

. . . I wonder what those guys are up to.

N—not that it matters. I'm busy huntin' and killin'! Something that I should absolutely get right on to.

I take a deep sniff. There's a lot of smells, many of them very different from the others, but all of them are both nostalgic and enough to make my mouth water. There are a ton of different critters in this forest. It might take some time to get all of them, but if I just sprint from one to the next, it should be fine. I'll need to pause to butcher everything, but that shouldn't take too much time either.

Sni—iff. Wolves, deer, squirrels, rabbits, boar, elks, and what I think might be two bears. All and all, they easily number over a hundred, but that's fine. I've got time.

I get to sprinting.

Zipping through the woods at the fastest speeds I can muster, I stop only to sneakily dispatch an animal or two. Most range in levels between one to five. After killing them, I butcher them into as many parts as possible before stashing them. After doing this for a couple of hours, my butcher skill evolved.

\<You have learned: Butcher Lv.10\>
\<You have learned: Disassemble Lv.1\>

It made the whole butchering process a fair bit faster, to the point where I became very confident in being able to break my former goblin skinning any% world record. It almost makes me watch to find another goblin, but, sadly, I can't smell any. All day, I kill and I kill, a—ll day long. It's great fun!

The only break I take is at three in the afternoon to eat a few pieces of gobling meat. As I've now discovered, gobling meat is more tender and juicier than regular goblin meat. I'll need to keep my eye out in the future.

Even when day turns to night, I keep going. Even when night turns to day, I keep going. Even when the days pass like minutes, I keep going.

I kill all the deer until I can't smell them anymore.

I kill all the boars until I can't smell them anymore.

I kill all the squirrels until I can't smell them anymore.

I kill all the wolves until I can't smell them anymore.

I kill all the bears until I can't smell them anymore.

It's kind of funny. I fought wolves, and it wasn't that hard anymore. Sure, one of them disemboweled me, but I got better. I just need to rip and tear at them and bite right back and I win. They have so many soft parts. Neck and bowels and eyes and mouth. Anything that can bleed, or spill organs is a weak point. It might as well be flashing in RED.

I even fought the two bears. They were in the same cave, both sleeping. I almost died, but I lived. That's all that really matters, because in the end, after healing up and re-challenging the bears around four times, I finally won.

I have so many lovely pelts now.

Bear pelt, deer pelt, boar pelt, cobbled-together patchwork of squirrel pelts, wolf pelt . . . everything.

And when the dawn of the fifth day rose, the forest was empty, and only I remained.

But it wasn't empty for long.

Footloose

Now, which way is the exit again? I'm pretty sure it should be toward the hut, but I'm not entirely sure, it could really be any wa—

No. It's in the direction of the hut.

There's . . . there's a lot of goblins appearing from just beyond it. I can smell them. It smells as though they're spawning in, but I think it's more that they're entering the designated *forest* area. You see, there was an invisible barrier keeping me inside a certain area, but that's unimportant now.

It isn't a dozen. It isn't two dozen, or three dozen, or even four dozen.

It's in the *hundreds*.

Huh. Uh. Um . . .

Realistically speaking, they shouldn't be here for me specifically, right? I mean, I'm just a little guy. I've done nothing worthy of getting an entire army sent after me, have I? Exactly—never in my days! This must be for something else entirely. Like, uh . . . Maybe one of those goblins was a war criminal hiding out here? Or those bears that I killed had a history of eating royal babies? If either of those two are the case, then there's no reason to come here, army. Your faithful friend and servant has destroyed both dangers, which means that you have no reason to fear—none whatsoever! Your savior is here.

. . . Why are they still approaching? For some reason, they seem to be heading straight for my position. Not a single little goblin is out of formation. All of them smell the same, too. Metal. Sweat. That sort of stuff. The determination is palpable around them.

Should I run? *Can* I run?

They're coming from the hypothetical east, right where I think the exit is, so they're blocking it. On the other hand, I could just hide. Fetal position blowover will keep me hidden, and if I remain in that position in some secure place for a few days, they should leave.

But will I still get the complete clear from that? I mean, it's *enemies*. To win, I have to kill all the enemies. That's just how it works.

I don't have much of a choice, do I?

<THE GOD OF COWARDICE IS WORRIED.>

Oh, come on, Coward, don't be such a spoilsport! If I can kill twenty-seven goblins, how different could—sniff—around four hundred be? It's practically the exact same thing!

Yup, this will work out great. I wonder how high my level will get? Four hundred goblins . . . That's a lot. That's quite enough to get me to level 40, right? Yeah. With this, I'll be able to easily give Moleman a show of what-for! Hehehe.

And, since we're hunting goblins . . .

Undressing, I stick my leopard pelt into my inventory and pull out the good ol' gobster. He's torn in places and some of his joints got a bit stretched, but he's still green, and that's all I need. Jumping inside, I tighten the teeth-clasps again, closing it up fully. I am vengeance. I am the night. I am . . . *goblin-man.*

It's only a shame that it's daytime. I'd look much spookier at night, but whatever. Grinning from behind the distended goblin lips, I move out.

Jump, jump, jump, jump. And, within time, I find the army. Not all the troopers have armor, but a lot of them have at least a helmet. That said, all of them carry a weapon, and for most of them, this seems to be a spear and a shield. Metal spear. Iron. Some also have bows, and a couple have halberds. The typical level is 10 among the infantry and archers, but there's more than that.

In the back rows of the army, there's a group of what seems to be the commanders, all of them mounted atop what seems to be scaly, lizard ostriches.

<Goblin (Lv.11)>
<Goblin (Lv.11)>
<Goblin (Lv.12)>
<Goblin (Lv.10)>
<Goblin (Lv.11)>

Right. I think that might be dangerous.

Four of them are dressed like stereotypical knights, with swords slung on their belts. The one goblin at level 12 also looks like a knight, but his armor is more ornate, and he also has his helmet off to show his face. I have no idea how to properly express this, but I think he might be slightly more handsome than the other goblins. N—not that I can tell that sort of stuff; he just looks, well, you know . . . His skin looks kind of smooth, you know? Argh, I'm just trying to say that he looks like an aristocrat, that's all!

A—anyway, there's also a sixth one, but for some reason, the status box isn't popping up. I'm looking at him, but I can't see what level he is. Which is . . . weird? Maybe it's a glitch or something. Either way, this goblin isn't dressed as a warrior. I can't completely tell what he's supposed to be dressed as, but he doesn't have any weapons and is just dressed in fabrics. Long tunic and stuff. But he doesn't look like a typical wizard, or even a cleric. I don't know what he is. Maybe a priest? I don't know, but that book he's holding looks mighty holy. Hmm. I kind of want it.

Well, as they say, go for the cleric fir—

Did he just point at me?

Hang on, I need to rub my eyes and squint. Yeah, that robed goblin is absolutely pointing at me. What the heck is he—

<Chain.>

Chain? Chain . . .

Hm. What a conundrum. Let me scratch my chin for maximum brainage.

Huh? My hand can't move. That's weird . . .

Ohhh, wait, no, I get it. He *is* a mage! And he just cast an immobilization spell on me. Hm. That's great. How interesting. Does that mean he can see exactly where I am? Oh, that isn't goo—

Approximately three dozen arrows whiz through the air, and my brain instantly flashes back to almost two months ago, with the winds and the darkness, and my body moves on its own as I tense everything that I am and everything that I have to leap off the tree I'm perched in, succeeding in avoiding most arrows but still getting hit by one, two, five or seven or so, and I only just have time to count them before I hit the ground below.

<You have learned: Immobilization Tolerance Lv.1>
<You have learned: Divinity Tolerance Lv.1>
<Chain Broken.>

Yeah, I can feel that last one.

Ignoring the arrows fully, I scuttle over to another tree and climb it so fast I can barely hear the arrows thudding into the trunk below. This isn't good. But it could be worse. The arrows aren't poisoned, at least. Quickly, faster than I've ever climbed, I make my way up to the scrubby foliage at the top of the tree before leaping to another tree, and then yet another, as many times as I can until I can't be properly seen anymore.

Sniff sniff sniff. The commanders have taken on a new smell. But I can't smell the priest. Weird, very weird. I almost want to get hit by his spells a bit more to get my tolerance up higher, but I need to take him out first.

Circling around the army, I head for the commanders.

And then, once I'm close enough to see the tops of their heads through the foliage . . .

A barrage of arrows crashes through my hiding spot, my body only moving by sheer instinct to leap back and willingly crash through the foliage and straight down on top of the commanders. Or, rather, on top of the raised sword of one of the commanders. O—w.

It's a shame that this just happens to bring me delightfully close to him.

"Gra-jit . . . ?" he mutters, which is the same word a lot of the goblins muttered when they saw me Scooby-Doo-ing them the other night.

I pull off his helmet and gorge myself in his expression of pure fear before completely eviscerating his now-exposed head and neck, first blinding him, then pulling off his jaw and tearing out his wiggling tongue alongside it, and then tearing out whatever arteries I can get a hold of within his neck.

<You have learned: Piercing Resistance Lv.10>
<You have learned: Piercing Protection Lv.1>
<Goblin (Lv.11) Defeated.>

The second I receive the message that he's dead, I leap away from his corpse, dodging another stab by mere millimeters.

The priest is only a few feet away from me. Can I get him? Should I escape instead? Will he—

The priest points at me with his ring finger. Now that I look at his hand, he's got a ring on each finger. I wonder what that's abou—

<Curse.>

Okay?

An arrow whizzes toward me and I leap on top of the fallen commander's lizard ostrich.

<Sprint Drake (Lv.6)>

Startled by my mounting, the ostrich starts running. Right into the thick of the army. Shoot.

Jumping right off its back, I find myself in the middle of the archers, who stare at me like I'm not supposed to be here, which I'm probably not. But strategically speaking, this is my best position, because the spears can't get to me, and the archers can't fire at me, and they don't have much face and neck protection. Hm. I should really thank that ostrich if I can catch it again.

Without a pause I throw myself at the nearest goblin, tearing up his face and neck to the point where I know he'll die, and then leaping to the next without waiting for the message of his defeat to pop up. From goblin to goblin, eviscerating as much as I can. At least, that is, until something bad happens.

I get pointed at again. Did nobody teach that priest that pointing is rude?

<Chain.>

Midclawing, I suddenly freeze completely in place, my arms and legs turning completely immobile. But now I know how to deal with this, so I just exert every inch of effort I can muster in order to . . .

<Chain Broken.>
<You have learned: Immobilization Tolerance Lv.2>

Great stuff. Now, to continue my little slaughter—

Something goes through my chest. Why, hello there, little spear. That's a very interesting tooth you've got there.

At the shout of one of the commanders, about a dozen arrows stab into my back. I fall off the goblin I was just about to finish off. Ah. It hurts. I'm bleeding. This is too much. It hurts.

<You have learned: Piercing Protection Lv.2>

Piercing protection . . . aren't you supposed to be strong? How come I'm still very much being pierced? Dummy. Ah, it hurts . . .

A goblin holding some weird, barbed hook thing approaches me where I lie on the ground, and I only barely have time to recognize it as a man-catcher before he thrusts it at my neck and catches himself a man. Ah. This is bad. Did I lose? No, I'm still alive, I just need to get back up on my feet, and then I can continue. I still haven't died. I need to win. I need to beat the dumb goblins. Otherwise, I'm a . . . bad . . . gamer . . .

<You have learned: Oxygen Deficiency Resistance Lv.4>

Before my hazy eyes, one of the commanders steps forth. It's the guy in the fancy armor.

"Jurt er't stutt," he tells someone I can't see. I wonder what it means. I don't think I could survive getting stabbed in the neck. My lung feels weird. I think that spear went into my right lung. That isn't good. It's collapsing. But my left lung works fine. If I could only meditate, then I could get better. I need to . . .

Oh, a goblin is stepping up behind me. I think that's one of the commanders. I wonder what he's going to do with that sword he's got.

Huh? Uh, okay, this is weird, two random goblin troops are grabbing my feet. Th—this is . . . I didn't know goblins were into this sort of thing. I am very disturbed. Please, God, protect me.

The commander lifts his sword high.

Huh? Wait a sec—

He brings it down. My left foot goes tumbling. Huh. Huh. Huh. What?

He lifts his sword again.

Wait. Wait just a second. Hang on. Please, wait, I'm not—

He brings it down. And there goes my right foot. Ah. Ahh. Ahhhh. I see.

This is . . . This is a new kind of pain, yes. Hm. Yes. I don't think I ever want to experience this again. My brain feels fuzzy. Like my head is filled with cotton.

<You have learned: Dismemberment Tolerance Lv.1>
<You have learned: Dismemberment Tolerance Lv.2>
<You have learned: Dismemberment Tolerance Lv.3>
<You have learned: Bleeding Protection Lv.2>
<You have learned: Slashing Tolerance Lv.5>

Ahh. I feel . . . Not so good.

The fancy commander steps closer to me. He has a weird facial expression: determination and mourning, mixed so strangely you could only really see it in a warrior. I don't like it. I don't like it. I hate it. It's too human. You're a mob. A goblin. What do you have to mourn?

"Gra-jit . . . Tu bin ish vir nerh," he says, almost gently, right to my face. "Trie mir ut chit-chit." He holds out his hand, and after a few seconds, a dagger is deposited in it. He brings it to my neck. Ah. Is it too late to tell him that I don't want to die?

But instead of stabbing it well and deep into my supple soft neck, he just starts cutting the skin of my pretty disguise. H—hey, that's my goblin disguise! Stop that, I spent a lot of time on it! Hey-ey-ey-ey—!

After cutting around the full circumference of the neck, he unmasks me. He stares at me. I stare at him. His expression turns a step more difficult.

"Gur fra hik?"

And only a second later, the priest appears at his side and points a big finger at me, and I expect him to do some magic at me, but instead he just shouts, "Hoeksak!"

Yeah, yeah, I'm a hoeksak. What else is new?

With that exclamation, though, the goblin soldiers who had crowded around me and the commanders all start stepping back, a murmur running through them that sounds an awful lot like *hoeksak*, whatever that means. Is that their word for *human* or something? For some reason, it feels like they don't recognize my species, but that might just be me. I don't look too typical right now, I'm aware. But a little ashen paleness never hurt anyone, right?

While my brain chugs along at half the speed of a kiddie ride at funland, the commanders start discussing among themselves, talking about this or that. It can probably be boiled down to something like *Should we kill him now or later?* I'm not entirely sure what conclusion they arrived at, but after the priest gave a rather long speech, they decide to postpone my death-by-goblins and instead bind me up properly.

Chains and chains and chains and chains. Like, real ones. Without trying to pull out the several dozen arrows and the spear stuck inside me, they pull me to my feet—or, rather, to my stumps. I don't know exactly what they expected me to do, but they seemed a bit surprised when I started walking. What else were they going to do: drag me along? Eh, maybe.

To answer your question, yeah, I'm not struggling. Look, I'm chained by several meters of heavy chains, surrounded by hundreds of goblins and already harmed to the point where I can't climb, much less run. Fighting means death. And unlike the common perception of the pro gamer, I do not want to die.

Two of the commanders are at my side. The priest is at a small distance, constantly checking over his shoulder. The main commander is far ahead, leading the army back from whence they came.

After an hour or so of marching, we pass the wooden hut, where you can still see a few darkened splotches in the ground.

Hm. Hang on. Are we hypothetically heading east?

W—wait a second. Hey, if I go there, I'll clear the stage! Just—just wait a moment, I can't . . .

Ah, shoot, I can see the forest ending just up ahead! No way. Nuh-uh. I didn't completely clear the stage! Step on the brakes! *Stopppp—!*

Grinding the stumps of my legs into the dirt, I pull myself to a stop, but the goblins holding my chains have other thoughts and start trying to pull me like an owner trying to drag their dog back inside the house. Nuh-uh. Nuh-uh. No way. I am *not* leaving this forest. I've changed my mind!

The commanders start trying to pull me too, but I am steadfast. No way. No way. Absolutely no—

<Chain.>

My entire body freezes in place, and the goblins using all their might to pull me all tumble over, with my light body flying through the air and landing atop them. In horror, they scramble out from under me. Not that they needed any haste, because I can't move.

Hey! Not fair! Magic is cheating!

The priest frowns at me. I growl at him like an animal.

But there's nothing I can do because the stage has shifted.

<A CHANGE HAS BEEN MADE.>

<Tutorial stage, Hell Difficulty Third Floor: True Boss Stage>
<[Clear Condition] Defeat the wicked goblin king who rules the Shore City of Acheron with an iron fist.>

True boss stage?

This is . . . Is this . . . ?

Does this mean that I was *supposed* to get caught by the army? Or would I still have gotten this if I killed them all? More importantly, since I was the last one to get dragged out of the forest, does that mean that I technically completely cleared the stage? I mean—really, you don't get into the secret bonus stage unless you did something right, so . . .

Whoopie! I'm going to beat the super-secret hidden true boss! I'm such an awesome gamer! Take *that*, Moleman! Bet you didn't get to fight the goblin king, hahahaha!

Ah, it seems the goblins didn't like my expression of pure glee. Whoops. But who cares about the opinions of mob enemies? I certainly don't! Hehehehe.

Kill a king . . . Easy peasy. I mean, it's only one goblin, right? A single goblin. That's no problem at all. Even if he has a few guards, that's no trouble. Just got to go for the arteries, that's what my mother always used to say. Actually, that's a lie. She never said that. I don't know why I lied about it.

By now the chain spell thing has worn off so I'm back to walking on my own, but apparently I got a bit too deeply stuck in my thoughts, as I almost walked right into a bunch of goblins.

Hey, what's the holdup for? Let's go to the castle already. I want to kill—errr, *meet* your king! Meat your king . . . hehehe. I wonder if goblin king meat is tastier than gobling meat? You never know. That said, I still have no idea why we paused.

Since I'm at least full head taller than all these green rubes, I have a pretty good view of what's ahead. Ah, it looks like the head honcho commander goblin has taken a brief pause to talk to some dude. Another goblin, one who's unusually well-dressed, all things considered. He looks old, though. Saggy green skin, like a certain famous alien. After talking for a few minutes, the old guy hands the head commander a rolled-up piece of parchment, and then we continue our trek.

After half an hour or so, we reach a village. Or maybe what used to be a village because it's completely empty. There's a mill and a few houses and the ground around it is tilled, and some of the plants being farmed are even blooming. I can't recognize what kinds of crops these are, but they are clearly being grown purposefully. But there isn't anyone here. Nobody that isn't wearing military garb, at least.

It seems that the army has set up camp here. There are a few tents, and a few flags are raised. I'm trying to put them to mind so I'll kill the right king and not some unrelated monarch. It's kind of hard, though, since it's a very ordinary flag, with a shield on it portraying a bridge and some water and a city.

There's a lot of stuff here in the village, though. Most noticeably, a large cage on wheels. Like, large enough to hold a small *T. rex*. And right as I start to wonder what they're supposed to use it for, they lead me into it. Uh-huh.

The inside is pretty big. Large chains with massive clasps are hanging from the roof, and even more chains are stuck to the floor. Right as I start to wonder how to best escape this situation, three heavier goblins push me to the ground and undo the chains I'm already wearing, and before I can even consider fighting them . . .

<Chain.>
<You have learned: Divinity Tolerance Lv.2>

Damn it, this again. Once my eyes find the priest, I glower at him. Weirdly enough, he stands his ground.

As I wonder what they're about to do to me in my poor defenseless state, they do the one thing I had hoped they would have forgotten about. They remove my goblin disguise completely. At the start they tried cutting it off, but then they found my tooth clasps, and after mumbling something, they undid those and removed my beloved goblin hide. Those meddling goblins . . . !

Apparently, the sight of my completely nude body was too much for them to take because they quickly retreated, though not before chaining me inside the cage.

Most of the clasps are too big for my wrists and ankles, so they chain up my abdomen and my arms and my neck and my thighs. I feel like this might be too much. I mean, I can't even break out of one, so what's the point of having a dozen? But I can't exactly ask them, so instead, I just give them a slight raise of the eyebrow once they're done. They don't react.

Reverently carrying the skin and the teeth, they exit the cage and lock it behind them.

Damn. This is probably the most humiliating thing that's ever happened to me. Assuming you don't count my entire life until this very moment, of course.

With nothing else to do, I let my eyes follow those goblins as they bring the skin to the head commander. He looks it over, mumbles a few words, and tells them something before pointing away. It's hard to see what they're doing since I'm chained in a weird position where I can't move all that much, but I'm pretty sure they just went and dug a grave for the skin. The priest even did some last-rite-looking things for it. Interesting. But such a waste.

Maybe they just want to spite me? It's possible.

Because of the way my chains are placed, I can stand and sit up and walk a foot or two in either direction, but not much else. I could probably escape the clasps on my limbs if I broke all my bones, but the ones around my midsection and neck are too much. I'm stuck. There's basically nothing for me to do but wait for them to bring me to wherever the king is. Assuming that it won't take more than . . .

<Top—Status—Community>
<12:03:12 Day 76>
<The fourth attempt will begin in 14:11:56:48>

. . . about fourteen days, I should be fine. I really don't want to have to redo this kind of quest. Hunting all the animals was thrilling, but kind of boring compared to hunting goblins. Besides, I might only have a single chance at doing the secret boss. You never know.

Man. I'm starting to feel really bored here. Are there any tolerances I can try to increase while in here? Probably.

Speaking of this place, I've noticed an interesting detail. Sure, it's obvious that this cage is meant to transport big live monsters, but I can't for the life of me understand the point of the tiny cage a bit ahead. It's closer to the front of the cage, stuck to the ground, with a—*get this*—tiny chair inside it. Just a chair. I have no idea what to make of it. Seriously.

Since there's nothing else to look at on the inside of the cage, I let my attention move outside to the goblins.

Oh, they're having a lunch break of some sort. Yeah, that makes sense. I think I can smell it. This is the kind of situation where I'd expect stew, but it smells creamier than that. Pea soup? Is that what it is? It's something similar, at least. Lunch break. Mobs are eating lunch. That's very silly.

I hope they finish lunch soon so we can go. This smell is starting to make me feel a bit . . .

<You have learned: Starvation Resistance Lv.8>

H—hey, I'm not *that* hungry! I ate just a few hours ago! I'm fine. There is nothing for me to worry about. I don't need to eat. Yup. Not at all.

The sound of footsteps reaches my ears.

. . . Someone's approaching.

I try to turn my neck, but the iron brace is making it hard, so I have to turn my entire body, but I don't even have time to do that before—

<Chain.>

Oh, of course it had to be *this* guy. Damn it. Such a bother.

Alright, priest, whaddya want?

He looks at me. I look at him. He's holding a bowl of whatever soup it is they're eating. His whole face just exudes hatred. Wow. Not one to be defeated, I give him the kind of look you give your sibling when they snitch on something you both did wrong and because they snitched, they didn't get punished for it.

The priest doesn't say anything. I can't really move, so I don't say anything, either. Unlocking the cage, he enters within, locking it behind him.

<You have learned: Immobilization Tolerance Lv.3>

Slowly, he circles around me until he's in front of where I'm sitting. He's been keeping eye contact the whole time, and I've dutifully returned it. Even then, I can't help but give him a closer look. He's young. I think so, at least. The robe he's wearing—although it appears plain—is actually finely woven, with a few embroidered details that must have cost a pretty penny. His blond mane is braided in parts and seems very well-kept. For some reason, as I'm mentally judging him, it seems like he's doing something similar to me. *What are you looking at, huh? Got something you wanna say, punk?!*

"At." As he says this, he puts the bowl in front of me, at a small distance. I don't take my eyes off him. He doesn't take his eyes off me.

After having a staring match for almost a full minute I accidentally blink because I got sand in my eye, which means I lose. The tension breaks and he stands up, walks over to the gate, and leaves, locking it behind him. Shoot.

I almost want to growl at him like a proper caged animal, but I think I'll avoid doing so.

I look down at the bowl.

If they think they can kill me by simply poisoning me, boy do they have something else coming. Had I been some ordinary animal, then yes, a bowl of poisoned stew would absolutely have killed me. But I am not a standard beast. I am a gamer. Poison doesn't work on me. In fact, should this increase the level of my poison protection, that only strengthens me. It's your loss, goblins! Hahaha!

Grinning because I'll be proving those bastard green-scalps wrong and absolutely not because I'm hungry and have forgotten how good real food tastes, I dig in. But since it's soft soup, I can't exactly use my hands, so I just bury my face in the bowl and gulp and gulp and gulp and gulp and gulp and gulp and gulp.

<You have learned: Drowning Tolerance Lv.1>
<You have learned: Choking Tolerance Lv.2>
<You have learned: Oxygen Deficiency Resistance Lv.5>

Haah, haah, haah, haah, haah . . . Okay, uh . . . Um . . . Yeah . . . Uh . . . Right.

I think, maybe, possibly, within some definitions, in some situations, that, maybe, just maybe, I might prefer stew cooked by goblins to raw goblin meat. Maybe. Possibly. I'm just . . . I'm just suggesting it, okay? There's a certain possibility that this is the situation. It's plausible. I mean, when you think about it, it's not like I had any spices for the raw goblin meat, and I didn't exactly cook it either, but . . .

Even if I had . . .

—No, that's not important. That just a—a *hypothetical* sort of situation that hasn't happened yet, or maybe even ever. Also, just so we're clear on it, unless a food gives me some sort of tolerance, what's even the point of eating it? Yeah.

S—so, by that definition, um . . . If they gave me more food, since it gives me, uh, tolerances, then . . . Yeah. I'd better eat it. Because, you know, they might try to do that sort of stuff to me, with the poisoning and whatnot, so I'd better, uh . . . Keep on my toes. Or stumps. Yeah. Yeah . . .

I look down at the bowl in my hands. It's completely empty, except for one little spot. Without really thinking, I lean forward to give it a lick.

<Chain.>

Oh, damn it, you . . . !

The door to the cage unlocks and the priest stomps right on in and is just about to grab the bowl out of my immobilized hands before he notices my fiery eyes. We have almost a full minute of silent staring.

"Sere," he says with a sigh. I have no idea what that means. As I look at him in confusion, he steps over to the bars, keeping his eyes on me. Once he's too far away for me to even consider doing any clownage . . .

<Chain revoked.>

I can feel my body turn mobile again. Honestly, I almost drop the bowl, but I'm able to keep it together.

He crosses his arms. "Gur? At."

Well . . . If you say so.

I lick the bowl. I briefly consider if I can throw it at him hard enough to break his skull, but even if I did, it's not like I'd be able to escape.

He points his finger at me but I'm way too tired of suddenly being totally immobilized, so I just hold up the bowl to him. *Come on. Just take it, man. It's not like I'll win anything by killing you. I think . . .*

His eyes widen slightly, but after a second or so of hesitation, he still magics me.

<Chain.>

My body freezes. Damn it. That's what I get for being nice, huh? Next time I see you, I'm tearing your face open. Yeah? I'm going to steal your nose and wear it as a necklace with your guts as string. That cool with you?

He steps up to me and slowly takes the bowl out of my hand. "Takk."

And off he goes.

But before he totally leaves, he turns around and . . .

<Chain revoked.>

I stare at him as he leaves.

But he isn't gone for long. It seems the lunch break has now formally ended, as less than an hour after he came to take the bowl, the whole army is back at it again, all up in a hubbub of movement and things. A bunch of weird lizards are tethered to the front of my cage, which the system categorizes as *pull drakes*, with an average level of 7. Four of them are needed to pull my huge cage, but right as I thought we were about to get moving, I finally learn what the purpose of the tiny cage at the front is.

The priest climbs into it from below. He takes a seat on the chair.

Am I seriously stuck with this guy for the entire damn ride?

Fun and Games

I'm sitting on the floor; he's sitting on a tiny chair. Somehow, we're at the same eye level. I don't like it.

After a minute or so, the army starts moving again, slowly. I'd like to enjoy the scenery, but I can't allow myself to look weak in front of this stupid priest.

The stumps of my legs are itching. I need to do something about that.

After a few minutes, he pulls out a book out of nowhere and starts reading. In the meanwhile, I'm going to see if my meditation can heal this or I'm going to have to do a footless playthrough.

Step one, I need to clean the stumps as best as I can. They got really mangled by the gravel and the dirt. I think I've got pebbles all the way into my bone marrow. Cleaning them would probably be almost impossible at this point.

I don't like the idea, but I'll probably have to slice off the bad parts, like you do with bologna. It's as simple as that. I have fairly good mobility with my arms, so it should be possible. I just hope that the priest won't notice and try to do something about it.

Inconspicuously, I glance up at him. He's reading his book. Yeah, he won't notice. I can do this.

I can't physically turn around, so I'll have to do it like this.

Silently, I summon the only sharp sword I own, namely the one I got from the first big goblin. It's sharper than my knife and will probably be able to cut through bone if I do this right. Yeah. I just got to do this the right way. It doesn't have to be perfect. I can heal an imperfect cut. Yeah. Just got to . . . cut . . . it!

Slash!

—Gh . . . !

Shoot. Heck. Damn it. It didn't get through my bone. Heck. Okay. I just need to try again. Once more. One . . . more . . . slice!

Chop!

<You have learned: Fracture Resistance Lv.2>

It didn't slice. It just broke. Shoot. But that also works. I just need to slice off the last bit and I'm good. Yup.

Saw saw saw saw saw saw, *pop.*

Fresh blood gushes forth. Ahh. Right.

But now . . . Now, it's controlled. I've already lost a foot once, so I know I won't die. Yeah. I just need to wait until it stops bleeding and it'll be fine. Yeah. That's all.

Just need to . . . wait . . . a . . . little . . .

Ah! Can't sleep. Sleeping kills me. Yeah. Can't sleep. Absolutely can't sleep. Sleep is death.

<You have learned: Unconsciousness Resistance Lv.2>

Gulp.

Right. One stump done. One left to go.

Haaah. I really hope these grow back so I didn't do all of this for nothing. Right. Next one. I raise the sword. My hand trembles. One good chop and it'll all go away. I clench my jaw. My teeth grew back. That's proof enough. If teeth grow back, then so do feet. It's basically the same thing. Yeah.

I steel myself and bring down the sword on my ankle.

And for the first time in a long while, maybe forever, it goes just as I wanted. The sliced-off stump soars through the air with a firework display of blood, and then it falls back on the wooden floor with a thick, meaty *slap.*

. . . I did it. I really did it. One chop was all it took. Hahaha. Haha. Haaah . . . I want to sleep . . .

I put my sword back into my inventory. Since I might need them someday, I put the stumps in there as well. And then, even though I want to sleep for real, I draw the stumps of my legs close, and I begin to meditate.

After a few minutes, they stop bleeding. An hour or so more and a thin layer of baby-bottom-soft skin forms to make them into proper stumps. If I scratch at them, they start bleeding easily. But it's a first step. Whether I'll be able to grow back my feet is still up to chance. I wonder if lopped-off appendages grow back in the lobby? Hmm. This might actually be a very important thing to know about . . .

Unfortunately, I know just the guy to ask. Damn it. I hate that I keep having to crawl back to him.

Huffing, I open the Community tab and enter the only chatroom I'm still a member of.

<Status—Community—Top>
<NORTH Europe chat>
<HookedOnBach[F6]: You really don't know who the secret leader is supposed to be? :(>
<HerringFerry[F3]: tbh i think only the Hard exec actually knows.>
<TerriblePretender[F20]: Does it matter tho. Whoever it is we'll just take him down too.>
<LionMawMadness[F10]: Your dumb>
<PrissyKittyPrincess[F3]: were is moleman>

I couldn't see him scrolling up a little, but there should be some way of getting hold of him.

<LionMawMadness[F10]: omg lol guys look Miss Kitty returned. have you reached level 40 yet kitty lol>
<PrissyKittyPrincess[F3]: fuk off>
<TerriblePretender[F20]: I don't appreaciate your tone but to answer your question Moleman is currently challenging the 23rd. It's very hectic.>
<PrissyKittyPrincess[F3]: don care didnt ask>
<HookedOnBach[F6]: Kitty, if you want to ask him something, just send him a PM. Also, stop being so rude. >:(>
<PrissyKittyPrincess[F3]: ur a slag>
<HookedOnBach[F6]: That's not even a real curse word. :/>

I exit the chat. Send a PM . . .

But that's so . . . *personal.*

If I do that, it'll look like I care about his opinion and what he has to say or something. And that's weak. Ugh.

But I don't have much of a choice. I kind of need to know whether I'll get my feet back or if I should just start looking for peg legs. Although it hurts, I go into the members list of the North Europe chat and look up Moleman. Once I'm on his profile, I press the Send Personal Message button. And now, I just stare at the screen. It's empty. Blank. Tabula rasa.

My fingers tremble. I take a long, deep breath.

And then I get to typing.

<PrissyKittyPrincess[F3]: hey do limb regen in lobby or like if u hve high healing or do they jus not>

I stare at the message I've typed. After a moment of thinking, I pull up the keyboard again and add a little word.

**<PrissyKittyPrincess[F3]: hey do limb regen in lobby or like if u hve high
healing or do they jus not thx>**

Send.

I feel hot and ashamed. But there's nothing more for me to do in the Community tab, so I put away the window.

We're still moving. I guess I'd better keep meditating. I need to heal a bit more. If I tried to walk right now I'd just scratch up my stumps again and the situation from before would repeat.

Ah, hang on. The priest is staring at me. I stare back at him. His eyes slowly fall to the pool of blood below me that's currently soaked into the floorboards. I say nothing and he gives no comment. After a few seconds, he goes back to reading. Yeah, you better!

Mrr. My back itches. Oh, yeah, I'm still prickly with arrows. I should probably push them out, or pull them through, depending on the situation. And then there's also the huge spear. I guess I'd better get to it. Haaah, this is starting to feel eerily nostalgic.

I start with the spear because it's the easiest. I really do just have to push it through, but then the hole that it plugged and that I had healed around is opened again and I'm bleeding like an uncorked wine barrel. I think I can feel someone looking at me with worry, but it doesn't matter. This much blood is still fine, I think. The most important thing is my lung. I close my eyes and start to meditate.

<You have learned: Oxygen Deficiency Resistance Lv.6>
<You have learned: Regeneration Meditation Lv.7>
<You have learned: Auto-Regeneration Lv.6>

And then, after some time . . .

<You have learned: Salamander Healing Lv.1>

Is this what I think it is?

I open my eyes wide and stare at my stumps. There is no change from before. Alright, so it's going to take a while. That's fine. Since it took this army at most five days to get to the forest, I should at least have a day or two to heal.

Right as I have that thought, the army's march rolls to a stop. The sun is still relatively high. I think we've only been going for a few hours, so this is probably just a break. Before I continue meditating, I push through a few arrows, including a few along my legs and arms. Apparently, having the arrows not be poisoned makes this slightly worse, because—apparently—the poison dulled the pain a smidge. The pain still isn't too bad, though, so it's fine. After around half an hour of pushing out arrows, a small pile has formed next to me. I stare at them, hard.

Pushing them out felt familiar. *Too familiar.*

I would be a fool not to notice that these arrows aren't just similar to those on the first floor but rather the exact same arrows. Same kind of material, same sort of design. Sure, most arrows look the same, but it's a bit too similar for my tastes. Silently, I put the pile of arrows into my inventory, just in case.

To stifle the bleeding, I spend a few minutes meditating before continuing.

I resume pushing through the arrows and pulling out those that sit too close to my interior organs.

And then I hit a roadblock.

I—I can't reach them. There are three arrows that are stuck in such a way that I can't physically reach them. I can't push them through either because they're right in front of where I'm pretty sure my heart is. Either I pull them out, or I don't. But maybe if I contract my body in such a way that . . .

Oh, I just noticed the priest is staring at me.

Faster than humanly possible, I return to my normal position. You didn't see anything. You got that, gob-gob?

Apparently, my eyes are at least somewhat effective at conveying my thoughts, because he quickly resumes reading his book. Unlike the normal foot soldiers, he didn't leave his post, which is interesting. This guy is weird. I still can't see his level. I'm not sure what to think of him. And the easiest way to handle that sort of stuff is to just not think about it at all. Isn't that clever? Hah!

I return to meditating, but now I feel more aware than ever that I'm being watched. As long as he isn't watching some embarrassing part of me, I guess it's fine. I guess it's—

<Curse.>

My eyes flare open. Hey, what the heck was that for?!

Still pointing at me with his ring finger, the priest shows an expression of deep focus and concentration, but I don't care. If I had anything I could throw at him, I would. Not counting the stuff in my inventory. Or the fresh arrows next to me. This is more of a monkey-throwing-doodoo situation, you know? Not that I would throw that sort of—okay, now I'm just talking myself into a corner. Back to the issue, why did he do that!?

He points at me again.

<Curse.>

And then again.

<Curse.>
<Curse.>
<Curse.>
<Curse.>
<Curse.>
<Curse.>

Dude, what the heck are you doing?!
I can't even feel any effects!

<You have learned: Paralysis Resistance Lv.2>

Okay, so it *is* doing something; it's just too weak for me to notice. Right, gotcha.

For some reason, he keeps cursing me for, like, several minutes, increasing a few of my tolerances and resistances, all the way until the gem of the ring on his finger literally explodes. I stare at him. He grumbles what I think might be some sort of goblin curse before reaching into his little satchel and pulling out a small gem. He holds it up to the light, puts it back into the satchel, pulls out a different one, holds that up as well, and then puts it into the ring. Okay. Exploding rings is just normal here. I sure hope that wasn't his engagement ring or things might get complicated.

I had almost expected him to continue cursing me, but when he instead picks his book back up, I feel strangely upset. My seizure tolerance has almost reached the resistance level!

Well, good enough, I suppose. I return to meditating.

Once the sun goes down, the whole caravan stops, and the goblins set up camp. The priest also goes away to help, leaving me alone.

An hour or so passes and the smell of food begins to waft across the simple plain they decided to set up camp on. Slowly, I inch over to the bars, as close as I can get to them, dragging my chains behind me. Sniff sniff sniff sniff. Mmm. Whatever it is they're making, I can tell that it's activating my great values sniffer, because the smell is going double. It's weird. I wonder, before today, when did I last eat a proper homemade meal? . . .

Sniff sniff sniff sniff sniff sniff sniff sniff . . .

The door to my cage opens and closes behind someone and I leap back to my standard position. I—I wasn't doing anything. Nothing at all. Nuh-uh. Nope. Just . . . normal human prisoner behavior. Yup.

<Chain.>

There it is. Ugh, I really hate the way this feels. My body just completely seizes up. It's less that I can't move and more that all of my muscles flex completely stiff. It's weird, and it's bad.

<You have learned: Immobilization Tolerance Lv.4>

But it is increasing my tolerances, so it isn't all that bad, I guess.

A steaming bowl of something is placed in front of me and I have to physically restrain myself from willingly breaking the chain spell to attack it. The second the priest leaves, I'm attacking. That's what I'm doing. Hehehe. Oh, yes, I'll do it. Hehe. God, I'm so hungry. I didn't know I could get this hungry. It smells so good.

. . . The door hasn't been used again.

Confused, I look up just in time to watch the priest take a seat on the other side of the cage, a few meters away. He places a bowl on the floor of the cage, alongside a spoon.

What in the world is he . . . ?

My confusion must have been more obvious than I thought, because almost as if to prove his intention, he starts eating out of his own bowl with the spoon, taking little sips. And then he takes a piece of bread he brought and breaks off a piece to dip into his soup. It looks really yummy. I drool a little. He notices my gaze, and before I have time to look away, abashed, he breaks off a piece and walks over to me. He holds it out to me.

The chain spell isn't active anymore. I can move. My eye hops between the piece of bread in his green hand and his face. His wrist is right there. Exposed. As fast as I am, I could quickly grab his wrist, claw it up, and then go for the throat while he's too stunned to use any spell. Even if he used chain, I think I could break out of it fast enough to kill him now. He wouldn't even be able to fight back. It would be over in less than ten seconds. He has the key to the cage. I could probably escape. If I take him as a hostage, they might let me go.

My gaze slowly falls from his exposed wrist to the piece of bread in his hand.

I take the piece of bread.

The priest walks back to the other side of the cage, sits down, and continues eating as if nothing had happened.

Gently, I squeeze the bread in my hand. It's soft. Freshly baked. On the other side of the cage, I see him dip his bread into the soup. Slowly, without thinking about much of anything, I mirror his actions, dipping the bread and bringing it to my mouth. Chew chew chew chew chew.

It didn't give me any tolerances or increase any of my resistances. It didn't hurt.

My eyes blur and something warm and wet goes down my cheeks, but I don't care about it. I dip the bread again, and I eat it. Dip, eat, dip, eat, and once the bread runs out, I drink the soup from the bowl. But I don't choke on it, or drown, or anything like that. I drink measured gulps. I taste what I drink, and when the bowl is empty, and I've licked it all clean, I wipe the edges of my mouth with my wrist and put the bowl back down.

Looking up, I find that the priest has finished his meal. How long has he been watching me? Meekly, I look away.

After a few moments of silence, he speaks. I don't know what he's saying, or what it means, or if it's directed to me or to the silence around us, but nonetheless, I listen. I put the words to mind. That's the most I can do.

And when he's finished speaking, he stands up and picks up the bowl from in front of me. His bare neck is mere inches from me, but I don't think anything of it. When he leaves and locks the cage behind him, I don't think anything anymore, either. What's there to think? I feel numb. Number than I ever have.

I'm almost able to respond before the door to the cage suddenly opens again, and the priest returns. He's carrying a bowl of water and a towel and a small bottle of something green. Furrowing my brows, I draw back a little as he steps closer to me. When he then puts his hand on my shoulder, I freeze fully. I can't move. He didn't cast chain on me, but I can't move.

When was the last time someone willingly touched me?

The thought brings me back to reality just in time to watch him put the towel, water, and bottle on the floor. Right as I make to draw away from him, he says a single word, which I assume is urging me to do the opposite. Reluctantly, I stay.

His small hands touch the arrows still stabbed into my back. I twitch a little.

He isn't saying anything, but I understand exactly what he's going to do, and somehow, he seems to know that.

I can't entirely see what he's doing, but I can feel him pouring whatever was in the little green bottle on my back. And then, carefully—more carefully than I ever have—he begins to pull the arrows out, inching them out so slowly I can barely even feel it, with such care that it hardly hurts at all.

\<Cure.\>

I can feel my own warm blood trailing down my back, but I don't mind it. I've got enough blood in me to paint a house.

But if only to help him along, I slowly close my eyes and begin to meditate.

One arrow.

Two arrows.

And then, finally, he pulls out the third. It barely hurt at all. Whenever I remove arrows, I tear them out, gritting through the pain. But this was different. Gentle. Completely different.

I have no idea what to make of any of this. I feel confused, dizzy, and almost nauseous. But none of my tolerances are increasing.

I can't even repay him.

Once the last arrow is out, he dips the towel in water and gently wipes off my back. His mending combined with my meditation has allowed the wounds to mostly heal by now. And it didn't hurt one bit.

After wiping off my back, he gathers his things again and heads for the door to the cage. And before he leaves, he says one final word. "Yat'nett."

He leaves, locking the door behind him. And once he's out of hearing distance, I mumble back, "Thank you."

The next day, early in the morning, the army set out again. This was only after breakfast, which I spent eating with the priest.

I didn't sleep all night. In a sense, though, I did nothing *but* sleep. My brain feels weird inside. I don't think I had a single thought all night, but I also did nothing but think. About nothing. About everything. Inside the cage, I couldn't see the stars, but I could feel the night. Everything was so silent. But not completely. In the middle of the night, amid that great big silence, you could hear a bunch of young guys laugh and snicker among themselves, coming from a little tent. And then one of the commanders, dressed in nothing but a nightgown with a matching cap, marched inside to shout at them. But a few hours later, they were right back to it.

And I just have that information, and I don't know what to do with it.

The priest didn't use chain on me when he gave me a sandwich and something in a bowl that had the same texture as hummus. When he left, I heard someone call him *Simel*. I've heard people call him that before. I think, from now on, I'll call him that, too.

I look up at Simel. Simel looks back at me.

Without anything else to do, without anything else to say, I point at him with my right index finger, and before he can make a show of his confusion, I point it at myself. The arch of his brows goes up. After swallowing what was in his mouth, he opens it to ask something before remembering that it doesn't matter. So instead, he points his index finger at me.

<Chain.>

After a minute or so, the effect wears off. I take a bite of my sandwich to prove it. Then I repeat the pointing thing, but with my right thumb instead.

By this point, he has caught on to the game, and he quickly follows along.

<Crush.>

A weight falls on my shoulders, pressing me into the floorboards. Not hard enough to break any of my bones or the floorboards beneath, but enough to be a real bother if I wanted to move around. It lasts a bit longer than chain, though, so I guess that's the main difference. Still, it gave me a nice tolerance.

<You have learned: Pressure Tolerance Lv.1>
<You have learned: Pressure Tolerance Lv.2>

Excited to check out the next finger, I point my middle finger at him, only realizing once I was already flipping him the bird that it wasn't the nicest gesture to make. Hastily, I hide it. But he didn't seem to mind, so maybe that isn't an aspect of goblin culture? They probably have something, it just isn't the bird, specifically.

Simel, smiling slightly, flips me off.

<Call.>

Huh. For some reason, I really want to approach Simel. Like, physically. I almost get to my feet before realizing that one, I shouldn't be getting closer to him, and two, I don't have any feet. Once that understanding settles into my brain, the spell lifts.

<You have learned: Divinity Tolerance Lv.3>

Now *this* is what I call effective training.

As the whole army starts marching and Simel takes his place in the small cage, we continue the game. In the end, I'm able to recall all ten of his available spells.

Right thumb, Crush.
Right index finger, Chain.
Right middle finger, Call.
Right ring finger, Curse.
Right little finger, Cure.
Left thumb, Cover.
Left index finger, Catch.
Left middle finger, Cold.
Left ring finger, Char.
Left little finger, Crackle.

Weirdly enough, all the spells start with a C. Then again, in the goblin language, they might all be different, and it just translates like this by sheer coincidence. Who knows?

Once I knew all of them, the game shifted a bit. He'd use one of them, and I'd try to guess which one it was by the way it felt and then show it by using the proper finger. If I got it wrong, he'd use it again until I got it.

If it made me feel like my body was filled with icicles, it was probably left middle finger. If it made my brain fill up with static and make my legs spasm, it was probably left little finger. If it felt like a soft blanket of air befell me, it was probably left thumb. And if it felt like nothing at all, it was probably left index finger.

From what I can guess, *catch* does exactly what it sounds like. It locates you. And unlike the others, it doesn't show up as a pop-up message, so I couldn't even cheat if I wanted to. But it still raised my divinity and, weirdly enough, my stealth skills.

All in all, not only did I learn a bunch of new tolerances, I also got a few to the resistance rank. Considering how willing Simel was to play the little game, I'm pretty sure he gained something from it as well.

Once evening arrived again, the army stopped once more and set up camp. The dinner was some sort of soup that—for once—contained meat. It was alright, but I kind of preferred the more vegetable-focused ones. The bread was as good as ever, though. And then night fell.

And for some reason, I feel more relaxed than I have in a long time. Sure, I'm chained and footless, but this isn't all that bad. It could be worse, you know. They give me food, and I'm not really asking for much else. Food, and . . . company.

Company. That's . . . a bit new.

I have no idea what to think. I'm confused and unsure, but it doesn't feel bad. And I guess, right now, that's what's important.

Within what feels like only minutes, dawn arrives. I eat breakfast with Simel, and when we set out, instead of going into his little cage, he stays in the big one, beside me, sitting on the floor. We continue our game. After a while, my tolerances get so high that I don't take any damage anymore, but it still hurts, and through that pain I can tell exactly which one it is. If I wanted to, I could have won every time, but I didn't. On purpose, sometimes several times in a row, I let myself lose, if only because then I get to hear his laughter. If that's the cost of getting zapped several times in a row, then so be it.

After the lunch break, when Simel returns, he brings a small bag of wooden tablets with him. He spreads them out on the floor between us, and then the game begins. I have no idea what the game is. He tries to teach me, but I genuinely can't understand it. One side of the tablets has a picture, the other has a number of dots between one and seven, and somehow, you're supposed to stack the tablets atop each other to make towers. I have no idea what rules govern it, but he laughs whenever I accidentally make a tower topple, so it's okay.

In the evening, the army stops once more to set up camp, but somehow, the atmosphere is different from before. There's excitement in the air, alongside a strange sense of melancholy. Simel doesn't say anything, but for some reason, he seems blue. I wish I could ask about it.

We eat dinner, and evening turns to night.

In the middle of the night, Simel shows up at my cage. Even though I have literally never said a word to him, he hushes me. I feel indignant. Him hushing me made more sound than I have ever made in this cage. I would call this ironic, but it's something else, too. Not sure what, though.

While I'm trying my best not to make a mean face, he sneaks inside. He's holding something between his hands. Going by the way he keeps glancing around like a robber who just snatched a blood diamond, it could be either a very small frog or crack cocaine. I'm leaning toward the former, but Simel doesn't feel like the kind of guy to go and catch a frog, much less come to me about it. I raise a single brow at him. He hushes me again, even though I'm pretty sure facial expressions are mostly soundless. Then again, goblins have really big ears, so they might be able to hear that, but . . . I really hope not.

He sneaks closer to me, thrusting his closed hands in front of my face. *Alright, alright, I see that you've got something. Just show me what it is.*

He meets my eyes, and then he glances around a bit again, just one more check to ensure no one's around, and then he finally opens his hands.

. . . What even is that?

It's like a tiny RED crystal ball. Well, there are actually two of them, but that doesn't change the matter here. It's a tiny glass marble. Sure, it's pretty, but what do you expect me to do with it?

He gives me a large grin, as though he thinks I somehow know what this is. I've said this before, but I really don't know.

Not listening to my internal thoughts, he picks one of the RED marbles from his hands and holds it up to my face. Y—you better not be asking me to *eat* that piece of shaped glass, because even if I would probably survive, it's still not exactly something I make a habit of—

Once again not listening to my very rational thoughts, he literally shoves the RED ball inside my mouth. I'm not kidding. Who even does that? Just shoving balls into people's mouths is . . .

Hang on.

Mm. Mmmm. Mmmmmm!

Hey, this ain't so bad! It's like . . . It's like candy, but not quite as sweet, and . . . I really can't describe the flavor, but it is certainly sweet. It isn't fruity, but it tastes like how I would imagine rubies might taste if they were edible. It's *really* good. Where did he get this?

Noticing my enjoyment, Simel gives a chuckle before popping the other one.

For a few minutes, we just sit in the darkness, slurping candies and enjoying each other's company. Mm. Yum. It's good.

The darkness outside has fallen completely. As is my standard nightly tradition as of three days ago, I scooch as close as I can get to the bars in order to catch the slightest glimpse of the stars outside. I still can't believe how beautiful they are. Not very cool of me to say, but they really are. There's just so many of them. Like a swarm of petrified fireflies. It's nice.

I can feel Simel watching me. I glance back at him, and the expression on his face is just so melancholic that it makes me freeze, no spell needed. He looks down at the floorboards. A lot of them are covered in my blood. He frowns at it. For some reason, I don't like how sad he looks. There's no need to feel sad here, is there?

I don't really have time to think more than that before he approaches me. His face is set in a grim, deeply serious expression. And while I stare at him, almost dumbly so, he pulls out a bundle of keys. My eyes burn onto them, and then I lift my gaze up to his face.

When I look back down at his hands, he begins making a series of gestures. First at me, and my chains, and then outside. And then, he makes a movement, going back in. He's not setting me free or anything; he's just taking me out for some fresh air. I see.

. . . But why?

I wish I could ask him because I certainly can't refuse him either. In the time it's taken me to think this, he's already undone all the chains except for the ones linking my hands together. He takes a soft hold of my chains. Slowly, cautiously, he moves to the door and I follow after him out of confusion than anything else. As we emerge into the night, he points his left thumb at the both of us, and I can feel an invisible cover fall over us, making us partially invisible.

We move away from the tents. And once we're out in the middle of the field, the cover spell leaves us. A western wind rushes across the field, rustling through the nearby trees and combing through my short hair. I look up. The stars really are a sight to behold. Endless, eternal stars. There's so many of them that you'd think the darkness was the exception, not the light. I wonder what these stars are named. Can you even have constellations, when there are as many as this, or do you deal in clusters instead?

I take a deep, measured breath of the night air. It's nice. It's very nice.

For a few minutes, I just look up at the sky, and then when I've had my sip of the great glittery ocean in the sky, we go back to my cage, and he chains me again. Only once I'm once again in chains do I realize how easy it would have been for me to escape.

But the thought goes no further. I don't need to escape. It's easier to get to the king by staying here, so there's no reason for anything drastic.

It was much more enjoyable to just watch the stars, anyway.

[BLACK]

And the next day, around lunchtime, I finally get a glimpse of it.

The Shore City of Acheron.

It is, by all means, massive. From a distance, you can only really see it as a mass of houses. It's obviously not as large as normal cities, but it's certainly big. It could probably contain up to a hundred thousand people if the surface area were covered with modern housing, but as it is, I'd estimate a population of around ten thousand or so. Then again, goblins are smaller than humans, so they could probably fit more in a smaller area. This is all very important information and in dire need of research.

The outer area is covered with farmland and smaller houses, but farther in, the road is met with a pretty substantial wall that covers the inner-city part. It's hard to see, but I think I can spot—just above the wall—a spire or two that might be from a castle. And that castle is absolutely the kind of castle you might rescue a maiden or two from, assuming it was guarded by a dragon.

And that's exactly where this army is heading. Except, first, we take a lunch break. I had assumed we'd just keep going since we're so teasingly close, but nope. One more lunch break.

But, if I didn't hallucinate it, I'm pretty sure I saw a relatively well-dressed goblin ride on ahead toward the city, probably to herald our coming. Or something like that.

After a quick lunch, we head toward the inner city. Along the way, farmers and goblins and every sort of greenie you can imagine has collectively agreed that watching an army and a single human in a cage is the most worthwhile thing you can do with your time. Like a bunch of tourists, they all stand on the side of the road, gawking and pointing. I really want to throw them a sign or two, but not with Simel watching.

Also, currently, Simel is back in his small cage. This is probably to make it clear that he isn't part of the freak show. I get it. Mostly.

The walls surrounding the inner city are pretty high, at least eight meters or so. I really couldn't help but stare at them as we approached. Unfortunately, once we were close enough to make out the details, the roof of the cage kept me from seeing it properly. Bummer. But I still got a good look at the way the huge gates opened to take in the entire army, which was pretty cool.

On the inside, a large crowd several times larger than the army awaited us.

Small goblins, tall goblins, blue goblins, goblins in dresses, goblins in fancy furs, crying goblins, excited goblins, happy goblins, sad goblins, all kinds of goblins were in there, staring at the army parade, and, even worse, at *me*. Did I mention that I'm butt-naked? Because if I didn't, I'll say it again.

But even then, I'm no coward. If they want to see me, then they shall see all of me!

Hm. I didn't notice it before, but at the very front of the parade, the soldiers are carrying coffins. Huh. I wonder why.

Aside from that, the goblin soldiers all seem pretty excited, waving and smiling. I watch them. A few goblins are running up to the soldiers and hugging them so tight you can't tell one from the other. A few of the soldiers are picking up tiny goblings and putting them on their shoulders. Other goblings are just running around the soldiers, weaving between their legs like energetic puppies. I watch those, too.

And they watch me.

Many goblins are pointing at me and murmuring. If I look at some of the younger ones in dresses, they squeal and look away. Even some of the older goblins can't even look me in the eye. They seem utterly disgusted by my form. But not in the normal *Oh, that guy is really ugly lol* way; no, this is something different. It really feels like they've never seen a human before. For some reason, it really makes me want to show them what kind of violence a human is capable of.

But then I remember that Simel is next to me, and the urge goes away. They're just gawkers. It's no different. It doesn't matter. Just take a deep breath, and it'll all be over soon.

The parade moves slowly through the main roads of the city, which I notice— just for the record—are paved with cobblestone. It's well-made too, so my cage isn't as bumpy as it used to be, which is nice. What's less nice is obviously the fact that I'm in the nude, being stared at by thousands of people.

And after about thirty minutes of moving along, we reach what seems to be a large marketplace or something, where all of the soldiers start gathering in formations seemingly by habit alone. They really seem to know this, but I have no idea what's going on. There isn't much I can do as the cage is placed front and center, right in the middle of the marketplace. But as grandiose as this is, I am not the focus.

He is.

On a raised platform overlooking the marketplace, made with WHITE marble, and painted with murals of scenes that seem to be from a storybook, stands a goblin clad in the finest purple and RED robes, with a long leather cape, surrounded on all sides by countless fellow goblins. And on his head sits a crown.

<Goblin (Lv.11) [BOSS]>

That's him, then? The king. The target. That's him.

I rise from where I've been sitting and turn toward him. I can't turn fully, but I can turn enough. I see him, and I can tell that he sees me.

Can I escape from my bindings here and now? Possibly.

If I do, can I get to the platform before I'm recaptured? Maybe.

Once I'm on the platform, can I kill the king before his bodyguards kill me?

<Goblin (Lv.17) [BOSS]>
<Goblin (Lv.18) [BOSS]>
<Goblin (Lv.17) [BOSS]>
<Goblin (Lv.16) [BOSS]>
<Goblin (Lv.15) [BOSS]>
<Goblin (Lv.18) [BOSS]>

. . . Highly unlikely.

But will I ever get this close to him again? I don't know. I technically only need to kill the king, but to completely clear the floor . . .

I glance at Simel.

. . . Maybe only killing the king is enough.

It's not like the reward will be that good anyway. What do I get this time—a wolf pelt? Bad news for you—I've already got that one, so what's the point? Really, there's no point. Except for my stupid gamer ego.

While I silently contemplate the situation, the head commander of our little band steps onto the platform, the other commanders following suit. After briefly bowing to the king, they take positions along the side, alongside the king's guards. Now that I'm looking closer, there's also a well-dressed female goblin, and a few goblings that I assume are the queen and . . . royal spawnlings. I suppose.

Right as I'm starting to wonder what this whole situation is about, the king speaks.

He has a deep and heavy voice. Brassy. The kind you'd expect a leader to have. I have no idea what he's saying, but he's saying it with such charisma and sway that I feel compelled to listen anyway. It's like when you hear a foreign singer. Even though you have no idea what they're singing about, you can tell exactly how they're feeling about it. It's like that, except it's a goblin holding what I think is supposed to be a speech about . . . something? I don't know.

Everyone here looks absolutely enraptured by it, though. I mean, even Simel seems completely spellbound. It should also be noted that even though the king is just talking into the air, his voice still carries across the entire crowd.

I almost wish I could understand it just so that I could make something of it.

But there's one detail here that worries me.

How is this king wicked?

No, seriously. The city is as pristine and beautiful as a medieval city can get. The roads are prim, the soldiers respect him, his family seems to like him, and his subjects appear absolutely spellbound by him. He has an aura to him that just screams *I am a fair and just king.* So why did the clear condition describe him as wicked when he clearly isn't?

I guess there's a possibility that he's secretly evil and has a hidden cult and feeds innocent children to the city rats and his heirs are actually incest babies, but that isn't even important.

It isn't important whether the king is wicked or not. All that matters is that the system told me to kill him. They didn't need to tell me any of that. If the system says that a goblin is the [BOSS] of this floor, then I have to kill him. That's just how it works, and I'm not complaining about it.

But the fact that the system thinks that I'd need some moral reason to do this worries me.

Silently, I wait for the king's speech to end.

. . . Ten minutes pass.

. . . Twenty minutes pass.

. . . We're at the thirty-minute mark, and I'm starting to get a supernatural urge to tear off my own two ears. Sometimes, the crowd will periodically cheer or clap. I have no idea what's happening, but I want this to end.

And I get my wish in the worst way possible.

The king suddenly stops speaking and after a long pause points straight at me and exclaims, in a voice as loud as a thunderclap, **"Hoeksak!"**

And the crowd chants in reply, *"Hoeksak, hoeksak, hoeksak!"*

For some reason, I don't think they're cheering for me, but rather the physical opposite.

And then something hits the back of my head before thumping to the ground and rolling to a stop. Oh, it's a rock. And then another rock flies through the air, striking me in the chest. I don't move to avoid it. Another rock, and another. One rock hits me in the eye and only then does anyone step in as the king with a single word stops the crowd and they fall back into silence.

He speaks again. Whatever words he's speaking are making Simel turn away and frown, so I don't like them. And after he finishes speaking those words, he turns to the head commander and speaks some more. Then he puts his hand on his bald head and everyone in the crowd cheers. I almost want to cheer with them because—why not?—but I contain myself.

And apparently that was the final part of the ceremony, because after that, the cage starts moving again. Specifically, we're moving toward the castle. And it really is worthy of being called a castle. It's huge, and it's surrounded by a moat with a drawbridge, so what more could you ask for? The whole city is situated next to the sea, but the city itself is kind of raised, meaning that although the castle isn't connected to the sea, it has a really good view of it. And this is where my cage is brought.

The drawbridge leads inside the walls of the castle, into a large courtyard. This is apparently the final stop, because finally, after so long, I'm released from the cage, though not without a fair bit of trouble.

<Chain.>

<Bind.>

<Attach.>

I can't move. Two more magician-type people have appeared, both slightly older than Simel, both with what appears to be a profound apathy toward the whole mess. If it had been just Simel, I don't think I'd even need to struggle to break out. With all three, though? I am well and fully restrained. This means that I can't even walk on my own, though, so a bunch of buff goblins are forced to carry me while the three magicians follow closely along as we head inside the castle, down into the very bowels of it, beneath the dungeons, into some dark, empty, dank extra-deep-dungeon-for-the-extra-bad-meanies. And down there, so deep even the torches seem muted, in the only cell that's there, is where they leave me, chaining me to the wall by both of my arms and legs, pinned to it like an insect. It'd be easier to handle if the one who designed the clamps wasn't literally Satan. Who the heck puts barbs on the *inside* of these things?!

So dumb.

And just like that, they leave me. Neat.

. . . Was that it? No, that isn't it, is it? No way.

Hey, come back! You can't just leave me alone down here! Aren't I supposed to have a cellmate so I can turn this dungeon into a fungeon? I mean, what's the point of chaining me up right to the wall if I can't ask someone hanging right beside me *How's it hanging?* This is inhumane!

. . . Yeah, inhumane! So do something about it!

. . .

. . . Hello? Is—is there really nobody there? . . .

It's . . . it's really quite dark down here, huh.

My arms are starting to hurt a bit. You know, because I'm hanging on the wall? Yeah. The fact that the braces themselves have barbs on the inside is a bit bad too, but I've had worse, so, you know . . . I just . . . where did everyone go?

It's dark. I can't see so well when it's dark.

It's . . .

                                                                              dark

and BLACK

                                and dark

I feel myself slip.

Deeper, and deeper, and deeper, and deeper.

    Into the BLACK sea below, below, below, below, below.

        Where everything is night, and BLACK, BLACK, BLACK, BLACK.

When I open my eyes, it's BLACK.

When I close my eyes, it's BLACK.

I can't really tell if I've gone blind, or if that's just how it is now.

If I did, it wouldn't make any difference. The BLACKness is the same.

I hate this.

I hate this.

I hate this.

I hate this.

I hate this.

I hate this.

I need to kill that king.

I need to kill the goblins.

I need to kill the goblings.

I need to kill whatever gives me exp.

That's the only way to get out of here.

Time passes like sludge, giving the illusion that it could move, while actually doing nothing at all.

But the pain reminds me that I exist. The barbs remind me that I'm here, and that I exist, and that I'm not just in my head, and that I can do things, and that I can cause things. Pain. That's it. That's what's keeping me anchored. If I smash my leg against the wall enough, it breaks, and then I feel. If I bash the back of my head into the stone wall behind me, my brain quakes, and then I feel. If I lift my knees and stab them into my own chest just right, I can crack a few of my ribs, and then I feel. That's all I can do. Pain. Yes. That's it. How blind I've been. I'm so glad that there is no pain tolerance. Without pain, I would be dead. I would be lost to the great BLACK sea within me already. I would have sunk to the depths and been dragged deep into the BLACK sludge down there and drowned within all of that. But the pain reminds me that I'm drowning, and that I can feel. That's all I need. It's good. This is a good system. We are well-designed, to be able to feel. If I break my bones just the right way, it takes longer to heal, and I can feel for longer. Bash bash bash bash crack crack smash back crack splash crack splash bash bash smash crash bash crack crack smash smash.

Crack Smash Crack Smash
Smash Smash Crack Crack
Crack Bash Crack Bash
Bash Bash Crack Crack
It is music.

After an eternity and one second, the light returns. It blinds me with its grace, and I cry in its presence.

"Con de ur hoeksak? Ay, ay, ay," a voice says in a weird accent. I've heard enough goblins to be able to tell that this is a weird accent, even for them.

"Ik." I've already heard enough of them to recognize this one. My eyes slowly roll to look at Simel. He won't meet my gaze. I don't avert mine.

I look back at the one with the strange accent. It's relatively tall for a goblin, and slim. Its mane is long and silver. It looks old, and its ears are kind of sagging. No pop-up will show for it. As I look at it, its eyes sharpen. Saying nothing more, it points its left little finger at me.

<Restrain.>

My body seizes up completely. My legs and arms don't move, my eyes don't blink, and I can barely feel my own breath rasp out of my throat. Is my heart still beating?

<You have learned: Immobilization Tolerance Lv.10>
<You have learned: Immobilization Resistance Lv.1>
<You have learned: Immobilization Resistance Lv.2>

And while my body attempts to spasm and fails, the old goblin points his left ring finger at me.

<Rule.>

My body is moving on its own. The clasps on my arms and legs undo them-selves on their own and like an obedient puppet, I hop down and give a small, curt bow. If I weren't completely immobile, I would be trembling with more than just rage.

Completely uncaringly, the old goblin turns his back on me, and after a second of staring at me, Simel follows suit. They walk ahead, and I follow them. There's something wrong with whatever he's done to me because whatever it is that's controlling my body, it is currently completely straightening out my otherwise hunched back, putting me an additional inch or two taller than normal. But I don't care.

Every single inch of my body hurts. All of it.

Several of my bones are still broken, and still, I'm moving like that doesn't matter. The stumps of my legs are getting scratched up and I've started leaving a trail of blood.

It hurts.

We go up the stairs, into the normal dungeons, through there, up farther, through maze-like hallways and rooms, across places I can't understand, and up higher and higher and higher and higher, through a winding staircase that just keeps going around and around, and even though I can feel that I've broken both of my legs, my body keeps moving. If I weren't controlled by magic, I wouldn't even be able to crawl.

Eventually, we reach a room of some sort, filled to the brim with books and bottles and preserved body parts and anatomical showcases. And still, my eyes slide past all that, instead going to the middle of the room, where they fall on a stone bench. It reminds me of the ones you see in autopsy rooms because it's got little grooves carved that lead to a basin by the feet.

I lay myself on top of the stone table and stretch myself out completely willingly, preparing myself for the slaughter like a sheep shearing itself.

The old goblin points at me again.

<Restrain.>

Again. I can't move. I can barely even breathe.

Above me, I can see the old wizard stepping into my view. But Simel still won't meet my gaze.

The old goblin stretches his hand toward him. "Chit-chit." Simel won't look at him either. "Simel!" the old goblin barks, startling Simel out of his thoughts. The old goblin motions with his hand. "Chit-chit. *Nu.*"

Simel gives a choppy nod. With trembling hands, he gives the old goblin a small, sharp knife.

The old goblin snatches it out of his hand before turning onto me. Mumbling to himself, he brings the knife to my abdomen.

I'm frozen in place. But I can feel everything perfectly.

> <You have learned: Evisceration Tolerance Lv.1>
> <You have learned: Evisceration Tolerance Lv.2>
> <You have learned: Evisceration Tolerance Lv.3>
> <You have learned: Evisceration Tolerance Lv.4>
> <You have learned: Evisceration Tolerance Lv.5>

Before this, I didn't really believe in karma. But I think that might be subject to change.

> <You have learned: Bleeding Protection Lv.4>
> <You have learned: Immobilization Resistance Lv.3>
> <You have learned: Evisceration Tolerance Lv.5>
> <You have learned: Unconsciousness Resistance Lv.3>
> <You have learned: Evisceration Tolerance Lv.6>
> <You have learned: Divinity Tolerance Lv.4>
> <You have learned: Evisceration Tolerance Lv.7>
> <You have learned: Evisceration Tolerance Lv.8>

I glance up.

The old goblin is holding my large intestine in his hand and comparing it to one floating in a jar. The one in the jar is slightly smaller. He mumbles something, cuts out my intestine, and puts it in a slightly larger jar.

I think that, by now, I might be too far gone, because when I look at that jar, and when I look at the jar containing my spleen and the jar containing my stomach and the jar containing my appendix and the jar containing my left lung, I don't really feel all that much.

I should, but I don't.

Not even when I look and see Simel and he finally looks into my eye and his face twists in profound pain do I feel much of anything, because there isn't that much to feel anymore. Anything that isn't my nerves screaming at me that I shouldn't be here is too distant and fuzzy to make out. It isn't important.

The numbness is all.

> <You have learned: Evisceration Tolerance Lv.9>
> <You have learned: Evisceration Tolerance Lv.10>
> <You have learned: Evisceration Resistance Lv.1>
> <You have learned: Divinity Tolerance Lv.5>
> <You have learned: Unconsciousness Resistance Lv.4>
> <You have learned: Unconsciousness Resistance Lv.5>
> <You have learned: Blindness Resistance Lv.6>
> <You have learned: Evisceration Resistance Lv.2>

He flips me over. I follow along. He opens my skull and pokes around inside.
Poke. Poke pokeOoe

Poek poel poek. Poke. epopoe

Poke iiiiii poke   ee

Pok eke kkk eeee poke

Pokepokepeoe poeooe peo

Oooooo ooooo ooooo oooooo

Poeoepe pppppppppppppppppp

A piece of what is what might be what should be what ought to be me is put into a little glass cylinder holder thing jar that has liquid liquid liquid liquid in it and also a bit of me that is me which is me there is me I see me I am there there in there I see it me am in there I I I I I me I am I am there I am a little piece of me I am pink and I am swirly and I am squishy and I should not be in the little I am I am I am jar the jar the jar the jar it is me I am the jar but I am in the jar I don't want to be in the jar it looks cold and uncomfortable please stop mommy daddy I don't want to be in the jar please take me back please please please the jar is cold mommy it is so cold I don't want to be in the jar I don't like it please please please please please please please please

plea

aaaaaaaaaaaaaaaaaaaaaaaaaaaaaaaaaaaaaaaaaaaaaaaaaaaaaaaaaaaaaaaaaaaaaaaaaaa

aaaa

It is not good.

It is not good. It is not good.

\<You have learned: Brain Damage Tolerance Lv.4\>
\<You have learned: Brain Damage Tolerance Lv.6\>
\<You have learned: Brain Damage Tolerance Lv.7\>
\<You have learned: Brain Damage Tolerance Lv.10\>
\<You have learned: Brain Damage Tolerance Lv.2\>
\<You have learned: Brain Damage Tolerance Lv.9\>
\<You have learned: Brain Damage Tolerance Lv.5\>
\<You have learned: Brain Damage Tolerance Lv.1\>
\<You have learned: Brain Damage Tolerance Lv.3\>
\<You have learned: Brain Damage Tolerance Lv.8\>
\<You have learned: Brain Damage Resistance Lv.1\>

I don't like the dark, mommy
Can you leave the door open
And the light in the corridor on
So I know you're still there
Even if the monsters come

Simel

I wake up. I'm back in the darkness of the dungeon.

The clock screen hangs in front of me. Like it's always been there.

<Top—Status—Community>
<02:20:12 Day 85>
<The fourth attempt will begin in 5:21:39:48>

I don't know how long I've been on this floor, or how long I've been in the capture of these creatures, or how long I've been in this darkness. I can't remember. My brain feels fluffy. Flurry. *Fuzzy.*

I . . . I need to get out of here. If I stay here anymore, I don't know what will be left of me anymore. I don't think there will be anything at all.

King. I need to king the kill. Kill the king. He . . . if I just kill him, then I'll be out of here. That's all I need to do. It's so simple, and easy. That's all I need to do. It's so simple, and easy. Kill the king. He's kind of old anyway. Who cares.

I just need to get out of here first.

I begin by breaking every bone in both of my hands. Once I pull them out of the barbed shackles, they look more like shredded meat than shredded meat human hand meat. I look at the bars of my cell. In order to get through, I need to break my pelvis, rib cage, and skull. The rest will get through easily. I bash my pelvis against the bars until it's in pieces small enough to get through. Then I just squeeze my rib cage through. Crunch crunch crunch crunch crunch went a few of my ribs but that's okay. Then my skull gets stuck but that's okay. I just bonk my head against either side of the bars like the metal donger inside of a metal bell that goes *dong dong dong dong* and my head is the donger that goes dong and the bell are the bars and after *dong*

*dong dong dong dong*ing enough the plates that make up my skull shift and my skull slips through and I'm free.

<You have learned:
Brain Damage Resistance Lv.2>
<You have learned: Fracture Resistance Lv.3>
<You have learned: Brain Damage Resistance Lv.3>
<You have learned: Fracture Resistance Lv.4>
<You have learned: Fracture Resistance Lv.5>

Once I'm out I lie down and pull myself into a ball that resembles what a fetus inside the belly of its mother might look like.

My body slowly heals in the darkness. Once my brain is in the right way and place again, I start to move. I've thought of something. You don't have to lie down to be in the fetal position. You just need to be balled up. So, if I just crouch down, and pull my knees to my chest, then it works, even if I'm not lying down, in a ball, like a fetus, then I can still not be seen. Then I can roll like samus metroid man and get through the castle. Roll roll roll roll roll roll roll roll roll roll roll roll.

Roll past the guards and the knights and the magicians and the royals and out into the outside and the darkness but the bridge is up so I crawl up to the top of the fort and jump cannonball into the waters below and then I swim to shore and go up onto land.

Okay. How do I best completely clear the stage?

I think for this floor, the entire city is considered part of the stage. I just need to defeat all the goblins in the city. Easy. What's the easiest, quickest way to do that?

I'm going to assume that the floor will be considered fully cleared so long as there is no one here when I clear it, which means that goblins who flee will be counted as defeated. If this isn't the case, then it's honestly unfair to expect me to defeat all these goblins with anything less than an organized nuclear strike. But since I don't have access to that, biochemical warfare will have to do.

I have only a little over five days to do this. It isn't much, but it will have to be enough.

My first step is to fill every single freshwater reservoir with corpses. That way, disease will be spread like the plague at Ratlickers Anonymous. It could really be any old corpse, but I think I'll make new ones just for this purpose, since I do need to grind my level a bit. Hm. Oh, wait, that said, I *do* have some rancid meat in my inventory! Man, I'd almost forgotten about that one. I forgot to pick up the meat from the goblins I'd killed in the forest for a couple of days, so when I got there it was already half-rotten and bloated, but I still harvested them because it might be good tolerance training. If I hadn't cleared the forest of animals so fast, they might have gotten to them first.

Anyway, since I already have enough corpses to pollute the biggest water sources, I might as well get to it.

My problem is the way I look. The goblins don't see me as one of their own, but that can be changed.

It's late at night, but that doesn't mean the streets are empty. It's just that there are fewer roaming goblins, and that the ones that are there are weakened by being inebriated.

Merging with the shadows, I watch these drunkards tumble here and there. After a while, I notice a goblin close enough to my own height, if a foot or so shorter. As soon as he leaves the safety of the light, I ambush him and drag him into an alley where I disassemble him fully with only my fingers. New world record! The extra sharp claws are way more useful than I had expected. Nice!

With a new hide in hand, I dress up and set out. My first order of business is to get my disguise level high enough to make it viable.

Wearing the hide, I wander around the streets in areas that are visible enough to get me noticed by the goblins, but not to the point where they can see exactly what I am. And, like a charm . . .

<You have learned: Disguise Lv.2>
<You have learned: Disguise Lv.3>
<You have learned: Disguise Lv.4>

At around six in the morning, I finally reach the fated level.

<You have learned: Disguise Lv.10>
<You have learned: Impersonate Lv.1>

Perfect. I have no idea what that does differently, but it will be good enough. During my walk, I was able to find a couple of public-use wells, into which I quickly dumped all the rotted meat I have. Since this was so early in the morning, by the time the sun went up, almost every single well in the city was completely unusable.

Part of my goal is to just scare the goblins out of the city, so I obviously also took the time to violently eviscerate a couple of nighttime goblins and strew what I got from them here and there. Since my last wish is to be discovered, once the morning arrived, I made my hideout by breaking into some random house along one of the streets, defeated the goblins inside, and just used that as a hideout. There were a few goblings too, and their meat was just as soft as I remembered.

At noon, I got bored of being inside, so I snuck out while wearing my disguise. I kept to the back streets. A few goblins still spotted me, but it was worth it to see the horror and confusion taking hold of the mobs.

To make sure my day wasn't wasted, I spent my time quietly emptying each goblin house one by one without alerting anyone. I even took the time to break into a few taverns to place spoiled meat into their larger barrels of beer. I have no idea if that will do anything, but I certainly hope it will.

And then night fell again. Apparently, during the day, some goblins had illogically banded together to help clean out the wells, but they're easy to poison again. I was able to save up a lot of goblin innards by taking them out so effectively, so I just filled the wells to the brim with organs, if only to prove a point. And since I still had quite a lot left, I just threw it here and there just about everywhere. And then to make the situation just a little spookier, I made sure to defeat every goblin I encountered. And to make sure that they knew it was the same person, I disassembled each goblin I defeated while still leaving what I got out for everyone to find.

By the time morning arrived, the inner city was a bloodbath. Screams could be heard, but I didn't really care. No sleep for the wicked, as they say. Not that I'm wicked or anything.

And now, finally, I'm starting to get pop-ups about goblins dying from the poisoning of the wells. But it isn't enough. Only a few hundred are dying, and the experience I get from it is greatly diminished.

I need to do something drastic.

The following night, it seems the king finally got the memo. Not only are the regular goblins not roaming the streets, but instead, it's filled with armed guards. It would be a mistake to attack them, so I just hop from house to house, defeating all the goblins and leaving their bodies unbutchered to rot. The city is starting to stink badly, but I can still smell the goblins above it. I've been able to do away with maybe a tenth of the complete population, mostly through the water. But it isn't enough.

Another day, another night, and right as I'm about to consider changing my strategy . . .

<**Top—Status—Community**>
<**00:00:01 Day 89**>
<**The fourth attempt will begin in 1:23:59:59**>
<**The Server Symposium will begin in 23:59:59.**>

I no longer have time.

In only a single day, I will be forcefully summoned to the server symposium. I won't have a choice. I can't afford to assume I'll be able to choose not to attend, so I need to stick to this until the null hypothesis is proven.

I was careless. The city is still riddled with goblins. I had hoped that it wouldn't come to this, but I don't think I have a choice anymore.

I'll need to set this entire city on fire. That's the only way to do this. I don't know if it will get rid of all the goblins, but it will certainly make most of them flee. Besides, it's the only option I have left.

Since my final goal is the castle, I'll start the fire on the edges of the city. That way, I can keep lighting it as I go along. Effective.

I get to it.

By procuring a torch from the fireplace of a tavern, I start putting a few abandoned houses on fire. They're mostly made of wood, and a lot of them have thatched roofing, so they were basically designed to burn. The smell of smoke and barbecue was pleasant. Of course, I'm doing all of this wearing my goblin disguise. Any time a goblin spots me I quickly defeat it, basking only a second in the funny face it makes. After a while, the fire has begun spreading on its own, so there isn't much that I have to do to keep it going. Lots of running goblins all around. At the start a lot of them headed out of the inner-city gates but now the entire inside of the walls are covered with flames so there's no escape. The wind carries with it only smoke and charred flesh.

As I run right alongside the goblins, I make sure to personally kill as many as I can to make sure to increase my level. I'm at level 17 now. Since most goblins are only between level 5 and 9, there's no problem defeating them.

<Goblin (Lv.5) Defeated.>
<Gobling (Lv.1) Defeated.>
<Goblin (Lv.7) Defeated.>
<Goblin (Lv.6) Defeated.>
<Goblin (Lv.6) Defeated.>
<Gobling (Lv.1) Defeated.>
<Goblin (Lv.8) Defeated.>
<Goblin (Lv.5) Defeated.>
<Goblin (Lv.6) Defeated.>
< . . . >

I'm getting so many messages that I can't do anything other than ignore them. It isn't important.

The castle is getting close now. I had assumed that I would need to do some parkour or whatever to get inside, but instead, the drawbridge is actually down, letting the fleeing goblins escape inside the fort. Interesting choice, but hardly a good one in this situation. Because, see, all I need to do is wait for the king or whoever's in charge to eventually decide to pull the drawbridge back up to protect those already in here, and then I can just go ham.

It didn't even take as long as I had suspected before the fort was closed off. That leaves me in here with a whole lot of bags of exp.

Better get right to it, then!

Moving like a whirlwind, I make my way through the crowd, eviscerating every throat I can get hold of, tearing up whatever bowel I can reach, leaving those dying to do so in their own time and moving on to the next without waiting even a single second. It doesn't take long for the soldiers inside the fort to notice what's going on, but the crowd itself is way less perceptive. A general wave of terror goes through the entire collective, making the swarm flee with such energy that those too small or weak to flee with them get crushed underfoot. I didn't defeat them personally, but they're still defeated, nonetheless.

The soldiers try to calm the crowd, but it's become a stampede. The only way the soldiers can protect themselves is to fight back with force. The only other option is to lie down and die in return for not having to kill those they swore to protect. All and all, it works out very well for me, because even those that escape still end up defeated somehow. I think I can even spot a few jumping into the moat, which isn't very survivable when there's nowhere to climb to shore.

Soon enough, the courtyard is becoming far less crowded, though the ground is certainly more so than ever.

And as if on cue, a certain head commander rushes out into the fray, the face part of his helmet raised.

He looks at the bodies first, and then at me. Nice expression! Wish I could take pictures here, because this one would absolutely be worth having. My feet still haven't grown back. Moleman never did answer my PM.

Moleman . . . !

Fueled by several different kinds of emotions, I fly toward the head commander.

He raises his sword and I leap at him and stab myself onto it, which surprises him enough to get at his head and neck, but before I have time to tear off his helmet, another sword descends upon me, though I leap out of the way just in time. Another one of the commanders. But they're all only around level 11 or 12. It doesn't matter. Sheer force is enough to take them out.

I drop into a crouch that is compressed enough to register as a fetal position. The two commanders begin to frantically look around, and the second one of them looks the wrong way, and I leap at them from below, slicing their neck in two before they have time to react. The other one—the head commander—is too shocked by the sudden death of his comrade to react when I defeat him in the exact same way.

Leaving them behind, I hastily pick off the remaining goblins roaming the courtyard, and then I head inside the castle itself.

With the narrow hallways of the castle interior, it's easy for me to sniff out and defeat every single goblin in one-on-one combat. For some reason, I can't smell the old goblin wizard, but I'm not looking for him, either. I don't think I could beat him. He's too far beyond me. And going by what my instincts are saying, I don't think I need to kill him, either. He isn't part of the stage, so to speak.

But the king and his guards are. I know they are. I can smell them. They're the only ones left. The city only smells of smoke and cinders and the rest of the castle is nothing but blood.

I can tell where they are. I wasn't there, but going simply by the smells present, I can guess that it's nothing less than the throne room.

Since I won't need it anymore, I change out of my goblin disguise and into my leopard one. If I'm going to be instantly summoned to the Server Symposium, I want to wear something proper.

And then, once I arrive, without a single shred of fear, I burst inside.

<Goblin (Lv.11) [BOSS]>

The king is sitting atop his throne, wearing his crown. The rest of his clothing is a lot less formal than what he wore the last time I saw him. Somehow, he looks several years older than the last time.

<Goblin (Lv.16) [BOSS]>
<Goblin (Lv.15) [BOSS]>
<Goblin (Lv.18) [BOSS]>

And then there's the six bodygua— Hang on, where's the other three? It couldn't be that they died from the poisoned drinking water, right? Nah, that'd be . . . But I also can't smell the other three, so I guess these really are the only ones left. Huh.

Oh, and then there's also the queen and his three spawnlings.

<Goblin (Lv.5)>
<Gobling (Lv.1)>
<Gobling (Lv.2)>
<Gobling (Lv.1)>

Can't forget those four. If I miss them, I'm screwed. "Hoeksak—"

The king starts saying something, but that pause is all I need and more, and in the single second that he took to say it, I've already bounded across the hall and stabbed my entire hand into the supple throat of the level 15, and without a single pause in movement, I swirl around to aim for the level 16. But they have a moment to react, though not enough to foresee my crouch into the fetal position before rolling around to his back and leaping up, slashing his neck from behind.

<You have learned: Sharp Claw Lv.2>
<Goblin (Lv.16) [BOSS] Defeated.>
<Goblin (Lv.15) [BOSS] Defeated.>

The third and last one readies his sword. He's only a level higher than me. Negligible.

He's the only remaining fighter, so there's no need to fear wounds. Throwing caution to the winds, I leap at him and do the ol' shish kebab maneuver, which predictably enough stuns him good enough for me to slip my fingers into the gaps beneath his helmet to tear out his arteries.

The exposed vessel bleeds thumping sprays of blood for a few seconds before he, too, falls.

<Goblin (Lv.18) [BOSS] Defeated.>

And now, there's only a few left. Man, I've gotten effective, huh?

On the verge of humming, I do away with the king's remaining vassals. When I then take one final breath, the only smell that remains is that of the king, and blood. I turn to him. His eyes are so wide. I didn't know eyes could go that wide, but here we are. Hm, I wonder how I should do this best? There are still a few hours until the symposium, so there's no need for me to kill him straight away. If I instead use him as a punching bag of sorts to test out my skills, maybe even increase the level of TRT, I could spend these hours productively.

At least, that's what I think.

Well, no need to dilly-dally. Let's get right to it! I take a step toward the king.

<Chain.>

. . . Hm?

I look back toward the entrance.

<Chain broken.>

There's a goblin there. It's pointing at me. Did nobody teach it that it's rude to point?

I take a step toward it.

<Chain.>

Another step.

<Chain broken.>

Another.

<Chain.>

One more.

<Chain broken.>

Now I'm standing right in front of it. It's very small, almost more so than most goblins. It points up at me, but its hand trembles.

<Chain.>
<Chain.>
<Chain.>
<Chain.>
<Chain.>
<Chain.>
<Chain.>
<Chain.>

I grab its wrist.

<Chain broken.>

I can feel the bones creak inside my grip. But it's weird, because I can't smell it, and no pop-up is appearing above its head, so I can't tell what level it is, which in turn means I won't know if it will give me a nice amount of exp. How weird. It's very strange.

It points at me with the fingers of its left hand.

<Cold.>
<Cold.>
<Char.>
<Cold.>
<Crackle.>
<Cold.>
<Char.>

<Char.>
<Char.>

The gemstones adorning the rings on its left hand all explode into dust. Weird. It's a lot of weird stuff.

I toss the goblin to the side, feeling the way its wrist breaks as I do.

In that case, I might as well do away with the king right now. This all feels too strange. I turn to the king.

Appearing in front of him, I lay my hands around his neck and squeeze. His face slowly turns darker and darker, and then he stops moving, and then it's done. I can't smell him anymore. I can't smell anything in the city. Nothing at all.

<You have learned: Choke Lv.6>
<Goblin (Lv.11) [BOSS] Defeated.>
<[Level Up]>
<You have reached Level 18.>
<Agility has increased by 3.
Strength has increased by 3.
Stamina has increased by 2.
Magic Power has increased by 1.
Disassemble has increased by 1.
Choke has increased by 1.
Eviscerate has increased by 1.
Stealth has increased by 1.
Sharp Claw has increased by 1.
Clutch has increased by 2.
Brain Damage Resistance has increased by 2.
Coma Resistance has increased by 1.>

Ahh, sweet status screens.

<You have cleared the third floor.>
<You have received 1,000 points for clearing the floor.
You have received an additional 1,000 points for being the first to clear the floor.>
<For clearing the stage completely, you will receive an additional reward.>
<There is a God that sees you. You have received 500 points.>
<2 Gods have shown a positive response to you. You have obtained 2,000 points.>
<18 Gods have shown a negative response to you. 18,000 points have been deducted.>

<A CHANGE HAS BEEN MADE.>

<THE GODS WISH TO GRANT YOU A SPECIAL SKILL INSTEAD OF THE NORMAL STAGE
REWARD.>
<WILL YOU ACCEPT?>
<YES/NO>

So far, there's only been one correct answer to that one. Obviously, I'll have
to go ahead and accept it.

"Yes." I poke the Yes button.

<THE GODS HAVE MADE A VOTE. 19 TO 1 IN FAVOR OF GRANTING THE SKILL.>
<THE SKILL WILL BE GIVEN.>

<YOU HAVE LEARNED: [ALL-TONGUE (LV.MAX)]>

. . . An all-what now—

"Y—you really are a monster!"

I freeze in place. It's like my veins are filled with lead. Slowly, shakingly, I
turn around.

Simel is crying.

"I thought—I knew it was stupid, but I thought, maybe—just maybe, I don't
know, you were what you were *made to be*! But I was *wrong*!"

I stare at him. But I'm also staring at the screen in front of me.

<THE GODS HAVE MADE A VOTE.
18 TO 2 IN FAVOR OF EXTENDING TIME SPENT ON FLOOR 3 OF THE HELL
DIFFICULTY.>
<TIME REMAINING:
00:04:58>
<[ENJOY YOUR TIME!]>

What . . . is this? . . .

This isn't right. This isn't how it's supposed to be. The stage ends when I beat
the boss; it doesn't just keep on goi—

"I—I even protected you, you know? They wanted to execute you right away,
put you on display like a freak animal, to show off this weird pale stub-eared
tallthing, but I told them not to. I said . . . I said, '*No, there's more than that in
there.*' I tried to explain, I went and I even said, '*If it wanted to kill me, it already
would've.*' But now I know better. *You've* taught me better. Right, monster? You

didn't kill me not because you didn't want to, but because you wanted to savor the kill once it really mattered." Every word he speaks drips with venom.

The regal carpet beneath my feet sways.

That isn't true. I didn't kill you because it wouldn't have been right. I couldn't kill you because . . .

"I don't even know what manner of creature you're supposed to be, but I was a fool to think you sapient just because you had two legs and a face." My heart sinks through my chest and through the floor and into the core of the world. "You're a beast. That's all you are, and that's all you ever were. I knew you couldn't understand me—your feeble brain was too simple—but I thought I could at least teach you a little. And yet . . . *And yet . . . !*"

My legs move beneath me. The world I walk on shifts and sways with every step I take, making me stumble drunkenly, my brain a feverish, fuzzy nightmare, everything whirling and burning and turning like a summer tornado.

I'm standing close to him now again. It feels weird to look down at him. I shouldn't be looking down at him. It's wrong.

The perspective is wrong.

"If I had known that this is what you were going to do, what you—were going to *become*, I would have told Percht to kill you right there and then. That's all you deserve. Being put out of your *misery*."

<TIME REMAINING:
00:00:13>

I squat down in front of him until we're at the same exact height and our eyes are level with each other and then I give the biggest grin I can muster and I grab his shoulder with one hand and then I point to myself with the other, and I say, with a voice so drunk on joy it slurs, "Lo Fennrick," and then I put my clawed and bloodied hand on his chest and say, "Simel," and then, finally, I put both of my thin spindly arms around him and I pull him into a tight embrace that puts us so close we might as well be one, and breathily, like a bird taking to song for the first time, I cry, "*Friends!*"

<TIME REMAINING:
00:00:00>

FLOOR 4

THE BLIND PIT

Moleman

The floor shifts out from under me and all of a sudden, he isn't in my arms anymore. I'm in the lobby, and everything is WHITE, but for some reason, it doesn't feel as bad as it did the last time. All things considered, I feel weirdly energetic. Rejuvenated, you might say. Invigorated. Like I could run a short marathon. On that note, my feet are back! Hooray!

That floor went pretty well, all things considered. I mean, sure, it had its ups and downs, but my level went up and I even made a friend! My very first friend.

Mmhh. Hm. I really hope that the floor being cleared didn't make his mind get wiped, or just destroy him completely. That would be bad. Not a good way to lose my first friend, I'd say.

That said, I didn't get my complete-clear reward, so it should pop up anytime no—

<To repay your debt, the additional reward has been traded for 5,000 points.>

. . . Hm? H—hey, hang on, what's that supposed to mean? Debt? What the heck are you talking about?

I'm not in debt to anyone; that loan was in bad faith, so—

Hang on. H—hang on just a minute. I think, maybe, that I might remember, uh, a certain message about a few gods reacting in a maybe-not-so-positive way. Um. D—don't tell me that you wanted revenge on me or something? . . . That said, what even *is* a point? From what I've understood, a point is just a made-up little thing with no real-world equivalent. It isn't paper or metal, so it has no intrinsic value.

So how can I be indebted when the currency itself doesn't work? I demand to speak to my lawyer!

Ah, then again, if he couldn't get me off the hook for those bogus second-degree attempted murder charges, he might not be too useful in this situation . . . Besides, what use do the gods even have for points? This is horsecrap!

But as is the usual, no god has the balls to answer me. Standard. They all hate me eighteen to two, anyway.

Eighteen to two . . .

Hey, which of you three reacted *negatively* to my amazing all-clear 100% no-feet complete run of the third floor?!

<THE GOD OF CRUELTY CHUCKLES.>
<THE GODDESS OF WANT SMILES.>
<THE GOD OF COWARDICE PRETENDS NOT TO HEAR ANYTHING.>

You old coward geezer . . . ! This is all your fault, damn it!

Ahhh, my points! . . . My yummy, yummy points . . .

Trying not to cry, I open my inventory. The only way to decide how to act in the future is to know how much debt I'm actually i—

It's empty. M—my inventory, it's empty! Well, not completely, I still have all my pelts for some reason, but everything else is gone! My goblin ears, my goblin organs, my goblin-gut ropes, my weapons, everything . . . !

<To repay your debt, your inventory has been sold for 2,327 points.>
<Current debt: 3,673 points.>

M—my inventory . . .

At least my pelts were spared. But, why? . . .

<THE GODDESS OF WANT EXPLAINS THAT ALL DEBTS, IF THEY ARE TO BE REPAID, MUST BE REPAID IN STYLE.>

I think this might be the first time I've even felt the slightest urge to thank Want. I'm not going to, but just the fact that I can feel the urge makes me want to vomit. If her sense of fashion is what I'm wearing, then I hope I never have to see her with my own mortal eyes. Oh, assuming this isn't the kind of setting where seeing a god makes your eyes melt and you go insane. But if that were the situation, then just hearing their voices would also do the same, so I think I should be okay.

But seriously. My inventory is empty. I have nothing. I can't buy anything, either.

The WHITE is starting to get on my nerves.

<Top—Status—Community>
<20:05:22 Day 89>
<The fourth attempt will begin in 1:03:55:38>H
<The Server Symposium
will begin in 3:55:38.>

Right. Plenty of time.

Before I do anything else, I paint the lobby the appropriate color. Ah, there we go—a pleasant RED.

<The Server Symposium will begin in 1:32:10.>

Lookin' good. In that case, I think I should check—

<You have received a message.>

. . . Hm? From who?

Curious, I open it.

<SuperMoleman[F24]: Hey, sorry, I only just now saw your message. Floor 23 took longer to beat than expected.

But, to answer your question: yes, limbs do grow back in the lobby. Even limbs you lost before the tutorial grow back; however, these limbs, although technically functional, often don't move as one would want. If you lost the limb long before you were invited, even when you get it back, you often can't make it move at all. So it's easier to just tie it behind your back and to not think about it too much.

What did you lose? Ears and fingers can usually be healed with a strong potion, but anything larger will need a special potion.>

Oh, him. I already got my answer, but I can't really buy potions anymore, so . . . Yeah. I mean, frankly, even if I had enough points to buy those overpriced energy drinks, I still wouldn't do it. You can't increase skill levels from a closed wound.

I start typing.

<PrissyKittyPrincess[F4]: goblinstook ma feet bt they grew back in lobby so its kk bt can u grow thm back wit like a skill or watver>

And, after a few minutes . . .

<SuperMoleman[F24]: I haven't encountered or heard of any skills that can grow back entire limbs, but I think there are some spells capable of doing something similar. Goblins cut off your feet? Did you get captured by them?>
<PrissyKittyPrincess[F4]: ya bt its not important k bye>

And I'm just about to close the Community tab again when yet another message drops in.

<SuperMoleman[F24]: Always glad to be of help, see you at the symposium!>

And even though there's no real reason for me to give any response, I still do.

<PrissyKittyPrincess[F4]: k im still gona beat ur *** tho>
<SuperMoleman[F24]: Haha, yeah, I bet you will. Good luck!>

Grumbling, I close the window. I hate his type. You just can't win. Even if they get insulted and even if they lose, they still find some way to be all happy and smiling about it. Ugh. Makes me nauseous.

Hm. Now that I think about it, I almost completely forgot about that skill I supposedly received as what I assume is a punishment. What was it called—something about *tongue*?

Opening my stats, I look around. Oh, here it is!

<[All-Tongue [Lv.MAX)]
Granted by a collective vote among the Gods.>
<The user is capable of understanding all languages spoken or written by goblin- and humankind. Likewise, all goblins and humans can understand the user's words.>
<[SOVEREIGN SKILL]>

Interesting. I have no idea if this is useful or not, but . . . Yeah.

That said, I've still got about an hour left until the symposium opens, so I might as well do something useful with the time. I hate the idea, but I think the best thing to do here is to go jogging.

And that's exactly what I do. For about half an hour I use sprint, never taking a break even as my bones break and begin to crumble, because even though it hurts, after only a few seconds, it all heals anyway. Within only half an hour of this, the sprint skill finally evolves.

\<You have learned: Sprint Lv.10\>
\<You have learned: Hurry Lv.1\>

Alright. From what I can understand, hurry is the same as sprint, except it works for every action you do. Walk, reach for things, hit things . . . anything except other skills and—*I think*—natural regeneration. It also doesn't work on my brain, which is probably good, because battle focus and field focus have already sped it up to what I think is the max. If it does things with any more focus than this, I'll probably have a seizure and die for real.

Still, just because hurry is an active skill doesn't mean I can't use it constantly. It just means that instead of only my legs breaking all the time, now my arms and ribs and everything else breaks, too. Useful!

And right as I've gotten used to my body moving in a choppy, almost animatronic-like fashion, it happens.

\<The Server Symposium will begin in 0:00:00.\>
\<The Server Symposium has begun. You will be automatically summoned in 00:10.\>

In other words, I don't even have to press a button to go there. Sweet.

Patiently, I wait until the timer goes down, and then the world shifts around me.

I stumble a little as my feet leave the familiar half-dried floor of the lobby and instead touch down on harsh, sandy rock. When I look up, I find myself inside what seems to be a room in a castle. Not any room from the castle I was in a few hours ago, mind you, just a standard medieval-castle-looking thing. The room itself is small, and all it contains is me, a large wooden table with two matching chairs, a single woven rug beneath said table, and . . .

She meets my eyes.

A girl.

. . . A woman? I can't tell if she's younger or older than me, but she is almost certainly a girl. As is customary, she has a short buzz cut, which looks as awful as it does on anyone. However, since it's grown out slightly, I can assume she didn't arrive at the tutorial just now. Clothingwise, she's wearing a tracksuit, but not one you can buy from a shop. She looks pale.

Her eyes widen at the sight of me, and her entire body jerks. I can't tell if she wants to approach or run away from me.

"Ah, uh, uhm . . ." she stammers, her voice wavering with each syllable.

I stare back at her. What do you even say in this situation? *Hi? Hello? What's up?* No, it feels wrong. Come to think of it, I haven't really talked to another human being in, uh . . . three, four months? What's the first thing you say?

Usually, you introduce yourself, and then you try to find common ground and similar interests, and you work your way from there. Yeah. I read that in a guide for making friends once. It never really helped, but maybe this will be different?

I take a step toward her and hold out my hand. "He—"

Hey eyes dart down to my hand, widen at the sight of what is mostly my own blood, and then she screams. "*AAAAAAHHH!!*"

H—hey, hang on, this isn't what it looks like! Most of it is just my own, so there's no need to—

Without giving me any time to say anything else, she practically flies out the door. Huh.

That was rude, wasn't? It's not just me who thinks running away when someone reaches out for a handshake is rude, right? Yeah, I thought so. Did nobody teach her any manners?

Though, since the room is now empty of anything of interest, I make to leave, though not before checking if I can put the chairs into my inventory. Spoiler, I couldn't. So, I leave the room, exiting into a narrow hallway. Just to orient myself properly, I try to take a look at how the door to the room compares to the hallway. What I find is a little different, though. Above the doorframe of the room I just left, a single sign hangs.

<Hell Lobby>

. . . Hell lobby? Hang on, don't tell me . . . ?

That girl was the one who stayed behind in the first lobby?!

Man. For someone so clever, she sure is rude. Then again, maybe this just confirms ye olde stereotype about how smart people are socially incompetent. Possibly. Who knows, really? That said, I should probably try to find her. I'm not sure if I've mentioned it before, but her presence kind of changes the whole game. If she can tell the challengers of the fourth attempt about what the first floor entails, then there may be some people who can beat it with fewer casualties than I did. Or so I hope. If nothing else, she can just tell them not to even try it. Then again, we're dealing with people who willingly chose the highest difficulty, so they may very well be too arrogant to follow her clever advice.

Either way, there is only one thing I must do.

I've got a girl to catch.

Sniff sniff sniff. Okay, she went *that* way. Down the stairs, and from there on . . . Alright, yeah, I know where to go. I'm not in too great of a hurry since I've got twenty-four whole hours to hammer this information into her, but the sooner I start, the better.

I start running down the stairs. Hurry doesn't make me all that much faster than sprint when it comes to running, but it's still useful. While running down the stairs, I happen to pass quite a few people, most of whom react quite rudely at seeing me. Sure, I'm not the prettiest face in the tutorial, and I'm not exactly wearing Armani, and I haven't washed myself in a couple of months, but that doesn't justify their screaming like schoolgirls in a blender.

Running like this, I eventually make a fun discovery. See, running on two legs is good, sure, but if I run on all fours, I can use my arms too. That means I can use hurry on both my arms and legs, increasing my fracture tolerances twofold while keeping approximately the same speed. Not to mention the aerodynamics, though I'm not quite fast enough for that to matter yet.

Running like a beast, I leap through the hallways, climbing onto the walls to avoid crashing into people who all react in pretty much the same way, and after just a few minutes of running, I finally find her.

I leap out of the main gate to the castle, out onto a green grassy field that stretches seemingly endlessly before conjoining with the bright blue sky above, and right out there, among a small crowd of people, in the arms of some guy wearing what seems to be really expensive armor, she stands. They both notice me at almost the exact same moment I appear into the air. Mm. The grass feels nice.

I stand up properly. Now, I just need to—

"Beast!" he shouts, pointing a sword he wasn't holding a second ago right at me. "Are you the enemy we must conquer in this castle? How dare you assault this poor girl!"

. . . Okay, those two sentences are completely unrelated. How do you even expect me to respond to that?

As my mind whirls, looking for a proper response, the crowd slowly turns to us and the pressure to say something increases tenfold. Sweat runs down my back. Gulp.

I take a deep breath. "Okay, um, first of all, no, and, second of all, I didn't do anything to her because I was just, like, trying to shake her hand, and she ran away, which I think is very rude, because I was just trying to greet her and say hello, because we're both the only challengers for the Hell Difficulty, so it's important for me to talk to her because she's very important right now, and her running away was actually very rude, so I'm not trying to be accusatory or anything, but it was almost kind of mean, and if it had been someone else they could have had their feelings hurt, and that would be bad, because I think we should have, like, a good relationship, since we're kind of like coworkers right now, right?"

A thick silence falls over the crowd.

Did I say something wrong?

The guy holding her makes a strange face. "You're from the Hell Difficulty?"

I nod at him.

"What floor are you on?"

That's a very private question, but there's no reason not to answer it if it helps defuse the situation. "I just beat floor three and it was super hard."

The guy's eyes narrow. "Give me a second." Without really knowing what else to do, I watch as he brings up the Community tab, reads a post, and then turns back to me. "So, you're—pfft—PrissyKittyPrincess?"

Blood rushes from my toes all the way up to my skull and I turn RED on every conceivable level. It feels like I've got blood up to my eyeballs. A tremble takes hold of my body and I glance down at the grassy ground. "Uh, um, uh, uh, n—n—no. That's not, um, my username at all, my username is actually, uh, um, GentleNight, that's, uh, wh—wh—what my username is, 'cause, um, what kind of, uh, person would have that kind of, um, stupid username, huh? I mean, she's also from Hell Difficulty, and she's a girl, so it makes way more sense that—"

"M—my username . . ." the girl mutters, "is GuideOfVirgil . . ."

The guy looks down at her and back up at me. "Sounds like a standard system-generated username to me. Since there's only one other Hell Difficulty challenger, that's got to be you. And according to the Delegate Commission, you're wanted."

The hot shame perforating my entire body is instantly replaced by cold rivaled only by the North Pole. Oh, right. I was going to get executed, wasn't I? "Um," I say. "No. That's . . . wrong."

With a twist of the wrist, he turns his screen around, nodding to it. Hesitantly, I inch closer.

<OrthodoxPox[F3] List of Wanted Persons:
Since challengers cannot see each other's level or usernames through the system, we hereby ask that the following list of persons be found. Turning in one of these will grant a suitable reward. Let's all help each other find these people.
1: HookedOnBach[F7] Hard
2: LeagueOfWill[F13] Normal
3: AnotherUndercover[F12] Normal
4: SuperMoleman[F24] Easy
5: LionMawMadness[F11] Normal
6: MilkInACupboard[F10] Easy
7: PrissyKittyPrincess[F4] Hell>

< . . . >

I feel a bead of sweat slip down my back. "Actually, um, I'm secretly an Executive Delegate, like, for the Hell Difficulty, so this is, like, uh, wrong, and I need you to talk to this Pox guy, because he'll totally clear everything up, because, like,

I really am an executive, so actually, in reality, for questioning my, like, authority and stuff, I could totally have you executed, because, like, I'm an executive, you know, and you don't want to mess with executives. Yeah."

He smiles down at me. "If you want to discuss this with Pox, how about you do it yourself?"

Ah. Oops.

Something hard and heavy hits the back of my skull like a sledgehammer, and when I turn around, I find that it really *was* a sledgehammer that did it. Wack. I blink at the armored guy holding it. He blinks back at me. Hm. It shouldn't be too hard to take him out. Not too hard at a—

The hammer comes down again, and then again, and I stumble once, twice, because my skull plates have shifted a bit too much again, and that doesn't feel good, but the darkness is coming, so there's nothing I can do but stumble and stumble and stumble and stumble and then I fall and the last thing I really see from the world of light is the face of that girl, that girl from Hell, looking down at me with such a meek expression that I can't really imagine that this was what she wanted.

<You have learned: Brain Damage Resistance Lv.6>
<You have learned: Fracture Resistance Lv.6>
<You have learned: Unconsciousness Resistance Lv.6>

The darkness fades and the light stabs me through the eyes so I startle awake.

"—Unfortunately, despite our best efforts, only a few of those who are wanted by our great Commission were captured. The few that we now have in our grasp will act as the final dying breath of the old generation, of the chaos that came before, of the world that once was. In this great moment, we can finally say with full confidence: *Out with the old, in with the new!*"

Hm. Okay, first things first, I'm having a bit of déjà vu. I'm back in the dungeon. Well, not *the* dungeon, just *a* dungeon. A relatively nice one, too, now that I have the time to look at it. The bars aren't completely rusty, the floor isn't muddy with my blood, and although I'm once again hung perpendicular to the wall, the good news is that, at the very least, the clasps I'm hung with aren't barbed on the inside.

Even better, I'm not alone!

There are three other people in here, though I'm the only one hanging on the wall. This means that if someone's going to pull the classic *How's it hanging?* joke, it sadly won't be me. Bummer. Anyway, I can see them pretty well because there's plenty of light streaming in from a barred window just above my head. In other words, I can't see anything, but I can hear it.

It's a speech. I have no idea who's talking, but it is absolutely a speech.

"From this moment on, this great Commission, as well as the tutorial it represents, will no longer be some cobbled-together group of good people. Rather, we will be a true community, where each and every one of us has a word to say and a voice to be heard! We will have our roles, and we will follow the rules that all of us have agreed to. That is our noble pursuit, and that is what we will now, finally, commit to!"

Eugh. Gross, he's talking like a real moderator here. So, I guess, to do this, he's going to execute me. And these lumps of sadness I share this cell with too, I suppose. And, sure, I would love to stay and chat and try to increase a few of my tolerances, but I've got places to be, things to see, and I can only really do that if I'm alive, so I'll have to decline.

Escaping the dungeon is simple since I've already done it once. I just have to break both of my hands, as well as both of my feet since there were clamps there too, and then I'm basically free. Hm. For some reason, my cellmates are staring at me weirdly. Well, that's their problem.

I make my way over to the bars. They're about the same size as they were at the other castle, so if I just break my pelvis and my ribs again and jimmy my skull through, I'm free to go. Yippie!

<You have learned: Brain Damage Resistance Lv.7>
<You have learned: Fracture Resistance Lv.7>
<You have learned: Fracture Resistance Lv.8>

Mm, good stuff.

Before continuing, I briefly roll myself into a ball, meditating only enough for my feet to heal, and then off I go. I'm not entirely sure where the best hiding spot is, but I kind of want to see what'll happen outside, so I just head upward to get a good vantage point. At least, that was my plan, because right as I head up the stairs . . .

"Hm?"

"Huh?"

I'm met by a small band of people who could've been pulled straight out of an RPG. Which is to say that they look exactly like all the other challengers I've seen so far, but I don't care about that. My eyes are glued to one of them and one alone. Even if God Himself had been standing in front of me, I would not have seen it. Among them, clad in simple wizard's robes, with his right arm tied behind his back by a leather band, stands the only man who has ever bested me.

LetsFraternizeTogether.

I freeze in place. The turbulent winds of hell could not have moved me. All the storms that rend the sea would not have been able to twist a single hair on my head. The world itself could have opened to swallow us whole and I would remain rooted in place.

I stare at him. He stares at me. Not even time moves me. His eyes narrow slightly.

And then his hand flies up and the points at me with his index finger, and—

<Tie.>

Honestly, he didn't need to. At this moment, no matter what he might have done, I would not have moved. It was superfluous, really.

One of the people next to him, a girl in light leather armor, steps forward and points at me, less because she's about to magic me to death, and more to actually accuse me of something. "Who are you?" she barks. "What is your relationship with the Delegate Commission?"

Another two-in-one. I glance at him. He's still looking at me. I turn back to her. I have no idea if this will work, but it's worth a shot.

"I'm the Delegate and also the executive of the Hell Difficulty, which means I'm super important and also I have all of the authority so you better not use any more of that magic stuff on me or I will go tell whoever our leader is and he'll kick your asses so bad you'll never do another squat in your life."

She blinks at me. She glances back at one of the people behind her. "Is that, uh, true?"

They all shrug.

She turns back to me. "It's not like we can just let this . . . *guy* . . . go free, so, uh . . ."

Hey, why did you say *guy* like that? That's totally suspicious!

She snaps her fingers. "Tie him up."

Huh? Hey, wait a second, didn't you hear what I said? Hey! I'm an *executive*! Treat a guy with some respect, damn it!

But, alas, with chivalry's recent closed-casket burial, they ignore my internal pleas and tie me up with ropes. I really wish I could pull off some Superman bit and easily break out of them, but they are *way* tighter than I had expected, so there's nothing I can do other than wiggle my shoulders pathetically. For some reason, I've got a feeling that even if I break every bone in my body, I won't be able to escape. Damn it. You just can't win with these sorts of people.

The girl holding my rope presents the end of it to . . . him.

"Here, Mole, you keep an eye on him since you'll be in the back anyway, okay?"

. . . Mole?

His eyes hop between the rope and my face. He seems like he's about to say something, but she just thrusts the rope into his hands. Since there's nothing he can say or do to refuse that wouldn't be at least slightly rude, so he unwillingly accepts it.

I'm starting to really believe in karma. That said . . .

Mole? As in . . . ?

I look at him. He's looking back at me. For some reason, he's squinting, kind of like when you're watching a movie and you can't place where you saw that actor before. Hang on for just a second. Y—you know, now that I think about it, it *was* like over half a year since he last saw me. And that was before I started my homelessness speedrun, and before any of this, and now I look pretty different, so, you know, there's a chance that, well . . .

Maybe he doesn't recognize me?

There's a chance. A possibility, really. It's . . . plausible, right?

I try to muster some sort of positive facial expression, like I only just recognized him, too. "H—hey, uh . . . she called you Mole, so, um . . ." He looks at me oddly. I wish I could wipe the sweat from my brow. "Any chance you're, uh . . . Moleman?"

He furrows his brows. "I am. But I generally don't make a habit of hanging around execs for the Commission, sorry."

"No, no, that's not it!" I say with maybe just a dash of too much desperation. "I—I might not look like it, but it's me! P—Prissy—" The word gets stuck in my throat like a lump, refusing to come out. "Prissy—" I can practically feel his eyes burning into me, even more than the embarrassment of my own username. I take a few long, deep breaths. "I'm . . . uh . . . *Kitty.*" After that wasn't enough, unwillingly, almost in a whisper, I continue. "I asked about, uh . . . dismemberment. Losing feet to goblins. That . . . sort of stuff."

"Oh!" he exclaims, eyebrows shooting up. "Wow, really?" I nod at him. "Really, that's . . . I'd say it's a pleasure to meet you, but . . ." He gestures at the whole of me. "Yeah. Still, I didn't take you for an *executive* type . . ."

"Oh, that's, uh . . ." I try to shrug but the bindings make it hard. "It was really just a, uh, matter of, like . . . availability. You get me?"

After a second or so, he nods back at me. "I suppose that explains why they put you on the wanted list. Contacting you normally might have been a bit too *challenging*, so they went with a more direct route. Do you think that makes sense?"

I jerk at the question. "Makes sense? Oh, uh, yeah! Of course it does, perfect sense! Couldn't think of a better solution myself, really."

His facial expression turns difficult. I don't like it when people look at me like that. It's been happening way too much recently. After a minute or so of walking, Moleman continues, in an almost hushed voice, "Do you have any idea what's happening right now?"

"Uhh, not really, to be honest. There was some kind of ceremony outside, but that's about all I know."

"They're going to execute people," Moleman says gravely. "They're going to take dissenters, and they're going to line them up, and right before they swear in their new leader, they're going to kill them. One by one. But they aren't dissenters, not really. They're our *friends*. They didn't do anything wrong—nothing to warrant *execution*—and still, they're going to die. Not because of any sin they committed, but rather to make a point." His voice turns low. "It's wrong. So, we're going to put a stop to them."

Hm. I don't really get it, but there isn't much I can say, so I just hum. "Hmm, sounds complicated."

Moleman looks me straight in the eye, his face deathly serious. "The Commission will be punished. Severely. All of the members to some extent, but the executives more than all of them. *Way* more than all of them."

XVIII

Executive Execution

Alright. That makes sense, I think. I'm not sure what these executives are supposed to have done, but it's not like I can tell them not to or anything.

Hm. Executives . . .

Hang on. "When you say, uh, *executives*, does that happen to include *me?*"

"You *are* an executive, aren't you?"

"Well, heh, yeah, *technically*, but, I mean, it's not like I've actually done anything as an executive—I just held the title, and that's about it, you know?" A pause. "I mean, sure, if I *could* have done something with my title, I totally would've, but I kind of couldn't, so this is all pretty much just, like, empty accusations and stuff. You get me?"

He makes another one of those dreadful, difficult faces. "It's not up to me to decide."

"H—hey, wait just a second, I'm not—"

But before I can say anything else, our party of rebels have burst out of the castle and into the light of the outside field, weapons held high and ready, and I have no other choice than to watch as all hell breaks loose.

The girl who captured me first fires off an arrow toward a man standing on a platform in front of the large crowd, and he gets hit in the shoulder, crying out in pain as he stumbles and falls over. With this starting shot, the crowd explodes into turmoil, some of the members raising their own weapons while others look around in a panic and yet more attempt to quell the chaos. And, in the meantime, I'm just sort of watching.

"Pick up your weapons, rebels!" the girl who caught me shouts. "And let us finally tear down this cruel rule!"

Her rallying cry echoes across the crowd to thunderous cheering. On top of the stage, alongside the man who got shot, stand three other administrative-looking people, alongside several others. Oh, and those three I saw down in the dungeon. Looks like they aren't dead yet, huh. At the sudden attack, the executives try to grab their weapons, but a few of them suddenly freeze in place. I glance at Moleman. Yup, he's pointing, alright. Those who didn't go stiff at the magic or were able to avoid it try to make their defense, but the tide has already turned. It almost makes me want to cheer for these rebel guys, but since I have no idea why this is happening to begin with, I'm just sort of watching on.

I can't even try to escape in the chaos since Moleman is still dutifully holding my rope. Blast it.

The whole revolution takes only a matter of minutes, with its shouts and rallying cries and everything in between, and by the end of it, all three of the executive-looking people have been tied up, much like me. In direct contrast, the prisoners who had been moments away from execution have been freed. A number of people have been more or less injured, some almost fatally. Only the ones fighting with the rebels were healed, with the rest being left to writhe in pain on the ground.

And here we are. That girl who caught me is standing at the lectern, here on top of the stage. The executives—and me—are all lying on the ground like a row of wrapped-up maggots. It's a bit awkward.

"Comrades! Rebels! Friends and fighters! For almost four months, our band has lain in wait, silently planning our resistance, waiting for the right moment to do what many considered impossible. For four months, we have been under the cruel rule of these power-hungry fascists. We have seen our friends executed for the most trifling of reasons, our fellow challengers physically abused for the mere crime of saying *no*, and our very own lives being made into the playthings of these ruthless, uncaring creatures!"

The crowd cheers and boos, and a few throw things at the executives. Ow! Hey, don't throw it at *me*!

"They are wolves in our midst. While we should have been allies, we were made into enemies. In our demanded fight for resources to fuel the needs of the elite, we were made to fight each other. But in truth, we are not many peoples! We are not of different difficulties, or floors, or levels. We are only one group, and that is *challengers*!"

Wild cheering. She's a surprisingly good talker, it seems.

"This tutorial will no longer be ruled by an elite that does nothing but govern. It will be ruled by us challengers! As we fight, we will be rewarded. We shall not take from our fellow challenger, we shall not kill our fellow challenger, and we shall not cause harm to our fellow challenger. These are the rules we will follow, together, applicable to each and every one of us."

She gestures to the executives, and also to me.

"For the crime of breaking all these rules, these four shall face punishment. They shall receive what they have given, and they shall be an example of how we challengers will never allow ourselves to be ruled ever again!"

Hm. Huh. Come again? Miss, what exactly do you mean by *these four*?

Four small vials of BLACKish liquid appear in front of her, on top of the lectern. "As they have forced innocent men and women to go into death seemingly of their own volition—to enter a floor with nothing but their own flesh and blood—they shall now likewise be forced to enter death of their own volition."

I look to the right. Closest to me is a pretty big guy, dressed in BLACK armor, his jaw clenched so hard I can see it bulge. Next to him is a younger man, lying perfectly still, the only hint of his inner thoughts being how deathly pale he is. And, farthest away, a young boy, younger than me, silently sobbing.

Leaving the lectern, to the sound of screaming cheers, she walks up to the young boy first. Untying him, she pulls him up to a sitting position, and the second he's seated, a sword snakes around his throat. I can see him tremble all the way from here. "I—I don't want to," he says in a trembling whisper. "I don't want to die."

She hands him the small BLACK vial. His hands tremble something awful. I didn't know the human eye could hold so many tears, but there it goes. After taking a few shaking breaths, he brings the vial to his lips and tips it in, swallowing it all in one gulp. The bulge going down his throat bumps against the blade of the sword. He stares straight ahead. "Mommy—"

And then he drops dead. He just . . . dropped. Didn't even kick or foam at the mouth or jerk or anything. Interesting.

And the crowd cheers so loudly it's almost deafening.

She turns back to the crowd, grinning, spreading her arms. "And like that, JustAPrankBro has finally tasted his own medicine!" Cheering.

They undo the bindings of the next one. He won't sit up on his own, so they pull him up. His head is so limp he almost slumps right onto the blade, but the small cut the blade makes along his neck is enough to get him out of it and he jerks upright, chest heaving, eyes wide and wandering. She hands him the small BLACK vial. He doesn't even look at it before taking a gulp. And then, just like before, he drops. Thump.

"HuppiGupp has met his match!" she exclaims, almost like a sports commentator. The crowd certainly reacts to it like they're watching a match, that's for sure.

She steps up to the final one before me. As soon as they undo his ropes he tries to attack, but a blade to his throat is enough to change his mind, and he ruefully sits down. She tries to hand him the poison but he just glares at it. "I won't take it. No matter what you do, I won't take it. If you want to kill me, be a real leader and do it yourself."

She almost smiles at him. I don't know what else to call the way her mouth twists, but it isn't quite a smile. It just sort of looks like it. A dagger appears in her hand and before he even has time to close his mouth again it's shoved deep into his throat. His eyes widen a little, but not much else. And when he drops, the knife she's holding goes out of him, and only then does the blood spurt, but just before that, just before the blood comes, there's a single half of a moment where you can see the RED of his inside, and it looks just like goblin meat. It makes me drool a little.

"TalonsOfRage is no more!" Cheering.

She steps up to me and undoes my ropes. Whew, thanks, I was really starting to get uncomfortable in that posi—

What's this sword doing around my throat?

She hands me a vial of BLACK liquid. Um. See, you know, I really don't want to be a bother or anything, but, heh, funny story, there's actually been a bit of a mistake here. I'm not an exe—well, I am, but it's not like I've done anything bad, so, like . . .

She nudges the vial closer to me. Ah. I get it. I just, um . . .

I sweat a little. "I'm not very thirsty."

She waggles her knife at me.

. . . But I can make a bit of space, haha. Bottom's up!

Slurp. Gulp.

. . .

. . .

. . . I look at the vial. I look at her.

She looks at the vial. She looks at me.

She waves a hand in front of my face, and I shrug at her.

After glancing at her fellow rebels, she opens her inventory and pulls out another one, handing it to me as she does. I uncork it and drink it. You know, on second swallow, it surprisingly has a pretty nice, mellow flavor. Kind of like how I'd expect aged sap to taste.

It doesn't do anything either, so she hands me a third. I drink it. The crowd starts murmuring. A fourth. I drink it. And at the fifth . . .

<You have learned: Poison Protection Lv.2>

. . . Hey, nice! She looks weirdly dismayed but I've still got to ask. "Hey, you got any more of those? It's kind of nice; my poison protection finally rose!"

She frowns at me. "You mean your poison resistance?"

I blink at her. She blinks at me.

She makes one of those difficult faces again that I hate before standing up and going over to her little band of rebels. They talk in hushed tones for a minute or so before she finally comes back over. She squats down next to me. "Mind telling me what level your poison resistance is at?"

"My poison *protection* is now at level two, *thankyouverymuch*."

She sighs and massages her temples. "Alright. Okay. Fine . . ." Standing up, she turns to the crowd. "Since the final executive has refused to go on his own terms, we will now send him off in a more classic fashion!"

And, predictably, the crowd goes wild.

Classic fashion? What's that supposed to—

The guy behind me drags me off my feet before shoving me headfirst, putting me on my hands and knees. Okay, not very polite, if you just asked, I would have done it on my own, but—

Hang on. Is that an axe?

W—wait just a moment. Listen, poison? Poison is fine. I can survive that sort of stuff. I—it's just that, you know, axe to the neck? Personally, I just think that's a bit too much, because, well, there isn't much I can do to defend against that, so I really just—

He lifts the axe. Higher, and higher, and higher, and with each inch higher it goes, the crowd cheers just a bit louder, more and more, until the axe blocks out the sun, and his body tenses, and . . . !

"*Stop!*"

Moleman rushes onto the stage, positioning himself in front of the axe, stopping it just moments before my beheading. As I stare at his back, the prisoners from before run onto the stage, alongside some guy I think I saw when I was captured.

"Bach," Moleman says to the girl, huffily. "You can't—you can't execute him."

The girl—Bach—stumbles back. "Wh—why not? He's an executive, isn't he?"

"He is, yes, but"—Moleman glances at me, still breathing deeply—"he didn't do anything. In fact, he was going to be executed, right alongside our comrades. He just happened to break out before he could be brought out for the ceremony."

Her eyebrows crunch together. "Escape? How? Did he use some skill to turn immaterial?"

Moleman's jaw snaps shut, and he turns to look first at the other prisoners, and then at me.

One of the prisoners steps forward. "Um, he, uh . . ." She makes a face as if looking for the proper words. "I'm pretty sure that he just . . . broke every bone in his body?"

Bach gives her a completely blank face. "Uh-huh. Right, so, uh . . ."

Moleman takes a step closer to her. "Listen to me, Bach. This guy . . . he's done a lot wrong, but I don't . . ." He heaves a sigh. "I don't think he's guilty of this particular crime. Not right now, at least." Pulling his lips tight, he closes his eyes for a second. When he opens them again, he somehow looks almost defeated. "We agreed that we wouldn't judge people for what they did before coming into the tutorial, right? That's behind us, so . . ." A deep breath. "He hasn't committed any crime."

As she looks at him, her eyes soften, and her expression turns a lot less grim. "Fine." She turns away from him. Walking over to the lectern, she takes a stand and faces the crowd. "We have come to the agreement that since PrissyKittyPrincess—the executive of the Hell Difficulty—has not technically committed any crime, he will not be punished, as it would be unjust." First, silence. And then, jeering. Just a huge wall of jeering.

They don't even know me! What do they care that I'm not being executed? Dumb idiots. Normies, the lot of them.

"That said . . ." Her grip on the lectern tightens. "Since it was SuperMoleman who requested this pardon, from here on out, he will be in charge of ensuring that should PrissyKittyPrincess break any of our agreed-upon rules, he will be punished just as we would be."

. . . Excuse me?

In nigh-on terror, I look up at Moleman. His lips are pulled so tight they've turned into a thin WHITE line. I kind of hope he isn't regretting all of this. That would be, uh, not good. I've got a feeling that even if Bach just made that statement to the whole crowd, she wouldn't mind going back on it. All things considered, she seems kind of, I don't know . . . bloodthirsty?

As if she could hear my thoughts, she turns toward us, nailing Moleman to the spot with her gaze. "Is that acceptable, Mole?"

After a pause that was just a little too long for comfort, he replies, "Yes."

And so it begins. Moleman grabs my arm and brings me up to my feet. Someone throws something at me, but I can't really feel it, even when a second and a third follow. Moleman hurriedly takes me off the stage and back into the castle, and all the while I can hear Bach talk in a grandiose fashion about how the former Delegates will all be banned from making parties and that from now on there will be order and peace.

But just one question weighs on my mind, heavier than any other. Once we're inside, Moleman drags me through the entire castle, into a back room and up winding stairs until we reach a small room. He sits me down, and he takes a seat across from me, burying his face in his hands. I look at him. I'm not sure I recognize him at all.

"How did you know?" I ask him. He doesn't lift his face from his hands. "I haven't told anyone. I look completely different now. Nobody should recognize me. So how did you know?"

"Know what?" he asks, but we both know how that might as well be a rhetorical question.

"That I've done something . . . bad. Before all of this."

He gives a chuckle, but not a real one, not a happy one. Finally, he looks up from his hands. His eyes are REDdish. "How could I not know you, Fennrick? How could I ever forget the face of the man who killed me?"

I can't feel the chair beneath me.

"I didn't kill anyone."

"You did, Fennrick." And carefully, gently, he unties the strap around his chest, removing his right arm from its position and placing it on the table with a thud. "They had to amputate, you know. It took too long to get to the hospital, and they had to amputate. But I wasn't aware of that. For me, the last thing I ever really saw was your face. How are you supposed to forget something like that?"

"I didn't kill you," I say again, a little louder than last time. "You're here, aren't you?"

He just smiles. "There's a theory you might have heard of. People have been considering it for a while, about how and why some people were invited here. *Why us? Why then? Why?* And it all brought a theory to the forefront of our minds. You don't seem like you're too invested in that sort of theorizing, but . . . In what state were you in when you were invited to the tutorial?"

"What state?" I look down at my lap. At my blueish, REDdened hands. "I was just . . . playing games. Lost a match. That's all." When I look up again, I hate that it's *his* face I see. Any other face would be fine. Any other face I could strangle and be out of here and not have to care anymore. Any face but that one.

"A heart attack, then? Pretty common," he says softly. His eyes go distant. Hazy. "I'd been in a coma for six months when it happened. Lack of oxygen and all that. If it makes you feel any better, it was a painless death, once I was actually there."

"But you aren't dead!" I shout, standing up so fast the chair behind me topples over. "You're alive, and you're sitting right there, and *that's that!*"

He goes silent for a second. The only sound in the room is my breathing, huffing, dragging breaths down by the ankle, scraping through my throat.

"I'd almost call it ironic that we died at the same time if it weren't like this. I've talked with a lot of people who feel the same thing. They were about to die, about to bleed out, about to eat a handful of pills, and then the invitation appeared. They weren't dead, but if it wasn't for the invitation, they would've been. So, in a sense, you didn't kill me. But I can't say that I was alive for those past six months before being invited here."

My chest heaves. Up and down. In and out. My brain buzzes as though filled with a million crammed-in wasps. Mutely, my eyes fall to the table between us.

Another question bubbles up in the stormy sea of my mind. A little question, so quiet it might as well be a hummingbird's whisper. "Why?" I ask. "Why, if I killed you, did you save me?"

And for once, he's the one that looks away. His face pulls itself tight. "I don't know. Maybe I shouldn't have." He looks back at me. "Do you think it was a good idea?"

"Uh," I say, without really thinking. "Rescuing people about to die is . . ."

"If you were in my position, would you have done what I did?"

I can feel the lines of my face deepen. Okay, hypothetically, a guy kills me. I get him into a position where he would rightfully be killed for that crime by someone else. I wouldn't even need to get my hands dirty. Everything would be left up to the world. It would do itself. Inaction isn't a sin. Nobody would even look at me wrong.

It'd be perfect. "You've got your answer, then." He leans back in his chair. To that, I can give no response. I feel mute. It's like he isn't even speaking real words. "I said it to Bach, and I'll say it again, but whatever happened before the tutorial . . . it isn't important, you know? It's alright."

Something bubbles up within me and without acting on any rational thought, without speaking with any logical guidance, I slam my hands on the table so hard he jumps, head flashing toward me, and I roar, "*It's not alright! I killed you!* You should hate me for it! Come on, strike me down; I'll let you get the first hit! You're level forty-something, right? One hit should be all you need, and then you won't need to think about me ever again, simple as that!"

Panting, I stare down at him, but my mind is still whirling.

Why did I say that? I—I don't want to die. I don't care about killing him; he totally deserved that, so why . . . ?

He chuckles and I twitch at the sound. "Wh—what's so funny?" I think my voice is trembling. I must sound so pathetic.

He looks at me, and he smiles. A real one. "You really regret it, don't you?"

What? What the hell is he—

Standing up, he takes three measured steps toward me, and I stagger backward in response, almost expecting him to really hit me or something; I did tell him I'd let him do it, and it's not like I'm a coward or anything, so when he brings up his hand, I stand steadfast, willfully awaiting the darkness with only the slightest tremble.

But his hand goes no farther. He's just holding it out. I stare down at it.

He waggles it a little. I look up at him. There's a weird sense of mirth in his eyes that wasn't there before. "You wouldn't take it the last time we met. How about it, Fennrick? Good game?"

I stare at his hand like it's radioactive. My mind releases a puff of steam.

I slap his hand away. "You—you can't say 'good game' if we haven't, like, had a rematch or something!"

He blinks at me before erupting into a light grin. "What, you want to have a go? Here, now? What level are you even?"

My jaw clamps shut. Okay, maybe I didn't think that one through. I could probably lie, but where's the point in getting into a fight you know you're going to lose? Grumbling, I look down at the floor. My toes are a weird mixture of bluish skin and dried RED blood. I wiggle my toes a little. "I'm . . . level eighteen."

"See? You're only at floor four, so it makes sense that—" He freezes in place, face petrified in sudden realization. "Hang on. Level *eighteen?*" Meekly, I nod at him. His pronounced brows furrow deeply, and he pinches his chin, looking a lot like a detective figuring out how and why the dog killed the master of the house. In the end, he looks up to me, an immeasurably nerdy glint in his eye. "Describe the past four floors to me. What enemies appeared, what level were they, what were the boss stages like . . . *everything.*"

"Everything?" I echo.

He nods sharply. "*Everything.*"

Well, that's quite the story, but after a little while of piecing together my thoughts and what I remember of it, I tell him about most of it. About what happened when I first entered the first floor, how I bested the beasts, my brief and/or eternal stay in the lobby and my creative solution to it, what little I can remember of the second floor apart from the colors and the party and the guests, and then finally my most recent adventure. And by the end of it, after an interesting shift through many kinds of emotions—recognition, surprise, understanding, dumbfoundedness, confoundation, secondhand pain and embarrassment, some measure of disgust—he finally ends up at *pity*. Honestly, though, out of all the emotions, pity is the one that I want to see the least.

"You . . . The entire city . . . you just—?"

I nod at him. "It got kind of hectic at the end since I had to finish it before coming here, but I was able to do it in the end and still get a complete clear, though since the gods didn't like my play style, they put me in debt and now I own nothing except a bunch of animal pelts."

"You don't have any weapons? Not even a sword?"

"Not a one."

He squints at me, his face contorting as if he ate something sour. "This is all . . . I'd assume you were lying if I didn't know that this really was the case. I shouldn't have to say this, but I can't believe you're still alive after all of that. I'd give you a weapon, but . . ." His eyes jump down to my REDdish hands before jumping back up to my face. "I have a feeling you won't need it. And even if you did, there's a fair chance, assuming the gods don't like your actions on the next floor, that you'll lose your points again—including everything in your inventory."

I stare at him. "They wouldn't be that cruel, though, right?"

For some reason, he's giving me a look usually reserved for hypocrites and line cutters. "I'm not going to give any comment on that except for the fact that the god of cruelty took an interest in you."

"Hey, I did nothing to deserve that! I was being *humane!*"

A long pause. "You don't think there's a reason why the gods didn't appreciate your . . . *creative methods?*" I'm not sure how to answer that, so I say nothing. He scratches the back of his head and looks off to the side, his eyes finding a mural on the wall to inspect. "I'm not sure exactly how to tell you this, but some of us on the higher floors have started considering the fact that, um, goblins might be, well . . . sapient."

Sentient? I almost snort. "Well, of course they're sapient. They speak and everything."

Moleman opens his mouth, but just as he's about to say something that he seems to consider very self-evident, his eyebrows twitch and he looks at me with emotions I can't recognize. "You . . . knew? And you still—?"

"It's pretty obvious. But it's not like it matters, right? When in war, different rules apply. And we *are* in a war, of sorts. Even if you're fighting other humans, as long as you have your objective, and as long as that's the only real choice you have, it doesn't really matter that they can talk or not, right?"

His mouth opens, closes, and stays closed for about half a minute before he finally speaks again. "I'm not going to argue with you, but, in the future, if you're facing goblins specifically, maybe just . . . tone down the—the . . . *creativity.*"

What's that even supposed to mean? If I hadn't been "creative" on the last floor, as he puts it, I would be dead. That's just how it is. I did nothing wrong and—frankly—it's very unkind of him to try to make me out as some sort of bad guy here when I only did what was absolutely necessary.

But before I can voice my very rational objections, he continues. "I'm just saying that, as your . . . *caretaker* of sorts, it would be bad for the both of us if you broke any rules. Goblins aren't currently recognized as anything more than enemies and all, but, in the near future, they may very well take on the same importance as us humans. Killing a goblin when it isn't necessary might be as bad as killing a fellow challenger."

I roll my eyes at him. Pssh, sure, whatever. It's not like he can actually prove whether I've killed any goblins. Also, since it isn't a rule, he can't try to enforce it, either.

"I can tell you're thinking about still killing them. *Please.* Didn't you tell me you had a goblin friend? What would Simel think, huh?"

I freeze up. A slight tremble takes my hand, so I clench it to make it go away. "I won't kill Simel, so it's fine. He's different."

He frowns at me. For some reason, it feels bad.

Grumbling, I look down at my feet. "We'll see." He smiles and I quickly add, "N—no promises! If I need to defeat all the goblins to win, then that's exactly what I'll do."

"Just try to send me a message first and I'll try to figure out if there's any alternative, okay? I've got a lot of people waiting for me in the wings. I mean, you didn't get a very good impression of Bach, but she's good at pulling people together. With her, it wouldn't be easy to figure out if it's fully necessary to, well, *defeat all the goblins*. It might not seem like it, but this place does actually reward creative solutions. You've seen it yourself, with the gods."

I give him a look. Hm. "You didn't react too much to them. The gods, I mean."

He shrugs. "Bach also has it. The god of combat took interest in her a while back and even gave her a sovereign skill. It was a huge deal in the chat. But I guess you weren't in a place to really keep an eye on it at the time, huh . . . Anyway, as long as you try not to anger them too much, I think you'll be fine."

"I'm surprised you haven't written a guide about getting noticed by the god-*senpais* yet."

He chuckles warmly. "If I could, I certainly would have. It's a very interesting concept. Unfortunately, since I've yet to be noticed myself, I can't say anything for certain. Though, all things considered, I doubt it's a coincidence that both people I know who've experienced this are in the higher difficulties. Whatever the case, as time goes on, I'm sure we'll learn more about these mysterious all-seeing entities."

Hrm. I hope not. Learning more about these voyeurs . . . sounds like a nightmare. I'm better off not knowing.

"Your next floor is the fourth, right? It's pretty simple, but the floor after that . . ." Jerked out of my thoughts, I nod for him to continue. He smiles strangely. "Would you like any tips? It's a pretty straightforward floor, but it might help to have a bit of an idea of what you're getting into, right?"

Slowly, deliberately, I cross my arms. "So far, your guides haven't been very applicable to my . . . situation."

"Haha, yeah, I'm not surprised. Though . . ." He frowns. "If there's one thing I need you to know, then it's this." He leans in closer to me. I can smell the scent on him. Grassy. Weird. Not sweaty at all. "Don't fight the minotaur. You'll die."

Minotaur?

He continues. "I've seen a lot of challengers enter the fifth floor and not leave it. The first part is fine, but the minotaur . . . you aren't meant to win that fight. I don't think anyone I know that has tried to fight it has even *survived*. It's a death sentence. Just do as the stage requirements say and you'll be fine. Just please don't—"

Minotaur, huh . . . I wonder what its meat tastes like? A minotaur is a big beefy cow-man, right? Hmm. The pelt on it has to be insanely good quality. And the beef? I like beef. Beef is the best meat. Always tender, always good. Combine that with a humanoid build and I can't imagine anything better. The thought is already making me drool . . .

"Hey, hey, hey, don't do that! Don't have those thoughts! You aren't *meant* to defeat it; that's like trying to destroy the boulder chasing you in an Aztec temple level! Just . . ." He makes a sound of actual, genuine frustration as he huffs. "Just be careful, alright?"

I look at him.

"Alright. Sure." And, after a pause, I add, "I will."

Virgil

After talking a little more to Moleman, I accidentally notice that over half of the symposium has already passed on by, so after saying a hasty goodbye, I leave to try to find that girl. Her name was Virgil-something. I don't really remember her full name, but I can recall her face well enough, and that's all I really need.

Let's see, Virgil, Virgil . . . Sniff sniff sniff. Yup, I can smell her.

I crouch down to start running, but then Moleman gives me a weird look. O—okay. I stand back up. I guess I'll just walk toward her.

The hallways are still pretty much stuffed with people, but, thankfully, they all part as I approach, though not without staring at me. Hm. Last time I remember being this harshly stared at by countless (human) strangers must have been at the courthouse. In the movies you'll usually see one or two people with a sign saying something like *The killer is innocent!* Then again, there was no one like that at my own trial, either. Life really is too unfair, huh?

"Hey, kitty!" someone shouts. I ignore it. "Psspsspss, come on, kitty, don't you want a treat?" I glance back at him. He's holding out a vial of something that looks very, very poisonous. I scowl at him and make to continue but stop in my tracks completely when I hear what he says next. "Come on, I thought furries like you loved being submissive to a loving master!" A few chuckles resound at his line.

I turn back to him. Ah. Alright. It's like that, isn't it?

I tense my legs. His neck isn't armored. His face is visible. He doesn't even look like a warrior. His hair is short. Perfect. I just need to—

A girl jumps in between us, holding out her arms, her face set in a tight expression of determination. I blink at her. "It's me you're looking for, right? I'm—" I think she bit her tongue. After a second or so of recollecting herself, she continues. "We . . . we met before. And I ran away." She gulps. "I think, maybe, that we should redo our introduction. Okay?"

I furrow my brows. Hm. "Alright."

"Hey, wait a minute!" my loathsome bully shouts from across the hallway. "I'm not done with that guy! The leaders may have pardoned him, but us challengers won't forget!" A few cheers of solidarity ring out across the hallway. Okay, but I literally haven't done anything. What's there to remember, huh? "Commies like you shouldn't even be allowed in the server!"

. . . What the hell did you just—

"Come on, let's go back to the lobby!" Virgil whisper-shouts at me, pushing me away from the guy, which is probably a good thing because otherwise I would've leapt across the room and torn up his face like a cocaine-fueled chimpanzee. Still growling and scowling, she pushes me up the stairs and into the Hell Lobby room, all the way into one of the two chairs there. She sits down in the other one across from mine. "This place is safe," she says. "I talked with a few guys who said that the lobby rooms are exclusive in that people who aren't in the difficulty can't enter. It's a safe room, of sorts."

I look her up and down. "Why did you decide to stay in the lobby instead of going into the first floor with the others?"

She brings up both of her hands in a form of surrender. "Just—let's take first things first, okay?" I raise my eyebrow at her in a silent question. Isn't this the best place to start? Apparently not, because right as I have that thought, she extends her hand across the table. I stare at it. "I'm sorry for running away from you. I thought you were some sort of . . . I don't know. It doesn't matter, though, because, well, as you said . . . It *was* rude of me. I'm sorry. Can we take it from the start again?"

My eyes widen a little. Slowly, hand trembling, I reach out across the table and take hers in mine. It's small. Smaller than mine. Soft. My palm is so sweaty in hers. Oh, God, this is horrible. Limply, I shake it up and down, three times, and then I dislodge. A bit of RED got stuck to her palm. She makes a face at it before wiping it off on the table.

"It's, uh," I say, "mostly my own, so it's okay, yeah?"

She frowns. "What do you mean by *mostly*?" But before I can answer her, she shakes her head. "No, never mind, it isn't . . . it isn't important. What *is* important is that, well . . . is it okay to call me Virgil?"

"Why not your real name?"

Her frown deepens. Ah. I chose the wrong option in the dialogue tree. "It's a long story, but . . . I just don't like my name." She chuckles weakly. "Maybe one day, I'll tell you. It's not like I'll die anytime soon."

"Virgil, huh . . ." I parrot. This works for me, actually. I kind of don't want people to know my real name since they might recognize me, so her calling me by my username is alright. I told Moleman to do the same, even if it hurt to ask him to call me *Kitty*. I wanted him to call me *Gentle* or *Night* first, but he said people wouldn't know who he was talking about, and everybody's already calling me *Kitty*, so . . . Even though it hurts, I have no choice. "Then, I wouldn't mind you calling me *Kitty*." I would, but I'm not saying that.

Her face loses all emotion. "Is there really nothing else I can call you?" she deadpans.

I return the expression of complete emotional bereavement. "Your only other options are *Prissy* or *Princess*."

She looks down at her lap. "I—I see."

I try to look down at her lap to see if there's anything of interest, but the table is in the way. Bummer.

"To answer your question," she says after a period of silence, "I just . . . I was scared, I guess. When I saw the screen, I didn't know what it was. I thought I was hallucinating from the—the . . . But I wasn't. I tried to wave it away, and I accidentally pressed *yes*, and *hell*. When it asked me to pick a weapon, I just grabbed a staff because that's all I could lift. And when I got into the lobby, and there were a bunch of excited people, I didn't know what was happening. I didn't know what to do or what to say, so when the floor opened and they went in, I just . . . didn't follow. And then when I looked at the screen, I saw that they were all dead. But there was still someone else in the difficulty. I looked all over the lobby, but there wasn't anyone there."

I lean forward slightly.

"And—and then . . ." Her eyes mist up. "I was stuck in there. With all the horrid WHITE and the echoing silence. I couldn't take it. I thought not eating would take it all away, but it just made a bunch of tolerances rise. Bashing my skull against the floor didn't work either." The edges of her lips dip down so hard it forms creases that go all the way up to her eyes. Creases that her tears find themselves sliding down. Every breath she takes trembles. "A—and then, at the end, just now, when I saw the timer tick down, I thought, oh, Gods, I thought to myself, even if I would die from going into the floor, that would be better than this horrible WHITE. Anything would be better." Abruptly, her mouth twists up into a smile, a trembling one. "But then I came here. And there were people. And I saw you, and . . ."

I hold up my hand, stilling her. "Okay, I know what came after that, and also, I totally get that feeling about the WHITE—I had that myself, and there's a very easy solution that I figured out, kind of unrelated, but if you just bleed yourself you can paint over all the WHITE with your RED, but that's kind of beside the point, 'cause I need you to listen to me here." I affix her in place with my gaze. "When the floor opens, you're not going to enter it."

Her eyes widen, but I continue before she can protest.

"I know you hate the WHITE, and I do too, but you absolutely need to keep being in the first-floor lobby. Otherwise, you won't be able to guide future challengers. If you go and die, everybody who joins after you will also die. I know you want to die, but you can't be selfish about this kind of stuff, because if you die, there won't be anyone left to guide those who come next, which in turn means that you're giving up on a lifesaving responsibility."

She sniffles once, but she's stopped crying now. "You want me to be—hic—a *guide*?"

I nod sharply. "Yeah. Listen, floor one is hell, but I survived it, right? Personally, I don't think anybody else is going to survive it 'cause it was totally super hard, but if they want to attempt it, we need someone to be there to tell them how the stage works. That someone is you."

"Me . . ."

"Yes, *you*. I'd ask you if you're cool with this, but you kind of don't have a choice. Either you guide the future challengers and tell them that they maybe shouldn't go kill themselves, or you go kill yourself. Before you came here, I'm sure you knew your answer. But back then you only had one option. So? What'll it be?"

Her lip trembles and I think she's going to cry again, but then she raises her eyes from the table and there is enough determination in there to make me completely freeze in place.

"I'll do it," she says firmly. "I'll guide them, so they don't have to go limp like the executives did. And so I don't have to do that either."

I feel a smile rise to my lips. "That's great to hear, Virgil."

She smiles back at me. "So, what's the information I should be able to give?"

I tell her everything I know. Not just about the first floor and the beasts and the arrows, but also about the second floor, and about the system, and how to best paint the lobby in the fastest, most effective way. I explain what the forums are for and what should be known, and about this symposium. She can't take any notes, but with the focus she's keeping here, I can honestly say that she won't need it. Talking to her took up the last of the symposium's hectic hours.

And after I've told her everything I know, and the symposium is only a few minutes from closing, somehow, we ended up talking about completely different stuff. Innocuous stuff. Stuff completely unrelated to the tutorial and to the people in it and even to who we were before. Now, even though it doesn't matter in the least, I know things about her. Her favorite color is blue. Before this, she still had her hair short. She only barely passed high school, and her parents were so proud of her.

It feels weird to know things about her. It feels weird that she knows things about me.

"So, circular motions, starting from the top of the pillars?"

"Yeah, if you can get help from the new challengers, you can probably reach higher since you don't have any spears to use as stilts, but all in all it should only take a few hours. That depends on how effectively you do it, though."

"And I don't need to reapply it?"

I pause. "I'm actually not sure. I've moved from the lobbies before I could see how it developed, but yeah, you might need to reapply it every attempt or something."

"Right."

I glance at the time.

<Top—Status—Community>
<23:58:50 Day 90>
<The fourth attempt will begin in 00:00:01:10>
<The Server Symposium will end in 01:10>

I look back at her. She smiles meekly. "Not much time left now, huh?"

I nod. "When you go back, the next challengers will already be there. You'll have twenty-four hours to explain it, so . . ."

"I've got my work cut out for me, right?" Her smile turns mellow. "I'll try to convince them to stay. But if they don't . . ."

"If they want to die so badly, leave them to it," I say. "That's up to them. You've done what you could—leave the rest to them. If they don't want to listen, then they're the stupid ones."

She nods.

Outside, cheering and applause are in full effect. Bach's been holding some sort of ceremonial speech, but we didn't go to listen to it. It doesn't really affect us anyway. If anyone messes with Virgil, I'll take care of it. Simple as that.

<Top—Status—Community>
<23:59:47 Day 90>
<The fourth attempt will begin in 00:00:00:13>
<The Server Symposium will end in 00:13>

"This is it, then?" she says.

"Yeah," I respond.

She turns to me one last time. "It was nice meeting you, Kitty."

I nod back at her. "Same to you, Virgil."

<The Server Symposium will end in 00:00>
<The Server Symposium has ended.>
<Thank you for participating! You will now be returned to your lobbies.>

When I open my eyes again, I'm back in the lobby.

<Top—Status—Community>
<00:00:02 Day 91>
<The fifth attempt will begin in 29:23:59:58>
<Floor 4 will open in 23:59:58>

And so, the fourth attempt has begun. Before I do anything else, I pull up the server list to check how many new challengers we have. Though, in the end, I only really care how many new people we have in one specific lobby.

<Status—Community—Top>
<Europe Server>
<Easy Lobby: 301/319
Normal Lobby: 107/110
Hard Lobby: 22/24
Hell Lobby: 8/8>

Six new people, huh? Not too shabby. If they're smart about this, they might make it.

In hindsight, unless you're really, really, really, *really* lucky, I think there's only one real way to beat the first floor. Simply put, you've got to train for it. You work up your resistances, specifically piercing and bleeding, and then you protect your head and chest right as you go into the floor. You could probably form a circle around the smallest challenger with your backs to them and hope to protect them like that. I spent a really long time nailing the idea that the very first minute is the deadliest into Virgil's head, so I'll just hope they follow her advice.

Even then, though, the best option would be to just remain in the lobby. At least you can live there. Some might say it's a dreadful way to live, and that it might be better to die rather than simply survive. I don't think those kinds of people have ever been in this sort of situation.

Dying is the worst alternative every single time. That's just how it is.

Anyhow, I've got around twenty-four hours to waste, and I think I might know just how.

I really want to train up my quadrupedal running. I need it to be my first instinct. It needs to be faster than normal running.

With that goal in mind, I get to it.

<You have learned: Hurry Lv.2>
<You have learned: Hurry Lv.3>
<You have learned: Crawl Lv.1>

<You have learned: Hurry Lv.4>
<You have learned: Crawl Lv.2>

The hours pass in a literal blur.
I only notice that time has passed at all when a message dings in.

<You have received a message.>

I open it.

<SuperMoleman[F24]: Hey Kitty. Just wanted to do a quick check-in. Floor 4 shouldn't be any problem at all, as long as you just do what the floor clearly wants you to do. Since there aren't any real living enemies, there's no problem if you want to be a bit more creative. Good luck!>

After a second's thought, I type in a response.

<PrissyKittyPrincess[F4]: kk thx>

And just like that, it begins.

<Floor 4 has opened. Do you want to enter?>
<Yes/No>
Oh, absolutely.
Without even a second of hesitation, I press Yes.
And the world buckles from down under and I only barely have time to catch my falling body before I'm standing again, staggering, my body swinging back and forth like I'm on a tightrope before I finally pull myself together and plant my feet firmly on the ground.
. . . Where the heck am I? It's so dark it almost feels like I've gone blind or something. But I can feel grass beneath my feet, and I can hear a gentle wind blowing, and what seems to be leaves rustling, and it smells like a forest, so it has to be a forest. The question of whether I've gone blind or if it's just extremely dark is easily answered by the one thing I can actually see.
A few feet in front of me, at the height of my knees, sits a bush. A bush that's on fire. Surrounded by a few sticks shoved into the ground.
But it doesn't sound like fire does. It isn't crackling or anything, and I can't feel any real heat from it. It's just . . . on fire. It's so surreal I can hardly react at all. But since I am not swayed by weird stuff thanks to my gamer constitution, I inch closer.

It really isn't warm at all. If I run my hand above it, it doesn't feel like anything, and my hand won't even catch fire. Another weird thing is that although I can feel that the wind coming from the hypothetical north, the fire is swaying toward the hypothetical east, as though there's a hypothetical western wind blowing. It both looks and feels beyond odd. On the other hand, the whole phenomenon can be explained by one simple line.

It's the tutorial.

\<Tutorial stage, Hell Difficulty Fourth Floor: The Blind Pit\> \<[Clear Condition] Bring the divine fire to the holy chalice to banish the shades.\>

Okay, first of all, this is clearly not a pit; second of all, I'm not technically blind; third of all, how do you expect me to bring this entire bush all the way to . . . wherever that chalice is?

Also, even more importantly, what the heck do you mean by shades?

Sniff sniff sniff. I can smell the chalice, I think. Metallic. Coming from . . . the hypothetical north. But I can't smell anything else. Maybe by *shades* it just means the darkness itself? I can imagine that this sort of supposedly holy fire could do something like that, but still. No need to word it so cryptically.

Well, guess I'd better get going. If there are no enemies to fight like Moleman claimed, then it should be fine to just walk there.

Squatting down, I thrust my hands into the soft dirt around the bush, sawing around the circumference of it before uprooting the entire thing. The fire sways in the air, but it remains pointed toward where I can smell the chalice. I wonder if this thing is actually any important?

Still, this forest sure is spooky. I almost trip on rocks and crawling roots several times, which is, indeed, very spooky.

I walk. I walk. I walk. The chalice isn't getting much closer, so it seems to be a longer trek than expected. Hopefully it won't take more than a week or so. It'd get awfully dull if I had to walk like this for an entire—

Something leaps out of the darkness and crashes on top of me, sandwiching the burning bush in my hand between my body and its own, and I stare up in wild terror at what I can only recognize as my own face.

It says nothing. I say nothing.

And then it starts clawing at me and like some caveman. I start waving the burning bush at it, trying to scare it off, but it just leaps at me again, and with my hands occupied holding an entire damn bush, there isn't much I can do as its claws tear into my exposed abdomen.

Hang on. I know this skill.

Is that . . . *Eviscerate level 6?*

<You have learned: Evisceration Resistance Lv.3>

My mind goes blank but before it can tear open my bowels completely my instincts kick in and I put the bush into my inventory—something I didn't know I could do. With the bush gone, all light drains from the forest, leaving us in pitch darkness. I leap to my feet, away from his claws.

<You have learned: Blindness Resistance Lv.7>

Great, that doesn't help at all.

I can't see him. I can barely even hear him. The only reason I know he's there at all is because I can just barely smell my own blood on his hands.

Slowly, I begin moving, just to keep on my feet. If I stand still, he'll get to me. My entire body and mind are on high alert. At least, that is until I trip on a rock, and I hear something fly through the air and I only barely have time to stretch out my clawed right hand before I feel something stab itself onto it, and my hand goes through soft, wet bodily tissue. But I can tell he isn't dead yet. I know this strategy.

Before he has time to start clawing at my face, I throw him to the side and leap a step back. As soon as I hear his bony body tumble to the ground, I leap on top of him, my hands acting on instinct alone to completely tear up his bowel area, clawing and clawing and clawing and clawing, and as I feel his warm innards spray onto me, I can also feel his own clawed hands going after my own bowels, tearing up a hole and doing his absolute best to do to me what I am doing to him, but I was able to do him in first, which means that I am the final definitive victor.

His hands and arms slowly lose motion, but I know how tenacious I can be. So even when there's nothing left in the cavity that remains of his abdomen, I still keep ripping and tearing, pulling out his lungs and his heart and his spinal cord and his brain until I know for certain he is no more.

<Shade (Lv.18) Defeated>

Haah, haah, haah, haah . . .

Th . . . *That* was a shade? But it was—he was . . . That was *me*, wasn't it?

B—but, then again, this might just be like a doppelganger thing, and once you beat it, it returns to its original form. Yeah. That's got to be it, right? I can't see it, but right now, I must be sitting on top of, like, some sort of faceless worm-creature or whatever. That has to be it. Yeah. Yeah . . .

Tentatively, I pull the bush out of my inventory.

There, just below me, lies my own corpse. Eviscerated. Every organ torn out and strewn around. My throat pulled out, my rib cage broken, my arms bloodied, and my abdomen emptied. I look down and my trembling eyes slowly find my face. It's pale. Deathly so. And ashen, too. Weirdly enough, the WHITEs of my eyes are starkly yellow, as though I've got liver failure or something. I look horrible. My cheeks are sunken, and my entire body is bony and thin, like someone grabbed the display skeleton in a biology classroom and stretched a piece of dead skin over it. I look horrible. There's no other way around it. The fact that I'm dead changes nothing at all. If I compare the skin of my hand to the skin of my dead body's chest, it's the same color, even though one is completely bloodless.

Breathing shallowly, I stagger to my feet.

Moleman . . . !

That lying cheat . . . ! I ought to send him an angry PM, but I've got a feeling that doing so won't help. And also, I've got good reason to believe that there's more than one of these . . . *shades.*

I look at the bush in my hand. It's my sole source of light. Without it, I can't see at all. But with it, I won't be able to fight.

Biting my cracked lips, I put the bush back into my inventory, letting darkness rule once more. The only smell I can tell from the shade is that of my own blood. It's weird. My blood smells exactly the same as goblin blood.

. . . I wonder if it tastes the same, too?

I pause where I stand. I was going to just keep moving, but . . .

It's not like it's actually me. It just looks like me. And fights like me. And acts like me. But, in reality, it's just a shade. An enemy. That means if I loot it, it's not like I'm looting an actual human being. It just looks like one. It's basically like a goblin.

After only a second or so of further hesitation, I finally decide to just go ahead with it. It's going to be sold by the end of the floor anyway. Might as well get it over with.

Hunching down, I begin by collecting my organs and putting them in my inventory. Compared to goblin innards, mine are a bit bigger, but they feel like they are of worse quality. Is it something to do with my diet and lifestyle?

Nah, can't be.

I'm not sure how long it took to disassemble my entire body, but once I'm finished, I feel like I've gained a newfound understanding of my own anatomy. Lots of lean muscle. Little fat. Most of my weight is in bones.

<You have learned: Disassemble Lv.3>

Once I'm done, I spend a minute or so just groping around on the ground, trying to make sure I didn't miss anything. Nope, I got everything.

<THE GODDESS OF SOLITUDE WATCHES YOU WITH PITY.>

Now hang on just a minute. I normally try to ignore you people, but really? You're the goddess of *solitude*! Shouldn't *you* be my greatest advocate?

Got no response to that, huh? Well, whatever. I'm in a forest of weird creatures, so it's not like I have time to hang around in one place anyway. Since the shades will apparently be banished once I do the thing with the chalice, there's no reason to spend a stupid amount of time personally defeating every single shade. I just need to get to the chalice.

Getting back to my feet, I start to head out, but I soon have a thought. I wonder what shade meat tastes like?

Summoning a lump from my inventory, I give it a quick once-over. It's very thin. I wasn't able to make any specific cuts since there was so little meat to work with. I mean, this is my entire left breast and it's barely enough to hold in my hand. Still, it's better than nothing, I guess. I bite in. Hm. Eugh. It's super stringy. Really tough meat, all things considered.

<You have learned: Indigestion Tolerance Lv.8>
<You have learned: Indigestion Tolerance Lv.9>
<You have learned: Ulcer Tolerance Lv.3>

For some reason, it feels like I should take offense to this. But on the other hand, since I'm the one actually eating this suspicious meat, it feels perfectly warranted. It really is that bad. Ah, I want to eat more gobling meat. I hope I'll get to meet more goblins so I can—

Something rustles. My feet lock in place.

<You have learned: Enhanced Hearing Lv.4>

It's subtle. Incredibly subtle. Barely even there at all.

Sniff sniff sniff.

It's hard to tell over the smell of blood clinging to me, but if I focus hard, if I focus very, very hard, then I can barely, just barely, make out the smell of blood clinging to it.

<You have learned: Enhanced Scent Lv.1>

I really hope that doesn't mean I have a stronger smell now than I did befo—

My brief distraction is enough to give the shade incentive to strike, and from the eternal darkness flies the sound of wind and the smell of blood, and only by a deft side step am I able to avoid a slice to the throat that would otherwise have been fatal. Instead, it simply rips a small incision along the length of it, peeling a bit of my skin and bringing forth a little burst of blood.

I leap toward where I'm pretty sure he went and am met with a face-full of tree. O—owwww . . . !

But I don't exactly have time to recover from my arboreal snogging before he's on me again, and in turn I'm on him, and we roll and claw at each other like foul beasts, snarling and spitting, and clawing and drawing blood that I'm sure is splattering everywhere. But although we are equally matched, there is one thing I know that he doesn't. Namely, how I fight, and how I think.

<THE GOD OF COMBAT GROANS.>

Despite what I might think and feel, I'm not actually that quick to take to biting.

I can't see him. I can barely hear him, our scents are mingling together since our blood is the same, but in a brief pause, in a tiny moment where he pulls in a breath, I go for it. Thrusting my head into the gap between us, I hook my teeth into his throat, making him squeal like a pig and claw at my back. My shoulder blades are getting exposed, but it doesn't matter and I just keep gnawing into his throat, chew-chew-chewing until I can feel his throat get crushed between my teeth. But if he has the same resistances as me, then it won't be enough. So I keep chewing, and I chew up his arteries and his tendons and his flesh and his throat and his spinal cord and his neck and his brain stem and in the end his entire head goes rolling.

<You have learned: Fang Lv.9>
<You have learned: Fang Lv.10>
<You have learned: Sharp Fang Lv.1>
<Shade (Lv.18) Defeated.>
<[Level Up]>
<You have reached Level 19.>
<Agility has increased by 2.
Strength has increased by 2.
Stamina has increased by 4.
Magic Power has increased by 1.
Sharp Fang has increased by 1.
Eviscerate has increased by 1.
Stealth has increased by 1.
Sharp Claw has increased by 1.
Enhanced Hearing has increased by 1.
Enhanced Scent has increased by 1.
Blindness Resistance has increased by 1.>

Fair Bout

That's a pretty nice sight. A sight for sore eyes, one might say. My only question is: does this mean that the shades will now *also* be level 19? Because, frankly, I would rather for that to not be the case, thankyouverymuch.

<Top—Status—Community>
<PrissyKittyPrincess
Human Level 19
Agility: 61
Strength: 41
Stamina: 72
Magic Power: 32>

Lookin' good, all things considered. I still have no idea what to do with my magic power thing. There are magic books and things you can buy in the shop, but I'm not exactly in any place to buy them.

. . . Shoot, I should have asked Moleman about it! Man, with how stupidly kind he is, I'm sure he would've handed it all over for free. I'll have to ask him about it next time we meet. Assuming there's another symposium, that is.

But right now, I can't really afford to consider those kinds of thoughts. I'm stuck in a completely BLACK forest together with a supposedly unlimited number of clones of myself who can appear at any time to try to rip out my throat. Yeah, that sounds reasonable. Was this difficulty even designed to be properly beatable? Who knows.

However, the fact remains that I fight better with food in my stomach. So, even though all I really want to do is lie down and take it easy, I squat down and start disassembling the shade.

But just as I start flaying the meat off the right femur, I feel something. Some little hint of what's to come.

I pull the leg out of its socket and spin around just in time to thrust the entire bony thing into the jaws of another shade. But I've got more weapons than just my teeth, and within only fractions of a second it starts wheeling its claws at me. Grunting, I use my feet for once and kick it away from me, the femur flailing out of its gnashing grip. I hunch down, and the moment it leaps at me again, I'm ready. Grabbing it from below, I lift it high into the air, ripping and biting into its soft, exposed underside. Warm blood streams down onto my face and body as the creature on top of me howls in pain. It scratches feebly at my back, its final dying attempt being to bite into the back of my neck, but by that point it's too weak to fulfill the attempt.

<Shade (Lv.19) Defeated.>

And so began my hellish three weeks in the forest.

It would have taken a lot less time if it weren't for the shades. Still, even if they hadn't been around, I'm sure it would still have taken at least two weeks just to trek the distance. Running in the darkness is just asking to face-plant into a tree, or trip on a rock and break your jaw, or fall down a small cliff to break even more than just your jaw. Climbing trees to get around doesn't work either. Not to mention that the shades also like being up in the trees, so a nice nightly climb just turns into a battle royale, tree version.

Regarding the shades, I have discovered three things. First, and most important: they do not have sovereign skills. I'm sure they don't have fetal position blowover, though I can't be certain of the great values sniffer one. They might have TRT, but since it wouldn't have any effect on me, I can't tell if they use it or not. But they have all the other skills, including resistances. Second, their level and skill levels update alongside mine. The one and only trump card I have compared to them is FPB, which I have now become a frequent user of. But FPB is purely defensive and distractive. The third and final thing is that they really do look exactly like I do. If I'm covered in blood and guts from the last shade, then the next shade I meet will also be covered in blood. They even wear my beloved leopard pelt, which I of course steal every time. I now have five dozen leopard pelts. Is that enough or too little? How much does one pelt sell for? Will these even be sold? I have no idea.

As I'm musing over all of this, a soft wheezing reaches my ears and I narrowly but accurately dodge a strike from a shade. The moment after his attack misses, I attack in the small gap, gouging my clawed hand into his lower back, jimmying it around until I can grab his spine properly, which I quickly pull out, the stringy nerves getting severed like bowstrings as I do. The shade mewls incomprehensibly, and I finish him off by biting into his neck hard enough to break his upper spine and sever the lower brainstem. And with that, he drops. The wheezing dies with him.

<Shade (Lv.23) Defeated.>

To explain, these things really do spawn in with the exact same body as me. So, if I have—purely for the sake of example—a small, calculated hole in my windpipe that causes me to wheeze with every breath I take, then the shades will also have that. I think this alongside the FPB is the only reason I've survived. If a shade breaks my arm, then the next one I face has a broken arm.

It's a simple concept that has led me to this point.

Sniff sniff sniff. I can smell the chalice. It's close now.

It's high up, though. But I can't smell blood on anyone but myself, so I think that maybe, just maybe, I won't have to face any shades on this climb. All I have to do is to go straight up. Yup. That's it.

I walk forward and walk right into a smooth, stony surface, possibly breaking my nose in the process. But it's fine, because I can unbreak it enough to use it for sniffing just by wiggling it around and clearing out the blood. I run my hands over the surface in front of me. Yeah, it's relatively smooth. Still rock, though. Going by how close the chalice is, I assume the thing is on top of a small rocky cliffside or something. Well, nothing to do but climb.

I thrust my clawed fingers inside the gap between the rocks and heave myself up. Sometimes I jimmy my fingers too far in and they break, and I have to tear the fingers off afterward, but it's fine. As long as I climb, it doesn't really matter what happens in between.

<You have learned: Salamander Healing Lv.2>
<You have learned: Climb Lv.5>
<You have learned: Falling Tolerance Lv.4>
<You have learned: Organ Rupture Tolerance Lv.5>

And after an hour or so and falling only two times, I reach the top. Heaving myself up, I'm surprised to find myself falling down face-first onto the platform in front of me, breaking my nose yet another time. Damn it.

But I'm here.

I pull the bush from my inventory, briefly blinded by the light it exudes.

In front of me stands a large ornate chalice seemingly made of silver, kind of like the ones they have at the Olympics. Well, not much else for me to do, I guess.

I toss the bush into the chalice.

The whole place erupts with such intense light I might as well be standing next to a small sun and the terrible WHITEness of it is enough to temporarily blind me and probably also cause permanent optical nerve damage and I'm so shocked by the whole thing I stumble down and fall onto my back, clutching at my face, trying to cover my burning eyes as best as I can. The light is so bright that even with my hands in front of my eyes and even with my eyelids squeezed shut, the light still comes through, making everything I see RED.

H—holy heck, what even—

And then the blinding light turns mellow, and after a few minutes of hyperventilating and grinding my molars in pain, I'm finally able to muster enough courage to open my eyes.

It's . . . light.

The sky above is blue. I can see the sun.

I stand up. A nice fire is burning softly in the chalice. If I look out to where I came from, there's a huge forest. Very green. But if I look at where I'm standing instead, I can notice something just slightly disheartening.

. . . This is a castle, isn't it?

I'm standing up on an exposed tower, at the very top of a big castle. I say *castle*, but it's half-eaten by the forest and mostly in ruins. If I look down at where I came from, there's a trail of blood and abandoned fingers along the wall. If I look at where I started this whole climb, I can see a simple door leading into the castle. Behind where I'm standing, right beside the chalice, is a staircase.

. . . I didn't need to do any of that climbing. I could've just gone up the stairs like a normal person. I hate my li—

<Tutorial stage, Hell Difficulty Fourth Floor: Boss Stage>
<[Clear Condition] Banish the unhappy king of poets.>

Uh-huh. Alright. And where do you expect me to find this guy?

No answer? Yeah, that's about what I expected.

Anyway, my left hand is only hanging on by a few stray nerves and a sliver of skin, so I think I'd better heal up. I couldn't see any shades looking out across the forest, so I'll assume they've all gone and croaked. Which in turn means that, for the first time in around three weeks, I can sit down and meditate and heal up fully. Isn't that just swell?

Almost excited, I sit down and cross my half-shredded legs.

I close my eyes.

<A Canto appears to you.>

Aaaaand there it is. Alright, stage, show me what you've got.

<And to a place I come where nothing shines.>

Right, useless as usua—

Hang on. I can read it?! H—hang on, this is completely new! I mean, sure, I could understand what Simel was saying and everything the people in the symposium were saying as though it was all my own language, but this is different!

It feels like I'm not supposed to have access to this kind of information. Isn't this, I don't know, *secret?*

Well, apparently not, because I can read it just fine. And now that I can understand it, it's actually even less useful than before, somehow. I mean, *And to a place I come where nothing shines?* What is this even for? Yeah, nothing shines here because the sun was gone. What did you expect, man?

But now the sun is back, so there's no need to worry. Yup. None at all.

<You have learned: Regeneration Meditation Lv.10>
<You have learned: Moving Meditation Lv.1>

Ohh, nice! New skill!

. . . What does it do?

<[Moving Meditation (Lv.1)]
The effects of [Regeneration Meditation] can be used even while not actively meditating. Requires strong concentration and mental focus.>

How useful! From what I can see, I still have regeneration meditation too, so if I use them both at the same time, my regeneration speed can increase massively!

To test things, I do the old test of trying out how fast different injuries heal with or without everything. With just moving meditation, I regenerate with an extra speed of about ten percent. Combined with regeneration meditation too, I get twice that, putting me at a total recovery speed of two hundred twenty percent! If I can get moving meditation high enough, I'll be unstoppable . . . !

The only problem is that, as the description says, it drains my mental energy like crazy. So even though I want to use it constantly, if I do so, I might get stuck in some half-Zen drooling state. Even though it hurts, I'll have to stick with only using this in battle if I really need it.

But after an hour or so of testing out my meditation healing techniques, I can finally say that my body has fully healed. My fingers are back and so are my toes, and the teeth that fell out are back, too.

In other words, it's time for me to head out and try to find that unhappy king of poets, or whatever. I can't smell him or anything, but I've got good reason to expect him inside this very castle. I mean, really, where else would he be?

Getting to my feet, I briefly consider jumping down the side of the castle so I can enter it properly through the front door. But after remembering that my falling tolerance isn't even a resistance yet, I decide to just take the stairs.

I go down winding stairs, through countless slim hallways, poking my head into look-holes and small closets, oohing and aahing like a tourist, accidentally exiting the castle through a window and falling two stories before entering through the main entrance normally, wandering around a bit more, and after what feels like at least half a day, I finally find the throne room.

"Took you long enough to get here, friend," some guy with an annoying voice says as I open the door. My eyes fall to the long RED carpet lying on the floor, and I look the whole length of the room until my gaze finally lands on the guy himself. He grins at me. "You don't seem especially surprised by my appearance."

Um, no.

In front of me, sitting on a throne of wood and wearing a crown of olive leaves, is me. Except this me is twice as tall as the real deal and five times beefier. At either side of the throne stands a guard, just as big, both carrying a shield each. Now that I look at it, the *poet king*—as he must be—has a sword in his lap. Just lying there.

<**The Poet King (Lv.28) [BOSS]**>
<**Guard (Lv.25) [BOSS]**>
<**Guard (Lv.25) [BOSS]**>

I glance at my status.

<**Top—Status—Community**>
<**PrissyKittyPrincess**
Human Level 23
Agility: 74
Strength: 45
Stamina: 87
Magic Power: 36>

I was actually feeling pretty confident about my level before this, but it seems I might be just a little underleveled. Should I have tried to personally kill all the shades before coming here? Hm. Not sure.

On the other side of the room, the poet king gives a massive wave of his hand. Man, he's huge, alright.

"Come, now. Speak with me, won't you? You have nothing to fear."

Hm. He isn't being too aggressive or anything, but I should still keep my distance. Also, if talking to him can give me some sort of opening to strike, then I will do so. "Who are you?"

"Who am . . . ?" He chuckles deeply, with mirth my voice shouldn't be capable of. This is super weird. I really, really hate the sound of my voice coming out of him like that. It's like listening to your voice in a recording but even worse, because he's saying things I wouldn't say. His eyes gleam. "What does the little box say I am?"

I try to stand my ground by straightening my back, but I've got a permanent gamer hunch, so all I can do is stand slightly taller. "You know about the system?"

"Of course I do, friend!" he says warmly, waving his hands about. "Am I not borne of this great all-mother, as you are to be shaped by that same all-father?"

I stare at him. "Okay, before you go any further, I kind of need you to define whether you're describing the system as like some sort of Gaia-like mother or if it's a father kind of guy, because saying they're both is very strange, but if you want to I'll totally accept that it would be like something completely different, but calling it both a mother *and* a father isn't, like, suitable. Make up your mind, weirdo."

His smile doesn't even waver slightly. "It has birthed us, and it has molded us. Comparing it to a human mother and father is simply a metaphor. In truth, it can hardly be compared to either one, but rather an amalgamation of bo—"

Chance!

I leap from where I stand but the instant I get even slightly close, I slam into a pair of wall-like shields, making my ears ring and my brain quake. Okay. Okay. Okay. Um.

\<You have learned: Concussion Tolerance Lv.2\>

From a gap between the shields, I can see the poet king's eye glinting with mischievousness. The two guards step back to their original positions, and I fall to the floor with a splat.

"Why don't you calm down for a second, my friend? There is no reason to hurry this."

"My clear condition is to kill you," I groan as I pull myself back up. "You should know that, right?"

"Of course I know that." He replies as though we're talking about the color of the sky. "I was made to be defeated. Or to defeat you. In that case, I would simply die at the hands of the next challenger."

He's playing with me. He *wants* to talk. I don't, but I need another chance. I'm closer to him now. The next time, I'll be able to get to him.

"Plenty of people in the tutorial have passed this floor before," I say. "Shouldn't you have been killed by them already?"

He waves his hand like it doesn't even matter, and as though the question is frivolous at best. "Those challengers simply killed my brothers. I am the poet king of the Hell Difficulty, not of the others." His face lights up. "And, until now, you are my first visitor." His expression falters a little, his mirthful smile taking on notes of tragedy. "And, possibly, my last."

"And why should I be your last?" I ask, not daring to consider the fact that I'm supposed to be the first. Somewhere deep inside, I hope, maybe stupidly so, that he's only the poet king for the Europe server.

His large, almost ancient eyes look me up and down; from my bloodied, bluish feet to my yellowed eyes. A little sigh escapes his lips.

"To be frank with you, my friend"—his eyes pierce through me—"the Hell Difficulty was never meant to be possible for your kind."

Huh?

Something hollow settles into the pit of my stomach. "What?" a voice that might be my own says. It's hoarse. "What do you mean by that?"

He shakes his mighty head. "It is very simple. From what the rulers of this tutorial could understand, beating Hard was as high as you could go. And this is not strictly in terms of your body and your physique. You were chosen for your large, highly metabolic bodies; but here, it is not your bodies that break with the strain. It is your *mind*." I can feel my own head shaking, all on its own. Words and accusations are trying to make their way out of my throat, but they won't emerge. "I had not expected to be met with anyone, as low as my floor is. Though, looking at you, I am starting to hope that you make it no further."

His eyes burn with cold fire. I can feel sweat bead along my back.

"If you defeat me now, eventually, I believe that you will wish you hadn't."

That isn't true. That's false. He's wrong. That isn't the case. He's just making things up. He's trying to demoralize me; that's what he's doing. That's it.

He leans back on his throne. "But it doesn't need to go that way, my friend. The next attempt will begin in only a week. If you stay here with me, in my castle, I will not harm a hair on your head. When the timer runs out and you are returned to your lobby, you may start this floor over again. You've made your way through the blind forest once. You can do so again. Return here, and we may continue our chat. I will remember you. You need not die, for if you continue beyond this, even if you should defeat me—even if you should defeat the floors that come next—at some point, you will reach a moment when you will wish you had died earlier." "No," I say, barely a whisper. "No, I will not . . . I won't . . ."

But it's not easy to deny the words of someone when they look so deeply, deeply compassionate. I didn't even know my face could make such an expression. I look wise beyond my few years. I can feel my voice tremble as I say, "I—I have to . . ."

"There is nothing you *have* to do, my friend. No one expects you to clear this tutorial. There is no need to shoot for the impossible. Please, stay here, and let's talk instead. The shades that roam the blind forest cannot talk with me; all they do is snarl. And these guards of mine are the same. Please."

Something switches in my brain. I can't tell what, but something takes a turn.

If nobody expects me to clear the tutorial, isn't that all the more reason to *do it*? Just to prove them wrong? To prove to whoever invited us here that even the impossible isn't too much? If I stop here, then if someone tries to get to this point, if they try to get beyond it, then all that awaits them is blind darkness. Someone needs to pave the way.

If I give up here, there will be no road for those that wish to follow.

"I can't do that," I say. When I look up at him, I can feel my jaw clench. "I need to defeat you."

His smile turns sad. "I see. I had hoped it would not come to this, but if it helps, then I understand. As I have been taught, I will let you fight this boss room normally. Guards?" The two guards at his side turn to him robotically. "One at a time, please."

I take a step back. The right guard steps forward.

<Guard (Lv.25) [BOSS]>

I can't be sure of it, but I think he has the same skills as I do. In that sense, him choosing to fight with a shield is more of a handicap than anything. His size is the same thing. His being literally twice as tall as I am may put us in a David-and-Goliath sort of situation, but it doesn't mean his size is a purely good thing. Really, if anything, it's just more flesh for me to claw at.

<THE GOD OF DUELS LOOKS ON WITH INTEREST.>
<THE GOD OF COMBAT TELLS HIM NOT TO GET HIS HOPES UP.>

The poet king solemnly raises his hand. "Take your positions," he says, and the guard follows his words exactly. I never really learned what position is best for me, though, so I don't do much other than crouch down a bit. "And on three. One, two . . ."

Before the third number hits, I leap across the floor, rolling myself into a ball and activating fetal position blowover before the guard has time to respond. With immense dexterity, I roll across the floor, all the way around behind him, where I jump onto the back of his calf and hook myself onto him with my claws before chewing into the tendons at the back of his knee in an attempt to cripple him fully.

The guard makes a grunting sound and I barely have time to chew through his skin before a massive hand reaches back and grabs my leg. My grip is fast, but if I lose my leg I am one hundred percent dead, so even though I want to stay here, I have no choice but to let him rip me off like an adamant tick. Once I'm removed, he lifts me high into the air, all the way above his head, probably to slam me into the ground, but I can avoid that by just grabbing his thumb with both arms and breaking it. As large as it is, his thumb is only the size of my hand, so against the full might of my spindly arms, it breaks and I tumble out of his hand, right back onto the floor.

I land into a roll, and as soon as I have time to, I start rolling again, though this time the guard seems to know the game, so he begins stomping at the ground with his feet, each one as long as my shoulders are broad. He almost gets me several times, but by deftly dodging his strikes, I'm able to roll around to the back of his body once again, where I again leap onto the back of his knee. This time he isn't quick enough to remove me, so with fierceness only rivaled by cats unwilling to take a bath, I tear up his entire back, making him completely unable to use his left leg.

Grunting, he has no choice but to fall to his knee, which is an excellent moment for me.

Leaping to the front once more, I avoid a few of his strikes before leaping at his face. I shove both of my arms into his eyes, blinding him at once, and just to make sure he won't regenerate them, I tear out his eyeballs and toss them behind me.

But apparently the guard for all his seeming normalcy is still a clone of me. So while I'm straddled to his face like a rabies-infected raccoon, he bites my left arm with enough power to instantly break almost every single bone I've got in there.

\<You have learned: Fracture Resistance Lv.9\>

Putting my left hand so close to something as blood-full as his tongue was a mistake.

Not really caring about my arm, I grab hold of his tongue and pull with every inch of what little muscle I've got, the surprise of it loosening his jaw's grip enough for me to tear it out completely. Blood spurts from his mouth like he's puking, and I change focus to his throat, ripping and tearing with as much power as I can muster.

\<You have learned: Sharp Claw Lv.5\>

And eventually I get hold of his carotid artery and I pull it out. Bleeding alone won't kill him, so before he has time to remember that he has arms, I rip and I tear until I get to his spinal cord. By that point, all it takes to make the most of it is to give him instant spondylolisthesis, thereby taking his discs on a one-way trip through slip-'n'-slide land.

With his neck fifteen steps beyond broken, he stumbles one step, two, and then finally falls, his head thumping on the floor like a knocker.

<Guard (Lv.25) [BOSS] Defeated.>
<[Level Up]>
<You have reached Level 24.>
<Agility has increased by 3.
Strength has increased by 2.
Stamina has increased by 3.
Magic Power has increased by 1.
Sharp Fang has increased by 1.
Eviscerate has increased by 1.
Sharp Claw has increased by 1.
Enhanced Hearing has increased by 1.
Enhanced Scent has increased by 1.
Hallucination Protection has increased by 1.
Concussion Tolerance has increased by 2.>

<THE GOD OF DUELS TRIES TO SAY SOMETHING BUT CAN'T FIND THE WORDS.>
<THE GOD OF COMBAT PATS THE GOD OF DUELS ON THE BACK.>

I pull my arms out of the guard's neck and look up at what's in front of me.

Ooh, level up! Now the gap between me and the next guard is just slightly slimmer. Which obviously means he should be far easier to the point where I won't need to try at all. Hehehe.

The poet king looks at me with a melancholy expression on his face. No, hang on, he's a poet, so I guess the look on his face is . . . lugubrious? Lachrymose? Something like that.

"You do know that it is common courtesy to wait until *three* to start the duel, don't you?"

I shake my hands, making a spray of blood splatter onto the floor. "Give me the next one."

He looks at my left arm. It's bent into awkward angles. "Should you choose to, I would not stop you from meditating to heal up before the next duel. As a matter of fact, I demand that you return to a healthy state before continuing. It is the most basic of courtesies. If you must know, it is likewise courtesy to face your next challenger in full health, so as to show respect to him."

I wipe some of the blood off my mouth. "If you don't send him out right now, I'm just going to attack him where he stands, and you won't even get to do your little counting-down bit."

He sighs. That smile of his is nowhere to be seen. Without even saying anything, he waves for the guard to step forward. "Take your positions, please." The guard moves to stand right in front of me. I hunch down where I stand atop his fallen comrade.

"On three. Three—"

I go on *three* and leap at the guard, rolling into a ball as I go for the back of his calf again. Apparently, though, he has the capability to learn, because instead of just letting me do a repeat of the last battle, he almost instantly slams his massive shield against the floor, right atop where I was mere seconds ago. Alright, the game is different, but that doesn't mean I'm about to die like a chump. Rolling behind him, I leap onto his back and begin clawing through his skin. See, he's buff. And there's one insurmountable weakness that such people have.

No matter how much the guard tries, his beefy arms can't reach me. Hahaha, take *that*, you damn gym rat!

Clawing like mad, I activate moving meditation if only to get my left arm good enough to help me claw at his back. And right as I start to see his spine . . .

My whole world shifts as the guard purposefully falls backward, something that surprises me so badly I can do nothing but stare as his back falls atop me and crushes me underneath.

<You have learned: Fracture Resistance Lv.10>
<You have learned: Fracture Protection Lv.1>

Perfect timing, but honestly speaking, it kind of doesn't help when my ribs are already broken beneath approximately four hundred kilos of meat. However, unlike what he may think, this doesn't remove me from his back. Just the opposite, as a matter of fact. So even though I can feel my lungs strain under the weight atop me, I still keep clawing. His spine is in my grip. I just need to break it and he's done for.

Grabbing the spine in both hands, I pull it in two different directions, severing it completely.

The guard rolls over and I scurry out of the hole I had made in his back. I didn't get any message from him, which means he's still alive, but that'll change soon enough. Apparently, I only succeeded in crippling him. Though, then again, in a fight like this, do I need any more than that?

I make eye contact with the poet king. He seems . . . sad, but in a pretentious way. I grin at him.

Following this, over the course of around five minutes, I use his guard as a scratching post, staying on his back and just doing small damage to him while watching him squirm.

<You have learned: Sharp Claw Lv.7>
<You have learned: Sharp Fang Lv.4>
<You have learned: Eviscerate Lv.9>

And all the while, I use moving meditation in order to heal myself back up.

<You have learned: Salamander Healing Lv.3>
<You have learned: Moving Meditation Lv.2>

By the time the guard finally croaks, I've healed completely.

<Guard (Lv.25) [BOSS] Defeated.>
<[Level Up]>
<You have reached Level 25.>
<Agility has increased by 2.
Strength has increased by 3.
Stamina has increased by 3.
Magic Power has increased by 1.
Sharp Fang has increased by 1.
Sharp Claw has increased by 1.
Enhanced Hearing has increased by 1.
Enhanced Vision has increased by 1.
Ulcer Tolerance has increased by 2.
Falling Tolerance has risen by 2.
Organ Rupture Tolerance has increased by 1.>

<THE GOD OF DUELS PLACES HIS HEAD IN HIS HANDS.>
<THE GOD OF COMBAT TRIES TO FIND THE RIGHT WORDS TO SAY.>
<THE GODDESS OF HONOR SHAKES HER HEAD.>

An Empty Win

Finally, I turn to the poet king. I don't think there's a single inch of me not covered in blood, and the floor of this throne room is no different. Slowly, I step down from atop the guard's mangled body.

This would be the perfect moment to say a speech or make a cool pose, but I don't really have anything like that to give. Really, it's the poet king's fault. If he'd sent both his guards at me at once, they would have defeated me easily. Even more so if he went with them. But now it's just me, and him. And I'm ready.

The poet king's eyes slowly move from one corpse to another before turning to me. "Do you truly feel nothing at this?"

Feel nothing . . . ? That's, well, uh . . . I feel pretty happy to level up? That counts, right?

He shakes his head. "Forget I asked." Slowly, carefully, almost like an old man rising, he stands up from his throne. He takes the sword on his lap into his hand. It's as long as I am tall, which isn't actually that much. Even so, I don't think I could lift it if I tried. His eyes meet mine and I watch with a fair bit of fascination as they harden. With a single, magnanimous movement, he raises his sword toward me, holding it in only one hand. "I suppose, if anyone should beat this difficulty, they must be a beast, in both body and soul." The gleam of mirth in his eye dies. "Expecting you to be anything else was arrogance on my part."

I'm not sure how to respond to that, so I just hunch down, ready to pounce the second he lowers his guard.

And for a second or two, we just stare each other down. Me, waiting for a chance. And he . . .

He draws a deep breath. "Take your posi—"

And that's the chance I'm looking for. With wild abandon, I rush at him, claws spread and ready, my mind whirling with all the different ways I can kill him, all the soft spots he has, every artery on his body that might weaken him.

He doesn't move.

But that only lasts until the very second I get into range. As soon as I'm close to him, as soon as my mind brings up the inevitable question of *Why hasn't he made a move?* I get my answer as his sword falls, inches away, and I stare dumbly as it crashes down toward me. My body reacts on its own to only barely avoid having our entire body bisected from head to toe as I instead lunge to the right, leaving me to only lose my left arm rather than my entire body.

\<You have learned: Dismemberment Tolerance Lv.4\>
\<You have learned: Dismemberment Tolerance Lv.5\>
\<You have learned: Dismemberment Tolerance Lv.6\>
\<You have learned: Slashing Tolerance Lv.6\>
\<You have learned: Slashing Tolerance Lv.7\>

At this moment my brain might as well not exist, because it's only my body that reacts to this, throwing itself into a roll as I bound across the floor. I roll to a stop several meters away from him, my brain whirling as though it's still stuck on the first floor in order to get some understanding of the situation.

What happened? What happened? Shouldn't he only have the skills that I have? How can he use the sword like that? I couldn't even see it move! This is way beyond unfair.

But it was only an arm. An arm is okay. It'll come back when I'm in the lobby, and it was only my left arm anyway. I'm still fine. I can still win this.

It's a shame my vision is so bad while I'm rolling, or I would've been able to keep moving.

Rolled up in a ball, I look at him.

Slowly, he lifts his sword back up again, resuming his prior position. He looks like a samurai or something. Whatever pose that is supposed to be, it isn't something a chump like me should be able to take. I should have thought of this before, but this guy really is only a shade in name. He only sort of looks like me. That's all. His musculature and size and especially his brain is completely different.

Unlike me, he's an actual warrior.

To win this, I'll need to treat him as such. But I know his weakness. His one, single weakness. *Unlike me, he's genuinely chivalrous.* That's why I'll be able to beat him.

Carefully, forcing my body to tremble like a wounded puppy, I unroll myself, and while making sure he can see me, I stand up. Breathing shallowly, I stagger toward him. He isn't moving, but he isn't attacking either. Looking up at him, I can see his eyes shine with pity. Perfect.

Shivering, I raise my right arm in surrender—the only arm I have left—and while making sure to keep my voice wavering and pained, I choke out, "I—I think, um, I think . . . I've changed my mind. You're—hic—you're right. This isn't the life I wanted. All this battling, all this fighting, all this *killing* . . . I hate what it's doing to me. It's making me into someone I can't recognize, and—and it *hurts*. I see myself in the shades and I can't even recognize myself. I don't want to do this anymore. So please . . ." Staggering, trembling, I walk up to him. I'm so close he could easily strike me down right now. But he won't. I know he won't. I can see it on his face. And then when I look up at him, and I make my face so pitiful even a bear would hesitate, I finally say, "Please, can we stop this . . . ?"

He looks down at me, and his eyes widen a hair, and his sword falls a little, just slightly, and his face softens and that hard iciness melts from his eyes and into pure sympathy, and right as he begins hunching down to me, to say something soft, something nice, something calming, right at that very moment . . .

I strike.

His eyes don't even have time to widen before I fly up at him, right into his face, and just like with his guard, I tear out his eyeballs, but before he can bite me or tear me off, I deftly fly to the back of his neck, and I tear and I rip and I rip and I tear.

<You have learned: Eviscerate Lv.10>
<You have learned: Maul Lv.1>

Yeah, that's it. I *maul* him.

Blind, he bats at me, trying to get to me, but I simply jump off him, and before he can try to find where I am, I roll between his legs, briefly disorienting him right before I leap toward his soft-skinned belly. Although it's protected by enough muscle for an entire banquet, once I start ripping, it's surprisingly easy to get in there.

I tear a hole in his abdomen, and then I stick my entire upper body in there, ripping apart anything and everything I can get my hands on. And once his abdomen is nothing but a slurry of sliced organs and blood and bile, I go further up, gripping hold of his quickly beating heart, and just as I have hold of it, I feel him grab hold of my right leg, effectively assisting me in such a way that when he tears me out of him, so too is he tearing out his own heart, not that he can see it.

I stab my hand through his heart.

His body gives a twitch.

His hand loses grip, and he drops me to the floor. I watch with interest as he staggers back one, two, three steps, back to his throne, finally collapsing into it. His chest is still going up and down even though his heart isn't there to pump anything.

I approach him. Maybe it wasn't enough? Maybe I need to destroy his brain too?

I step up to him where he sits so still and soundless, and right as I start to think that *maybe he really is dead*, his hand shoots out and I'm just about to tear up his wrist when it instead falls softly onto my head, like a big hat. Since he's so big, and I'm so small, it feels sort of like when you're a kid, and your dad puts his hand on your head.

I stare up at the poet king, and his empty, bloody sockets meet me. He smiles at me. But it's a sad smile. "*I pity you*," he breathes. "But I nonetheless hope that you find peace."

And then, without me even being able to find the words to say in response, he dies.

\<Poet King (Lv.28) [BOSS] Defeated.\>
\<[Level Up]\>
\<You have reached Level 27.\>
\<Agility has increased by 6.
Strength has increased by 5.
Stamina has increased by 5.
Magic Power has increased by 2.
Disassemble has increased by 1.
Maul has increased by 1.
Dismemberment Tolerance has increased by 2.
Sharp Claw has increased by 1.
Sharp Fang has increased by 2.
Blunt Tolerance has increased by 3.
Slashing Tolerance has increased by 2.
Divinity Tolerance has increased by 1.\>

I feel numb looking at it.

\<You have cleared the fourth floor.\>
\<You have received 1,000 points for clearing the floor.
You have received an additional 1,000 points for being the first to clear the floor.\>
\<For clearing the stage completely, you will receive an additional reward.\>
\<To repay your debt, the additional reward has been traded for 5,000 points.\>
\<3 Gods have shown a positive response to you.
You have obtained 3,000 points.\>

**<21 Gods have shown a negative response to you.
21,000 points have been deducted.>**

. . . It's even more than last time, huh?

**<To repay your debt, the floor clear reward has been traded for 1,000
points.>**

So, in other words, I gained nothing at all from this, huh?

FLOOR 5

THE INFERNAL HURRICANE

Butterfinger

The floor shifts beneath my feet and I'm back in the horrible WHITE lobby, but my eyes are staring at the screen in front of me.

<To repay your debt, your inventory has been sold for 1,899 points.>
<Current debt: 11 774 points.>

My debt is even worse now. So, in other words, beating this floor awarded me exactly nothing, huh? I just went deeper in debt? Right? Is that the situation? Any chance I could get a bank statement on the situation here? Really, I don't know about you, but this whole *we-don't-like-you-so-go-into-debt* system feels a bit rigged. I mean, if you liked me, I would've been rich by now! Imagine that, huh? If every god that disliked me liked me instead, I would've had enough points to buy the whole damn shop!

This is a travesty. I can't believe this. Then again, it's not like being in debt has any effect outside the shop, so I think it's fine if the gods don't like me as much as they—

<The God of Duels thanks the God of Combat after a long and fruitful discussion.>
<The God of Combat has come to a decision.>
<The Goddess of Honor is in favor.>
<The God of Adventure is in favor.>
<The Goddess of Solitude is in favor.>
<The God of Cruelty is in favor.>
<The God of Wild is in favor.>
<The Goddess of Children is in favor.>

< . . . >
<THE GOD OF COWARDICE IS IN OPPOSITION.>
<THE GODDESS OF WANT IS IN OPPOSITION.>

<22 TO 2 IN FAVOR.>
<THE GOD OF COMBAT HAS DECIDED WITH THE SUPPORT OF 22 BACKING GODS
THAT HELL CHALLENGER LO FENNRICK WILL BE STRIPPED OF THE BLESSINGS THAT
THE GOD OF COMBAT HAS SO GRACIOUSLY GIVEN HIM.
REASONING:
HELL CHALLENGER LO FENNRICK DOES NOT APPEAR TO APPRECIATE OR REQUIRE
THEM IN HIS FURTHER CHALLENGING OF THE HELL DIFFICULTY TUTORIAL.>

Uh . . . Huh? . . .

H—hang on just a moment. If I may ask, and if it isn't too offensive for your divine palates, I have just one question.

What the fuck?

There is so much wrong with this that I don't even know where to start, but I guess the easiest place is . . .

Hey, Cruelty. How come if you like me so much, you still agreed with all these sourpusses to go against me, huh? We may not agree on a lot of things, and I personally don't think you should like me at all since I'm such a kind and virtuous person, but is that any reason for you to go and side with all these dumbos? I mean, really now. Coward and Want got the hint, so why not you?

<THE GOD OF CRUELTY ATTESTS THAT HE ENJOYS ALL FORMS OF CRUELTY, BE THEY
COMMITTED OR ENDURED.>

. . . Uh-huh. So you're the ultimate switch? Right. Got it.

Second, and maybe finally, what the heck do you mean when you say *blessings*? You haven't given me anything! You haven't even taken interest in me, Mr. Fight Right or Die! How am I supposed to be stripped of a blessing I don't even have? Hm? Riddle me *that*, you supposed god.

Bleh. Yeah, of course I don't require your blessings—you *haven't given me any*. Stupid god . . .

So anyway. I got a lot of skills this floor, so I think I'd do best to check on the—

Hm. Hm? Hm . . .

Hu—h. Huh. Huh . . .

If I'm not seeing things wrong, and assuming I didn't court Lady number 2, there's a fair chance that, um . . . Again, assuming I'm not currently experiencing hypnosis, that, ah, uh . . .

All my combat skills are gone?

Intermediate Spear Arts level 2: gone.

Intermediate Knife Arts level 3: gone.

Intermediate Axe Arts level 1: gone.

Intermediate Shieldwork level 4: gone.

Intermediate Swordsmanship level 5: gone.

All of them. I've still got Maul and Eviscerate and my claws and fangs, but anything pertaining to a weapon is just . . . gone.

So, in other words, um . . . Are these the supposed blessings the god of combat had supposedly given me? Huh. Um . . .

Okay, honestly, I'm not especially upset at losing these skills in particular. I haven't used them in a while and I don't think I need them much since all my weapons get automatically sold anyway, but . . .

There's an insinuation here that I don't like. Namely, these skills—whatever they are—come directly from some god or another. As, like, a blessing, I suppose? Or something?

I—I just . . .

Maybe I should have figured this out earlier—it makes absolute sense considering the way, well, *everything* is formatted around here—but, somehow, some way, the system I have, the skills I get from it, the levels it gives me, the *entire tutorial itself* . . . is most likely made from the powers of these gods. They could absolutely do a vote to just kill me.

For some of them, I'm basically just a plaything. For others, by what I can see, they're just hate-watching me. And, sure, being hate-watched is nothing new for me, but the difference here is that the losers who sent me hate mail and angry PMs on Earth didn't hold any physical power over me. They couldn't just press a button and have me explode into confetti on the spot. And, sure, maybe these gods can't do that either. But if they band together, and hold some stupid democratic vote on it . . .

There wouldn't be a thing I could do to stop it.

And that wouldn't be too bad if these supposed gods actually acted like honest-to-God divine creatures. If they were aloof and didn't care for mortal quarrels or anything like that, then they wouldn't care *what* I did because no matter what, I would still be a pathetic, foolish mortal. But as it is, right now, I'm stuck in some sort of half-Greek pantheon. And I don't know about you, but I would *not* want to meet Zeus personally.

This is not a good situation, but there's also nothing I can do about it.

Frankly, I'm starting to think that if the gods really wanted me dead, then I'd already be floating down the river Styx in a one-piece and cement floaties. *But I'm not.* The worst they can do, from what I can see, is to strip me of my skills. And sure, that's already bad enough, but the god of combat couldn't just do that as he pleased. He not only needed the other gods to concur with him, but also a logical reasoning behind it. In this case, it was because I didn't appreciate them, and he didn't think I'd need them in the future. And maybe he's right about that.

Either way, they can't do this stuff out of nowhere and for no reason. The god of keeping-me-alive can't suddenly decide to strip me of all my tolerances because, well—I'm using those! And diligently, too.

As weird as it is to admit, at least within the walls of the tutorial, the gods can't just act however they please. They can try, but they need to have solid reasoning and democratic backing behind whatever they do.

I am not receiving power from a single human-acting god.

I am getting it from *many*.

And some of those gods happen to understand the sound logic and reasoning in why I act as I do. And even if one of those gods happens to like nothing more than watching me suffer, the other two will at least *try* to protect me. Hm. There's got to be some way of using this to my advantage, right?

I just know there is.

But, for now, since there isn't much to do about this whole thing—I certainly can't alter my winning play style—I guess I'd better put it to the side.

The next floor . . . That's the one Moleman warned me about, right? Specifically, about how the boss was supposedly *unbeatable*. In my personal opinion, there's no such thing as a truly unbeatable boss, only bad players. I mean, yeah, some bosses are invincible during certain stages of the battle, but that's always temporary. A boss, no matter how seemingly invincible, will always be beatable somehow, even if it is only inside a cutscene.

Minotaur . . .

Yeah, I've got to beat him. Ain't no way I'm letting a perfectly fine pelt-plus-meat combo slip out of my grip just because the entire tutorial is filled with losers.

That said, I haven't really had time to check the time in a while. How long is it until the floor opens?

<Top—Status—Community>
<06:59:55 Day 112>
<The fifth attempt will begin in 8:18:00:05>
<Floor 5 will open in 23:47:31>

One hundred and twelve days have already passed, huh? Somehow, it feels like it's been both way longer *and* way shorter than that. I guess time really does move fast and/or slow when you're in constant life-or-death situations. Now that I think about it, I haven't been to the forums in a while. I don't feel like posting anything, but there might be some new information or whatever. Can't hurt to check, right?

<Status—Community—Top>
<Europe Server>
<Easy Lobby: 202/278
Normal Lobby: 49/95
Hard Lobby: 10/16
Hell Lobby: 2/2>

Ah, I forgot to check if—

Oh. Looks like Virgil didn't exactly . . . yeah. Man. If she could access the Community boards, I would've sent her a PM or something, but as it is . . . Ouch. I can't really do anything for her. Assuming it is her, of course. I mean, technically speaking, she could have left someone else behind, and . . .

No. I don't want to think like that. That isn't . . . that isn't something she'd do.

Whatever the situation, I hope—maybe in vain—that she at least feels some solidarity with the fact that I'm also alive. We're both alone, but we're alone together, you know? Yeah.

Yeah . . .

W—well, anyway. Next time we meet, if there's such a time, then I'll just hear her out. I don't think there's much I can tell her; I don't exactly have the skills myself to teach her how to best convince people not to go kill themselves, but the least I can do is to listen. With any luck, she'll learn the ropes after a while. It doesn't look like either of us will leave the tutorial anytime soon, so she has all the time in the world. I guess.

Without much else to do, I go into the Community boards.

<Status—Community—Top>
<Discussion Boards>
<HerringFerry[F6]: List of all known former Delegates and Executives.
[28]>
<PetrolPatrol[F2]: What is this place? How is everyone so cool with
this[2]>
<HookedOnBach[F7]: Lawbook for all challengers in the tutorial. :)[397]>
<SuperMoleman[F27]: Moleman's Guide to the People's Rulership of
Rebel.[78]>
<Thanks4All[F15]: wat happened at the Symposium i was on the loo wher
did the delegate commission go[0]>
<ZebraPhonic[F2]: hi uwu[3]>

Same old, same old.

From what I can tell, those rebels decided that *someone* had to make sure everyone was following their agreed-upon rules. So they appointed themselves as our new leaders, with the whole organization being called the People's Rulership of Rebel. PRR for short.

Bach is the leader of it all. I'm not surprised. It doesn't appear like this was democratically voted on or anything, but nobody's complaining, so I'm sure it's fine. The rulebook she posted is just a standard thou-shalt-not-kill. I tried reading whatever Moleman posted, but it was so dry and boring I had no choice but to drop out after only half a paragraph. Anyhow, the PRR has a general leader for each floor who will stay there and make sure that nobody causes trouble, and if someone *does* cause trouble, the issue will be brought to the representative of the difficulty itself, who will decide on the punishment from there.

It's pretty similar to what we had before, but now it's the *people's*, so it's fine. It doesn't really make any difference to me, and nobody's complaining or anything, so there isn't any problem. Easy stuff.

The only other thing of note is that I've received a bit of hate mail.

\<Status—Community—Top\>
\<Personal Messages\>
\<[NEW] Nevermore[F5]: please go and die in the next floor.\>
\<[NEW] FranticRomantic[F3]: ok a Delegate literally killed my friend and now u are just going free witch Is totally dumb so plz go a[. . .]\>
\<[NEW] VatOfBrain[F12]: you are a furry. please put yourself down.\>
\<[NEW] WhitherAndFall[F6]: i wanted to see you die an now im disappointed please kys next time ok.\>
\<[NEW] LethargicSand[F4]: im glad your on Hell Difficulty so youwill die soon.!\>
\<[NEW] Jormungand[F16]: thx 4 the 3 months ******.\>
\<SuperMoleman[F27]: Good luck with Floor Four!\>

Yeah, I'm not reading those. If I wanted to go blind, I might as well tear out my own eyes again.

So, since there's nothing of value to be found here, I just exit out. Back out into this horrible WHITE lobby. Thankfully, I now know how to handle it. So, with no time to waste, I get to painting.

By the time the whole room is a nice fleshy RED, six hours have already passed, which means I've still got eighteen hours left to waste until the next floor opens. Thankfully, I've got a lot of tolerances that need increasing, alongside a few related skills.

Fun fact! I can use maul on myself, and if I disembowel myself just right, I can keep it from healing long enough to raise my tolerances. Useful!

Unfortunately, though, the maul skill isn't too quick to improve, which is fine since it's already very effective. Faster than I expected, my hours are up, and the time has come.

<Top—Status—Community>
<06:46:24 Day 113>
<The fifth attempt will begin in 7:17:13:36>
<Floor 5 will open in 00:00>
<Floor 5 has opened. Do you want to enter?>
<Yes/No>

As usual, I press Yes, no thinking required.

And before I know it, I'm there. Let's see here . . .

Above me is a dark abyss. Below me is a somehow even darker abyss. From what I can tell, I'm standing on a tiny, solitary platform, high enough to make just about anyone feel a little bit agoraphobic. N—not me, though. I'm perfectly fine standing up here. No problem at all, whatsoever—none. The fact that my legs are trembling is just because of the winds. Yeah, that's it. It's just the winds . . .

<Tutorial stage, Hell Difficulty Fifth Floor: The Infernal Hurricane>
<[Clear Condition] Descend the mountain.>

Ah. Ho-hum.

Leaning forward, I look down again. Yeah. That's deep. Can it even be called a mountain? Honestly, it's more like a . . . Well, whatever it is that's one size above mountain, I guess. Really, I wouldn't be surprised if we were above the clouds. Then again, I can't tell the difference between the darkness above and the darkness below, so I can't be sure either way. But what I *do* know is that I'm starting to feel just a little woozy.

<You have learned: Oxygen Deficiency Resistance Lv.7>

Mm-hm. Ah. Yes, I see. That makes sense. Mountain climbers *do* climb with oxygen tanks for a reason, don't they? But I don't have any, so I guess I'll just die.

Alright, alright, strategy time. I've got a little over a week to descend this mountain and encounter beef royale. That should be doable, right? If the time gets too tight, I can always just jump and probably die when I hit the ground. Yup. Yup . . .

W—well, no time like today! I'd better get started.

I walk over to the ledge and look down. It—it sure is steep, huh? It's basically a vertical drop, right down to God knows where.

Tentatively, I sit down on the ledge, putting my feet over the side. I just need to drop down, and then I'll make my way to the bottom at least relatively quick. It's totally doable. Slowly, carefully, I inch farther and farther down the ledge. That is, at least, until something bites my foot, and I pull it up to find a little bat stuck to my sole, biting, and chewing at my arch.

<Bat (Lv.1)>

H—hey, no freebies! Get outta here!

I shake my foot vigorously, but when the bat won't let go, I just rip it off and stick its head into my mouth. I crush it between my molars, making its skull pop in a really gross fashion. I don't know what else to do with it, so I just stick the rest of it in there, chew and swallow. Simple stuff.

<You have learned: Bacteria Tolerance Lv.7>
<You have learned: Bacteria Tolerance Lv.8>
<You have learned: Bacteria Tolerance Lv.9>
<You have learned: Parasite Tolerance Lv.5>
<You have learned: Indigestion Tolerance Lv.10>
<You have learned: Indigestion Resistance Lv.1>

. . . In other words, eating raw bats isn't good for me? Gee, who woulda thunk it.

Anyway, with this, I think I finally know what that weird sound I've been hearing is. I thought it was just the wind, but it seemed a bit too animal. On the other hand, now that I've had a taste of this here bat, I think I just might know what this smell is. That darkness above and around and below me isn't just darkness. It's *bats*.

Hundreds of millions of bats. Enough bats to completely blot out both the sky and whatever's below. And by descending this mountain, I'll be going right into that swarm.

. . . I've got my work cut out for me, then.

Giving a silent prayer to whoever will listen, I heave myself over the ledge and begin my descent. The very second I place my exposed, supple flesh and skin in front of the bat inferno, the lot of them decided that just flying in circles was apparently not good enough for them. Suffice it to say, they decided to have a bat mitzvah on my legs, and my back, and my arms, and even my face. Trying to bat them away was like trying to use a towel underwater. Every bat I ripped off and clenched in my hand was just as soon replaced by yet another, and another, and another.

Countless bats. So many bats I couldn't have counted them even if I had all the time in the world.

I can't count the times I wanted to just stop bothering with the bats. Killing them would just replace them, so what was even the point? But if I stopped trying to kill them then I wouldn't have any way of replenishing energy. Grabbing every bat I could get and crushing it to paste and then stuffing it in my mouth was the only real way of dealing with the swarm.

Within only minutes, I was so covered with bats I had turned completely brown and furry myself. They were everywhere, even in my own damn eyeballs. Since I couldn't exactly focus on the ones in my eyes alone, I had no choice but to accept the fact that I would just have to be blind the entire way down. That wasn't much different from floor 4, so it wasn't too bad. The only difference from my climb to the chalice was that this time I was going down, and this time, I was carrying about ten kilos worth of bats.

<You have learned: Indigestion Resistance Lv.2>
<You have learned: Indigestion Resistance Lv.3>
<You have learned: Parasite Tolerance Lv.6>
<You have learned: Parasite Tolerance Lv.7>
<You have learned: Parasite Tolerance Lv.8>
<You have learned: Virus Tolerance Lv.4>
<You have learned: Virus Tolerance Lv.5>

After some time, I could swear my stomach contained more bats than were on my back.

I feel bloated. I can hear nibbling and suckling across my entire body. I think I can even hear some bat teeth scraping against my bones. They started chewing not long ago. They just weren't happy with my blood alone. But the bats are one thing. I can tolerate them, to some extent. The issue is that my feet and hands are starting to get too bloody to have a proper grip.

<You have learned: Climb Lv.6>
<You have learned: Climb Lv.7>

I'm compensating by forcefully shoving my clawed fingers into whatever crevices I can find. Nevertheless, the second I lose one finger too many, I'm a goner. Losing one or two fingers is fine. I can grow them back with salamander healing and moving meditation. But this whole situation is starting to get to me just a bit too much. The bats are one thing. The steep descent is one thing. But together? Not a fun combo.

The only good thing is that a stupidly high number of my tolerances and resistances are rising at a nice and steady pace.

My head is spinning. Now that I think about it, it's been spinning for the past hours or days or years or so. I can't really think. I pluck a bat from the back of my neck, crush it in my hand, and stick it in my mouth.

\<You have learned: Clutch Lv.6\>

I wonder if the bats are endless. Do they count as enemies? Will I need to defeat all of them in order to get a complete clear? They have levels, though all of them are at level 1. If I had my touch of reverse tolerance at the resistance level, I might have been able to, like, spread a plague of some sort among the bats. Ah, but even then, they're already diseased as it is. I don't think any bacteria or virus I can give them would even be able to stand on the same stage as whatever they've already given me.

Ah, bats . . . I think, if I weren't covered head to toe with bats, I would probably have frozen to death at this point. Though, then again, they are also actively chewing away at my flesh and bone, so the price is heavy. These past hours or so, I've been catching bats, crushing them and putting them into my inventory instead of eating them. My plan is that if I can just string together enough bat skins, I should be able to make a pretty cool cape of some sort. Or something. Assuming all of them don't get sold for whatever reason, that is.

I take another step down.

I tear a bat off my back and stick it in my inventory.

I take another step down.

I tear a bat off my leg and stick it in my inventory.

I take another step down.

I tear a bat off my face and stick it in my inventory.

I take another ste—

My foot slips on something, possibly my blood, possibly a loose rock, and my hands grip for something, anything, in sheer blind panic, unfortunately only finding smooth rocks and I only have six fingers right now anyway so even if I had grabbed something this would still have happened so as vertigo takes hold of my body and the screeching of bats turns louder and louder my body slips off fully and my heart sinks as I begin to fall, and fall, and fall, and fall, and fall, and my mind whirls and my body whirls and I spin round and around and around with the bats clinging to my body like mad, and somewhere deep inside my head, inside the only part of my head that can keep calm no matter what, I start counting, slowly: one, two, three, four, fi—

And then I hit the ground.

My head bursts open and my bowels burst open and the only reason I didn't die on the spot is because I'm covered in a layer of bats but even that isn't enough as my body spasms violently. My brains are on the ground. I'm on the ground. My jaw moves robotically in circles. My spine is broken. I can't feel my legs. I don't want to die. Where did my eyeballs go. If the bats weren't dead beneath me they would be eating me.

Ooo—ooww.

<You have learned: Brain Damage Resistance Lv.8>
<You have learned: Brain Damage Resistance Lv.9>
<You have learned: Brain Damage Resistance Lv.10>
<You have learned: Brain Damage Protection Lv.1>
<You have learned: Falling Tolerance Lv.7>
<You have learned: Falling Tolerance Lv.8>
<You have learned: Falling Tolerance Lv.9>
<You have learned: Falling Tolerance Lv.10>
<You have learned: Falling Resistance Lv.1>
<You have learned: Organ Rupture Tolerance Lv.7>
<You have learned: Organ Rupture Tolerance Lv.8>
<You have learned: Fracture Protection Lv.2>

The darkness takes me.

XXIII

Minotaur

I open my eyes. I'm lying with my back against the ground. The ground below me is soft, even though it should be rocky.

Slowly, I sit up. I rub my head. It kind of aches, but it doesn't hurt. I feel funny.

\<Tutorial stage, Hell Difficulty Fifth Floor Boss Stage\>
\<[Clear Condition] Escape the minotaur by climbing the mountain.\>

I read the message in front of my eyes. And then, like an office worker pressing snooze even though he's already late, I lie back down. Above me stretches that immense mountain. Compared to most mountains I've seen, this one is really more like a needle. It's slim and sharp and it has little to no slope to it. It's almost a complete ninety-degree drop. Interesting. A swirling, squirming swarm of bats covers almost the entire mountain. Outside this swarm, it's nighttime and BLACK, but the stars are so numerous that you can still see pretty well.

For example, I can see that minotaur pretty well.

. . . Hm?

Hm.

\<Minotaur (Lv.37) [BOSS]\>

Huh. Yeah, that's a minotaur alright. It's standing a pace or so away, just kind of looking at me. It's larger than the poet king, and broader, too. And then, just to really ram it home, it's carrying an axe. Oh, and did I mention that it's got a snake for a tail? Yeah.

But it isn't really moving, so I don't know what . . .

Hang on, wait, I just made eye contact with it. Uh. Hum. Erm . . . Hi?

As if on cue, the minotaur roars and raises its axe, the little snake it has for a tail also roaring, which makes it shoot fire from its mouth, because obviously that's something minotaurs do. And then, much like minotaurs also do, it charges at me. I'm still lying on the ground. Now that I think about it, this might not be the most favorable position.

Leaping to my feet, I start to frantically claw at the barren rocks of the cliff just above, almost slipping once, twice before finally pulling myself up. Scrambling up the side of the mountain using every relevant skill I can muster, I try my best to ignore the sound of the minotaur, seemingly mere inches below.

I glance down. Oh, wait, scratch that, it really *is* mere inches below! Who would've thought it?

Right as I begin to question the sense of it all, the snake it has for a tail shoots toward me, spraying fire at my feet.

\<You have learned: Heat Resistance Lv.2\>

Ow, ow, ow, hey, that's unfair, cut it out!

Breath in my throat, trying not to think about the sound of the minotaur huffing and panting, I clamber farther up.

Okay, remember when I said that some bosses were only temporarily invincible? Yeah, uh, that only counts if you aren't completely underleveled compared to them. I mean, I'm ten levels below it! How is that fair?!

It sure as heck isn't, that's what!

Ah, I'm already starting to lose fingers. This sucks. And no matter how high or how fast I climb, the minotaur always seems to be mere feet behind. You know, if I was a little less optimistic, I might have assumed that the whole *you-shouldn't-defeat-the-minotaur* thing was part of the floor's *design*! Hahaha, but there's no way that that could be true, right?

. . . Right?

Okay, let's think here. I can afford to think because the bats have started descending on both me and the minotaur, putting us on equal ground. See, if I don't remember wrongly, when I fell down the cliff, I literally bashed my brains

out. I'm honestly surprised I'm not dead, but it isn't the first time I've been partially lobotomized, so . . . But that isn't the issue here!

When I woke up, the minotaur was just . . . there. It didn't even attack me
until I'd looked at it first. That is, until I'd read the boss stage's clear requirement.

It was waiting for me.

An axe flies toward me and I only barely dodge it by making a quick jump
a step higher.

That isn't to say that it isn't currently trying to kill me; but I have a feeling
that it isn't exactly trying its best either. It's keeping me on my toes, while still
pushing me higher. It is, by all means, fully sentient. This is both a good and a
bad thing. I mean, frankly, if it were trying its damnedest to get me, I'd be dead.
To reiterate for the slow ones in the audience, me being dead is a bad thing. But
just because I'm not dead doesn't mean that this doesn't have any downsides.

\<Top—Status—Community\>
\<07:07:59 Day 118\>
\<The fifth attempt will begin in 2:16:52:01\>

Two days is a lot of time. But that's only if you don't think about the fact that
it took me five days to descend the mountain. Going up it? I can already tell you
that my body and brain aren't quite up to the task, and especially not while being
chased by an axe-wielding, fire-breathing minotaur. If I hurry, I might be able
to survive until the next attempt starts and I can do this all over again without
falling.

But where's the fun in that?

Didn't I tell Moleman I'd beat the minotaur? Didn't I decide that I was going
to prove the whole tutorial wrong? To show them that this here minotaur was
just a chump, and anybody who decided to escape it rather than kill it was—in
turn—even less than a chump?

Yeah. That's right. Because I'm a real gamer.

And someone has to prove that this strat is viable.

I pull one of the many bats off my face and toss it at the minotaur, a tactic I
have long since learned was useless. Fun fact: no matter how many bats you toss
into the minotaur's wide-open maw, it won't die. I've tried for a while now, and
it just swallows them down. By this point, I think it might have eaten more bats
than I have, which is impressive.

Holding one hand over my eye to shield it from the bats while using the
other to heave myself farther up, I look down, but not at the minotaur.

We're pretty high up now. If I fell from up here, I'd be falling for . . . five, six
seconds? Something like that. Either way, this should be high enough.

I survived a fall from this height once, didn't I?

After less than a single moment of hesitation, I let go of the rocks.

Within only half a second of falling I crash into the minotaur's face. The image of his cow eyes widening at the strange sight is enough of a delight for me to say with full certainty that even if this fall kills me, it will be worth it. And, as expected, the combination of me smashing into his face and the surprise of the whole thing is enough for him to lose his weak grip on the rocks. If he had agile toes like I do he wouldn't have any problem staying on, but all he has for feet is a pair of worthless hooves.

We both fall.

I'm on top of his face, madly grinning, ripping at his flesh and trying to open his mouth so I can tear out his tongue in some strange desire for a fitting last meal. Who doesn't like ox tongue?

"*GROUUGGHHHHHH*," the minotaur cries, the sound of which makes all the bats around and above us scatter like mad, and we fall and fall and fall and fall, and even though I am engorged in a bloody, ruthless mania, deep in that one sane corner of my mind, I hear a voice counting, carefully, making sure that each number is exactly as long as it should be: one, two, three, four, five, six . . .

Seven, eight, nine . . .

Hm. Did I perhaps miscalculate the height we were at just the slighte—

The ground greets us firmly and I smash on top of the minotaur, and even though I had expected its body to sound like popcorn since I'm sure every bone in its body just shattered into a million pieces, instead, all I get is a single resounding *CRACK* and a *SPLAT* and my body, despite being cushioned on top of its massive one, also makes a similar sound.

<You have learned: Pressure Tolerance Lv.5>
<You have learned: Falling Resistance Lv.2>
<You have learned: Organ Rupture Tolerance Lv.9>
<You have learned: Organ Rupture Tolerance Lv.10>
<You have learned: Organ Rupture Resistance Lv.1>
<You have learned: Concussion Tolerance Lv.5>
<You have learned: Concussion Tolerance Lv.6>

Even though my body hurts in just about every way you can imagine, a single realization brings me back to the here and now. *I didn't get the boss defeat message.*

My arms are broken but I still pull myself up. Below me, the minotaur lies broken and dying but still alive. Although faint, it is still breathing, and although muted, I can still hear its heart beating.

And you know what? This is good for me.

You see, I realized something with the poet king. If I beat the floor, I can't loot the boss's corpse. Furthermore, since I'm in crippling debt, I can't get the normal floor rewards anyway, so even if I do get one or two of the boss's drops in there, I still lose it. What a conundrum! A dilemma, one might even say.

But here, staring at this bull's magnificent horns, I can tell exactly what the solution is.

I just need to loot the boss *before* I defeat them. Effectively putting the horse before the cart. Isn't that just clever?

Almost smiling to myself, I begin my bountiful harvest. I don't really care too much for its organs since they'll just get sold anyway. Really, it's the pelt that I care for. Sure, it isn't exactly of the finest quality or anything like that, but I *need* to have it so that I can prove to Moleman that I really did defeat this supposedly invulnerable being. Oh, and I also want the horns. And the tail. And the tongue. That last one is mostly as a snack, but the tail is important. I need to check if it can still make the fire. I *need* to know.

<You have learned: Disassemble Lv.5>

And after only a few hours of disassembling, working as slowly as possible in order to keep the minotaur alive for as long as needed, it's finally done. I have my new favorite skin. It is *so big*. I cannot overstate how big this hide is. If I wanted to, I could use this thing as a tent, or as a blanket, or as an entire cape-cloak combo! I am so happy.

<The Goddess of Beasts pities one of Her own.>

I sigh. Well, first of all, just because I wear beast skins doesn't make me one of your own; second, I didn't ask for any pity, and that includes yours.

<The God of Adventure rolls His eyes.>
<The God of Wild isn't sure what to say.>
<The Goddess of Forgiveness pities the God of Harvest.>

Hey, stop ganging up on me! I didn't do anything wrong, you hear me?! Come on, all gods who like me, come to my defense!

. . .

. . . Guys?

<The Goddess of Want finds the minotaur coat displeasing.>

Wh—what for? Okay, frankly, now I'm just confused. Why wouldn't you like it? Is it because it was made from a cow, someone clearly of your own family?

. . . Was that too far? Nah, can't b—

<Minotaur (Lv.37) [BOSS] Defeated.>
<[Level Up]>
<You have reached Level 29.>
<Agility has increased by 5.
Strength has increased by 4.
Stamina has increased by 7.
Magic Power has increased by 2.
Disassemble has increased by 1.
Organ Rupture Resistance has increased by 1.
Oxygen Deficiency Resistance has increased by 1.
Pressure Tolerance has increased by 3.
Falling Resistance has increased by 2.
Concussion Tolerance has increased by 3.
Climb has increased by 1.
Hurry has increased by 1.>

Ah, there it goes. Can't keep an old ox alive forever, I suppose. But at least I was able to take what I wanted from it, so that's nice.

<You have cleared the fifth floor.>
<You have received 1,000 points for clearing the floor.
You have received an additional 1,000 points for being the first to clear the floor.>
<For clearing the stage completely, you will receive an additional reward.>
<To repay your debt, the additional reward has been traded for 5,000 points.>
<2 Gods have shown a positive response to you.
You have obtained 2,000 points.>
<27 Gods have shown a negative response to you.
27,000 points have been deducted.>

Wow. Wooo—ow. Is my authentic minotaur fur coat really *that* ugly, Want? Or is this Coward going at it again because he doesn't like my drive and passion?

<To repay your debt, the floor clear reward has been traded for 1,000 points.>

Yeah, yeah, I get it, I get it, so just take me back to the lobby alrea—

FLOOR 6

THE ETERNAL RAIN

XXIV

Spooky

—dy. Well, well, well. Here we are again.

<To repay your debt, your inventory has been sold for 32 points.>

That's—that's actually sad. My entire collection of several thousand bats was only worth that little? Thirty measly points? And now that I check my inventory properly, everything I took from the minotaur is gone too, including the pelt. I guess Want, in her eternal graciousness, couldn't bother to protect my ugly low-quality no-good cheap second-hoof minotaur hide, huh? Well, whatever. Let her do as she pleases. If she can't understand my sense of fashion, that's *her* problem!

<Current debt: 28,742 points.>

Is this what my life has become? Debt upon debt, piled like stones atop my chest? There really is no win for the little guy. The whole system is rigged against me. I wonder if there's some way to tear down the system? Sure, the ones I'm trying to tear down are literal *gods*; however, unlike a certain Someone else, they aren't truly omnipotent.

That means, as long as I keep my hands in my pockets, there's a chance I can do something. Something *cool*.

. . . Nobody's going to react to my joker speech? No one? Oh, well.

<Top—Status—Community>
<13:05:01 Day 118>
<The fifth attempt will begin in 2:10:54:59>
<Floor 6 will open in 23:59:12>

Hm. I see I've found myself in somewhat of a situation. When the next floor opens, I'll only have a little over a single day to beat it. That's . . . not a lot. From what I can remember, almost every floor I've completed so far has required over a week to beat. I doubt this one would be different. However . . .

My eyes slowly lift to take in the horrible WHITE around me.

—I absolutely can't stay here. If I refuse to go into the floor, I'll have to stay here for an entire month. I can't do that. If I do that, I might actually somehow find a way to kill myself even in the lobby.

I really don't have any choice but to enter the floor, scout it out for a single day, and then come back. This one will be a bit weird, I guess. Then again, this will probably happen again, so there's no real use in mulling over it.

But before I do anything else, this lobby really needs a makeover. And I know just how to do it!

Four hours of painting later and I'm left with a wonderfully mellow RED covering every inch of the floor. Wonderful! Is there anything better?

<You have received a message.>

I can't be sure if this is a hate message or something else, but I'm feeling frisky. Sure, system, show me what's up.

<SuperMoleman[F33]: Hey, sorry about the delay, I wanted to wish you good luck with the fifth floor, but it seems like I'm a little late, haha. How did it go? Did you beat the minotaur? It's pretty chaotic on my side. Apparently, Floor 34 marks the end of the first part of the tutorial, and since one of my party members has gotten it into her head that we're way too underleveled to face whatever's there, she's having us grind like mad on the 33rd floor. It's crazy.>

He's already at floor 33? How the heck is he climbing these floors so fast?!

Man, these Easy Difficulty guys really have it on a platter, huh? I'd envy them if I didn't already pity them. Anyway, we're both online, so I guess there's no reason not to respond.

<PrissyKittyPrincess[F6]: ya aktually i DID beat da minotard cuz he ws a CHUMP n so is evry1 who cant beat him they r also CUMPS bt lolz ya flor 5 ws ttly super hard i aktully fell an splettred my brainz at 1 point an it rlly hurt bt i live>

After a minute or so, an answer dings in.

<SuperMoleman[F33]: I'm glad you survived! Be more careful in the future, alright? I'd love to hear how you defeated the minotaur. I've got a feeling nobody else will be able to implement your strategy, but I'm still very curious.>
<PrissyKittyPrincess[F6]:
droppd cow off cliff>
<SuperMoleman[F33]: Haha, that sure sounds like you! Good luck with Floor 6, it isn't too bad as long as you bring a few potions. Best wishes!>

I literally can't buy anything, but okay.

Best wishes . . . How do you typically reply to that?

<PrissyKittyPrincess[F6]: thx u2>

There. Perfect.

And now I just need to waste around twenty hours doing menial harm to myself. I'm actually pretty happy I was able to unintentionally get my brain damage tolerance all the way up to protection because I don't think I could raise it in a safe and appropriate manner. Anyway, back to mauling myself, I guess.

Sooner than it feels, the floor opens.

<Floor 6 has opened. Do you want to enter?>
<Yes/No>

I press Yes.

And then, just like so many times before, the world around me shifts.

I fall down into a patch of disgusting mud and within only seconds of slipping and sliding on top of the gloopy gross goop beneath me, I finally keel right on over, splashing into the mud face-first. Ugh. Everything is cold and goopy and slippery and I'm sure my beloved leopard hide is completely soiled now. Wow. Great. I love this floor already. Ah, wait, my leopard hide slipped off. It's just gone. I can't find it because it seemingly conjoined with the mud to a most literal degree. It's just me and the mud now.

I try to stand up, but every time I move even slightly, I just wind up slipping again. At first, I think a single square inch or two of my body might have remained clean, but now I'm just completely covered. From afar, I'd probably look like some sort of mud monster. If a particular mystery-solving Great Dane had seen me now, I'd probably get my face ripped off.

And, to make things just a step worse, it's hailing. And I don't mean that it's almost snowing—no, I mean hail. Hail that can be likened only to a machine gun in the sky, firing pellets of ice and death onto my back hard enough to scrape off my skin entirely.

It's a very simple process, really. First, it freezes my skin. Then, it tenderizes my skin by pelting it. And finally, after enough of that, the skin on my back just slips off like a wet blanket.

Since I've yet to even stand up yet, there is basically nothing I can do to stop this. Ah. That *really* hurts.

<You have learned: Cold Resistance Lv.2>
<You have learned: Hypothermia Tolerance Lv.2>
<You have learned: Hypothermia Tolerance Lv.3>

Yeah. Yeah, that makes sense.

It feels like my back is on fire. At the same time, I can vibrantly feel every single ice crystal slowly forming in my back, not unlike a little fly maggot worming inside me.

In that sense, the mud is a good thing. It isn't frozen, even though it is far colder than me, so it acts as an insulating layer. And even though it hurts even worse than not having skin on my back does, I grab a blob of mud and slather it onto my back. Saying it stings is like saying the Fat Man had an adverse effect on the population of Nagasaki.

Hissing in pain, I'm eventually able to pull myself up to stand on both feet. No matter how much I'm trembling, the fact that I'm standing is good enough in my book.

<Tutorial stage, Hell Difficulty Fourth Floor: The Eternal Rain>
<[Clear Condition] Pass across the marsh to reach the lair.>

Two things. One, this is hail, not rain. Two, can this really be called a marsh? It's *nothing but mud*!

It's pretty dark, but I can see plain as day that from the north side to Kentucky, there ain't nothing but mud. Mudmudmudmudmudmudmud. Oh, and the hail beating down on it.

So this is what it feels like to get flogged? How novel!

I raise my nose into the air. Sniffsniffsniffsniff. Okay, it's really hard to smell it above the wind and the hail and the mud, but I think I can sort of tell the approximate direction of the lair. I wonder who the lair belongs to? I'll be sure to find out when I get there, but I'm still curious. Not curious enough to message Moleman—he'll probably say something wildly different from the truth—but still.

Nowhere else to go but toward it.

I take a step toward the lair. I instantly slip and face-plant in the mud again. The hail beats me into the mud like a million hammers. If this isn't the perfect metaphor for my entire life, I don't know what is.

I try to get back up to my feet. I slip and face-plant in the mud. I try to get back up to my feet. I stand for three seconds or so before I slip again and kiss the mud. I try to get back up to my feet. I slip and face-plant in the mud. I try to get back up to my feet. I stand. I take one step, and then one more, and then I fall. Plop. Splat. Eugh.

<You have learned: Enhanced Balance Lv.1>

Great. Wow. Thanks. You don't say?

Okay, you know what? Normally, I try to do whatever's best to increase my skills. We've established that, right? Yeah, but right now, if increasing my skills requires me to slip around in the mud like some clown-pig hybrid, then I'm not doing it. I'm just going to embrace the pig part and do this on all fours.

It's still slippery, and I still end up eating mud an untold number of times, but if I just do this on all fours, I'm at least able to move forward. And I do so pretty well, until I start noticing hard, sharp things in the mud.

At first, I just assumed they were rocks or whatever, but after a bad slip that sent my hand deep into the mud, what I pulled out wasn't *just* my hand, but also a skull.

A child-sized skull.

I blink at it. It doesn't blink back because its eye sockets are filled with mud. Its jaw is missing.

In a panic, I throw it as far away as I can, which isn't all that far. It splashes down in the mud a few paces away, leaving me to quietly hyperventilate in the mud. Th—that, um, that was . . .

My other hand touches something hard, just inches below the mud. Gulp. Slowly, with hands trembling definitely only from the cold and no other condition mental or otherwise, I pull it out. It's another skull. Small. But this one still has teeth, and that's the only reason I notice something's afoot. The teeth look . . . weird. The canines are just a little bigger, and it's got pronounced molars. Hm. Suspicious.

Curious, I dig around in the mud until I've unearthed an at least somewhat complete skeleton. The hail naturally cleans off all the mud caking it, so I don't have to do any real cleaning myself. And with this complete skeleton in hand, I can say with at least some certainty that this is probably not a child. From what my amazing inductive reasoning can gather, this is most likely merely a goblin. False alarm, crisis averted, no need to feel any fear.

Sighing, I toss the bones over my shoulder. I wish there were something fun I could do with them, but even if I make something cool, it'll just get taken away at the end of the floor anyway.

I pick up a femur. From above, I can feel the hail drumming down on my exposed spine like it's a xylophone. Hmm. I feel like I read somewhere that you can use bone to waterproof leather, but you probably need some kind of special technique to do that. Frankly speaking, I don't know any such techniques. I'll just have to make do, I guess.

Throwing away the femur, I continue.

Man, the wind is really becoming a fair bit loud, huh? If I hadn't heard winds that howled even louder than this, I would have assumed I was surrounded by a terrifying whirlwind of ghosts or something, haha. Haha. Hahaha . . .

Um, it isn't ghosts, right? Ghosts are—pardon the expression—spooky.

I don't know why, but ever since I was little, ghosts have irked me. You can't touch them, you can't kill them—they're already dead—and they can do anything they want to you. Most monsters you can kill with a bullet or faith in the One God, but ghosts? Nuh-uh. Invulnerable. Unkillable.

I know some games have killable ghosts, but I think that's very unrealistic. Ghosts are already dead. Where are they supposed to go when you kill them? Superhell? Makes no sense.

B—b—b—but, I mean, it doesn't sound *all* that much like spooky ghost moaning. Only a little. But the wind makes that sound all the time. Ooooooooohh: that's the sound the wind makes. Oooohhhhh.

"Oooooohhhhhh . . ."

Yup. Just the wind. No need for me to do anything except keep crawling at a nice, reasonable pace. Haha. Hahaha . . . Erm, is it just me, or is that ghastly moaning that's totally only the wind coming *closer*?

In the smattering hailstorm, across the muddy marsh, in spite of the clawing winds and biting gale, I see a shadow stand, almost relaxed in the horrible tempest.

My blood freezes to ice and I can feel my heart cease its drumming.

"Ooohhhh . . . Oooohhhhhhh . . . *Whyyyyyyyy* . . ." the shadow moans, its cries conjoining with the weeping wind and the grating hail.

Slowly, I draw myself back. But my movement, as driven by sheer fright as it is, only serves to bring the shadow closer to me. With every step I take, the shadow moves forward by three, its legs only barely moving while still bringing its body forth, sliding atop the mud like a phantom, its approach unhampered by the need for physicality in movement.

I try to crawl backward but the haste in my limbs makes me slip and slip and I can do nothing but slip around like a soap bar in an oiled bathtub as the shadow steps closer, and closer, until it is just above me. With eyes as wide as saucers, I stare up at it, my jaw trembling and a word hanging just on the tip of my tongue.

. . . Zombie?

\<Shade (Lv.22)\>

Its body—flayed by the hail—is skinless, the muscles covering its limbs torn and exposed to such a point where the individual strands of muscle hang like thick hairs from both arms and legs. In various places, bones hiding just beneath the surface of the hairy muscle break through in flecks of WHITE. From within the pried-open sockets of its face, a pair of staring eyes emerge, lacking both eyelids.

. . . Okay, so it's a zombie.

Phew, that was *scary*! Turns out it was just a simple zombie, so there's no need to get hysterical.

Man, I really thought I was going to die there! If it's just a zombie, there's no need for fright. Zombies are easy to take care of—all you've got to do is bash their brains in and they're gone. No silver or cross required. Wonderful.

The zombie raises its index finger and points it at me. I stare at it. Is it a common thing in this place to point rudely at people? It isn't very polite, even if the one doing it is a dead man. Or, in this case, going by the drooping ears and the small build, dead *goblin*.

Its eyes pierce into me.

"You . . ." it says in a long, hoarse drawl. "*You did this . . .*"

Huh. Did I? I can't remember dabbling in necromancy, but if you say it, then it must be true. Never doubt the words of a dead guy, that's what they always say. I mean, they're already dead, so what's the use in lying? Then again, if they've already died, then it's not like sinning even more will get them any worse off than they already are.

But that's a sticky subject, and I'd do best to refrain from it. After all, right now, I've got a brain to bash in.

That exposed skull worn by that zombie goblin looks just right, wouldn't you say?

Since it's standing and I'm on the floor, my first order of business is to get us both on the same ground, which is easily done by grabbing hold of both of its cold, soggy legs and pulling them out from under it. The zombie-shade-goblin makes a weird croaking kind of sound as it falls into the dirt and mud with a splash. Not waiting for it to recover, I jump on top of it and just kind of start whaling on it.

Out of curiosity, I made a mental list of which types of attack could actually harm it and which ones did exactly zilch.

Clawing and slicing was ineffective since it didn't bleed.

Dismembering it was also sort of ineffective, as the removed limbs continued moving.

Evisceration, disembowelment, and similar removals were also useless. It was already lacking several internal organs, and the rest were necrotic and mushy, so removing them was, funnily enough, more beneficial than averse.

Blunt attacks didn't do much.

I bit off its head by severing the neck, but it was still going, so no luck there either.

Out of sheer curiosity, I used TRT to check what else didn't do much of anything. Turns out, basically nothing had any effect on it whatsoever.

But, by the end of it, I did level up my TRT, so that was nice.

<You have learned: Touch of Reversed Tolerance Lv.3>

I continued using TRT until I got bored with the whole thing, at which point I was at least able to get it to level up again.

<You have learned: Touch of Reversed Tolerance Lv.4>

The whole thing would be a lot more interesting if the goblin-zombie-shade reacted by doing basically anything other than limply writhe beneath me, but whatever.

I bash its brains in, but it's still moving. Huh. Is that not how zombies are defeated here? Okay, uh, what about the heart? Oh, yeah, it's half-necrotic. Never mind. Hmmm . . .

After a few minutes of careful consideration, I finally find the solution. If I were in a zombie movie or something I'd never do this, but since this isn't technically a zombie of the viral disease sort, it works, I think.

I eat the zombie.Out of all the things I've eaten in the tutorial so far, this is probably the worst one. The muscles are stringy and tough, the organs are slimy and have a rotten taste, the brain is basically just a grainy jelly . . . Not good stuff. But once I ate the whole thing, and all that remained was the skeleton, it finally stopped moving.

<Shade (Lv.22) Defeated.>

Great success! Not to mention all the tolerances and resistances I got out of it.

Though, now that I think of it, I might have been able to just put the whole thing in my inventory. I guess it depends on whether the system recognizes the zombie as being dead or alive. That age-old argument will probably be answered with the next zombie I encounter, though. I've got a feeling that I'll be meeting more of them real soon.

That aside, um . . . I'm starting to feel kind of, what's the word . . . queasy? Yeah. There's a rumbly in my tumbly and I'm starting to think that maybe I shouldn't have eaten that half-rotten goblin zombie. I could probably have left the organs alone. Did I really need to eat them? I don't know.

I continue crawling, but my pace soon turns rather slow as my entire body breaks out in a cold sweat. All I can hope is that whatever this infernal heat that's melting my head and fusing my peanut brain to my eggshell skull is, it isn't deadly. I hope. I don't know. My whole body feels kind of shaky. It's not supposed to be shaky, right? Or maybe I just absorbed so many super-zombie calories that my body has started metamorphosing into a super-zombie, too. The question in that case is: is the price of immortality worth it, if it means eventually losing everyone you care about and being left in an empty void, the only super-zombie around, forever?

Heck yeah it is! Man, immortality's so dope; you get to play every single video game to completion, forever, and you'll always be able to play the latest games. Unless they make it so that you can't play the old games, but new games are being released so fast it doesn't matter.

Ah, I wanna play games. I'd kill to play a game of Pong right now . . .

Hmm . . . I don't . . . feel . . . so good . . .

<You have learned: Necrosis Resistance Lv.2>
<You have learned: Necrosis Resistance Lv.3>
<You have learned: Hypothermia Tolerance Lv.4>
<You have learned: Hypothermia Tolerance Lv.5>
<You have learned: Fever Tolerance Lv.4>
<You have learned: Bacteria Resistance Lv.2>
<You have learned: Ulcer Tolerance Lv.6>
<You have learned: Ulcer Tolerance Lv.7>
<You have learned: Indigestion Resistance Lv.4>

Status messages are filling my screen, but I can't really see them. No matter which buttons I mash or where I point the joystick, my player character won't move anymore. This game is garbage. You're telling me a little bit of half-rotten meat is enough to go this far? Pathetic. Ahhh, my character is getting surrounded by zombies. Bummer. I'll have to retry the level next time, I guess. Oh, wait, this game is a *roguelike*. No retries. Game over is game over. Man, I can't believe I'll have to start over again. I wonder what kind of character I should do this time? Hopefully someone more charming. This guy was pretty annoying.

<The fifth attempt has begun. You will now be returned to the lobby.>

Hm? Oh, I forgot that this was part of the ga—

I wake up. The world isn't whirling and moaning and sighing anymore. I have no idea where I am. What is this RED stuff?

<Top—Status—Community>
<00:00:01 Day 121>

<The sixth attempt will begin in 29:23:59:59>
<Floor 6 will open in 23:59:59>

Hm. Oh, wait, yeah, I'm in the tutorial. That's right. The tutorial . . .

Okay, so the lesson for today is as follows: maybe I shouldn't eat a whole shade-goblin-zombie.

But half of a shade-goblin-zombie should be no problem, right? Right. Exactly.

I just need to wait twenty-four hours and then I'll be right back at it again. Now I know how to handle the floor, at least. The zombie-shade-goblins are all chumps, and their attacks are super weak. And as if they couldn't be pathetic enough, it just so happens that they can be defeated by simply consuming their mortal remains. How convenient!

<You have received a message>

Wonderful! Take it away, system!

<SuperMoleman[F33]: Sorry, I forgot to ask, but have you learned any kind of magic yet?>

Magic? You mean the choice weapon of the mythical nerd-coward hybrid? Unfortunately, I haven't had the opportunity to dabble in it. Though, just to be clear, if I happened to own a magical book somehow—say that I got it second-hand from a certain nerd—then I wouldn't mind giving it a quick read-through. Mainly to understand the enigmatic minds of the nerd populace. And if reading a magical tome just happens to also grant me magical powers, then that isn't really my fault, now is it?

<PrissyKittyPrincess[F6]: nt yet>
<SuperMoleman[F33]: That might not be good. If I remember correctly, on Floor 6, you get accosted by the dead shades of whatever you've killed until then, and they can only be defeated with magic. Then again, you seem to have a knack for finding alternative ways to beating floors.>

Magic-only enemies? That's so unfair.

On the other hand, there doesn't seem to be any specific requirements to learning magic, so it might be surprisingly common to be able to do at least one or two spells. If that's the case, then I'm the dummy here for not being able to learn it. Hm.

<PrissyKittyPrincess[F6]: ya i eat da zombs vrry good strategy an any1 can do it>

That's right. Unlike Moleman's unfair strategy that only rich challengers with lots of points and no debt can pull off, this one is for *everyone*.

After a minute or so, I get my response.

<SuperMoleman[F34]: Haha, outrageous as usual! Eating zombies . . . I'll update my guide to suggest it.>

Hm. Uh. Hmm . . .

<PrissyKittyPrincess[F6]: kk bt umm mayb say tht its only doable if u hav high resist an tolerances k cuz otherwise u prolly die>
<SuperMoleman[F33]: I'll be sure to mention it. Good luck with the sixth floor!>

I type in a quick response.

<PrissyKittyPrincess[F6]: kk thx>

But then I change my mind. After a moment's reconsideration . . .

<PrissyKittyPrincess[F6]: kk thx u2>

Right. Good enough.

Since I'll need to have my eating-bad-things resistances pretty high to deal with the floor, I spend the time until the floor opens by eating my own flesh. When this wasn't enough and my progress stalled a bit too much for my tastes, I made the executive decision that since I wasn't going to use all the hides I kept in my inventory, I might as well use them . . . productively.

Chewing leather is only possible thanks to my sharp fang skill, but once I'd chewed my way through three of my hides, I actually gained a new skill from it.

<You have learned: Chew Lv.1>

Sure, why not?

After I get the chew skill to level three, the floor finally opens once more.

<Floor 6 has opened. Do you want to enter?>
<Yes/No>

I stick the hide I was chewing on into my inventory. And then I press Yes.

Good Boy

I'm back in the mud, but this time I'm ready. I know what to expect, so the spooky wailing wind isn't all that spooky anymore. Just a little spooky. K—kind of spooky.

"Oooohhh . . ."

Time to show these zombies what for.

Without waiting for it to appear, I start clomping toward it on all fours. My great values sniffer can't smell the shades, but I can still smell them normally because of the whole rotting-flesh and necrotic-tissue deal. Not to mention the sound of the pained moaning.

\<You have learned: Enhanced Scent Lv.4\>

I'm not sure if I want that, though. Now the smell is even worse. Wow, gee, thanks.

\<You have learned: Enhanced Balance Lv.2\>

—That I do like. It's subtle, but it lets me run better and with more agility, so when I leap off the muddy ground and hook my teeth into the neck of a poor gombie (goblin-zombie), I don't slip in the slightest. Wonderful!

And now, I need to do some experimenting. What's the least amount of flesh I need to eat in order to kill the zombie?

Let's see here . . . Nomch. Nomch. Nomch. Nomch. Chewchewchewchew.

Okay, so, from my observations, if you eat the entire head, put the skull in your inventory, slurp up all vital organs, dissect the rest of the gombie, and then put that in your inventory, then it dies. Yes.

<Shade (Lv.21) Defeated.>

And now that I've got a simple and easy-to-do way of defeating these gombies, there's no need to fear anymore.

With a skip in my step, I continue crawling across the mud. If I were in a cartoon, I'd be walking with a comedic bounce. I can already feel the necrotic meat in my belly start to have adverse effects, but it's fine!

Sniff sniff sniff. Is that rotten meat I smell?

Bounding across the mud, I make my way to my next victim.

And so begins my gombie slaughter.

The closer I got to the lair, the more gombies there were, and the more bones littered the mud. It was becoming kind of a hazard. No matter where you stepped, there would always be a piece of bone. Watching. Waiting for you to step on it wrong and leave you howling like a kid on Christmas morning accidentally stepping on a Lego.

It actually got to a point with the gombies where I was being ganged up on by not just several of them but several *dozen*. They're all pretty weak—they don't actually do any real damage—but once there were enough of them, the little scratches of damage they made amounted into real wounds. Wounds that *festered*.

Or, at least, they *tried* to fester, but by this point my bacteria, virus, parasite, necrosis, nausea, ulcer, and inflammation tolerances had all reached the resistance level, with necrosis and bacteria even being at protection, so it was more of an annoyance than anything else.

A general observation, however, was that the gombies would always approach me. It didn't matter where I was or what I was doing. If I stayed still, they would flood my position.

So that's exactly what I did.

Once I had the supposed lair in sight, which really was just a little cave, I set up camp and waited for the gombies to come to me. After only a few days of this, no more gombies would come for my head, which supports the realistic conclusion that I've done away with all the gombies. Great success! And it only took me a little over a week. Neat.

That leaves me with the lair.

I have no idea what awaits inside it, but I think it's fair to say that whatever it is, it's probably what made all these bones. Considering that the bones are in a relatively whole state without much damage, it wouldn't be strange to assume that whoever made them ate the person whole. But this is a magical fantasy world. It doesn't *need* to be a huge frog or a huge lizard or a huge snake. It *could* be a huge boar, or a huge cat, or even a huge bird. It isn't fair to assume these sorts of things.

I stare at the lair from a few paces away.

See, it's moments like these when I wish I wore armor and had a cool sword or something. Then I could hunker down and spend an hour or so polishing it and readying armor and sharpening my sword. Preparing myself and all that. As it is, when I now enter that lair, we'll be on equal ground. No, now that I think about it, I'll be at a slight disadvantage! If the thing in there isn't sleeping, then we will actually be fighting on its home ground. It's not that I'm screwed or anything, I just think it's unfair that I don't have an advantage while it does. That's all.

But enough about that. Into the lair I go!

I've barely even had time to set foot inside the maw of the lair's entrance before the boss stage message pops up.

\<Tutorial stage, Hell Difficulty Sixth Floor: Boss Stage\>
\<[Clear Condition] Defeat the vile Cerberus.\>

Cerberus? As in, like, the three-headed dog?

Man, assuming it's as big as the mythologies make it out to be, I'm sure to get one heck of a hide out of it. Unless a certain goddess decides that it isn't fashionable and lets it get taken by the taxman, that is. I'm starting to get tired of being in debt. They did say in the forums that you can get a wish once you beat the tenth stage, so it might be a good idea to use it to clear my debt. Maybe.

But that's only possible if I beat this here doggie.

Since the inside of the lair isn't covered in mud, I'm able to stand back up on both legs. For some reason, after a week of crawling and running around on all fours, this feels weird. I'd better keep myself half-crouched just in case I get jumped.

That said, this cave really does have a lot of skeletons in it, huh? I mean, there are enough skeletons to fill an entire haunted mansion and accompanying cemetery. You could probably make a swimming pool full of the bonemeal you'd get if you ground them all up. I almost want to grab a few to put in my inventory, but they'll just get sold for one point per hundred heads anyway, so there's no real point to it. Sighing, I pass them by.

I can smell it. The dog. Wet dog. That's what it smells like here. But the path is very straight, and there aren't really any diverging paths, so there isn't any need to track it.

After only a few minutes of walking, I reach a large, dome-shaped cavern, with the farthermost wall covered up by a small mountain of bones and skulls. And in front of that great pile of bones sits a massive hound, roughly the size of a barge, with three heads in total, one in the middle and two resting just below its mighty snout. All three heads have the appearance of a grayish wolf. The lower two heads each only have one eye each while the greater head atop them sits eyeless and blind. The two eyes roll to me as one and I freeze in place. The head on the right, with its eye of yellow, whines at me.

\<Sit.\>

I sit down. Something slimy slithers its way across my brain and I remember something important that I hadn't thought about before.

I've forgotten who my Master is.

The head on the left barks.

\<See me.\>

I look up, and I see my Master. He sits before me, draped in gold and silver, with a coat of finest BLACK velvet. He is disappointed in me. I broke another vase. How could I have been so clumsy? I'm pathetic. I shouldn't be allowed in the house.

\<Did I permit you to meet my gaze?\>

My face falls to the floor in mere milliseconds. N—no, Master. I'm sorry. I didn't mean to . . .

\<Raise your head.\>

I hesitate, but he hates when I hesitate, so I lift my head to face him. His expression softens.

\<I didn't mean to raise my voice at you.\>

You were right to, Master. I was being bad again. I didn't mean to, but I still did wrong. Thank you for your mercy, Master.

Master reaches out his hand. I look at it, wide-eyed.

A bark resounds through the back of my head.

\<Paw.\>

I place my hand on his.

My hand disappears.

It isn't there anymore. It hurts but then I hear a droning whine in the back of my head and I'm okay. Master is so good to me, to only punish me with so little as taking my hand and nothing more. Other masters would have killed me because I'm foolish and clumsy. But he is so kind to me. I am grateful, Master.

<You have learned: Delusion Tolerance Lv.1>
<You have learned: Delusion Tolerance Lv.2>
<You have learned: Delusion Tolerance Lv.3>
<You have learned: Hallucination Protection Lv.3>

My head feels weird. I'm . . . what is happening . . . ?
His gaze meets mine and mine meets his.
Master has three heads.

<Cerberus (Lv.35) [BOSS]>

My hand is in his jaw. He's chewing with a wolf's jaw. But Master isn't a dog. If anything, I'm the—

Master's left head whines. I'm not in a cave; I'm in a mansion. A wonderful, beautiful mansion where I live with his many other servants, and we are so happy, and he is so kind to us, and every day we eat delicious meals, and we are so happy, and every night we sleep on beds of softest cotton, and every day is sunny and bright and warm, and we are so happy, and sometimes we even get to eat yummy yummy yummy treats like candies and cookies and cakes because he is so kind to us and we love Master and Master loves us.

But Master is a dog. No, he's a *wolf*.

Master isn't a wolf. I know he isn't. Master is just like me . . . He's . . .

What is Master? Master isn't a human. He isn't a goblin. What is a human? I am a human. Master is . . . Master is like me. Whatever I am, Master is like me, because he's good.

But I can see Master in front of my eyes, and he has the heads of three wolves and he's eating my hand. Master shouldn't be doing that. Master is a fine gentleman—a noble of great status, who with his great compassion and his great love and his great intellect has ruled these lands with compassion and love and intellect.

But he's a dog.
But he's Master.
But Master is a dog.

<You have learned: Delusion Tolerance Lv.4>
<You have learned: Delusion Tolerance Lv.5>
<You have learned: Delusion Tolerance Lv.6>

< . . . >

<You have learned: Delusion Tolerance Lv.9>
<You have learned: Delusion Tolerance Lv.10>
<You have learned: Delusion Resistance Lv.1>
<You have learned: Hallucination Protection Lv.4>

I look at the creature before me. It is a three-headed hound, and I have never seen it before in my life. I have not lived a happy, content life in the service of this being, and it is not a merciful master. My right hand is gone. That's how it is, and that's what happened. I let my guard down. I should have rolled inside in the fetal position. I should have—

<Paw.>

My body jerks.

That slimy thing is inside my skull again. I can see the world in front of me in double, one being this hell that I now inhabit, the other being the heaven this creature wants to lull me into. But there's one sense it hasn't fooled. No matter what I see, no matter what I hear, no matter what I feel, no matter what I think, I can still smell what this thing truly is. And it smells like a wet dog.

And still, and yet, my body moves. Robotically, on all fours, like a pathetic, drooling, slobbering dog, I crawl toward that massive being, the stump where my right hand used to be leaving a trail of blood in my wake. It isn't Master. I am not a servant. And still, I can't help it.

I can't help it.

I'm beneath it now. It's massive. The sound of its heart is as loud as a base drum. The two eyes of its lower heads pierce into me.

My hand trembles, and yet I raise my left hand.

<Good boy.>

Master's upper head lowers toward my hand, his maw opening wide, his WHITE teeth glistening in the dark, and even though I see him for what he is, even if I see the massive beast he is, I still think to myself, as his jaws clasp around my hand, slicing it off as neatly as any knife would, that *he truly is a gentle Master.*

Blood spurts.

Blood. RED.

RED blood. Blood RED RED RED RED RED RED RED RED RED RED.

<You have learned: Delusion Resistance Lv.2>

I fly to my feet, one step back, but then my mind and instincts flip into gear, and instead of trying to escape the Cerberus, I instead leap toward him, the stumps where my hands used to be spurting blood left and right, and without so much as a hint of hesitation, I shove both stumps into his two eyes, deep in there, and his whine and his bark almost shifts the world back into that rosy lovely happy wonderful perfect excellent happy lovely wonderful yummy perfect place, but I won't have it, and instead of falling, I shove my stumps in deeper and deeper into his sockets until I can feel his eyeballs pop.

With the Cerberus blinded and panicked, I leap back down, pausing only for a moment before I go at it again, throwing myself at the left head's supple throat. I may not have any hands, but my teeth will have to be enough.

\<You have learned: Chew Lv.4\>

I chew my way through his simple living leather and into his throat, letting my weight tear it out by letting go with my feet.

The Cerberus's massive paws swat at me but I'm as nimble as a bobcat, leaping aside and quickly doing the same thing to the right hand as I did to the left. When I return to the ground, all that's left is the final middle head.

I stare at it, my eyes narrow and focused. It stares back at me, eyeless.

And then it howls.

A high, stable tone slips out of its rounded lips, filling the cave like a single hallelujah in a massive cathedral. It is ethereal. It is inhuman. It is a sound only Master could make. The pitch is steady, beautiful, and so divine that I can feel warm, salty tears stream down my face. I've never heard anything prettier.

\<Be me.\>

I lift the stumps of my hands to my face, to my eyes, and then I press them into my sockets so hard that I can feel my eyeballs pop. I can't see anything anymore.

\<Be me.\>

Using my clawed feet, I tear off my own ears.

\<Be me.\>

I bite off my own tongue.

\<Be me.\>

A sound emerges from my bleeding throat. "Oou . . . Oooouuuuhh . . ."

It is a foul sound. It's wrong. It isn't good. It's horrid, and terrible, and the kind of throat that would produce such a sound must be purged. It is only right. It is justice.

But I have no hands with which to claw out my own throat, and my feet won't reach, either. A hollow horrid haunting lump of lead settles inside the pits of my stomach. I can't be him. I will never be him. I can't even punish myself for my sin of not being him. I am worse than imperfect. I am an insult to him.

Staggering, I approach him, exposing my throat, begging him, pleading, urging him with all of my heart to undo what I am.

Gently, his massive wolf's head falls toward me, his great maw opening.

<Be me.>

Something shifts. As his maw closes to take my throat, that great humming of the cave fades, the final verse of his hymn dying, leaving behind an empty numbness that reverberates within my chest like the final mumbles of a dying man, and with swiftness that surprises even myself, I pull my throat back just in time to avoid an unfortunate de-throating. But I don't flee, I don't escape. Instead, I throw myself at his throat, my legs snaking around his furry throat, my teeth sticking deep into his throat, chewing through his soft hide, into his throat, where I crunch crunch crunch it, so that when he scrambles back, jaw opening to sing his song again, no sound will emerge.

He, much like me, has become less than imperfect.

<You have learned: Chew Lv.5>
<You have learned: Chew Lv.6>
<You have learned: Sharp Fang Lv.9>
<You have learned: Sharp Fang Lv.10>
<You have learned: Dagger Tooth Lv.1>

I bite and then I stop biting because he isn't fighting back anymore and there's nothing more to bite because his divine throat is gone and through the hole that's left I hear his final divine breath leave his divine body and the breath smells like dog's breath.

<Cerberus (Lv.35) [BOSS] Defeated.>
<[Level Up]>
<You have reached Level 32.>
<Agility has increased by 4.
Strength has increased by 6.
Stamina has increased by 6.
Magic Power has increased by 2.
Dagger Tooth has increased by 1.
Chew has increased by 1.
Hurry has increased by 1.
Ulcer Resistance has increased by 1.
Indigestion Resistance has increased by 1.
Delusion Resistance has increased by 2.
Parasite Resistance has increased by 1.>
<You have cleared the sixth floor.>
<You have received 1,000 points for clearing the floor.
You have received an additional 1,000 points for being the first to clear the floor.>
<For clearing the stage completely, you will receive an additional reward.>
<To repay your debt, the additional reward has been traded for 5,000 points.>
<4 Gods have shown a positive response to you.
You have obtained 4,000 points.>
<26 Gods have shown a negative response to you.
26,000 points have been deducted.>

Four gods? Who's the extra one? The gods have been kind of radio silent this entire floor, and I have no idea why they would react negatively, but who's this fourth one?

<To repay your debt, the floor clear reward has been traded for 1,000 points.>

No answer? Alright, then.
I look down at the Cerberus corpse beneath my feet.
Wait, hang on, I need to loot the boss before I—

FLOOR 7

THE MEDIATION

Gorilla Warfare

—get tossed back into the lobby. Wow, real nice throw, guys.

. . . My brain feels weird.

I have no idea what Maste—what that *dog* did to my brain, but I don't like it. I didn't get any divinity tolerance level-up from it, so I don't think it was magic. But if it wasn't magic, then what the heck was it? I don't want to try to delude myself into thinking it was just some random dog power, but I genuinely don't know what else to consider it as. Maybe a skill? But so far, no enemies apart from the shades have had any kinds of skills. There's tolerances and stuff like that, but a skill to make people do . . . that?

It just sounds too strange, I guess. Maybe I'm the one being weird about it, but that's what it feels like.

Anyhow, time to gloat to Moleman about my win.

<To repay your debt, your inventory has been sold for 3 points.>
<Current debt: 42,739 points.>

Ah, there it is. I was almost starting to think they'd forgotten to sell all my gombie parts and balls of mud.

That said, being returned to the lobby really doesn't clean you off at all, does it? I'm still muddy from head to toe. If I were rich, I could probably buy a bunch of water bottles to wash off with. Ah, the struggles of the poor.

<Top—Status—Community>
<02:06:08 Day 130>
<The sixth attempt will begin in 20:21:53:52>
<Floor 7 will open in 23:59:40>

Same old, same old.

Just for the sake of it, I give the boards a quick look through, but there's nothing much of interest being discussed, so I just leave it. My PMs are filled with nothing but hate mail. Nothing new from Moleman. If I check his profile, it seems as though he's finally on floor thirty-four, which would suggest that he's probably busy, all things considered. Messaging him while he's in the middle of a floor might not be the best idea, so I just leave him alone.

That leaves me with basically nothing to do except to prepare for the next floor.

I look around at the horrible WHITE lobby.

I hate this place. I wonder if I can make a wish to not have to go back here between attempts and floors. That'd be sweet.

But for now, I'd do best to simply get ready for floor seven. You never know what'll happen. Oh, and I also need to make sure this lobby won't drive me insane.

So, once the lobby is nice and RED, I spend the rest of my hours just casually mutilating myself. Since I've got nothing better to do, I eat the mud covering me. Apparently, it contains a stunning number of parasites and similar creepy-crawlies, so I come out of the whole thing pretty diseased. However, since the lobby automatically heals you, it goes away fast.

Right as I start to wish I'd been allowed to keep some gombie meat to have as a snack, the floor finally opens.

<Floor 7 has opened. Do you want to enter?>
<Yes/No>

About time, don't you think?

Glad to finally leave this horrid lobby, I press Yes.

The moment I press the button I'm swept away and into the next floor, where I'm already hunched down and ready to attack or be attacked. But before I can even wonder about enemies and clear conditions, I'm suddenly overwhelmed with just how much green there is around me. Last time I saw this much green must have been on floor three, and that was . . . a few months ago, I guess? One attempt is roughly one month, floor three was on the third attempt . . . so, it's been over two months? Oh, and then again, I was only in that lovely forest for the first week or so, so it's probably closer to three months. Hm. Going by that math, it would mean that I've been in the tutorial for over five months now.

Five months . . . My birthday is on the twenty-ninth of July, so that would mean that my birthday is eighty days away. Huh. My birthday will be on the final day of the sixth attempt. Interesting. Not that I'll be able to get myself anything, since I'm so deeply in debt that even getting three hundred points to buy a measly cake would be impossible. Well, not that it really matters.

For now, this here forest is quite a bit more interesting. If it can even be called a forest at all. Considering the vines and the general humidity, it could probably be better described as a jungle of some sort. That would also explain the sounds I can hear. Strange birds whistling and whooping in the distance, animals braying and neighing, people arguing loudly, monkeys howling . . .

Hang on. People?

Slowly, stepping cautiously through the thick foliage, I approach the voices. I'd be a lot more cautious if it weren't for one thing. One little detail that makes me too confused and uncertain to properly prepare myself for any fight.

You see, as I approach, closer and closer, I can eventually make out the exact words they're saying.

"Well, where is he, then?"

"Why do you expect me to know?"

"*Because*, out of all of us, you're the supposed creep-charmer. You should know when he's going to show up."

"When have I ever called myself that? Just because I'm the only one here he didn't hate doesn't make me—"

Even if I hadn't had the all-tongue skill, even if I had only ever learned Swedish, I would still understand exactly what they were saying. Dumbfounded, I step out of the brush.

One of my former classmates turns toward me. She rolls her eyes. "Ugh, *finally*. You do know we've been waiting here for, like, four months, right?"

I freeze in my step. Before me, a little screen pops up.

<Tutorial stage, Hell Difficulty Seventh Floor: The Mediation>
<[Clear Condition] Solve the conflict between the shades.>

Shades?

"Hell—o? Fennrick, are you listening to me?"

I look up at her. Her name was . . . I can't remember. But she was the popular girl in class. Everyone liked her. I'm not sure if she ever talked to me before this. When her eyes meet mine, I look away, down at my feet. They're still a little muddy. "Y—y—yeah," I stutter. Oh, God. I can feel my face turn RED. "I'm, uh, I'm . . . I'm listening."

She sighs—exasperated—and glances back at the others. My whole class is here. Everyone. I've forgotten most of the names that I had bothered to put to mind. The last time I saw them was our second year, when they leered at me and snickered when I exclaimed that since I was going to become a pro gamer, I wouldn't need any useless normie education.

She steps closer to me. She's wearing armor, like what a medieval soldier would have. It looks out of place on her but she's too pretty to not look good in it. I'm embarrassed. She's slightly taller than me, but if I had a straight back, that probably wouldn't be the case. Combined, these two factors mean that I'm looking up at her. I wish I were a turtle so I could go hide in my shell.

"Okay, *great*. You saw the message, right? I'm kind of totally bored so I need you to settle this fast, but—"

The popular guy in class steps up behind her and gently pushes her to the side. He's wearing similar armor, but the crest on his chest is different. He smiles down at me like how you smile at a confused child. "Hey, man, glad to see you!" I don't think I've ever talked to him before, either. He puts his hand on my bony shoulder and I want to escape my skin. "Look, just like Jirya said, this is really a very simple situation. There's us"—he gestures at himself and a group behind him—"and then there's *them*." He gestures at Jirya and her band. I look over at her.

\<Shade (Lv.34)\>

I look back at him.

\<Shade (Lv.34)\>

He smiles down at me.

I don't think *Jirya* was the name of my classmate. I don't recognize it at all. Either he's making it up, or there's something else going on.

I look him up and down. "So, um . . ." I try to draw away from him, but his grip on my shoulder is fast. "Wh—what's the, uh, problem?"

His smile broadens just a little. I don't like the way it looks. "I'm glad you asked, Fennrick. You see this big open field here?" I follow the direction his hand gestures in. As sure as he said it, there's a large, open field. It looks weird since it's surrounded by a big, thick forest, but I'm not about to question it. "A while back, my army and hers fought each other, and we both kind of died. Bummer, right? But, see, then we both came back, and now we can't decide on who deserves to spend their eternal rest here. Between you and me, though, since our army reached this place first, it's only obvious that—"

"Ugh, seriously, Het?" Jirya says, butting in. "This place is *literally* ours. It's part of the kingdom we hailed from, so it's clearly ours to rest in. This shouldn't even be a question."

Above me, Het's smile turns a little strained. "As I've said before, Jirya, your kingdom *fell* to the rest of our army. Which, in turn, means that this place is *ours*. How hard is that to understand?"

She growls at him.

Behind them, the rest of my classmates squirm. "So, um . . ." I say, intercepting them. "What exactly do you want *me* to do about it?"

"Obviously," the both of them say in unison before glaring at each other, with Het continuing. "We need you to decide—"

"Fairly!" Jirya chirps.

"*Fairly*, who deserves to rest here."

I gulp. "Um, and I, uh, guess that saying b—*both* is out of the question?" The look on their faces says enough. "Okay, then, uh, um . . ." I look them both up and down. I could just pick one at random. It probably doesn't even change anything, which one I pick. Both sides seem equal in strength. I know the two leaders equally badly.

"In that case, I think that . . ." A little thought snakes its way inside my brain, wriggling inside the folds of my lobes and all the way into the very center of my brain. There's a simple solution to this. A solution that I have no choice but to choose, considering that I want to clear this stage completely. Is there really anything else I can say? Looking up at them both, I open my mouth. "*Neither of you* should rest here."

Het grins and opens his mouth but his jaw instantly snaps shut again and when he looks down at me again, the only thing shining through his eyes is pure, sheer confusion. His grip on my shoulder tightens. I don't react to it. "What do you mean by that? Fennrick?"

Jirya's brows knit. "That's not an answer," she says. "Obviously, one of us deserves to—"

"No," I say. I pull Het's hand off my shoulder. "N—neither of you. You're all, um, alive. You've got meat, and bones, and everything else, so you can't rest here, like, uh, at all. Since you're alive, you shouldn't rest here."

Het's gaze burns into me like a branding iron. "So, what do you think should be done?"

I look back down at my feet. I wring my hands. "You, um, you should . . . I can . . ." My hands are so sweaty. I'm glad I put on one of my backup leopard pelts before I came here, not that it helps any.

"You're going to kill both sides or something?" Jirya says sharply, butting in close. I draw back. "Is that your grand solution? Wow, that's so clever, Fennrick! This explains why you dropped out to pursue your *pro gaming* career. Obviously, you didn't need to learn anything anymore, unlike us normies. I never knew you were so smart. If I'd known, I would've totally mooched off your smarts to get a perfect score on all my tests. Oh, wait, you didn't do all that well on your tests, did you, Fennrick? That's so weird! It must have been the school being pitted against you, that's all. These tests are made to cater to the normie elite, so obviously a pioneer of gaming like you would be left outside."

She smiles at me. I hate it.

I look down again. I don't want to see their eyes. My face feels hot. My pulse beats quickly against my throat. "I—I—I was just—"

"You—you—you were just . . . what? Giving us the super-smart secret to how best to beat this floor? Just kill everyone? Psh," she continues. "Is that really it? You can't honestly be thinking that *Ooohh I'm gonna be super edgy and cool and kill everyone wow look at me* is the solution to *every single floor*, do you? Mediate between us. That's all you need to do. Hear out both sides, understand which one has more valid points, and decide which of us deserves to win more. That's all this is."

Het steps closer to me. "Listen, Fennrick . . . You aren't making this more complicated or something. If anything, you're making this *less* complicated. But it's not a good answer. It's like how in a riddle, you aren't meant to just give whatever answer works. You're supposed to give the *one* answer that works the *very best*. You can't brute-force riddles like you can put a hammer to a nail." He puts a hand on my shoulder again. I want to shake it off but it's too soft. "That's your problem. You think all your issues are nails when they're really riddles. If you just met your problems with more grace, less violence, then—"

Something hot and RED wells up inside my head and I can't really see anything anymore and he's close enough so without really thinking without really acting at all in any form of logical and sound manner I leap at him like a Tasmanian devil and I claw at his face and I claw at his throat but he grabs me by the neck and he pulls me out of range. His arms are just a bit longer than mine, but I claw at his arm, tearing off his armor and exposing his flesh but before I can do anything to him deeper than a mere flesh wound, Jirya attacks me, a sword she's suddenly holding cleanly slicing off my right arm.

Bad bad bad bad bad bad *not good*. I need to get away this isn't good this is bad.

Using my left hand I break the fingers Het is holding my throat with and once I'm freed I jump down onto the ground landing on all fours, but my classmates—those horrible shades—are quickly upon me, and it is only through a combination of fetal position blowover, haste, and four-footed running that I'm able to escape, first by leaping on top of their heads and then once I'm on the ground again rolling myself into a ball to escape into the forest.

I leap into the trees with the swiftness of a cat. My classmates follow me, but after only a few minutes, they realize the obvious in that they won't be able to find me. When they return to the open glade, I follow them, if at a safe distance.

<You have learned: Stalk Lv.10>
<You have learned: Stealth Lv.10>
<You have learned: Hidden Lv.1>

As we reach the open field, I find that it has changed a fair bit.

There are now a number of tents all in different colors yet placed together. There are far more people now than there were before. I think, if I look closely, I can notice people from the classes above and below mine, and even a few teachers.

My entire school is here. I can't exactly count all the people here, but I wouldn't be surprised if there were over a thousand people here.

Did I make a mistake?

<Tutorial stage, Hell Difficulty Seventh Floor: Boss Stage>
<[Clear Condition] Defeat the undeserving shades.>

Hm. Okay, so, from what I can see, most of these people have a level between twenty and thirty. And as for me . . .

<Top—Status—Community>
<PrissyKittyPrincess
Human Level 32
Agility: 98
Strength: 65
Stamina: 117
Magic Power: 45>

Level 32. It's slightly higher than the average among these guys, but the problem is that, well . . . I'm just a single guy. They're over a thousand strong. Sure, most of them have the bodies of tweens and teens, but to many, that isn't exactly a detriment.

As I'm looking at them, I actually have a pretty good view of how Het and Jirya discuss things together. Het's got his arm all nice and bandaged, and since they haven't exactly turned on each other, the case right now is most likely that they've joined forces. Hm.

Okay, I need to check something real quick.

I go into my personal messages and check Moleman's profile. It's still at F34, but whatever. This isn't exactly urgent—I'm just a little desperate to know.

I start typing up a message.

<PrissyKittyPrincess[F7]: hey um k quik question bt umm 4 f7 how do u
normally beat all da shades>

Aaaaand send. Good enough.

See, I've got a sneaking suspicion that—

<You have received a message.>

Already? Well then, take it away, buddy.

<SuperMoleman[F34]: I beat floor 7 by mediating between the two sides. If you sit them down and discuss the matter, they can usually come to an agreement, but from what HookedOnBach[F16] has told me, on Hard, you can't mediate the conflict without rallying one side against the other. Since the shades normally look like your coworkers, classmates, or similar, I've heard that this is often a very difficult choice. I need to go now, we're almost at the boss, but I still wish you good luck!>

It is as I feared.

<PrissyKittyPrincess[F7]: kk thx u2>

So, in other words, my best strategy here was absolutely not to go right on ahead and declare war on both sides, but rather to rally with one group. And then, just before the other side was killed, while my side was weakened by them, I could kill them all.

That is, unless the system doesn't recognize the shades on *your side* to be enemies, which would in turn mean that you wouldn't need to kill them in order to clear the stage completely.

Huh. I seriously picked every single incorrect dialogue option, didn't I?

Is it too late to come out of hiding and rally one side against the other? . . .

Probably. Ah, man . . .

Hm. Then again, just because I pick one side doesn't mean I can't rally a side, right?

It just means that I'll have to be a little bit more . . . *creative.*

It's a simple plan, but in this case, I have good reason to believe it will work.

I have three weeks to kill as many as I can. This shouldn't be any issue. It's just that I need to kill them in such a way where I can pick them off not necessarily one by one, but rather in small groups. If they all come at me at once, I'm a goner. But since they don't know where I am currently, as long as that remains the case, they won't be able to do anything to me. It's just me, against them.

Simple, right?

Another positive is that I don't physically need to eat or drink or sleep, and I don't leave any, erm, *smellable* traces. I do leave marks on the trees I climb, but these would be hard to time-stamp, so I don't think there'll be much trouble with that.

Hmm.

I lift my nose into the air. Sniffsniffsniffsniff. Yup, I can smell them. I can even smell Het, and the way his arm is bloodied. Perfect.

It may be just slightly cowardly, but it is time for me to introduce this place to some good ol' guerrilla warfare.

First up, I spend a few hours simply observing their camp. My stealth skill, now called *hidden*, should be good enough to keep me out of their sights. But just in case, I still engage FPB. Like this, I carefully observe their comings and goings. Right now, their biggest weakness—and my greatest strength—is that they have human physiology. I can see them drinking, and eating, and doing all the other businesses a human would normally do. At one point, a small group of them—most of them being students with a single adult coming along—went out into the forest. I followed them without any intent of attacking. Simply observing.

As I watch them from the treetops, I see them go through the forest, and after a while, they reach a flowing stream. They fill a few buckets they were carrying and then they return to base camp. I follow them.

Back at the base camp, a lot of stuff is going on. But my interest lies on a certain group, all wearing blue—the same color that Het wore—carrying large bags and heading out into the forest. I follow them, but since they're wearing blue, I won't attack.

After going a fair bit into the forest, they set up a small encampment. Right.

I go back to the base camp, just in time to watch as a group clad in RED— the color of Jirya—does the same thing. I follow them, and once they're too far away to be seen or heard in time to be saved, I attack.

Most of them are just young teenagers, at the age of fourteen or fifteen, with only a single teacher following along with them. The math teacher. He gave me a really bad grade once.

The teenagers only have levels of around twenty, so even though they all have short swords and a few even have bows, I still kill them relatively easily. And that leaves me with only the math teacher. His wide eyes dart shakingly from me to the bodies lying in the high grass. "F—Fennrick . . . Why—"

Before he says anything else, I leap at him. He stabs his sword through my left lung but that's fine. Once I'm close enough to him, I tear off his jaw and push his loosened tongue deep into his throat to both choke and silence him at once. Very effectively. And then, before he's had time to die, I start disassembling him. By the end of it, I've got myself a perfectly usable huma—uh, *shade* hide. It's a bit bigger than me, but it should be enough to cause some funky trouble. I put it into my inventory, and then I do the same to the other bodies.

Normally, I want to take everything I can. But this is a different kind of situation. So, since I can't do much with or really eat them, I leave the hands, feet, and heads right where I killed them.

Before I leave, though, I go through the bags to check if there's anything useful. From what I can see, they have enough things to set up a small base, but since having a base would be to my direct detriment, I leave that stuff alone.

My very first goal in this situation is to freak them out. I need them all to be on their toes, constantly, always. That way, they'll have trouble sleeping, and they'll quarrel, and they'll eat poorly, and all this will in the end cause them to make bad decisions. Bad decisions that I can take excellent advantage of.

I go back to base camp, leaping through the trees like a monkey. Not much is happening, so now is the right time to set up some traps.

That's a classic part of guerrilla warfare, right? Traps everywhere? Yeah. My only problem is that I don't know all that many trap-setting techniques. It's mostly just to make them more freaked out by the jungle, so killing isn't entirely necessary.

Let's see, what kind of traps would be best? Falling pit with sharp sticks at the bottom? Regular falling pit? Tripwire? All very tempting. I would love to do something cool with tripwires, but I actually have no idea how I would make that work. I don't even have wire to make the tripping.

Disguised pits full of sharp stuff it is!

In that case . . .

Slipping back to where I'd killed that RED squad, I loot the swords and spears and arrows that I'd previously left behind. Hm. I'd better take these sorts of things more often. It also doesn't hurt to steal their stuff, so even if I won't use it or anything, I grab the tent stuff, too.

And now, I just have to make a bunch of pits and put this stuff at the bottom. My hands should be enough to dig with, right? Right.

I want to make my traps on the little paths that go from the small base they made earlier to the big base, or to make one on the path to the river, but there are people walking there, so . . . yeah. I could camp out the river path, but then they'd eventually catch on to my location.

They've already started sending out random squadrons to try to find me, and since killing a squadron would alert the rest, there isn't much I can do. At least, for now.

When night falls it's a completely different story.

Unlike the daytime, most people aren't up and about. Sure, they have some guards, but they don't mean anything. The really important thing is that the paths aren't being used, which means that my time to shine is now.

I choose the path to the river as my first target. Once I pick out an appropriate location, I get digging. And digging. And digging. And digging. And digging . . .

**<You have learned:
Dig Lv.1>**

Right, yeah, very useful. Digging an appropriately deep pit was a bit more difficult than I had imagined. The whole thing took me well over two hours to do, not to mention fastening the arrows at the bottom. Just for the sake of it, I also slathered the arrows with my own blood. Just because, you know? But the real challenge was covering it up. In the cartoons, the booby traps are always covered in a simple layer of leaves, but apparently you can't just put a bunch of leaves over it and be done.

Most of the trap-making process was actually just me trying to figure out how to make a convincing-looking cover for the trap. Once it was done, I was almost tempted to test it on myself just to make sure it worked, but I couldn't bring myself to.

And then, I had to repeat the whole process for the other path. Eugh.

\<You have learned: Dig Lv.6\>

Phew, that was a lot of work. I still have a couple of hours until sunrise, so it would be a waste to just . . . not do anything.

I make my way back to the main camp.

They've got a couple of guards, but they can easily be bypassed with fetal position blowover. Deftly, I roll toward one of the RED tents and sneak inside. Well, there I stand up, just to get a good look at what I'm dealing with. There are about two dozen sleeping teenagers, snoring softly under their covers. They look awfully comfortable, but soon, they'll be even more comfortable. Hehe.

I sneak up to the side of one bed. In a single movement, I press my left hand onto the lower half of his face, stifling his scream. The very second his eyes flare open in terror and recognition, I press my fingers into his neck, my claws stabbing through the soft skin, through the soft muscles, until I can close them around his quivering throat, which I deftly pull out. He jerks once, twice, before twitching a little as he stops moving completely.

\<Shade (Lv.21) Defeated\>

One down, approximately twenty-three to go.

I move to the next bed, but instead of just slashing his throat or something like that, I try something else. Honestly, I've always wanted to do this.

I place my hands on either side of his head, and then I twist as hard as I can. *Cr—ack!* And then, nothing. He didn't even have time to open his eyes.

\<Shade (Lv.20) Defeated.\>

Very effective! But I think I prefer getting my hands just a little dirtier.

Slowly, deliberately, I move through the room, one by one, like a specter of death.

But at the very last bed, I pause. This guy . . . I recognize him. Erik . . . Erik . . . Something with Erik. Erik Hansén? Was that it? I don't know. He was a classmate of mine. He wasn't too bad. He didn't laugh at me or pick on me too much. He was . . . nice. My trembling hands reach for his throat. I just need to kill him. That's all. Then it'll be over. That's all. That's the only thing I need to—

His eyes gently flutter open. They fall on me. I look back at him. My breathing is fast, shallow. He almost seems . . . calm.

His eyebrows knit together. "Fennrick? . . ."

I grasp both of my hands around his neck so tightly that he doesn't even have time to choke before I can feel something crack and he's just gone. But that look of pure, innocent recognition in his eyes doesn't leave. It just doesn't go away. Even when the light fades from his eyes, that simple, quizzical look remains.

<You have learned: Clutch Lv.7>
<Shade (Lv.20) Defeated.>

Haaah, haaah, haaah . . . S—see? That wasn't so hard. Not at all, in fact.

Sitting down, I carefully bundle myself into a little ball. After a second or two, I roll out of the tent. I had wanted to dissect them, to make them look horribly mutilated and horrific and bad, but I just . . . I didn't feel like it, okay? Isn't it frightening enough with them just being dead? Being dead is being dead. It doesn't matter if your guts have gone flying everywhere or if your head's busted open. Dead is dead. That's all.

Since there are still a few more hours left of the evening, I spend the rest of the night digging a few more traps, and then just for the sake of it, I don the shade hide I took earlier. Then, while wearing it, I deliberately waltz into camp, on all fours, waiting until several different guards can see me before I bolt forward and grab one of them, dragging him off while the others can do nothing but watch as he struggles in my grip, screaming all the way into the forest. Once we're in the depths of the jungle, I tear him up, disassemble him, and put most of what I got in my inventory.

I almost want to wait a bit before doing this, but the sooner the better, right?

I head to the river. It's relatively small, but anyway. Following upstream, I investigate the origins of the water. After a while I hit an invisible wall, so that plan was a bust. By scouting out a bit more of the forest, I find a small pond, which is more useful for my schemes. Pulling the internal organs and a few of the limbs I collected from my inventory, I dump the lot of it into the pond. Aside from the river, this is the only source of water in the designated area. So to make sure they have no choice but to use this soon-to-be poisoned pond, I'll just need to make them completely unable to get to the totally superior river.

This means doing a little camping.

But before that, I might as well set up a few more traps along the river. You know, just to make it even more unappetizing.

<You have learned: Dig Lv.7>
<You have learned: Dig Lv.8>

All things considered, I'd say that this whole floor is going pretty well. If anything, trying to side with one group would just have made it more difficult.

Probably.

Paranoia

I can tell when morning comes, because a loud, piercing scream emerges from the base camp.

Ah, my good work has already been discovered, huh? About time, if you ask me.

Even though there's no real need to, I go over to the base camp, just to watch the shades scramble. Some of them are even crying, which is interesting to watch. After a while, they remove the bodies from the tent and bury them on the outskirts of the camp, unfortunately not close enough to the forest for me to do anything with them. There should still be something I can do with those bodies to freak them out somehow. Hm.

All very important issues to think about, but even more fun is that I can both hear and smell the people walking into my booby traps. The first ones were the ones at the small base, and then a group trying to get to the river fell. Since I didn't get any message, I can assume that none of them died, but my main thing here isn't to kill, but to scare them.

Once the river gang returns to base and informs them of the traps, when others go out and don't come back, they won't instantly assume that I killed them personally. After all, it could just be that they got trapped.

Man, I really wish I had some way of making poison. Or to spread a plague of some sort. I guess the only real way to do that would be to level up my touch of reverse tolerance. The last time I used it was against a gombie, so I don't know how strong it currently is. General logic would, however, dictate that it won't be very useful until I get it up to the resistance level. Assuming it can even get there, of course.

I should probably train it a bit against these shades.

But first, I need to do a few hit 'n' runs.

They've started sending out a number of squads. They're trying to locate me at any cost, and to expand their base area to weed me out. Of course, this is very hard to do if they are dead. My only goal is to make sure they don't find exactly where I am. Once they know that a squad is dead, I'll already be too far away to pursue.

And so, I start systematically taking out every squad of RED-clothed shades I see.

But while I was doing this, I caught the scent of something else: a large group of people heading toward the river. And I'm on the other side of the glade—several minutes away even if I run.

I sink my clawed hand into the throat of a shade and click my tongue. They got me. The good ol' diversion got me, huh? I guess I underestimated these people. Not very hard to do when they all look like teenagers and regular teachers, but it was still hubris on my part.

<Shade (Lv.24) Defeated.>
<Shade (Lv.20) Defeated.>
<Shade (Lv.21) Defeated.>

Taking out the remainder of the squad, I head toward the river. But as I pass the main base, I have a thought. A large number of the shades are either aimlessly wandering around in the forest to get killed by me or have just straight-up gone away. The cat isn't home. That means it's the perfect time for the rats to play.

I approach the base. While I was away doing a good ol' slaughter, they've begun setting up an encroachment. A number of them are digging a small trench around the camp and putting spears at the bottom. But they aren't even covering it with anything, so I think it's more of a warning on their side. There seem to be four entrances where there aren't any spears, so for them, it seems to be a matter of being able to properly guard the few entrances that they have. The dirt they dug up from the trenches is being used in conjunction with some rocks to form a wall behind the trench itself.

It's all very complex, but it won't stop me in the least.

I'm not entirely sure whether this will work, but it's worth a try. Right in daylight, I pull on my math-teacher disguise. Wearing it, I approach one of the four entrances.

"Mr. Fredriksson?" one of the shades says. I just wave at him as I casually stroll by. "Wh—what happened to you? Are you alright?!"

<You have learned: Impersonate Lv.2>

Let's see . . . What did Mr. Fredriksson usually say in times like these? "Oh, it's no worry. I was attacked by that awful Fennrick, but I made it out alive. I just need to get to the barracks and I'll be fine."

The shade frowns at me. "You sound somehow different, but . . . Okay, hope you get better. And . . ." His eyes glance down at my nethers and up again. "Try to put something on, alright?"

"Alright," I say. "I will." But that's a lie, because, as a matter of fact, I'm already wearing something! Haha, get tomfooled! Man, these people sure are dumb. They really just let me stroll right on in, wearing the saggy skin of some old fart! This game is easy.

Now, where's the food court?

After wandering around for a bit, I involuntarily find my way into the infirmary, even though I had wanted to do the exact opposite. Hm. Funny way the world works, huh?

"Mr. Fredriksson? Is everything alright? You look pale—why don't you take a seat?" I look up to find the school nurse looking at me. She's younger than most of her profession, with an unusual liking for what she does. Most school nurses would just sneer at me whenever I came to them. Elementary school was the worst. If I didn't have a broken nose or something, they'd just send me away and tell me to wash it off myself. "Mr. Fredriksson?"

"H—huh?" I say, taking a step back. Oh, yeah, I'm in the tutorial. I—I forgot for a second there, that's all. "No, I'm fine. I was just . . ."

But then I look around. The sick bay isn't too big—barely the size of a standard building—but it's already full of people. Some with no visible injuries, others with pierced legs, an arrow still stuck in them. I recognize a few of the faces from my year. One of them is the economics teacher. When I told him I was going to be a pro gamer, he hadn't laughed or told me off for it. He'd just encouraged it and told me that the gaming industry was really taking off.

I swallow down a lump that hadn't been in my throat seconds ago.

"—I just wandered into the wrong tent, that's all," I finish.

She smiles at me. "When are you going to stop being such a ditz, Mr. Fredriksson?"

I know she's talking to me, but my brain is spinning with razor-sharp thoughts.

The sick bay is the heart of their operation. If I just take this place out, then no matter what I do, eventually, I'll be able to win. She's the base of it all. With her dead, recovery for the wounded will be impossible. If they get wounded, and if the wound starts to fester, then there won't be anything left to be done. They'll just die. That's all. That's it.

I should kill her. And then I should kill everyone else in the sick bay. And then I should escape before the other soldiers arrive. That's what I should do. That's what I need to—

"Mr. Fredriksson?" Her hand falls on my forehead. On the forehead of the skin I'm wearing. "Oh, my! You're freezing! We'd better get you something warm. Do you think you might have gotten a co—"

Her eyes meet mine. Not where she probably thinks Mr. Fredriksson's eyes are. Nothing like that. *My* eyes. The ones peeking out from beneath the empty sockets, the flaccid eyelids, the eyeless eyes. And for just a second, she's so still and so pale that anyone could have mistaken her for a marble statue.

I don't know what to do. I don't know what to do. I don't know what to do. I don't know what to do. I don't know what to do. I don't know what to do. I don't know what to do. I don't know what to do.

So I just act.

My hand, straight and firm, flies out and slices up her throat. She falls to the floor. She didn't even stumble or say anything. I look down at my hand. The skin gloves of the disguise are torn, and my sharp, clawlike nails are sticking out.

<Shade (Lv.21) Defeated.>
<You have learned: Impersonate Lv.3>
<You have learned: Sharp Claw Lv.10>
<You have learned: Dagger Nails Lv.1>

After she drops, I just act. I'm not even really thinking. It's like I'm wearing not only Mr. Fredriksson's skin, but my own, too. Like I'm peeking out from inside my own eyes, seeing but not acting.

I see myself fly through the infirmary, deftly severing the arteries of men and women, young and old lying listlessly in their beds, none of them so much as able to put up a fight. I just kill them. There's a scream in the room and I don't think it's mine, but it could have been mine because my lungs and my throat and my tongue aren't mine anymore. I'm just moving. I'm just doing. And when the room doesn't contain any breathing save for mine, when the skin I wear is torn and stretched and wrinkled in places it shouldn't be, only then does someone enter.

A young soldier. I think he's fourteen or so. He's holding a spear, but it won't do him any good. He looks at me with wide eyes. "M—Mr. Fredriksson? What happened here? What is—"

And then he's gone. It was so easy. He didn't even raise the spear to me. The last thing he does, moments before letting out his final breath, is to look up at me, and to see me, to see the me that is within the sockets of Mr. Fredriksson, and within the eye sockets of Lo Fennrick. He sees *me*. And then he's gone.

<Shade (Lv.20) Defeated.>

I leave the infirmary. Crouching down into a ball, I roll my way out of the base camp.

Once I'm far away, I remove the skin I'm wearing. I don't put it back in my inventory. I don't like the look of it. I don't know what else to do with it.

Far away from base camp, where no one can see and no one will check for newly dug mounds of dirt, I bury him.

Days go by. I can practically taste the paranoia in the air, surrounding the base camp like a thick cloud.

Once the defensive trench around the base camp was complete, they apparently felt confident enough to branch out into more, smaller bases. This is probably in the hopes of pushing me to the point where I'm crushed between their bases and the invisible wall surrounding us. But this won't happen, because it's not like I'm just letting them put up these bases wherever they want. Anytime a RED squad goes out into the forest, I kill them. Easy as that.

Why not those dressed in blue? Well, see, that's one of my little schemes.

And after about a week of this whole thing, after a week of them not being able to access the river because of how many traps I've got surrounding it by now, the whole situation has finally gotten to them. I don't know exactly how these shades are made, but despite their knowledge as soldiers, they still have the bodies and minds of teenagers. With lackluster food, poisoned water, traps, constant harassment from me, and not even being safe in one's own bed, the stress has finally gotten to them.

After all, only one half is getting attacked at all.

From atop a tree, crouched in the fetal position, I watch with interest as Jirya and Het quarrel right in front of everyone, in the middle of camp, without a care in the world. Though, of course, it *is* pretty one-sided. And for good reason.

"—Have you *sided* with him, huh? Is that it?"

"Of course not!" Het shouts back at her. "Why in the world would we even do that? You should know better than anyone that we are as bad off as you are!"

"Oh, is that it? You're as bad off as we are? Really? Okay, then. *Explain* to me, in simple terms, how it always is that whenever *you* send out troops, they return home without so much as a scratch on their pretty little heads, while mine always get ruthlessly torn apart?!" Saying so, she throws her hands in the air, and the people standing by begin to murmur among each other.

Het's head starts shaking back and forth. "Without a single—I don't know if you've noticed it, Miss *I-am-always-the-victim*, but my men die just as often to booby traps and disease as yours do! In fact, since you hardly send out anyone anymore, I'd say mine die *more often* to traps and disease than yours. Or are you trying to say that this sort of death is somehow preferable to being maimed? Is that what you're saying?"

"No—no, now you're twisting my words! What I'm *trying* to say is that . . ."

And back and forth it goes. This isn't their first time arguing over this—I've been sneakily listening in on their strategic conversations—but I've got a feeling that this may very well be their last. And as I watch them from above, after a few minutes of back and forth . . .

"Fine, then!" Jirya says. "If that's how you want it to be, then I don't suppose you'll mind it even a little if we split up a bit. How about that? We go on the left, you go on the right. If—according to your *amazing* and *flawless* logic—we still have the same number of men left alive, then sure! We're both equally screwed in this hell of a place. How does that sound, Mr. *high-and-mighty*?"

Het shrugs in return. "Sure. Do whatever you want. I'm not the boss of you."

"Great. Glad we agree, then!"

And so it happens. Both camps separate, splitting the meadow into two and making a wall between them. This is exactly what I wanted. Now the people who had until now mingled as friends and coworkers are forced into separation. For some, this will cause profound isolation; for others, harsh conflict is sure to follow.

Food and other basics of living are starting to run dry. Without access to the river, they can't do any washing, which means that any wound, no matter how small, has a relatively high chance of getting so much worse. Afraid of my nightly raids, the shades have started sleeping together in tighter clusters. People are already significantly weakened both mentally and physically by the situation.

It's the perfect condition for spreading a plague.

However, to spread a plague, I'll need an actual plague. Despite how much I would love to be sick right now, I am not infected by any cholera or bronchitis or whatever else might be useful. Since the water poisoning isn't going too fast and the diseases incurred by it aren't transmittable in the right way, I'll need to get my hands on a plague through some more . . . unconventional means.

Namely, touch of reversed tolerance. I've been trying to use it as much as possible, but I've still only been able to get it to level 6. At this point, though, it's finally starting to show a few effects. They're very minimal, but I think, in the right conditions, I might be able to make something of it. And I have the perfect plan for how to do it. All I need to do is to capture a shade at random, infect him with TRT, and then send him back to base camp. There, he'll infect the rest of the guys, and boom! Win.

It's simple, but I've got good reason to think it'll work. I just need to find a suitable patient zero, and then I'm set.

Sniffsniffsniff. Oh, another squad entered the forest. Let's see, it's on the hypothetical west side, which probably means they're from the RED group. Alright, let's set out!

Like a loosened arrow, I fly toward their location, leaping and climbing so deftly I couldn't have moved faster even on ground. After a few minutes, I reach their location. Let's see here . . .

<Shade (Lv.19)>
<Shade (Lv.22)>
<Shade (Lv.23)>
<Shade (Lv.21)>
<Shade (Lv.20)>

Only five of them, huh?

As the total number of soldiers has waned, the size of the probing squadrons and the scouts have likewise decreased. Just the other day, I saw a single soldier walking on his own. Poor guy. I tried to give him a quick death, but then my dagger tooth skill leveled up and I just had to test it out. It is what it is and all that.

"I—is it true what they say?" one of the shades asks one of the others. For some reason, I feel like I recognize his voice somewhat.

"About what?" the shade replies.

The first one looks down at his feet. Stopping in his place, he carefully pokes the pile of leaves in front of him with the shaft of his spear. I don't think I put any trap there, and since nothing happens when he pokes it, that seems to be the case. The shade looks back up at the other one. "That the, um . . . that Fennrick only attacks REDdies?"

The other shade shrugs. "Who knows? We'll all be killed anyway, so it doesn't matter whether it's us first or them. It's all the same."

The first one seems to want to say something, but I've gotten bored with their conversation, so I just drop down from above onto the second one's head, planting both feet on his shoulders and gripping hold of his head in both hands, snapping his neck with a single well-placed twist.

<Shade (Lv.23) Defeated.>

The body beneath me falls and I jump back, right at the other shades, first kicking their feet out from under them and then ripping out their throats.

<Shade (Lv.20) Defeated.>
<Shade (Lv.21) Defeated.>

That leaves me with only two left.

A spear flies at me and I let it stab itself into the gap between my ribs. Then, by twisting the spear, I get it stuck in me, meaning that the shade has effectively just given me his weapon. Jumping a step back, he loses his grip on the spear fully. In turn, I grab the spear myself, untwisting it before pulling it back out of my chest, then putting it in my inventory so he can't get it anymore. The shade is too stunned by the whole exchange to do anything but scream as I leap at him and rip his throat out.

<Shade (Lv.22) Defeated.>

There. Perfect. Now, only one le—

. . . Johan?

"L—Lo?" He stutters at me. If I were speaking, I'd probably stutter right back. His eyes are wide and staring and still he takes a step toward me. I know I should fly at him, claws at the ready, jaw open to rip his throat out, but instead, like a damn coward, I take a step back, one step for each one he takes toward me. But this just makes his expression of horror suddenly lighten into a small, trembling smile. "D—do you recognize me, Lo? You do, right?"

I don't want to answer him. I don't want to say anything. But the words come out of me on their own. "Johan . . . ?"

His smile erupts into an entire grin, and he almost throws himself at me, but I step back, only barely dodging a hug. He almost tries again, but now that we're so close, he can see all the blood on me. His smile falters a little and he takes a step back. I mirror the motion. "It's, um . . . It's been a while, hasn't it?"

I look down at my feet, awkwardly. "Y—yeah. I guess . . . I guess it has."

When I look back up at him, he's still smiling. Softly. I hate it. I hate that smile. I want to—

Sniffsniffsniff. Just a few dozen meters away, I can smell people approaching. More people. Over a dozen. Too many.

"Lo?"

My face snaps back to face Johan.

"Is everything alri—"

I can't afford him to give me away, but I can't just leave him here, but I can't just *do away with him* either, so with no other choice, I crouch down and leap at him, grabbing him by the chest and hoisting him up on my shoulder, and while still carrying him like that, without waiting for him to calm down, I jump up into a tree and away into the forest. I need to find a safe place. Somewhere I can put him down. Somewhere they won't approach.

Somewhere . . . like the river.

After a minute or so of near-frantic running, I finally reach the river. And there, I put him down. "G—gee, Fennrick, you could've, um, *warned me*, you know?" he says, still clutching at his head in an almost comedic fashion. We're at the river. Since I don't answer him, Johan looks down at the mirrorlike water. He's sitting on a nice round rock. I'm standing to his right, just slightly behind him. If I wanted to, I could break his neck before he even knew what was happening. He wouldn't need to know. It would just be over, and that would be it. Gently, Johan turns to look at me. I look down at him and then away. "Sorry if I took you by surprise, I just . . . I've never seen you look this *serious*, so—"

"What are you?" I ask him.

"H—huh?"

So many old questions are bubbling up to the top of my mind. "What are you actually? You aren't a human. You aren't the real Johan. So, what are you actually?"

"I'm not sure I understand the—"

I grab his neck from behind, my grip tightening.

<You have learned: Clutch Lv.8>

"You're a shade. What does that mean? Why do you look like Johan?"

His lips tighten into a line. Slowly, he turns his eyes back to the river. He almost looks melancholic where he sits. "I'm . . . *We* are just, I guess, shadows of your memories. Or something. We were put here to exist to train you in the— the art of *mediation* or something." He looks back up at me again, eyes glistening. "But that doesn't mean we aren't real! Just like you, we were also made by a god—several, in fact. Sure, to you, I'm just a fake version of your old classmate, but to *me*, this is as real as I'll ever be!"

His voice trembles but there's too much power in it for me not to listen. "We're alive, we breathe, and even though this forest and this meadow are the only things we've ever known, that doesn't make us any less real than you are. I remember who you are. To me, I'm as real as your Johan thinks himself to be. In my mind, I've lived the life you remember me to have lived. I remember how you used to be before you came here, how you were back in kindergarten. How the kids would pick on you for the slightest things, and how nobody would stand up for it because they all thought you were weird, too. I remember it like it was my own childhood. And I feel *bad* about it."

Slowly, I release my grip on his neck. Still, he continues.

"Is that feeling not real, just because your system—that cruel system—calls me a *shade* rather than a human? Your Johan, the *real* one—whatever it means to be real—isn't here. The last time he saw you was on a television screen. I don't know how that made him feel, but I can tell you that where I sit, next to this river, next to *you*, I still feel bad for those memories I have. That I didn't do anything. We were close enough to be friends, but I held off. Or am I not allowed to feel bad for it, since I technically didn't do anything?"

I look down at the ground. "I—I didn't say that . . ."

"You did," Johan says sharply. "And maybe you're right. Maybe I am just some sort of shadow of a real person. But if I feel that I am real, then am I not real?"

How do I even respond to that? "How should I know?"

His expression melts slightly. "Right, I forgot. You never did pass philosophy, did you?"

"Th—that was because Mr. Nilsson didn't like me! If he'd just read my fifty-page essay on why games are the highest form of art, he would've given me the best score possible!" I cry, waving broadly.

Johan chuckles. "You really are a geek." He smiles at me. "I'm glad you haven't changed too much since we last met, Lo."

Last met . . .

I feel my hands ball into fists. "I have, though," I mumble. I look up at him. "And so have you."

Adjusting his position on the rock, Johan shifts around to face me. His expression is back to being serious. "Lo, I need you to tell me one thing honestly. You can do that, right?"

I can feel my claws digging into the palms of my hands. "Yeah," I choke out. "Sure."

His expression turns muted. "What are you going to do with me?"

My jaw clenches. "I—I don't know. I was thinking of—"

His eyes pierce into me. "Don't lie to me, Lo." His smile turns teasing. "I know you can't look people in the eye when you lie."

I look up at him. Into his eye. Right into his eye—his eye that looks just the same as when I last met him. "I'm going to try to infect you with a viral disease and send you back into the encampment and once as many people as possible have fallen ill and have weakened I'll set a fire to the tents and kill them as they run out and then finally pick them off one by one while they're in the forest until none remain."

His smile doesn't even twitch. Carefully, he looks down at the ground in between us. "I see . . ." he says, after a long pause. And then he looks back up at me and my chest feels so tight. "Thanks for not lying to me."

I look at him. Right into his eye. "You aren't going to tell me not to? To ask me to spare your life, if only for old times' sake?"

He makes a difficult face, but I've watched Johan make that face so many times that seeing it again doesn't faze me. "It's not like it would help. I don't want to die or anything, but . . ." He shrugs. "You can't beat this floor without defeating us all, can you?"

"I don't think so," I answer honestly.

He looks back down at his feet. He's trying so hard not to show anything on his face, but his lips keep dipping down into a deep frown, the kind you only make when you're trying to hold in tears. When he looks back up at me, his hands are clenching the fabric of his armor and his eyes are pooling. "I don't want to go, Lo. I don't want to. But I can't stop you, so . . ." His voice wavers, trembling, dipping up and down and touching into a near-desperate falsetto. And yet, despite the tears now streaming down his face, despite the way his eyes are turning RED, he's still able to twist his lips into a strange, rebellious smile. His arms stretch out to me. "Before I go, will you hug me? Please."

I can do nothing but stare down at him and his outstretched arms, baffled.

"I can remember being hugged by Mom, and by Dad, and my sisters, but— but . . ." He gulps down a lump. "But I've never actually experienced it. Please." His tears are starting to stain the front of his armor dark. "Just . . . just once."

Stunned, uncertain, acting less by thinking and more by my body alone, I let him hug me. I take him into my arms, and I hold him, and I pat him on the back because I don't know what else you're supposed to do when someone is hugging you. I can feel his tears and snot soak into my pelt, but I still hold on to him for some reason that I don't know myself. I don't know exactly for how long I hold him, but during the entire duration, he goes from quietly weeping to loud, heaving sobs, and hiccupping, and sniffling whimpers, and quick hyperventilation, and then he calms down again, forcing his breathing back under control, clutching at me so tightly he might actually be leaving a few marks, and then, after some time, he finally stops. Carefully, he pushes me away, and I let him leave my arms.

He looks up at me, his eyes RED. "I—I'm ready."

I don't think he is. But I can't bring myself to say that. If he says he's ready, then he is. I take his head into my hands.

<[Touch of Reversed Bacteria Tolerance (Lv.6)]>
<[Touch of Reversed Virus Tolerance (Lv.6)]>
<[Touch of Reversed Ulcer Tolerance (Lv.6)]>
<[Touch of Reversed Indigestion Tolerance (Lv.6)]>
<[Touch of Reversed Parasite Tolerance (Lv.6)]>
<[Touch of Reversed Necrosis Tolerance (Lv.6)]>
<[Touch of Reversed Fever Tolerance (Lv.6)]>
<[Touch of Reversed Hypothermia Tolerance (Lv.6)]>
<[Touch of Reversed Nausea Tolerance (Lv.6)]>
<[Touch of Reversed Coma Tolerance (Lv.6)]>
<You have learned: Touch of Reversed Tolerance Lv.7>

Instantly, with every touch of my fingers, he looks visibly worse. Paler, weaker, more disheveled, more in pain . . .

His hand reaches up to grab mine. It's trembling.

"I can . . . I can still keep going," he slurs.

I don't want to. But I have to. I can. And he's asking me to. So even though it hurts, even though I want to do anything else, I continue.

<[Touch of Reversed Bacteria Tolerance (Lv.7)]>
<[Touch of Reversed Virus Tolerance (Lv.7)]>
<[Touch of Reversed Ulcer Tolerance (Lv.7)]>
<[Touch of Reversed Indigestion Tolerance (Lv.7)]>
<[Touch of Reversed Parasite Tolerance (Lv.7)]>
<[Touch of Reversed Necrosis Tolerance (Lv.7)]>
<[Touch of Reversed Fever Tolerance (Lv.7)]>
<[Touch of Reversed Hypothermia Tolerance (Lv.7)]>
<[Touch of Reversed Nausea Tolerance (Lv.7)]>
<[Touch of Reversed Coma Tolerance (Lv.7)]>

He stumbles into my arms. His breathing is haggard, rasping in and out of his throat. "Johan?" I say, but he doesn't respond. His eyes are half-closed and hazy. I don't even know if he can see me at all anymore.

I bite my lip.

Carefully, gently, I place him on my back. And then, I head back toward base camp. Since I'm carrying him atop me, I can't leap through the treetops, but that's fine. Once I'm at the base camp, I leave him by one of the many entrances, slumped against a wall. Climbing into a nearby tree, I watch intently, waiting impatiently for someone to find him. By the time he's discovered, I've already considered fifteen different ways of saving him. But it's too late for that.

They bring him inside.

Over the course of only a single week, almost every single person inside the walls of the camp falls ill. I can smell the sickness on them. I wait another week, killing anyone who tries to leave. Many people die. One by one. Sometimes in clusters, usually alone.

<Top—Status—Community>
<02:06:08 Day 150>
<The sixth attempt will begin in 21:53:52>

It's about time, then.

Once night falls, I sneak inside the camp. It isn't hard. There aren't many guards anymore. Inside, I can see bodies piled into mounds, many leaned against the walls, others tossed over and into the trench on the other side. The stench is indescribable. I move through this place like a specter. Outside, a single camp-fire remains lit, with a slumped-over guard next to it. I snap his brittle neck.

Grabbing one of the burning logs with my bare hands, I make my way to the tents. One by one, I set them alight. There aren't many left in there to struggle, but I still kill those that try to escape.

As I make my way along the base, fire in hand, I notice one of the bodies, lying in a pile among the rest.

Hunching down, I place Johan on my shoulder. Once I've lit the final tent on fire, I bury Johan in a grave just outside the base.

\<You have learned: Dig Lv.10\>
\<You have learned: Excavate Lv.1\>

A few shades remain. In the final few hours of the floor, I kill them. And once the last one falls, the sun finally rises once more.

\<You have cleared the seventh floor.\>
\<You have received 1,000 points for clearing the floor.
You have received an additional 1,000 points for being the first to clear the floor.\>
\<For clearing the stage completely, you will receive an additional reward.\>
\<To repay your debt, the additional reward has been traded for 5,000 points.\>
\<4 Gods have shown a positive response to you.
You have obtained 4,000 points.\>
\<31 Gods have shown a negative response to you.
31,000 points have been deducted.\>

. . . Right.

\<To repay your debt, the floor clear reward has been traded for 1 000 points.\>

Please. Just take me back to the—

EPILOGUE

THAT'S A FIRST.

YOU CAN SAY THAT AGAIN.

IS THAT ALL YOU HAVE TO SAY?

I THINK IT WAS A VERY CREATIVE SOLUTION.

PURELY IN TERMS OF GETTING LEVELS AND WHATNOT, THIS WAS CLEARLY THE BEST SOLUTION.

CRUELTY, YOU CAN'T HONESTLY MEAN THAT.

HAVE YOU NO PITY FOR THE POOR SHADES HARVEST MADE?

THEY WERE MADE TO BE KILLED.

I DON'T SEE THE BIG DEAL.

WHAT DO YOU THINK, COWARDICE?

IT'S YOUR HUMAN, ISN'T IT?

OH, THIS I WANT TO HEAR.

COME ON, COWARDICE.

WHAT DO YOU THINK?

. . .

NO ANSWER, HUH?

I GET IT. TOO HUMBLE TO ACCEPT FIRST CLAIM ON THE MOST PROMISING HUMAN.

MOST PROMISING?

IF WE'RE TALKING ABOUT WHICH HUMAN HAS THE HIGHEST CHANCES OF CAUSING MORE DAMAGE THAN EVEN HIM, THEN, YES, I SUPPOSE THIS HUMAN WOULD BE MOST PROMISING.

YOU'RE ALL MISSING THE POINT.

THIS HUMAN IS CLEARLY UNSTABLE.

IF ANY OF YOU HAD ANY REAL GALL, YOU'D THROW IT OUT AND PUT YOUR DIVINITY INTO A HUMAN THAT ACTUALLY HAS A FEW VIRTUES TO IT.

PARDON ME, BUT AREN'T WE LOOKING FOR A WARRIOR?

SOMEONE WHO CAN FIGHT?

YOU'RE BOTH RIGHT AND WRONG.

WE'RE LOOKING FOR A SAVIOR.

A HERO.

A HERO.

A HERO.

YOU'RE ALL DREADFUL.

IF YOU WANTED A HERO, YOU WOULDN'T HAVE HAD THE HELL DIFFICULTY AS A CHOICE. WE NEED TO SEED OUT THE ARROGANT SOMEHOW.

WE NEED TO ROOT OUT THE PRIDEFUL SOMEHOW.

WE NEED TO WEED OUT THE DANGEROUS SOMEHOW.

AND, BESIDES, IF SOMEONE DOES BEAT THIS DIFFICULTY . . .

I DOUBT HE'LL BE AN ISSUE ANYMORE.

ABOUT THE AUTHOR

Palt is a Sweden-based author of isekai, short horror stories, and some fanfiction. He is currently working toward a degree in criminology. In his spare time, Palt enjoys drawing and playing the trombone.

DISCOVER
STORIES UNBOUND

PodiumAudio.com

Printed in the USA
CPSIA information can be obtained
at www.ICGtesting.com
JSHW021939080724
66057JS00007B/26